PRAISE FOR *PERSIMMON TAKES ON HUMANITY*

"With a deep passion for his subject and a wonderful skill in storytelling, Christopher Locke opens an enlightening window onto the little-seen world of animals raised to serve human wants. Sometimes uplifting, at other times disquieting, it's a thoughtful novel that teaches as it entertains. The adventures and tribulations of this unlikely band of raccoons, squirrels and other animals make for an engaging, page-turning read that is hard to put down."

—David Robinson Simon, author of *Meatonomics*

"Christopher Locke takes young adult fiction in a bold, new direction with his novel *Persimmon Takes on Humanity*. Anyone who loves animals will cheer Persimmon, the plucky raccoon, and her friends in their quest to rescue animals from industrialized cruelty. I hope that readers will pick up this book, learn from it and perhaps adopt Persimmon's valiant crusade as their own."

—Robin Lamont, author of *The Kinship Series*

"With colorful characters and an enthralling story, *Persimmon Takes on Humanity* is not only enjoyable to read, but it might just change your view of humankind, and of the world that we have created."

— Mark Devries, director of *Speciesism: The Movie*

"The story of Persimmon, a raccoon on a mission, is at times magical and at times a searing view of the abuses animals endure, told from their own perspective. I'll never look at animals the same way after reading Christopher Locke's poignant portrayal."

—E. Van Lowe, bestselling author of *Boyfriend From Hell*

THE ENLIGHTENMENT ADVENTURES * BOOK ONE

PERSIMMON
TAKES ON HUMANITY

Christopher Locke

Dear Victoria,

Thank you for all of the amazing work you do for the animals of the world! I admire the impact you've had on our movement. Likewise, I hope this novel is my lasting legacy to make the world a more compassionate place. Enjoy!

Sincerely,

Christopher Locke

Edited by Jaya Bhumitra

Published by Fathoming Press

Fathoming Press
www.Christopher-Locke.com

For all the remarkable people out there who are working tirelessly to make the world a more compassionate place. You inspire me.

For all the critters of the world who are suffering at the hands of humans. I humbly wish that the words contained within this book will somehow, one day bring you peace.

For my brilliant wife. You set the standard for what a true partner and soul mate should be. Your creative input on this book was invaluable and your infinite support has made my dreams come true. In return... Everything. All my life. For you.

1

PERSIMMON IS FEELING restless. Her black-and-brown-striped tail bounces eagerly back and forth as she anticipates her next daring move. She scopes out the branches on the evergreen tree across from her, which are glistening in the moonlight. Can she make the leap?

Derpoke sees the determined look in his raccoon friend's eyes and immediately speaks up. "Persimmon, don't!"

Persimmon peers down at the opossum—her more cautious companion—on the branch below her. "What? You don't think I can make it?"

"I know you want me to say, no, so that you can prove me wrong, but I'm not going to fall for your foolish game."

"Come on," Persimmon baits him. "Where's your sense of adventure?"

"That's what you said to get me to climb so high in this tree," Derpoke scoffs. "Be sensible."

Just then, Persimmon's sprightly—and tinier—brother, Scraps, rushes headfirst down the tree trunk and stops with perfect accuracy just above her. Unlike his sister, whose fur is mostly brown with a sprinkle of gray, Scraps is all gray. Both of them, though, have the classic black raccoon mask around their eyes—perfectly fitting for their mischievous natures.

"Did I hear you say adventure?" Scraps jumps in excitedly.

"What is it with you two and adventure?" Derpoke questions, exasperated. "Adventure does not mean risking your life."

Persimmon's eyes light up. "But the risk sure makes it exhilarating."

"If raccoons were meant to fly from tree to tree, you would have wings instead of legs," Derpoke chides.

Persimmon shoots Derpoke a devilish grin. "Oh, really."

"Persimmon, don't twist my words to justify your whims," Derpoke scolds. "You're going to get hurt. Please!"

Scraps hops up and down. "A challenge! A challenge!"

Persimmon inches her way backward toward the trunk of the tree. It's an official dare. How can she turn back now?

She digs her claws into the bark. Derpoke quickly lifts himself up onto the branch where she sits, blocking her path. He holds his pink paws out to stop her. She is larger than he is, though, so he isn't much of an imposing force. "You can make it, Persimmon. Okay? I believe you. So now there's nothing to prove. Come on, let's see how many raspberries we can eat before our stomachs start to ache."

Persimmon digs her claws deeper into the branch. She takes a steady breath. She is so focused on the jump, it's as if she is looking right through him. At this point, his pleading will be in vain.

Derpoke slumps down onto the branch below and turns the other way. "I won't watch. I can't bear to see my best friend jump to her death."

Persimmon races forward. Faster and faster. The edge of the branch is nearing. Can she make it? The gap between the trees seems to be getting wider and wider as she gets closer. Faster, faster… there's no stopping now! The end of the branch bends down with her weight, which slows her pace dramatically. She keeps running forward, but now she is facing down instead of straight—she'll be jumping directly at the ground. She presses her hind legs hard into the branch and pushes off with all her might. Derpoke, who has just turned to watch, lets out a frightened squeal.

Persimmon falls quick and hard. Her heart is racing so rapidly, it hurts. Fear overcomes her. The branches of the next tree are not coming closer, but the ground surely is. Down, down she falls. She reaches out for a branch, but it zips through her claws. The ground is getting closer. Pine needles sting and slap her masked face. She wildly flings her paws around, trying to clasp onto anything that would break her fall.

Her body crashes against a flimsy tree limb, knocking the wind out of her. She wraps all four legs around the branch, clinging for dear life. She struggles to breathe. The tree limb bends down and then swings her back up into the air. She tries to hold on, but the force bouncing upward is too much. She flies into the air and loses her grip. She flails around before landing with a thud on a bed of dandelions.

Scraps bolts down the tree trunk toward his sister at lightning speed.

"Persimmon!" Derpoke screams, lowering himself as fast as his stubby legs will go, which is agonizingly slow for the distressed opossum. He finally waddles up to her and clasps her limp paw. "No, no. Be alive. Be alive."

The night is silent. Derpoke lets out a gasp and rests his pink nose on her paw.

Just then, Persimmon sucks in a giant gulp of air. She opens her eyes. She moans. Every inch of her body aches.

Derpoke lets out a sigh of relief. "Are you broken?"

Persimmon turns to him with a smile. "Told you."

Persimmon and Scraps playfully kick their back paws together, and Scraps dances on his hind legs in jubilation. "The winner!"

Derpoke pushes her front paw away. "You are the most impossible creature I have ever met. You infuriate me. What if you had died? Huh? What would I do then?"

"You would miss me every day for the rest of your life. You know why?"

"Ha," Derpoke dismisses her. "I would say you were silly, and…"

"You didn't answer my question. You know why you'd miss me so much?"

Derpoke starts to scamper away. He knows where this is going. Persimmon rushes up to him and wraps her legs around his body, knocking him to the ground as she squeezes him tightly.

"Because I'm your favorite." She tickles his belly and kisses his forehead and ears. "Your favorite creature in all the forest and beyond!"

Derpoke tries to wrestle free, but it's no use against his bigger, stronger friend.

A shadow suddenly forms over the two companions.

"Having fun?" Rawly, an imposing raccoon, stands over them on his hind legs, asserting his dominance. He glares at the playful pair. Derpoke goes limp with fear.

Persimmon lets go of Derpoke and leisurely rolls onto her side to face Rawly. "Well, well, well, if it isn't Grumpykins."

"Grumpy?!" Rawly replies, incensed. "How about rightfully annoyed that you're in my territory—again? You think you can just gallivant around all over my trees?"

"The forest is big enough for all of us to share," Persimmon responds defiantly. "I'm not intimidated by the silly rules you males force on everyone around you by rubbing your butts on everything."

Rawly moves closer to Persimmon and whispers sleazily, "It's nature, and nature tells me that a female coming into my territory wants only one thing."

Persimmon kicks him away with her hind legs. Derpoke pops out of his frozen stance and glowers at Rawly.

"You're gross, Rawly," Persimmon retorts. "Not that it occurred to you, but there are more important things in life than mating."

"More important? Yes. More interesting? No." Before Persimmon can snap back at him, Rawly continues. "The most ridiculous thing about you jumping between those trees is that you were doing it to show off to your puny brother and this cowardly opossum."

Persimmon pops up, indignant. "They both have more heart than all of the other raccoons combined. Besides, I did it to prove to myself that it could be done—and maybe to taste the thrill of it."

"Huh. Well, if you warriors are so brave, then why don't you venture past Oak Tree Forest on the other side of the river?" Rawly provokes.

"You're absurd," Persimmon jeers. "As if you're courageous enough to venture there. No raccoon has ever gone past that point and lived to tell the tale."

"Or so our parents would have us believe." Rawly pauses for a few moments to let that revelatory thought sink in. Then he laughs to himself. "Don't be so naïve. Where do you think the older raccoons go when the cold is coming in and food is scarce?"

Persimmon responds without hesitation. "They go to the human burrows that are all lined up in rows on this side of the woods, as we all do. Savvy forest creatures stay away from that side of the river beyond Oak Tree Forest because it is common knowledge that the humans there are more ferocious. There, the humans force other creatures to carry them around when they are too lazy to walk, they tear off animals' skin and fur and wear them proudly, and they beat animals to death for entertainment."

"Yeah," Scraps chimes in. "Those humans even go around killing us forest dwellers just for the fun of it."

Rawly grins smugly. "All of that is true, and yet I go there regularly to feast on all kinds of tasty treats without being bothered by the likes of you bugs."

Persimmon is unimpressed. "How do we know you've really been there? I could just as easily say I've been there too."

"Solid point," Rawly agrees. "But what if I told you there was a creature there that you had never seen before? Perhaps that would pique your interest?"

Persimmon is silent for a second. Derpoke doesn't like the look in her eyes, but Scraps smiles widely. A creature they've never seen before in a treacherous land? Now *that* sounds like a thrilling adventure.

2

DERPOKE STRUGGLES TO keep up with Persimmon, Scraps and Rawly as they trek through the woods. As if he's been holding the words in for a while, the anxious opossum finally blurts out, "Persimmon, I have a bad feeling about this."

"What harm is it to have a look?" Persimmon replies, slightly annoyed by her friend's endless obsession with caution.

Derpoke perks up. Maybe he can still talk his thrill-seeking friend out of this perilous excursion. "We all just acknowledged that humans there kill animals as entertainment. What if they keep us captive and force us to fight, and then we have to bite each other's faces and swallow each other's noses as they watch and laugh?"

Persimmon stops and turns to Derpoke in shock. "What?! Where do you come up with these disgusting thoughts?"

Derpoke sheepishly lowers his head. "I've heard stories."

"Yes, stories," Persimmon explains. "Maybe our elders made up those stories to keep us away from the best food sources in the area. I mean, think about it, why would any creature be entertained by watching another creature be beaten? Maybe the humans there aren't all that bad. Either way, I won't let anything happen to you."

"I'm not worried about me." Derpoke peers at her earnestly. "I'm worried about you."

Persimmon pats him on the back. "You really are too precious and I love you for it. But stop worrying so much. Just answer me this: Are you not even the least bit curious to see a creature you never even knew existed?"

"Of course I am," Derpoke concedes. "I have..."

Before he can finish his thought, Rawly calls out to them from twenty trees away. "Come on, you slugs. We'll never get there at this pace."

Derpoke sighs. He knows he's not winning this one, so he just follows the three raccoons as they travel briskly through the thick brush.

They cross the river using a large fallen tree as a bridge and then hike deep into a part of the woods where Persimmon, Derpoke and Scraps have never dared travel before. The trio is on high alert now that they're out of known territory. At this point, they can barely contain their bubbling anticipation for what lies ahead.

After walking for what feels like forever, a foul stench suddenly hits their noses.

Persimmon can hardly stand it. "What is that smell?" A vexing thought crosses her mind, and she frowns at Rawly. "Is this a trick? Are you taking us to see some rotting carcass?"

Rawly turns around. "I am not silly enough to play tricks. That is how these creatures smell."

Derpoke tries to breathe through his mouth instead of his sensitive nose. "Do they not have the decency to lick themselves clean or wade in a stream?"

Rawly pushes ahead. "Come on. We're close."

The foursome finally comes upon an incline and they climb it. What they encounter, leaves Persimmon, Derpoke and Scraps momentarily speechless. There is a fenced-in field surrounded by mud.

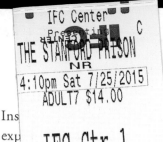

Ins   rhood full of houses, which is what they
exp   y one house off in the distance, and in
fro   mposing building with a shiny metal roof
tha   But it's not *what* they see that surprises
the... the most—it's the sounds and smell. The odor is the same heavy stench they came upon earlier, but it is so strong now that it burns their keen noses. It smells like a thousand piles of droppings. And the noise that fills the air is a sad mixture of moaning, wailing and weeping. The mysterious creatures inside that long building are suffering.

"Why are they crying?" Scraps whispers to Persimmon.

"I don't know," Persimmon replies, concerned. "You know what it reminds me of, though? Remember how I told you that I once came upon a fox who was howling hopelessly with her head caught in a trap?"

Scraps nods.

"It sounds like that," Persimmon explains.

Derpoke cuts in. "Wait, listen. They're not just crying. It sounds like they're saying something."

All four listen intently to the cries pouring out of the wooden building. Persimmon focuses her hearing on one particular animal and listens ever so carefully. Her heart breaks a little at what she hears. She can just barely make out one word being repeated over and over: "Mommy."

3

RAWLY SHRUGS. "THESE creatures cry like that every time I come here. So what?"

Persimmon shoots him a nasty look. "How can you be so callous? They're calling out for their mothers, obviously in pain. Or maybe they're crying because you're eating all of their food."

"Oh please," Rawly laughs. "They never have any food in there. They just sit in these wooden stalls whining all the time. I eat the food from the main burrow where the humans reside."

"Well then, have fun gorging on your feast," Persimmon remarks disdainfully. "I'm going to check on these injured creatures."

Scraps speaks up. "I'm coming, too."

Persimmon looks directly at her little brother. "Scraps, it's too dangerous. If they are hurt, they could be like that fox in the trap and scratch at you even though you're trying to help them."

"I didn't come all this way not to see them." Scraps holds his ground. "Besides, if they're in pain, I want to help, too."

Persimmon gives in. "Fine, but stay close."

She and Scraps start down the hill. Derpoke turns to Rawly. "Now who's cowardly?"

Rawly starts to respond, "I'm not afraid of..."

Derpoke doesn't stay to listen. He rushes to catch up with Persimmon and Scraps. Rawly is left squatting on top of the incline by himself—feeling foolish, although he keeps his head held high so no one will notice how foolish he feels.

The three critters crawl stealthily through the grass toward the building. No humans are in sight. They hoist themselves onto the wooden fence and when they get to the side of the building, Persimmon notices a hole in the wall up near the roof. She turns to her companions. "Ready?"

Derpoke and Scraps nod.

Persimmon climbs to the hole with ease and peeks her head inside. It's dark, but her eyes adjust quickly. She examines the interior and sees long rows of narrow wooden enclosures. Inside each one, she can make out shorthaired creatures with white and black patches. She squeezes through the opening for a closer look. Scraps and Derpoke climb the wall and follow close behind.

They scamper along the rafters high above the creatures. The putrid stench is unbearable. Scraps whispers to his sister, "How do they stand this smell? My nose is..." He stops mid-sentence, looking fearful. "Don't move. They're watching us."

Persimmon, Scraps and Derpoke peer down at the creatures, some of whom are now staring back at them. The creatures are bigger than they had imagined—five times the size of raccoons—and they each have four long legs. Their tails are longer than raccoons' tails and bushy only at the end. The trio is filled with a combination of excitement and anxiety. Their presence has been discovered. Now what?

Persimmon calls out with trepidation, "Hello?" Her voice gets lost among the moaning, though. She exclaims to her companions, "I'm going in closer."

She crawls down a wooden pole toward a set of crates. There are around a hundred in all, each containing one creature. She notices that the stalls are so narrow that the creatures cannot turn around. In fact, they can barely lie down.

Persimmon talks calmly to the two creatures she is crawling toward. "I'm not going to hurt you, okay?"

The creatures step back in fear as Persimmon approaches, but there's not much room for them to move. One of them slips on the messy wood slats and cries out as his back hits the wall.

"It's okay. I'm a friend." She sees that he has slipped on his own droppings. To her disgust, the wood below him is smeared with the foul substance, as is his black and white fur. "Goodness, sweet one, you need a dip in the stream." She notices that the creature beside him is also covered in his own droppings.

Now that Persimmon is closer, she realizes how big and soulful the creatures' eyes are. One of them whimpers in her direction, as if he's trying to say something.

"I'm sorry," Persimmon exclaims. "I don't understand you." She calls up to her friends. "I think he's trying to speak to me but doesn't know how."

Derpoke calls down. "Do they seem dangerous at all?"

"No," Persimmon remarks. "They seem scared. I... I think they're babies."

"Babies?!" Derpoke is stunned. "But they're enormous."

She gazes at the gentle giant. She half-whispers to herself, "There's just something about them. They seem so innocent."

The creature cries at her again.

"Are you hungry?" Persimmon asks, perplexed. "I'm sorry. I don't have any food."

Persimmon sees that he has a rope tied around his neck, connected to the wooden stall. "That's odd. Why would you be tied up? It's not like you can escape."

The creature moves toward her, whimpering.

Derpoke screams. "Persimmon, he's trying to eat you!"

"I'm fine." Persimmon dismisses her frantic friend.

The creature keeps crying as he nears her. Persimmon is slightly intimidated but she doesn't run away. Something in the creature's eyes makes her trust him. He moves his head—which is about half the size of her entire body—toward her.

"I'm sorry, sweetness," Persimmon apologizes. "I don't have any food. I don't even know what you eat."

The sad creature moves his head closer and closer, and for one second she fears he might bite her, but instead he rests his head against her soft fur. By instinct, as if he were her own little pup, she caresses his head by his ear. He lets out a sigh, closes his melancholy eyes, and unbeknownst to her, for the first time in his miserable life, he is calm.

"You just wanted a hug." Persimmon's heart aches. She rests her head on top of his and begins to hum a lullaby that her mother used to sing to her when she was a pup. And as she holds this sad creature close to her, she knows that she must help him. She doesn't know how yet, but she knows that somehow, some way, she must.

4

EVERY NIGHT FOR a month, Persimmon, Derpoke and Scraps go back to the large building to keep the shorthaired creatures company. The trio has learned from a rat that the creatures are called calves, that these particular ones are all males for some reason, and that they are the babies of cows (their mothers) and bulls (their fathers). The friends have given names to each one and throughout the nights, they take turns spending time with each calf. Persimmon's specialties are hugging and singing to them. She has grown especially close to Gilby, the calf who cuddled up to her that very first night. All of the calves enjoy her singing, but he's the one who nudges her to sing song after song.

Derpoke has bonded with Calvin due to the calf's curiosity about the outside world. None of the calves has ever stepped foot outside of their cramped stalls, so Derpoke describes things like streams and trees to them, and he even manages to teach them how to say certain words like "food," "yes," and "no"—without their mothers around, there has been no one to teach them verbal skills. Derpoke fancies himself a wordsmith, so he greatly enjoys having a room full of eager learners, Calvin being his best student.

Scraps likes to gather different types of food to share with the calves. He discovers that they thoroughly enjoy fruit, but refuse to eat insects and fish. Scraps is partial to a gentle calf he named Berry due to his seemingly endless desire for berries.

During the day, Persimmon observes the humans interacting with the calves and often has to restrain herself from interfering when she sees the humans get rough with the harmless beings. The farm workers never clean the calves—they'll kick them and slap them at times, and the only food they give these creatures are tiny portions of a white substance in a bottle. She guesses it's some type of milk but isn't sure why the humans don't let the mothers feed it to their babies naturally. After each meal, the animals always beg for more. Persimmon is overwhelmed with countless questions— *Why do they feed them so little? Why are they so rough with them? Why don't they clean up after them?*— but there are no easy answers to be found. After a month of spending time with the tormented calves, she can't stand it any longer.

"Derpoke, Scraps, come here." Persimmon leads them to one of the empty stalls. "Watch this." She fiddles with the door latch and it snaps open. Derpoke looks concerned, but Scraps is overjoyed. "You finally did it!"

"Shh. Yes. Keep it down. I'm excited too, but I don't want any of the calves seeing yet."

Persimmon motions for Derpoke and Scraps to follow her to where the calves won't be able to overhear, and they climb into the rafters.

"Look at them," she whispers. "They are sicker tonight than the first night we came in here. I thought that if we gave them food, spent time with them—sang to them, told them stories—maybe we could make them better, but they just keep getting more and more sickly."

Persimmon, Derpoke and Scraps look down at the calves inside their filthy, tiny stalls. Some of the calves are bobbing their heads back and forth, for no apparent reason. Countless flies buzz around, pestering them incessantly. All of the calves have constant, runny droppings. Their eyes and lungs burn from the putrid ammonia in the air—a nasty byproduct of the urine and feces mixing together. The stench is so foul that one could easily faint upon entering the room. The only reason Persimmon, Derpoke and Scraps can handle it night after night is because Derpoke came up with the ingenious idea of rubbing berries on their noses to make the hideous odor less pungent.

"We have to get them out of here," Persimmon declares.

"I know," Derpoke agrees. "But where do we take them? Are we supposed to hide them in a tree? There are so many of them, and they're so big."

"If we don't do something soon, some of them will die," Persimmon urges.

"Anywhere we go, the humans will surely come looking for them," Derpoke responds. "And who knows how fast the calves can run? On top of that, they don't have claws—I bet they can't climb. If the humans don't get them, mountain lions or coyotes surely will."

"Well, I can't just sit here and watch them suffer. They were already taken from their mothers—we can only imagine what the humans did to *them*. These calves have no one else to turn to, Derpoke."

Persimmon looks down at Gilby, who is cramped in his minuscule stall. "Do you know how much mint I feed Gilby every night? That's the only thing that calms his stomach, and he is in such pain he asks for it constantly."

"Persimmon, I worry about them, too. They're such sweet and smart creatures, and they spend every day and every night trapped in suffocating cages covered in feces. The other night Calvin asked if I would take him to see a stream. He just wanted to feel what it was like to dip his body in water. I didn't know what to say. I didn't want to lie to him, but I couldn't bear to tell him the truth, which is that I don't know if he'll ever step one hoof out of that stall."

Persimmon moves closer to Derpoke and looks him right in the eyes. "We can do this. We *have* to do this. If we were in those stalls we'd want someone to come and save us, right?"

"Well, yes."

"So, let us be the ones to save them."

Derpoke sighs. He looks away from Persimmon and finds Scraps staring at him with a beaming smile on his face, waiting excitedly for his response. "Well, of course you're on board, Scraps. You'd do anything that sounds thrilling, especially if there's danger involved."

Scraps hops up and down. "Come on! Please. They need us."

Derpoke sighs even louder to let them know how reluctant he is. "Ay ay ay. Okay, fine."

Persimmon hugs him. Scraps jumps on Derpoke's back.

"Alright, alright," Derpoke grouses. "Be exuberant in your own space."

Scraps continues to celebrate. "Yes! The Valiant Vermin emerge!"

Persimmon and Derpoke scrunch up their faces in disapproval.

Scraps looks surprised. "What? We need to have a team name."

"Okay, but the Valiant Vermin?" Derpoke retorts. "It sounds like we're a horde of heroic lice."

"I'll work on it."

"Sounds good." Derpoke turns to Persimmon. "And while he's doing that, we also need to find some help. I'm not so sure we can do this alone."

"I'm one step ahead of you, my diligent friend," Persimmon coolly replies.

5

RAWLY PUNCHES HIS paw through the surface of the cool stream, grasping the tail of a tiny fish. The fish thrashes around and Rawly tries to dig his claws in just as the fish slips out of his grip. "Rrrr. Come on!" He slaps the water in frustration.

"You know, berries don't swim away."

Rawly turns to see Persimmon sitting on the bank, facing him. He glares at her. "Don't you have some smelly beasts to sing to?"

"They're called calves, and how do you know I've been singing to them? Have you been spying on me?"

"Don't flatter yourself. I just wanted to see what you three were wasting your time doing every night."

"So you *were* spying on me." She smiles at him smugly. "Anyway, it's not their fault that they smell. In fact, that's what I was coming here to talk to you about."

"Aha, so you wanna know how I keep my fur smelling so fresh?"

"No, I want you to help us free the calves."

"What?! Are you rabid?" Rawly turns back around to look for more fish.

Persimmon steps into the water. She winces. The water is colder than she had anticipated. She pushes her way through the current, nearer to him. "Rawly, they're in a lot of pain. You don't see them every night like I do. It's been over two full moons, and they just keep getting sicker. If we don't get them out of there, I think they'll die."

Rawly focuses on the water, searching for another fish. "What are you gonna do with them if you free them—live inside a tree together? Those creatures are huge."

"But don't you see? They're just like us. They eat berries. They enjoy stories. Actually, they're sweeter than we are. I mean, you're about to catch a fish and rip him to shreds. They would never do that."

"Are you trying to tell me that I'm evil because I eat fish?"

Persimmon pauses. "No... maybe... I don't know. What I mean is that they need our help, and if you had any sense of decency, you would join us."

Rawly stops looking for fish and turns to her. "What's in it for me?"

"What's in it for you?! I just told you that they're suffering immensely each day and all you can think about is what you get out of saving them? Can you really be that selfish?"

Persimmon starts to crawl back out of the rushing water. Rawly calls after her. "We could die saving them. Don't try to pretend that our lives wouldn't be at risk."

Persimmon turns to face him. "Okay, yes, it is dangerous, but it's worth it. I'm brave enough to risk my life for them. Derpoke and Scraps are, too. Maybe if you exuded more courage, you'd have more females coming to your little territory." Persimmon splashes water at him. "I hope you accidentally grab a snake and he bites you."

Rawly's jaw drops open. "Whoa, I..."

Persimmon storms away without letting him finish, leaving Rawly sitting in the cold water, wondering what just happened.

6

THE GREAT ESCAPE!

Tonight, Persimmon, Derpoke and Scraps are going to rescue the calves from their dismal daily torment. All day, Persimmon rolls around in her tree trunk, unable to sleep—nervous, excited, hopeful.

"You can't let them down. You can't let them down," she repeats to herself over and over. "They're counting on you to save their lives, and if you fail, they will die." She has a plan, but she's still not exactly sure how she's going to pull it off. The only thing she knows for sure is that this is the most important task she's attempted in her entire life.

*　*　*

Persimmon, Derpoke and Scraps huddle together on top of the hill, looking down on the large building.

Derpoke turns to Persimmon. "I'm sorry I couldn't find even one opossum to help us. I made it clear that we rarely see humans at night, that the foul smell of the droppings washes out of your fur with a few deep dips in the stream, and that even though the calves are much bigger than us and, I suppose, could stomp on us, they're harmless. Despite all that reassurance, not one of my opossum friends or family agreed to join us." Persimmon and Scraps discreetly smile at one another over Derpoke's misguided persuasion tactics. Derpoke keeps going. "The part that boils me up the most is that they laughed at me, like what we're doing is silly. What is silly about trying to save lives?"

"I know you tried, my friend. I appreciate it." Persimmon pats Derpoke's paw. His heart begins to race, and he hopes she can't tell how flustered he is by her closeness. Persimmon continues, oblivious to the emotions she has just stirred in her friend. "The same thing happened to me. Every raccoon I talked to, including selfish Rawly, seemed completely baffled that we would take the time to free the calves, much less risk our lives to do it."

"Well, we don't need those naysayers. We've got the perfect team right here," Derpoke declares.

"That's the spirit, Derpoke! Okay..." Persimmon pulls in closer to them. "Don't forget, the moment we free the calves from the building and we all get out into the open, we have to sprint as fast as we can to the forest. Then, Derpoke, you keep watch on the first group of calves here among the trees while Scraps and I go back and get the others. Once all of the calves are relocated to this spot, we rush straight for the stream, no stopping. Got it?"

Derpoke and Scraps nod.

"Derpoke, remember who's in your first group: Calvin, Frederick..."

"Persimmon, I got it," Derpoke assures her. "We've been over this a hundred times."

"I know. I just want to be sure we're all set. If we make one mistake, it could cost all of us our lives. Scraps, stay within my sight, okay?"

Scraps nods again. He's not as talkative as usual and is breathing heavily.

Persimmon crawls closer to him and puts her paw on his back, scratching the part of his neck that makes his foot kick.

"You okay, baby brother? I don't mean to scare you. I just want to make sure we take the dangers seriously."

"I'm not scared… well, maybe a little, but mostly I just don't want to let them down. For the last few nights when Berry sees me, he keeps saying, 'Freedom?' He keeps thinking it's the night we're finally going to get them out of there."

"I know. I don't want to let them down either, but we have a solid plan and I believe in us." She turns to her opossum friend. "Derpoke, come here."

Persimmon pulls them into a huddle. "Derpoke, Scraps, you two are the most courageous and trustworthy souls I could ever hope to have by my side. Tonight, we are going to rescue these sweet creatures, and then we'll look after them as if they were our own pups. You have no idea how much it means to me that I can count on you."

She pulls them both in for a warm hug. Then they all kick their hind paws together and Persimmon exhorts, "To freedom!"

Derpoke and Scraps join in. "To freedom!"

$$* \quad * \quad *$$

The three friends crawl stealthily down the hill and into the large building. The nearly one hundred calves perk up at their arrival. Cheers of "Persimmon!" and "They're here!" can be heard coming from every stall.

Persimmon, Derpoke and Scraps waste no time getting their plan underway. "Listen up, everyone," Persimmon calls out. "Tonight, we're going to get you out of here."

The calves rejoice. Persimmon continues. "Now I need you all to remember who your team leader is. Does everyone know who they're following?"

Each calf calls out the name of his leader.

"Persimmon!"

"Scraps!"

"Derpoke!"

"Okay, good. Now I know you're excited to see the outside world, but there will be time for exploring grass and bushes later. Right now we need each of you to follow us as fast as you can until we get to the forest. Once we're there, we're going to head straight for the stream."

Some of the calves call out, "Stream!" They're very excited about seeing moving water for the first time. They've spent most of their lives stained with their own feces, so they can't wait to be clean and drink to their hearts' content.

"Okay, let's get going," Persimmon instructs.

Like clockwork, Derpoke and Scraps start their first major task: chewing through each calf's rope. As they begin, Persimmon crawls from one gate to the next, undoing the latches. Some are more jammed shut than others, but she pulls and prods until each one opens. Then she starts chewing the ropes herself. She first crawls down into Gilby's stall.

Gilby livens up. "Freedom?"

"Yes, Gilby. Tonight you're going to be free."

She steps down onto the grimy wood slats that are smothered in excrement and takes a hold of his rope. The smell of the stall is overwhelming and the rope tastes atrocious.

"We go swimming?" Gilby asks.

She stops chewing for a second. "Yes, later, but now we need to focus on getting you out of here." She goes back to chomping on the rope. She can feel her teeth slowly tearing through the threads.

Gilby moans in pain. "My tummy's owie. Have mint?"

"Not now, Gilby. I'm sorry. I need to focus on biting this rope, okay? Once we get out of here, then we can talk. You understand?"

He looks at her with those melancholy eyes. "Sorry."

"It's fine. I know your stomach hurts. After tonight you can have all the mint you want. And then one day you won't need mint, because you'll be all better." She pats him on the cheek.

Derpoke rushes across the stall wall above her, calling down as he passes by. "Three ropes down. Only around two thousand left."

"Keep up the good work, my friend!"

*   *   *

Persimmon has been chewing through ropes for what feels like hours. Pestering flies buzz around her face, crawling into her eyes. Her mouth is raw and sore. She is now in Dill's stall and as she bites, she notices the rope is stained red right where she was nibbling. She looks closer. It's blood. She's bleeding. She stops chewing for a second. A wave of discouragement sweeps through her. *Can we do this?* she wonders, frightened by her sudden doubt.

Dill notices the blood on her mouth. "Owie?"

"Yes, I have an owie. It's okay. It's nothing compared to what you're going through."

"Hey, Persimmon," Derpoke calls out. "Look who decided to show up."

Persimmon peers up to see Derpoke with Rawly at his side. She's worn out and covered in filth, but she smiles at the sight of a much-needed helper. This is exactly what she needed to keep her spirits up.

"Just in time. Thank you for coming," she says with a sigh of relief.

"Looks like a snake didn't bite me after all." Rawly pauses just long enough to make her uncomfortable over her snide comment the other day and then adds, "So, what needs doing?"

"Can you help chew through these ropes? It's taking way longer than I thought it would."

"Lucky for you, I have the sharpest teeth in the forest." Rawly trots off proudly, feeling mighty good about himself for saving the day.

Derpoke crawls into the stall toward Persimmon and whispers, "Surprising that he showed up, eh?"

"I'm so glad he did. This is…"

Derpoke cuts her off. "Persimmon, your mouth is bleeding."

"Yes, I just noticed. It's alright. I'm almost done."

"Why don't you let me finish that one? You should take a break."

"No. No time for breaks." Persimmon notices that Derpoke's mouth is bleeding as well. "Oh no, are *you* okay?"

Derpoke shrugs. "At least these things aren't made of metal. So can I finish that one for you or not?"

"No, I'll handle it. You and Scraps should start opening the gates for your teams, okay? All the gates are unlocked."

"Check."

Derpoke climbs back out of the stall while Persimmon chomps ferociously through one last rope. Finally, it tears apart. She lets out a joyous sigh and smiles at Dill. "We did it!"

Dill lights up. "Freedom!"

Persimmon pats him on the leg. "That's right, Dill. Freedom."

Persimmon pushes open Dill's front gate. "Okay, now remember, you're on my team, so you need to follow me. Got it?"

"Follow you."

Persimmon scampers out onto the main floor, followed by Dill. His legs are weak, so he more wobbles than walks, but he pushes forward, fueled by hope.

Persimmon looks around the main area and sees that all of the calves are struggling to walk. Derpoke is coaxing Frederick to stand up. "Come on, Frederick. You can do it."

Frederick moans in pain as he tries to lift himself up on his frail legs.

"I know it hurts, buddy, but you have to push through the pain," Derpoke coaches.

Scraps has four teams of ten all lined up and ready to go. Persimmon scurries over to him.

"Scraps, I'm so proud of you. You're more organized than the rest of us." She turns to the calves on his teams. "Berry, Tate, Manny, Peter, Twig…" She looks down the line of forty calves and realizes she doesn't have time to name each one. "All of you are doing an admirable job. Keep up the good work."

The calves beam, proud of themselves. Rawly trots over. "All of the ropes are done, Persimmon, but I think you should come here."

Persimmon follows Rawly over to one of the stalls. Inside, Calvin is lying on the wood slats, moaning. "He won't stand up," Rawly explains gravely.

Persimmon crawls over to him. "Calvin, I know it hurts, but we need you to get up now."

Calvin whimpers. He seems to be in unbearable pain.

"Come on, Calvin. Let me see you stand up. You can do it. I know you can."

Persimmon steps back to give him room. Calvin pushes with all his might to lift himself up. "Come on. That's right." Everyone around him—Persimmon, Derpoke, Rawly, some of the other calves—coaxes him. "Come on. You can do it."

Calvin pushes and pushes. He gets his front legs up, but he can't move his back legs. He cries out in pain and collapses back onto the ground.

Persimmon motions for Derpoke and Rawly to follow her as she steps away from Calvin. She makes sure the calves are out of earshot before anyone starts talking.

"If all four of us worked together, maybe we could carry him," Rawly whispers.

Persimmon sighs heavily. "No, I need all of us to focus on leading the calves out of here. If we're carrying Calvin, the rest of them will be all over the place."

Derpoke looks like he's about to cry. "So we just leave him here?"

"Derpoke, I know you're especially close to him. I don't want to leave him here either, but if we... we can't risk... let's focus on getting all of the other calves out of here first. We'll get them into the forest where they're safe. By that point, there will be too many calves for you to watch alone, so maybe Scraps can stay there with you, and Rawly and I will come back for Calvin. If need be we'll find some other raccoons to help. Okay? We're not leaving him. We'll be back."

Derpoke pleads with her. "But what if we run out of time? What if the sun comes up before we have time to get back here? Then the humans will be awake and..."

Scraps calls out from the main walkway. "Persimmon! I need your help."

Scraps is doing his best to keep the calves in line, but they're starting to wander aimlessly. Some are even trying to escape outside.

Persimmon rushes over. "Everyone, please. Calm down. Focus. Line up by your leader. Gilby, Dill, over here with me. Berry, Tate, Twig, please get back in line with Scraps." Persimmon continues to sort out the various calves with their leaders. She gets Rawly's attention.

"Rawly, follow alongside all the groups, and if we have any stragglers, help guide them back to their teams. Sound good?"

"Consider it done."

Derpoke stands beside Calvin, gently rubbing his ear. "Calvin, I need you to stand up, okay? I know your legs hurt, but you need to fight through the pain. Please."

Calvin moans. "Legs hurt. So much."

*   *   *

Persimmon stands at the front door, peering into the dark field. The forest is over a hundred yards away and there is no cover until that point—just open field with a lot of mud to trek through. Luckily, there are no humans around. It's now or never.

"Okay, first group, follow right behind me. Quietly."

She steps into the mud with her team of ten calves following after. Their legs are weak, so it's slow going. Dill slips and falls to his knees. He struggles to stand back up. Griffin falls too. Persimmon reassures them. "It's alright. You're getting used to walking. Just put one hoof in front of the other and keep pushing forward."

Scraps peeks his head out of the doorway with his first crew in tow. "Okay team, keep in line just like I showed you." Scraps steps out into the mud, bathed in moonlight. He catches up to Dill, who is at the end of Persimmon's crew. Dill is barely moving forward and his legs look like they're about to buckle. "You okay, Dill?"

Dill's legs give out and he topples to the ground. This sends Griffin, who is just as worn out, to the ground as well.

Scraps gently scolds them. "No, no, guys. You can't sit down. We have to keep moving."

Persimmon turns around to see two of her team members sitting on the ground. She quickly says to Gilby, who is right behind her,

"Keep steering the others along this fence. You're the leader right now, alright?"

"All right," Gilby exclaims, excited to take charge.

She zooms past the next few calves in line. "Ant, Little, all of you, follow Gilby. I'll be right there."

*   *   *

Back inside, Rawly steps up to Derpoke, who is still kneeling beside Calvin. "Derpoke, we need to go now. The first two teams are already out of the building, and we have to keep this mission moving forward."

"Give me a minute. Calvin can do this. He just needs some help."

"We'll come back for him. You need to take your team out."

Derpoke stands on his hind legs, defying Rawly. "I'm not leaving him here. Take my group. We'll be there shortly."

"You're risking everyone's life for one calf. That's foolish, Derpoke."

Rawly rushes up to the nine calves who are awaiting their turn to step outside. "Team, I'm Rawly. I know you don't know me, but I need you to follow me to safety."

Derpoke runs behind Calvin and leans into the calf's rear-end with all of his might. "Stand up, Calvin. Now. I'm not asking. I'm telling you. Stand up."

Calvin strains every muscle in his body. He huffs and groans. He struggles and fights. But it's no use. His back legs are useless.

Derpoke gets in Calvin's face. "Please. Please. Don't make me leave you."

Calvin has a look of sheer terror in his eyes. "Don't leave me!"

"Well, then get up!" Derpoke's eyes are filled with tears. He is frantic.

Frederick and some of the other calves start to cry, but Rawly attempts to rally them. "Come on, guys. I need you to follow me out that door." They won't budge. Derpoke is their team leader.

Derpoke looks at them. He knows what he has to do. His heart burns with guilt.

"Just rest, Calvin. We're going to take the others to safety and then we'll come back to get you."

Calvin sobs. "Don't leave me!"

"We're not leaving you. We'll be back. I promise."

"I walk. I walk." Calvin starts to pull his body forward, dragging his limp legs on the wood behind him.

Derpoke marches over to his first group of calves. He clears his throat, fighting the urge to scream in desperation. "Team, line up behind Rawly." The calves are staring at Calvin, who is still dragging himself toward them. "Focus, team!" The calves look at Derpoke. "Good. Now march forward." Rawly walks through the door with the calves reluctantly following him. As Frederick turns around to look at Calvin, Derpoke gives him a stern look. "Eyes forward! Keep going!"

They step through the doorway. Derpoke turns to shut the door. He sees Calvin pulling his broken body along the ground. "Derpoke, don't leave!"

Derpoke can barely see through the tears in his eyes. He tries to say something, but he can't speak. It hurts too much. What do you say to someone who you're abandoning anyway?

Other calves in the room see Calvin being left behind, and they mistakenly think they're being dealt a similar fate. Some wail, others trample over one another to push their way through the door.

Derpoke struggles to keep them in the building. "Stop! We're coming back."

A few calves push past him into the field. Finally, he pulls the door shut as calves bang against it and howl on the other side, as if they were being burned alive. He looks around to see some of the calves from his first group staring at him, scared. "We're not leaving them. We just can't have them escaping unsupervised."

The calves look unconvinced. Derpoke isn't so sure he's convinced either.

7

RAWLY STEPS UP to Scraps with his troop following him and Derpoke trailing behind. To Rawly's dismay, a whole gang of calves is sprawled out in the mud around Scraps, whimpering in agony. The calves are still out in the open, a full fifty yards from the edge of the forest.

Rawly is in shock. "What's going on? Why is everyone lying down?"

"Their legs hurt too much," Scraps explains, overwhelmed. "They say it's too painful to walk."

"Where is Persimmon?" Rawly demands.

"She's over there." Scraps points to Persimmon, who is off in the distance leading a group of calves. "She's taking the ones who can walk up to the edge of the forest, and then she'll be back for the others."

Rawly growls. "You can't just sit out here with no shelter. It's too dangerous."

"I know that, but they cry every time they move their legs. What am I supposed to do?"

Rawly runs up to the calves who are sitting in the mud and rams his head into them, one by one. "Get up! Get up! You don't have time to rest."

"Rawly, you're being too rough with them. Stop." Scraps protests. Rawly ignores him. "Do you all want to die? No? Then get up!" Some of the calves teeter to a standing position. "Good. Now follow me. We need to get to safety."

Rawly darts along the fence with about half of the calves following.

Scraps hunkers down next to Derpoke, who is now sitting in the dirt. "What do we do?" he asks. "We can't carry all of them. And there are still so many more calves back in the building." Scraps looks at Derpoke for an answer, but he just sees a hollow look in Derpoke's eyes. "You okay?" Derpoke shakes his head but doesn't say a word.

Scraps surveys the moaning calves lying in the mud. They look so helpless. He feels so helpless. "Everything's falling apart."

*   *   *

Rawly catches up to Persimmon. "I can't believe you haven't even gotten the first group to the forest yet. We need to get these calves out of the clearing."

"What do you think I'm trying to do?" Persimmon snaps back at him.

"Well, you're not doing a good job. Half of your team has collapsed in the mud. And the rest are panicking in the building."

"Just get…"

BAM!

A loud shot rings out. Dirt sprays all around Persimmon and Rawly. Persimmon keels over in pain. Her tail has been shot off. Blood pours out of the wound.

"Got 'im!" a farm hands yells out in victory.

"There's another one over there!" Another farm hand shouts as he eyes Scraps and aims his gun right at him. Luckily, Tate, Frederick and the other calves around Scraps scatter at just that moment, blocking the human's view.

"Hold on," the farm hand who shot Persimmon hollers frantically. "You'll shoot the damn calves."

Rawly drags Persimmon toward the woods. Persimmon is screaming in pain but she's more concerned with the calves. "Wait, we can't leave them."

Rawly doesn't stop. "The humans won't shoot the calves, but they *will* shoot us. We have to get to the forest now!"

*　*　*

Derpoke and Scraps dash under the fence, still only halfway to the forest. The mud is thick and clings to their fur, which slows them down as they rush for the trees.

A group of farm hands runs around, trying to gather up the calves. "How did all these damn animals escape?! What is going on here?"

A man pounces on Dill. "Stupid animal! Git over here!" He grabs Dill by the back legs and drags him toward the large building. Dill shrieks and clambers to break free.

Another man aims a gun at Derpoke as he strains to push his way through the mud. "I think I got a shot."

His buddy gleefully goads him on. "Then shoot 'im!"

The man unloads his shotgun.

SMASH!

The bullet crashes into the fence just above Derpoke, sending splinters of wood into his flesh. Derpoke trips face-first into the dirt.

The man celebrates. "I got 'im!"

Scraps skids to a stop and rushes back to his friend. "Derpoke! Are you okay?"

Derpoke lies frozen in the mud.

"Derpoke, can you move?"

Derpoke opens his eyes with pure terror etched on his face. "Go. Run!"

"Not without you," Scraps refuses.

The two men start walking toward Scraps and Derpoke. Scraps crouches down next to his injured companion.

"Derpoke, they're coming. Are you hurt or just scared?"

"Both."

"If you can get up, you need to move. You don't have time to be scared. I'm not leaving you, but I sure don't want to get shot, so I need you to get up. Now!"

Derpoke pushes himself up onto his feet, trying to ignore the searing pain in his back.

The men see Derpoke get up. "You missed him, idiot!"

"Not this time."

The man aims his gun again. He follows Derpoke and Scraps as they run toward the forest, lining up his shot. Just before he pulls the trigger a calf steps into his line of sight. It's Berry, standing there bravely, willing to take a bullet for his friends.

The man furiously shakes his gun in the air. "These calves are the stupidest animals on the planet. He don't even know that I coulda put a bullet in his head." He yells at Berry, "Get out of the goddamn way!"

The man aims his gun again, searching for Derpoke and Scraps in the mud, but they're nowhere to be found.

The other man laughs heartily. "Ha ha! Nice shootin'!"

"Shut up! I woulda got 'em if it wasn't for that goddamn calf." The man runs up to Berry and kicks him over. Berry screeches as the man hollers, "I shoulda shot you, stupid shit."

Another farm hand angrily yells at the two men. "Come on, no more playin' around. We gotta get all these calves back in that barn 'fore we catch some hell."

*   *   *

Persimmon and Rawly are hunkered down at the edge of the woods. They see Scraps and Derpoke racing toward the forest's edge. "Scraps, Derpoke—over here!" Persimmon calls out.

Scraps and Derpoke run into the cover of the trees beside their friends.

Persimmon hugs them both. "You made it. I was so worried."

Derpoke sees blood flowing out of a tiny hole where Persimmon's tail once was. "Persimmon, your tail!"

Persimmon shrugs it off. "I know. I don't care about me. We have to help the calves."

"But you'll bleed to death," Derpoke insists.

Persimmon isn't listening. She is horrified as she watches the humans kick and beat the calves with metal rods. The humans curse the crying creatures as they drag them back into the filthy building.

"Stupid animal! Where'n the hell you think you were going, huh?" One of the humans kicks Gilby hard in the back. "Maybe I'll break your legs. Then you won't be goin' nowhere!" The man slams the metal rod so hard into Gilby's right hind leg that he buckles to the ground, wailing in pain.

Persimmon almost rushes out into the field, but Rawly holds her back. "Persimmon, they'll shoot you. You can't help him. Not now."

"But they're beating him to death."

"No, they won't kill the calves," Rawly assures her. "They've been keeping them alive all this time for a reason. They're worth more to them alive than dead."

"But it's our fault—it's *my* fault this is happening to them. I can't just desert them," Persimmon laments.

Rawly looks her in the eyes. "Persimmon, if you go down there, you will die. You cannot help them right now. Not only do the humans outnumber us, but each of them has a gun. Running down there now would not be an act of bravery; it would be an act of stupidity."

Persimmon looks over at Scraps and Derpoke. They nod in agreement. Rawly's right, and she knows it.

As the rush of Persimmon's near-death escape begins to wear off, the pulsating agony of her wound starts to take over. She rests her stomach against the ground, slightly light-headed. "What have I done? How did our plan go so wrong?" she ponders aloud. "I know that we were going slowly, but we were quiet. How did the humans know we were breaking the calves free? Did some dog alert them? I never saw a dog."

Derpoke speaks up. "You need to lick your tail to stop the bleeding. That's a very serious injury."

Persimmon licks her wound in defeat, then notices the bloody spots on her opossum friend's fur. "Derpoke, you're bleeding all over your back!"

"Yes, it hurts, but it could have been worse. I think it's just a bunch of splinters. I almost got shot, but Berry put himself in the line of fire. He risked his life for us. What a remarkable soul."

Persimmon looks at the ground, frustrated, disappointed in herself. "All that planning we did—splitting the calves up into teams, practicing with them to memorize their groups, chewing through all those ropes, going over every detail so many times. And it all came crashing down because the poor babies can't walk. I knew they were weak, but how are we supposed to save them if they can't even stand upright for more than three steps? I'm so furious at these humans for making them so sick, for treating them this way!"

Off in the distance, the calves, who are now locked up again in their tiny stalls, can be heard crying. One human stands guard with a gun at the entrance to the building.

Derpoke steps over to Persimmon. "We did our best. We got in over our heads and underestimated how..."

"Oh, please," Rawly snarls. "All these excuses are worthless. We failed. And now..." Rawly stops talking, distracted by the upsetting sound of the calves' wailing. "I wish they would stop crying. I can't take it. I can't listen to them anymore." Rawly speeds off into the forest.

Persimmon calls after him. "Rawly, wait."

"Let him go," Derpoke interjects. "He's right. We should all get away from here. It's just going to break our hearts more to hear them whimpering in pain."

Persimmon doesn't look at Derpoke. "You can go. I..." She stops. "That's it. Their cries. The humans have listened to them crying all day and night for who knows how long, and then suddenly tonight, they were quiet when we tried to help them escape."

She pauses and thinks. "I thought the humans had somehow outsmarted us, but they're not more intelligent than we are; they're just callous. The only time they show any concern is when the calves are *not* suffering."

Persimmon closes her eyes. She feels slightly dizzy and is weak from the loss of blood. "I must sleep."

"Here?" Derpoke protests. "What if the humans find you?"

"They won't. It's fine. I can't leave the calves."

She curls up into a ball, licking the hole where her tail once was. Scraps nuzzles in close to her. Derpoke sits down beside her, keeping watch in case any humans make their way into the woods.

Persimmon starts to doze off, but her mind is already swirling with ideas for a new plan—a better plan. She knew the calves were sickly, but she completely underestimated the extent of their physical deterioration due to their malnourishment, unsanitary living conditions, and lack of exercise. Now that she knows their leg muscles have almost completely atrophied, she'll adjust for that. She'll have to rally more raccoons and opossums to help—even if she has to bribe them. The next rescue attempt may need to involve carrying the calves, so she'll have to come up with a clever way to accomplish that, but no matter the level of difficulty, this isn't over. She told the calves that she'd help them escape and she will. They deserve better than a life inside those cramped and sickening stalls. The humans are absolutely not smarter than she is; she just misunderstood how badly they had damaged these innocent creatures. She'll never make that mistake again.

8

PERSIMMON IS PERCHED on a rock at the base of a big tree, peering at the building in which the calves are held captive. A fire burns in her heart. She is irate at the humans for what they have put these calves through, and she is determined to save them. It has been a week since the failed rescue, and every night she has sat atop the hill at the edge of the forest watching over the farm. She dares not venture any closer until she can be sure there aren't any humans guarding the area—even if she can't see them, she knows they may be secretly monitoring the area. She has been racking her brain but still hasn't come up with a solid plan for a new exodus. Soon though, she will. She just needs to think harder.

The sun is starting to rise, so Persimmon calls out toward the building. "I'm going off to sleep now, sweet ones. I'll be back tomorrow." She knows that the calves are too far away to make out what she is saying, but it makes her feel better to think that just the sound of her voice might bring them some comfort. If only she could hug them and bring them food. *I bet Gilby could use some mint right about now,* she ponders sorrowfully.

At that moment, a little twig ricochets off her back. Persimmon turns around, annoyed.

"Excuse me," a voice from high up in the tree next to her calls down. Persimmon gazes into the thick branches above but doesn't see where the voice is coming from. Another twig plops onto her back.

"Who's there?" Persimmon calls out.

A female squirrel is crawling down the tree, but a male squirrel is pulling on her tail, trying to stop her from descending. "Tucker, let go of my tail," the female squirrel demands.

Tucker holds onto her tightly. "No, do not climb down this tree. Chloe, stop."

Chloe tries to push him off with her hind legs, but Tucker keeps holding on. Persimmon watches, confused. Tucker finally lets go of Chloe's tail, but she is struggling so hard to break free that she loses her grip on the tree trunk and falls straight to the ground.

Persimmon steps closer to Chloe. "Are you okay?"

"I'm fine." She glares at Tucker. "It's nice to meet someone with manners for a change."

Tucker harrumphs and scampers back up into the tree.

Chloe curtsies for Persimmon. "Hello. My name is Chloe."

"My name is Persimmon."

"Persimmon. Great. So I finally learn your name. I feel like I already know you, I have been watching you so long." She corrects herself. "That sounds a bit odd. You see, the thing is, I think you're brave. I saw you and your friends feeding those calves, and then trying to free them, and I thought it was valiant."

"And foolhardy," Tucker calls down from the tree. "It's not our problem to deal with."

"Don't listen to him," Chloe insists. "He's just sour because I said that we should help you, and when he refused, I called him uncaring and apathetic."

"Thank you very much for wanting to help, Chloe. I appreciate your even considering it." Persimmon looks up into the tree. "Tucker,

I understand you not wanting to join in on our mission. It was danger-ous and reckless, but if you had only seen the pleading in the calves' eyes. We raccoons and squirrels are lucky that we are free."

Chloe nods her head and sassily flicks her tail at Tucker. "I al-ways wanted to help, I just didn't know how. But you're actually doing something!"

Before Persimmon has a chance to respond, she is distracted by two giant trucks pulling up to the building where the calves are stored. She watches as humans open the back of the first truck and lower a ramp by the building's entrance. Her heart jumps when she sees some of the humans pull out the metal rods that they always use to beat the calves.

Chloe lets out a sad sigh. "Oh, no."

Persimmon's pulse races. "Chloe, what is happening?"

"They're taking the calves away. We've seen this many times be-fore. My family's lived in this tree for generations, and that farm has been in business even longer."

"Where are the humans taking them?"

Chloe hesitates. "They're taking them to be slaughtered."

"Slaughtered? You mean killed?! Why?"

"You don't know? The humans eat them."

Persimmon lets out a pained gasp, as if someone had ripped her heart straight from her chest. She can barely breathe. This is the deep, dark fear she never dared utter. All along, she had a terrible feeling that the humans were keeping the calves captive to eat them one day, but it was such a dis-gusting thought that she wouldn't allow herself to dwell on it.

Persimmon is aghast. "But they're just babies. And they're so frail and run-down."

"The humans think the calves taste better like that," Chloe ex-plains. "They call their flesh veal."

Persimmon can't believe what she's hearing. "The humans put the calves through all this torment and intentionally make them sick just because they think that makes them taste better?!"

Persimmon can hear the calves crying as the men hit the creatures with their rods to make them move. She sees Gilby, Berry and Dill being kicked and pushed out of the building and onto the ramp. They all struggle to walk. Then she gasps as she sees a man drag Calvin along the ground, using a chain tightly tied around his neck since his legs aren't working. Calvin struggles to breathe as he is yanked up the hard metal ramp and onto the truck.

"Persimmon! Persimmon!" the calves are crying out her name in terror. She must act now. They need her. Without hesitation, Persimmon rushes down the hill toward them.

Chloe calls after her but Persimmon doesn't stop.

Chloe looks up at Tucker. "We have to tell her friends." She rushes into the forest.

Persimmon crawls by the side of the building, as low as she can get. Half of the calves are already on the truck. She watches in horror as, one-by-one, these babies are kicked, hit, shoved and dragged onto the truck. *What can I do? What can I do?* she wonders desperately. She can't take on these humans all by herself—they have weapons.

"Persimmon! Persimmon!" Persimmon's eyes well up as she hears Gilby and some of the others begging for her to save them. They don't even know that she's right there; they're just calling out to one of the only beings in the entire world who has actually shown them love—but how can she possibly help?

With the first group of calves on the truck, the humans slam the back gate shut. Just then, Persimmon sees Rawly, Derpoke, Scraps and Chloe running down the hill toward her.

The truck's engine turns on. The humans close the truck doors. It's now or never. Persimmon rushes as fast as she can toward the vehicle. Gilby sees her running toward the back gate. "Persimmon!"

The truck shifts into gear and starts to roll forward. Rawly, Derpoke, Scraps and Chloe are alarmed to see Persimmon sprinting toward it.

"Persimmon! No!" Derpoke calls out.

Persimmon jumps with all her might and clings to the bumper. She hoists herself up and crawls along the metal slats into the carriage section with the frightened calves. She turns around and sees Derpoke running as fast as he can toward them. He is breathing so intensely that Persimmon worries he'll hurt himself, and he is hobbling because of his wounded back. The truck moves away from him, faster than his little legs can run.

Persimmon looks through the metal bars of the truck as it speeds away. She puts her paw against her heart to signal to Derpoke that she loves him. He watches helplessly as the vehicle carrying the calves and his best friend disappears beyond a bend in the road.

9

THE CALVES ARE frantic as the truck rushes down the highway. Persimmon does her best to comfort them. "Everyone, please. Keep calm. I'm going to get you out of this."

"Persimmon, where are we going?" Gilby cries.

"I'm not sure. I need to think of a plan. We just..."

Persimmon stops talking. She can barely hear her own voice. It is so noisy between the rush of the wind, the roar of the truck's engine, and the howls and moans of the calves. Her brain is swirling with ideas to get them out of this situation. *Maybe the truck will stop along the way, and when it does, I can pry open the back gate and they can run for their lives... But how can they run if they can barely even walk?... Not running isn't even an option any more. They'll run... Okay, that's a possibility for this truck, but what about the second truck? I'm sure they're not far behind.* She pauses. This is all happening so fast. *Just focus on this truck for now. You can figure out the other one later.*

Persimmon clings to the metal slats, but her legs are getting tired. She needs to find a safer place to sit where she won't be bounced out of the truck. Unfortunately, the cargo area is dangerously overcrowded. The calves are so tightly packed together that some of them are lying on top of others without room to put their legs on the ground. If she tries to squeeze into a spot on the floor, she'll likely be crushed. But there's no way she's touching that floor anyway. The calves were so panicked as they were being shoved onto the truck that they littered the ground with droppings and urine. She'll just have to hold onto the side and hope that the ride isn't too long.

The wind rips at her fur and slaps her so hard in the face that it stings. She watches the road, trying to memorize the truck's route. When this is all done, she'll need to find her way home with the calves.

"I'm scared, Persimmon." Gilby nuzzles his head against the soft fur on her back.

"I know, sweetness. I'm going to help you, though, okay? We're going to get through this." Persimmon tries to smile reassuringly at him, but it's difficult to sound convincing while she's clinging to the side of a truck for her own dear life.

Persimmon knows she can't show it, but she is scared too. More questions spin through her mind. *Will the humans really kill all of these innocent calves? What does it mean to be slaughtered? Will the humans beat them to death with their metal rods? Will they eat them alive?* She shudders at the thought. *I can't think about that. I need to focus on getting them out of here. They are counting on me to save them. They cried out my name when they were scared. Not their mothers*—me. Persimmon's maternal instinct kicks in even more at this thought. *I will not let my babies down. I will not let them die.*

She closes her eyes and thinks hard about what to do. The calves are still sobbing. The moaning gets louder as they try to move around and bang into one another. Each one is trying to find space to breathe and sit down. Their legs are frail and they need to sit, but there is no room. Each time one moves, another bangs into the calf beside him, and then another gets smashed against the metal slats. Someone is going to get crushed if this doesn't stop. Persimmon springs into action.

"Dill, sit still. Berry, no pushing." She climbs around the inside of the truck, quieting the calves as she moves from one spot to the next. "Calm yourselves," she whispers soothingly. "You're going to get hurt. I have a plan, but you need to listen." The calves stop pushing to listen to her.

"This is very important. At some point this truck is going to come to a halt and the humans are going to open the back gate. And when they do, you are going to charge them. You got it?"

They look at her blankly. "Do you understand? I know you think you don't have the strength, but when that gate opens, you need to push and shove, but not against each other—against the humans. They're going to swing their sticks at you, but keep moving forward. Try to get past them. And then run. Hobble if you have to. Help each other. Just get as far away as you can. There will probably be a forest near where we stop. Go into the forest and I will find you. Got it?"

"Run?" Dill calls out.

"Yes." She yells to the group over the noise of the truck. "I know it hurts to run, but you'll rest your legs later. Just follow me. I'll lead you into the forest. I know you're afraid, but you have to be brave. Do you know what brave is?" They look lost. If only she had more time to teach them how to speak. They need to understand her. "Brave. The opposite of scared. You can't be scared this time. It's too important."

She looks at their faces. They're worn out. They're terrified. Some of the calves aren't even facing her, because there is no room for them to move around. There's no use in overwhelming them with any more orders at the moment.

She crawls along the metal slats to the other side of the truck. Her paws are aching from grabbing onto the metal for so long. Luckily, she sees a small section of the ground that is raised to give room for the wheels below. It isn't quite big enough for a calf, but it's enough for a raccoon to rest on. She hunkers down onto the metal slab, and softly whispers to herself, "We can do this. I know we can do this."

10

PERSIMMON AND THE calves are insufferably hot. The sun has been baking the back of the truck for hours. They desperately need water. Persimmon's thick fur especially weighs down on her, but the most painful part is that her paws burn from holding onto the scalding metal, which has been getting increasingly hotter as the day wears on.

Gilby has been pushed up against the wall where Persimmon is sitting. He opens his eyes and notices the stub where her tail once was. "Owie?"

"Yes, my tail is gone. The humans shot it off."

His face scrunches up with indignation. "Humans."

Persimmon can't believe what she's witnessing. For the first time in Gilby's short life, he shows a sign of anger, but the endearing part is that despite all that the humans have done to him, he's actually more upset over learning that they harmed *her*.

What a loving, empathetic being, she reflects, warmed by her bond with Gilby. There's much she wants to say to him, but she is so over-heated that she can't think straight and just pats him on the head. Berry, who is squished beside them, rubs his head against her stomach urging her to caress his head too. She gently rubs his ear and hums her mother's lullaby. The other calves beside them quiet their crying and listen as she hums. Berry hums along.

"That's right, Berry. You hum to me."

Berry keeps humming the lullaby. Persimmon looks out the side of the truck at the trees and road zipping by. It feels like they've been traveling for days. She had no idea there was so much land. She has seen cars before, but never this many. Who knew there were so many humans beyond the forest?

She looks into the automobiles as they pass by. Some cars have kids in them; some have old people. And there are so many different shades of humans. But none of them seem the least bit concerned about the calves in the back of the truck. *Do they know that these calves are being driven to their deaths? Do they know how hot and thirsty they are? Why don't they stop the truck? Are they excited about eating the calves? Do they just see them as food? Don't they know that Gilby, Dill and Berry are back here suffering?*

She has seen humans be outwardly cruel to other animals before but never indifferent. She wonders if these humans' indifference is just as bad as the farm hands' beating of the calves since both ways lead to her babies' demises.

Just then, some of the calves start crying and pushing again. Persimmon hops up to see what the matter is. She notices that the calves are shoving one another to move away from a particular area, but she can't tell why there's so much commotion. She crawls to the top of the wall and looks down. There is an empty space where no calves are standing, but she can't see what they're moving away from. *Is it a snake?* she wonders.

Persimmon darts across the calves' backs to make it more quickly to the center of the scuffle. To her horror, she sees Calvin lying on his side on the ground. In their rush to get away from him, the other calves are trampling him.

"You're crushing him! Stop! You're going to kill him."

But she sees that Calvin is already motionless. He's already dead. He was weak before he got into the truck and the intense heat pushed him over the edge.

Persimmon doesn't have time to process the horror of what she sees. The calves are in an uncontrollable frenzy, wailing, "Calvin dead!" Persimmon gets shaken around and fears that she will fall to the ground, where she'll surely be stomped on. She hops her way to the side of the truck as it comes to a stop on the side of the road.

A human steps out of the truck and walks around to the back. Persimmon whispers emphatically. "Shh, everyone. Keep quiet." She fears the human will beat the calves to silence them. "Shh. Please."

The man angrily pops open the back gate. Persimmon hunkers down at the far back of the truck, hoping not to be seen. "Shut the hell up, you shits!" He hits a few calves with his metal rod. "What the hell is your problem?" He sees Calvin's dead body on the floor of the truck. "Goddamn it." He pushes and kicks his way through the calves toward Calvin. "Git the hell outta my way!"

The man hoists up Calvin's lifeless body, carries him out of the truck and tosses him onto the side of the road. The other calves gasp. Persimmon's eyes widen as she watches the man walk by the side of the vehicle.

"What a waste of good meat," he complains. The driver slams his hand against the truck. "Now shut the hell up!"

Persimmon rushes to the back gate as the vehicle starts up again. She stares in disbelief at Calvin's dead body. *They're just going to leave him there like that?!* She is in such a state of shock that she feels detached from reality, as if she is floating in a nightmare.

The truck pulls away. Persimmon doesn't take her eyes off of Calvin. She's heartbroken. Nauseated. Angry.

11

DILL IS DYING. Persimmon is watching over him as he breathes erratically from her perch on Frederick's back. "Dill, hold on. I know you're hurting. I know you're hot, but you have to hold on just a little longer."

Dill keeps repeating, "Water. Water."

"I know you're thirsty, but just breathe. Can you do that for me?"

Is this it? Persimmon thinks to herself. *Is this the slaughter? Do we just drive around in the sun and bake to death? No, that can't be. The man said "waste of meat" when he threw Calvin on the side of the road. So why are they letting us die back here?*

The truck turns off of the highway onto a smaller road. This feels different. Persimmon climbs to the top of the wall.

"Everyone, listen." She gathers their attention. "I have to tell you something. Very shortly the humans are going to open up the gate, and that's when our plan goes into action. We must fight for our lives. You saw what happened to Calvin. The humans are cruel. They don't care about your well-being. I..." Should she tell them that they may die? Will they freeze up in fear? Persimmon pauses. This is no time to sugarcoat things. "I think you may die, too. I mean, I think the humans are going to try to kill you."

The calves rustle around. Persimmon tries to read their puzzled expressions. *Do they understand?*

Gilby finally speaks. "Die, Persimmon?"

"Yes. You will die." Persimmon tries to sound authoritative to instill confidence in them. "You have to run the best you can. When the gate opens, follow me."

Persimmon crawls over to the back gate. She looks at Gilby and Berry. "You only have to gather the strength to use your legs for this one fast burst. Then, when we get to the woods, we can hide and you can rest. You can heal. Got it?"

They nod.

The truck pulls up to a giant building. There are humans walking all over the premises. Persimmon reassures the calves. "It's alright. We'll surprise them." Deep down, though, she knows that not all of the calves will make it. Some will be caught, but their capture will save the others by distracting the humans. It crushes her to admit this, but she has to be realistic or she won't be able to forgive herself afterward. She wants to save them all, but that may be too much to ask. She can't bear that burden. And even if only some calves get out, it will be a bigger success than the last escape attempt.

The truck backs up toward the building. Persimmon rallies the troops. "Okay, this is it, everyone! We can do it!" The calves steady themselves. They look fatigued but determined.

A few humans walk up to the rear of the vehicle. They bring a ramp to get the calves off of the truck. One of the humans lifts up the lock on the gate.

Persimmon readies herself. "Here we go!" She's prepared for battle!

The human cracks open the gate. With that, Persimmon jumps out at his chest with a ferocity she's never before shown.

"What the…" The man trips back onto the ground. Persimmon scratches his flesh, digging her hind legs deep into his flabby belly while tearing holes in his face with her front paws. He screeches in agony.

The calves run at full force out of the truck and down the ramp. They muster the last bit of energy in their broken-down bodies. Gilby runs right up to a human and slams his head against the man's stomach. The man falls to the ground, the wind knocked out of him. The other calves run straight ahead like a freight train.

Another human slams a metal rod into Frederick's and Berry's backs. Persimmon rushes up and latches onto the man's leg with her claws. The man screams and tries to pry her off. Frederick and Berry run ahead, following the other calves. They all run straight into the building. The humans rush after them, smacking them with metal rods the whole time.

Persimmon runs up onto a fence. She's trying to catch up to the calves, who are running down a chute deeper into the building, and the chute keeps getting narrower and narrower.

Persimmon runs alongside them. "Jump over the side! Turn around! Get out of there!"

The calves are confused. They can't run any longer. They're crammed into a narrow pathway and can't turn around.

Two humans run alongside the path. "Get that goddamn raccoon!" Persimmon sees them coming and races up a pole into the rafters high above the slaughterhouse floor.

"Forget it. We'll deal with the damn thing later. Get those fuckin' calves down the line."

A few humans hit the calves with metal rods to push them farther down the path. They curse at the calves the whole way. "Tryin' to git away, huh? Little fuckers!"

The calves cry out. "Persimmon!" Gilby looks around frantically, hoping she has not abandoned him.

Persimmon runs along the rafters. *What happened? How did they get trapped?* she wonders. She then sees at the other end of the pathway, right where the calves are headed, a man holding what looks like a gun. *Oh no! They're going to shoot them.* This *is the slaughter.*

She stealthily climbs down a rafter where no human can see her and rushes up to Gilby. She runs alongside him. "Gilby, you have to climb out. They're going to kill you. Berry, you have to jump. Jump!"

But the calves keep pushing their way forward in a panic.

"Persimmon, help!" Gilby belts out, terrified.

"You have to jump out, Gilby!"

Persimmon bites and kicks at the metal wall around the calves. *There has to be an opening.* She runs ahead, looking for some type of lever or handle that would pry open an exit. Frederick is at the front of the line, so she calls out to him. "Frederick, stop running. Dig your hooves into the ground."

Frederick stops in his tracks and tries to push against the ground, but the momentum of the calves behind him trips him up. The calves start to trample him as they advance and he yelps in pain.

"Stop! Everyone, stop," Persimmon hollers. "You're going to crush him."

Frederick finally pushes himself back onto his feet and moves forward with the rest of the calves. Persimmon's heart is pounding. *I'm just making it worse. What do I do?*

Just then, a metal rod smashes down onto Persimmon's back. She is paralyzed, in agony. Pain shoots through her body like lightning.

"Gotcha, vermin!" A man with scratches on his face is standing over Persimmon. Blood drips down his pockmarked cheek. He holds up the rod to strike again, but just then Tate reels up on his hind legs and kicks him. The man swerves back a little to avoid being kicked again and swats at Tate. "Stupid animal!" Tate is pushed forward down the pathway by the calves behind him.

The man looks down, hoping to hit Persimmon again, but she's gone. "Damn it!" He is furious that he wasn't able to crush Persimmon's skull.

The first calf is pushed up to the man at the front of the line. It's Berry. The man puts the gun to Berry's head. "Please. Don't kill me!" Berry begs. "I don't wanna die! Please!"

Without hesitation, without emotion, the man pulls the trigger. But there's no explosion as Persimmon had expected to hear. Instead, Berry falls to the ground and convulses. Another man drags his shaking body and wraps a chain around his legs. Berry is yanked up into the air and a man slices his throat. Blood comes pouring out, bathing the floor in red.

The other calves scream in fear, traumatized. They were scared when Calvin died in the truck, but this gory murder was brutal—and *they're* next. The man with the gun pulls Frederick toward him. Frederick kicks, trying to free himself. "No! No die! Please!" But the man just waits until he has a shot, puts the gun to the pleading calf's head and pulls the trigger. Frederick falls to the ground, twitching uncontrollably.

Persimmon drags herself along the ground near the metal chute, trying to stay out of sight of humans. The throbbing in her back is unbearable with every move, but she needs to help her babies. At just that moment, she looks down the line and sees Frederick's throat being slit. She can't believe what she's witnessing. They're all being murdered, one by one, and there's nothing she can do to help.

She gets near the front of the line and hides between two machines. Helplessly, she watches as each calf passes by, hearing their sobbing as they witness their friends being massacred. To make matters worse, more and more calves keep piling up behind them. Persimmon's heart sinks. *Oh no. The second truck must have arrived and they're already filing them in here.*

"Persimmon! Persimmon!" She can hear Gilby crying out for her. She must do something. She climbs to the top of one of the machines and looks around for him.

"Persimmon!"

They lock eyes.

"Gilby... I'm right here." She looks around the room. What can she do? How can she save him? She can't save them all, but she needs to save him—at least him.

She crawls over the side of the machine, but as she reaches down with her hind leg a shooting pain races down her spine, knocking her off balance. She falls to the ground, hard.

"Persimmon!" Gilby calls, trying desperately to see where she landed.

She turns over. The man at the front of the chute grabs Gilby and puts the gun to his head. The look in Gilby's eyes is one of sheer terror.

Persimmon cries out. "Gilby! I love you. I'm so sorry. I love you."

The man pulls the trigger. Gilby falls to the ground, convulsing. Persimmon looks away. She can't bear to watch what happens next.

She drags herself under a machine into the darkness. She can hear the rest of the calves shrieking for help as they're killed. Some scream her name, so she tries to cover her ears, but the their cries are deafening.

She promised she'd save them, but she didn't. She lied to them. She failed them.

After what feels like an eternity, the cries stop. They're all dead. Almost a hundred sweet, gentle calves dead. She didn't save even one of them. How can she ever forgive herself?

The room is filled with the noise of machinery buzzing, humans working... and the sound of a lone raccoon weeping.

12

DARKNESS. PERSIMMON IS consumed by darkness. She isn't asleep; she just can't find the energy or willpower to move. All of the humans have left the slaughterhouse for the day and she is completely alone, curled into a ball. She has wept on and off for the past few hours, and although she still feels like weeping, her eyes are empty of tears. The pleading cries of the calves haunt her, as if they were still being massacred a few feet away. Horrifying images keep flashing through her mind: blood spewing from calves' necks, them begging for their lives, Gilby's head being punctured by the gun.

I could have done more to save them. I ran them right into that narrow passageway straight to their deaths. It's my fault... But where else could they have run?... No, that's no excuse. They were counting on me to save their lives.

The image of Berry convulsing on the ground, his tongue flapping out of his mouth, pops into her mind. She cringes.

Oh goodness, they were such sweet creatures. And they suffered so much. Every day of their lives they suffered, and the humans couldn't have cared less. Why did the humans have to be so cruel to them? They were just babies. And they were killed in such a painful and horrific way.

Rage wells inside of her. She wants to scream, but it's a struggle to even breathe. What will she do with all of this anger? She thinks of Gilby nuzzling his soft head against her side and melancholy sweeps over her again. *I just wish I could hug him one more time. I wish he knew how much I loved him. What a gentle, loving soul. And now he's gone— all because humans think he tastes good.*

"Miss Raccoon?" a tiny black rat calls out. Persimmon doesn't stir, hoping that if she ignores him he'll go away.

"Can you hear me? You should get out of here. When those humans come back they're gonna find you and kill you."

Persimmon opens her eyes. She sees the little rat facing her from a foot away. He steps back when he sees her uninviting glare.

"Don't get any ideas. I'm trying to help you. I may look tiny, but I have a nasty bite."

"I'm not going to eat you. Please, go away. I want to be alone."

"Look, I know you're sad. I can tell those calves were your friends…"

"They were my babies," Persimmon utters, broken.

The rat looks confused. "Your babies? But you're a raccoon. It's not even…"

"I don't mean literally. Please, leave me alone. I appreciate you trying…" Persimmon gasps. There is blood around the rat's mouth. "Is that blood?! Are you eating…" She averts her eyes. She can't bear to look.

"Oh, jeez. Sorry. I didn't realize. I wasn't eating your friends— babies—I just… That's what we eat. We didn't kill them, though. We just…"

"Please go."

"Okay, okay. Sorry. I was just trying to help."

The rat scurries away. Persimmon closes her eyes again. She wishes she could fade away. She knows the rat is right, though. If she stays there until morning, the humans will surely seek her out and kill her. She has to make it to the forest before she can rest.

She starts to get up, but a shooting pain in her back abruptly stops her. Luckily, no bones are broken, but she is severely bruised. *Come on, fight through this. The forest isn't too far,* she tells herself. She pushes herself up again, but the pain is too intense to stand up straight. She decides to stay low and take a few short steps at a time. She puts one paw in front of the other, clenching her teeth in agony, and gradually makes her way across the cold concrete floor. She stops every few feet, breathing deeply, comforting herself with the thought of hiding deep in the forest, then continues on.

She thinks about Derpoke and Scraps. She could use a hug. Derpoke, especially, always gives heartwarming hugs, as if every time he sees her, he is suddenly the happiest opossum to ever live. (Of course, when he sees Persimmon, he is.) When will she see them again? *Will* she see them again? *We were riding in that truck for so long, I memorized some of the way, but not every twist and turn. I couldn't. It was too far, and I was distracted by all the mayhem—the heat, the calves dying.* She starts to feel panicky. *Focus. Just focus on getting out of this death trap first. You can worry about getting home later.* She proceeds on her agonizingly slow trek.

✳   ✳   ✳

Persimmon finally makes it outside. The soft dirt feels welcoming. She lets out a sigh. The last time she was in this spot she still had hope that she could lead the calves to freedom, but now she's walking out alone. She starts to slip into despair, but snaps herself out of it. *Focus. Keep moving.*

As she pushes forward, she hears scampering behind her. "Excuse me, Miss Raccoon? Excuse me? I'm all clean now. Do you need help?"

It hurts too much for Persimmon to turn around, but she knows who it is. The rat steps in front of her. "Miss Raccoon, you seem hurt. Can I help you?"

Persimmon stares at the rat, bewildered. "I don't mean to seem rude, but why do you want to help me so much?"

"Because you ripped apart that human's face. That was amazing! And because you lost your babies. You have no idea how many of my family and friends these humans have killed. They drown us, stomp on us, poison us. I've been wanting to fight back for so long, but I'm so small. And you're so small—compared to them—but you weren't afraid to fight back."

"I'm sorry you lost so many loved ones. I know how that feels now."

"I'm sorry *you* lost your loved ones. There seems to be an endless supply of those calves that humans truck in here to slaughter. That was the first time I ever saw anyone fight to save them, though. You should be proud."

Persimmon looks down at the ground. "No, I'm not proud. They all lost their lives because I wasn't savvy enough to save them."

"From what I saw, you did everything you could."

Persimmon doesn't look up, still feeling ashamed.

The rat looks behind her. A group of rats is staring at him and Persimmon. "Get out of here! Go find something else to do," he yells.

They laugh at him and scamper off. "I guess you should be getting on your way, Miss Raccoon. Not to frighten you, but some of my brothers and sisters thought you seemed pretty injured, and well—let's just say they were hoping you wouldn't make it through the night."

Persimmon is taken aback. "Oh, goodness. Well, my back is definitely hurt, but it's not life-threatening. That certainly would have been an appropriate ending to this horrendous day, though, to be attacked by hungry rats." Persimmon forces a smile. "Thank you for being so kind to me. I believe you saved my life in more ways than one. My name is Persimmon, by the way."

"My name is Jabber. I'm a bit of a talker, as you may have noticed. It was an honor to have met you, Miss Persimmon."

"Likewise," Persimmon replies as she hobbles away. Before the injured raccoon staggers too far off, she stops and calls out. "Hey, Jabber."

The earnest rat turns back around. "Yes?"

"You said earlier that you wished you were bigger, so that you could fight back against the humans. It's not about size, it's about smarts. My elders taught me some tricks for not tipping off humans that you're digging through their trash. Don't eat the food they want, only eat the leftover scraps, and never leave a mess when you're done. Don't leave your pellets for the humans to find. Try locating entrances you don't have to chew your way through. The reason the humans are so intent on killing you is that they see you as pests, but if you stay out of their way and leave as little trace as possible, I bet they'll lay off a bit. I hope this saves the lives of some of your family and friends."

"Wow. I never thought of it that way. I'm going to tell everyone I know. Thanks!"

Jabber watches as Persimmon slowly disappears into the night. He is not sure if he'll ever meet anyone so intelligent and brave again, but he surely hopes he will.

13

FOR DAYS, PERSIMMON treks along the road. She lives in fear of the moment when it stops looking familiar. When that happens, she knows that if she takes the wrong turn, she may never see her beloved Scraps and Derpoke again. Her pace is still slow, but it's improving. The first two days she slept in fallen tree trunks, hoping no one would bother her. But after being by herself for so long she is beginning to feel lonely.

I wonder what Scraps and Derpoke are doing right now. Are they thinking of me? Are they worried about me? Do they think I'm dead? I hope I'm not causing them too much anxiety. What was I thinking jumping onto that truck?... Don't be silly—you know exactly what you were thinking: You were trying to save your babies... Yeah, and look where that got you. Look where it got them.

Stop beating yourself up. You tried. You did everything you could. And if you hadn't jumped onto that truck, you never would have forgiven yourself. If you never make it home, at least you followed your heart... If I never make it home? Is that really a possibility?

Persimmon stops in her tracks. A house. And where there's a house, there is likely to be a trash can nearby. She has barely eaten since the incident—she's been too consumed by guilt and heartache—but she knows that she must keep up her strength in order to survive. She has also been avoiding humans at all costs. Any time she sees a car drive by, her blood boils. *Who knows if they enjoy eating calves?* This house looks quiet, though, and unlike in the neighborhoods she's passed in the last few days, there are no other homes in sight.

She moves in the moonlight toward the side of the residence. There's a tall wooden fence enclosing the backyard. *A perfect spot to hide a trash can*, Persimmon notes. She scampers over to the fence. Normally, it would be super easy to climb, but due to her back injury, she winces as her muscles strain to pull up her weight.

She crawls along the top of the fence, peering around the perimeter of the house for trash cans. Sure enough, she sees two, but they've been knocked over and the garbage is strewn across the lawn. *Drat. Looks like everyone in the forest has rummaged through here.* A foul odor attacks her nose. *Yuck. It's all rotten anyway.*

Suddenly, a vicious Doberman comes barreling down the walkway right toward her. His barking is so fierce that Persimmon leaps into the air, and when she lands, she almost impales herself on the wood slats on top of the fence.

"Git outta here! Stupid raccoon! I'll rip ya to shreds!"

Persimmon rushes into the brush covering the fence at the back of the yard. She sits in the darkness, trying to calm her pounding heart.

"Come back out here, raccoon!" the Doberman threatens. "See if I don't tear ya apart. Come on! Try me!"

Persimmon regains her composure. *Stupid dog. They're always but lying everyone, and for what—to protect a trash can?* She straightens up and steps out of the brush to where the dog can see her on top of the fence. *I'm going to set him straight.*

He growls ferociously. "Get off my property or I'll swing ya around by your tail until you split in two!"

"Silly dog, I don't even have a tail." She shows him the stub where her tail once was. "You know what happened? Humans shot it off, because I wasn't afraid of them, and if I'm not afraid of humans, I'm certainly not afraid of you. Besides, you can't even get to the end of your own yard with that chain around your neck."

"Oh, yeah? Why don't ya see what happens when ya git within bitin' distance? Then you'll know what happens to brave raccoons."

Persimmon is unfazed by his threats. "Just listen to me for a moment..." She notices his legs wobbling, as if he's having difficulty keeping his balance. She steps closer to him on top of the fence and continues. "You dogs think you can just push us around—raccoons, opossums, birds, anything that moves—when all we want is a little food. The humans are throwing it out anyway."

The dog teeters, as if he's about to fall over. He catches himself, but Persimmon can tell there is certainly something wrong with him.

"Git outta here, raccoon! You're not eating this food. It's mine."

"It's *yours*? It smells rotten, so I don't even..." Persimmon peers more closely at his back. *What is wrong with his fur?* It seems to be mostly scratched away, and his back is covered with scabs and wounds. "What happened to your back?"

"Leave me alone. I'll rip your limbs off." He has lost his gusto, though, so his half-hearted warning seems more pathetic than frightening. The Doberman can no longer hold up his own weight. He sits down in the dirt.

Persimmon examines the seething creature, and sees that not only does he have lesions all over his skin, but he is also so malnourished that she can see his ribs through his fur. "My goodness, what happened to you? Where are your humans? Are they not feeding you?"

Persimmon peers up at the house. She didn't notice before, but it actually looks empty—there is no furniture and one of the windows is smashed. *The humans are gone, so why is this dog chained up outside?*

"I'll be back." Persimmon hops down the fence and scampers into the forest as fast as her injured back will let her go. She sniffs around and finally comes upon some wild berries. She scoops some up and races back to the house. "Now, dog, I'm going to crawl down this fence and give you some berries, but I don't want any mischief, okay?"

"I don't want yer berries. They're probably poisonous, so ya can kill me and eat my food."

"You mean your decaying garbage?" Persimmon lowers herself down the fence. "Don't be so proud that you can't let someone save your life—even if it is a raccoon."

Persimmon steps onto the dirt and inches her way toward the dog. Even sitting down, he is imposing. It would take three raccoons stacked on top of each other to reach his height. As she nears him, though, she whiffs in a horrendous stench. That's when she notices the pile of droppings next to him. *Ugh, he's sitting in his own feces and urine.* She has a heartbreaking flashback to the calves. *What has happened here? Would a human do this to a dog?... But they love dogs.*

He growls as she gets closer, so Persimmon tosses the berries toward him. He looks at her with rage in his eyes. Then, without taking his eyes off of her, he swallows all the berries in one gulp. He scratches and bites at his back, ripping off scabs in the process.

"Dog, will you..."

"My name isn't Dog," he snaps at her. "It's Bruiser."

"Okay, Bruiser. Will you let me help you?"

Bruiser stares at Persimmon. His breathing is labored. He scratches again at his back, ripping his flesh with his elongated nails. "Why would you help me?"

"Because no living creature deserves this."

Bruiser looks down at the dirt. How can he let a raccoon help him? And yet, how can he not? He looks back up at Persimmon. "Ain't nuthin' you can do. I tried everything."

*　　*　　*

Persimmon and Bruiser strain with all of their might to rip the end of the chain loose, but it's no use. The chain is attached to pipes protruding from the ground by the house, and the metal is too thick to pull apart.

Bruiser falls to the ground, defeated. "Told ya. Ain't no use. I'm gonna die here."

Persimmon snaps back indignantly. "You will not die here. I am telling you right now, I will not let you. But you can't give up on me."

"Give up on you?! I'm exhausted. In pain. My back is bleedin' from scratchin' so much, but if I don't scratch, it drives me mad. And you talk to me 'bout givin' up? You see that puddle over there?" Bruiser motions toward a grimy puddle near him. Flies hover over it in droves. "That's my urine. The dirt we're standin' on is soaked in it. I haven't had water... for so long." He pauses. This is very hard to admit. "I've been so thirsty. I didn't know what else to do. I didn't wanna die."

He looks away from her. Persimmon puts her paw on his. "Bruiser, I am so sorry this has happened to you. I am going to get you out of here. I promise."

Think, Persimmon. Think. She looks at his collar. She was cautious earlier about not wanting to get too near him, but now he seems to have warmed up to her enough to not be dangerous—at least, she hopes. She sees that the collar is so tight around his neck that it is embedded in his skin. There is blood where he has attempted to pull it over his head.

"Bruiser, can I take a look?"

Bruiser is fatigued and out of breath. He just moves his head so she can see the collar more closely. She has never been this close to a dog before. She knows at any moment he could snap his teeth into her throat and tear her to pieces, but she is not afraid. She will do whatever it takes to save his life. She will not let another creature die on her watch.

She surveys the collar more closely and homes in on the metal buckle. *That must be where you undo it. But how?* She moves it with her hands, but to her horror, maggots are eating at the raw flesh underneath. She falls back, aghast.

Bruiser jumps up. "What?!"

"I'm sorry. There are maggots all around your neck. They're eating... I'm so sorry. You must be in so much pain."

Bruiser shuts his eyes. "At first I tried to scratch 'em off, but there are so many I gave up. Same problem on the back of my right leg."

Persimmon grabs at his collar with more vigor. She pulls at the strap in the buckle. *There must be a way to loosen this. How do humans do it?* She keeps pulling and prodding while the maggots fester below. She tries to pull them off as she goes, but Bruiser's right—there are just too many. She scratches at the collar and tugs. She screams in frustration. "Come on! Come on! Come off! Stupid humans. I will not let them get away with this. They will not win. I am going to get you free."

Just then, the strap loosens. "That's it!" She pulls at the strap inside the buckle, and it loosens more. "I got it. I figured it out, Bruiser!" One more tug and it's done. She pulls the collar off of his neck and tosses it away. "We did it, Bruiser. You're free!"

Bruiser doesn't move. He breathes a deep sigh. She knew he was worn down, but she thought he might celebrate with a joyous bark or two. But he just lies there and looks up at her. Tears are filling his eyes. He begins to howl, as if his heart just broke in two.

"They left me, Persimmon. One day, they packed everything up in a truck, and I thought we were movin'. I thought I was finally gettin' outta this filthy yard. But then they drove away—the whole family—without me. At first I thought they forgot me. What a fool

I am. I barked and barked for days, but then it hit me. They didn't forget me, they left me here with the garbage—to rot."

Tears stream down his face. He scratches feverishly at his neck, but the maggots just keep eating away at his flesh. "Why'd they stop loving me? Aidan was my best friend, and he left me here to starve to death. His father, I understand. He could be a real bastard. One minute he'd be wrestlin' with me, the next he'd kick me because he'd had a bad day. But Aidan? He didn't even say goodbye. That hurt so much."

Bruiser howls again. Persimmon rests her paw gently on his. "I don't know why they left you. You deserve better. But you're free now. I'll help you find a creek so you can clean off. I'll bring you some food. You're going to get through this."

"I never thought I'd leave this backyard. You saved my life. I'm sorry I was so growly with ya."

"Come on, let's fix up those wounds and get you something to eat."

Bruiser heaves himself up. He is weak, but he has renewed energy now that hope exists in his life. He surveys the squalid backyard that was to be his unmarked grave—overgrown grass, dirt, broken appliances and him. He spent many a lonely night here, in the rain, in the snow. They never once let him in the house. They never once took him for a walk. Often they neglected to feed him. Only Aidan would sneak him some scraps from dinner. But mostly he was alone, loyally guarding the house of the family who would one day leave him chained to a pipe to die of starvation in a pile of his own excrement.

"They never loved me. As I laid here dyin', I kept wishin' they'd come back. Now I hope I never see 'em again."

Persimmon figures out how to unlatch the gate and Bruiser slowly follows her. He hobbles as he walks. His skin is bleeding and covered with sores, but he is alive and escaping this wretched yard. Who knew, after all the raccoons he has terrorized over the years, that in his darkest hour, it would be one of these wily creatures who would save his life?

14

"GILBY! GILBY!" PERSIMMON jolts awake from a nightmare. It's dusk. Bruiser is sitting beside her, awakened by her screaming. He looks better than he did three weeks ago when she saved him from that dingy backyard.

The first thing Persimmon did after she rescued him was meticulously pick all the maggots from his wounds. It was squirm-inducing work, but it had to be done, and his sores now finally have a chance to heal. Her own damaged back is also closer to recovery. She has spent the days and nights watching over him as he slept and deterring other vermin from munching on his open flesh. He is by no means completely healthy, but he will survive. That's all that matters.

"You were screamin' Gilby's name again in your sleep," Bruiser comments.

Persimmon sits up, but her head lays low. "That day weighs on me heavily, Bruiser. I will never forgive myself for what I let happen."

"Persimmon, that story ya told me — ain't nuthin' else ya coulda done. Those stupid humans had ya outnumbered, and you had no idea what you were up against. You're lucky *you* got out alive."

Persimmon scoots closer to Bruiser; she has a secret to share. "I have an idea I want to run by you. I've been mulling it over ever since that hellish day with the calves—actually, ever since I met them. I want to save other animals—calves, raccoons, opossums, dogs, any animal who is suffering." Bruiser notices that, for the first since he met her, her face is lit up. Persimmon continues. "When I helped rescue you from that backyard, it was so rewarding. I felt this surge of lightning in me. That same surge I felt when I was trying to help rescue the calves. I think I'm meant to do this. I feel like this is my destiny." Persimmon seems aglow with passion. "I can't stand to see another animal in pain, and now that I know there are so many creatures out there experiencing so much cruelty, I can't turn my back on them."

"So you're gonna save other animals from humans?"

"Yes, but that doesn't mean I think all humans are bad. In your case and the calves' case, those humans were reprehensible, but I can't imagine that's the norm. Humans are animals too, and…"

"Humans ain't animals. They're nuthin' like us. They don't even understand what we're sayin' most a the time."

"They just aren't listening correctly. The elder raccoons told us that humans are animals. Think about it—they have babies, they eat, they breathe. They're more like us than that tree over there or that rock, right? They're simply animals who raccoons are supposed to steer clear of, like we do foxes or mountain lions—or dogs."

"Hmph." Bruiser clamps his teeth together. He's not sure what else to say.

Persimmon steps over to face the grumpy dog. "That said, here's why I wanted to share this idea with you. I can't save all these other animals alone. I want to form a team, and with your brawn and admirable survival skills, I would be lucky to have you as a member."

Bruiser's ears perk up. "Really? You want me to stay around?"

"Of course! What did you think, that I was going to leave you out here all alone?"

Persimmon didn't even consider parting ways with Bruiser, but it only makes sense that he would have abandonment issues. Relieved, he gives the raccoon a sloppy, wet lick across her cheek.

Persimmon cringes. "Ugh. I never thought I'd get dog drool all over my face."

Bruiser licks her again. "Get used to it. That's how we do."

*   *   *

Persimmon and Bruiser stroll at a slow but steady pace along the highway. Each day, they move as fast as they can, but their injuries keep them from charging forward at their usual brisk speed. They have been walking day and night until they're too fatigued to walk any longer, but today, they're both getting a bit overheated in the afternoon sun.

Bruiser decides to finally share something that has been plaguing him the past few days. "Do you think your friends will be frightened of me, Persimmon?"

"What's that?" Persimmon seems distracted and a bit flustered.

"Just wonderin' if your friends will be afraid when they see a giant dog alongside you."

"It'll be fine." She still seems distracted.

Bruiser can sense something is wrong. "Are you okay? Do you need to stop?"

"No, it's fine. Let's keep walking. I can make it." She seems slightly panicked but is attempting to mask it.

High above them, two crows caw. Bruiser peers up, but the sun burns his eyes. "Wow, that sun sure is bright."

More crows gather overhead and their chattering fills the air. "They musta found somethin'. Sometimes, when I was in that backyard, birds would circle above *me*, thinking I would turn into some good eatin'. But I never quit. No, sir."

The massive flock gathers together and swoops toward the ground. Bruiser marvels at the sight. "Huh, look at 'em go." He stops in his tracks. "Wait a second. Persimmon, run!"

But it's too late—the black mass lands all around Persimmon and Bruiser. Their high-pitched cawing is deafening.

Bruiser stands guard over Persimmon, biting and barking at any birds who get near her. The crows flap up into the air but keep landing back around them.

One crow calls out. "Raccoon, is your name Persimmon?"

Persimmon's heart jumps. She calls out over the loud chatter. "Did you say my name? Bruiser, hold on." Bruiser stops biting, but stays at a hissing growl.

All of the crows talk at once: "Persimmon! It's Persimmon."

"We found her!"

"Finally!"

"You were looking for me?" Persimmon can't believe it. "How do you know my name?"

The crows reply in unison: "Derpoke sent us."

"Derpoke and Scraps asked us to find you."

"We did it! Somebody owes us some corn."

"Corn!"

"You know Derpoke and Scraps?" Persimmon's face lights up. "They sent you to look for me?"

"Looks like we just got some corn!"

"And berries!"

"Anything we want!"

"Oh my goodness!" Persimmon can barely contain herself. She feels dizzy. She hadn't told Bruiser but after she rescued him, the road stopped looking familiar. After all Bruiser had been through, though, she didn't want to discourage him by admitting she was lost. "What a glorious day!"

The crows gather around her. "Follow us."

"Derpoke and Scraps can't wait to see you!"

Persimmon hugs Bruiser around one of his legs. "My friend, we're going home!"

15

PERSIMMON PRANCES THROUGH Oak Tree Forest with the sweet smell of home enthralling her senses. She feels like she's walking on clouds. Bruiser walks beside her, feeling a bit tense but trying to hide his unease from Persimmon. The crows fly high above the forest, anticipating their tasty reward for bringing the battered soldier home.

"Persimmon!"

She freezes. She knows that voice. She searches excitedly for where it's coming from.

"Persimmon!" There! Persimmon sees Derpoke racing toward her from among the trees. She bounds toward him at full force. The best friends embrace, sniffing and licking one another. Their joy is palpable.

"Derpoke, I missed you so much!"

"I thought you were dead. I thought I'd never see you again. How could you run away like that?"

"I know, I know. I thought I'd never make it back." Persimmon hugs him tighter and holds the embrace. She felt so hopeless and lost all these weeks, so guilty over the calves. But now she can unburden the weight of her sorrow in her friend's arms.

Derpoke is beside himself as well. He spent many anxious hours waiting for her, thinking of her, worrying about her, and he feared this day might never come. He does not plan to let her out of his sight again.

Just then, though, he opens his eyes to see a ferocious-looking Doberman staring at them off in the distance.

"Persimmon, don't move," Derpoke warns. "A dog is watching us, and he looks very angry."

Persimmon turns to see Bruiser, but he doesn't look angry—he looks uncomfortable.

"That's Bruiser. He's my friend. You're going to love him."

"You're kidding, right?"

"I have much to tell you, my dear Derpoke."

$$* \quad * \quad *$$

Rawly paces back and forth. "I still can't believe you brought a dog here."

Bruiser bares his teeth at Rawly. Persimmon is sitting with Scraps in her lap; the little guy hasn't left his sister's side since she returned. She snaps back at Rawly. "I just told you that all of the calves were slaughtered—hacked apart—and all you care about is picking on Bruiser?"

"He could tear us to pieces in seconds, all of us. Look at him; he's bred to be a killer."

Persimmon presses on. "Rawly, he's growling at you because you're yelling at him. Don't you have any sympathy? His people left him to starve to death."

"With all the terror dogs have put us raccoons through, one less dog in the world would be fine by me."

Bruiser lunges dangerously close to Rawly. He snarls and then barks violently, but he doesn't bite him—yet.

Derpoke and Scraps run for cover into the brush, while Persimmon quickly hops in between Rawly and Bruiser. Her instinct is to calm Bruiser down by patting him on the back, but she sees the savage look in the Doberman's eyes and fears he may lash out at her without meaning to. She attempts to get his attention. "Bruiser, Bruiser. It's okay. Look at me. I'm on your side. Everyone else here is on your side." Bruiser lowers his growl and she continues. "You're too smart to let him get to you."

Persimmon turns to Rawly and gets right in his face. "Shame on you. After all he's been through, you treat him like this? As far as I'm concerned he's a better friend to me than you are, and he has a better heart. How dare you sully my return with your prejudice. I thought I was going to die out there, never see any of you again, and *this* is how you greet me?"

"Well, who knew you'd bring a dog home with you? Dogs have been tormenting us since we were born, and our elders before that. They've killed countless raccoons, opossums—you name it. And just as bad, they're friends with humans. You know, humans—the ones who killed your 'babies.' Maybe you're okay with that, but I'm not."

Rawly storms off. Bruiser barks in his direction for good measure. Rawly's comments sting Persimmon, especially given her fresh emotional wounds, but she collects herself and turns to the Doberman. "I'm sorry he treated you like that. He clearly does not speak for the rest of us."

Scraps chimes in from the brush. "Definitely not, Bruiser. I can't wait to tell everyone that my new friend is a dog!"

Bruiser's furor has subsided. He looks away, ashamed. "Maybe he's right. Maybe it is too risky to have me 'round y'all."

"Absolutely not," Persimmon determinedly exclaims. "He was goading you. I suppose we could work on your temper a bit, but you spent a lifetime being neglected and mistreated. You're bound to have some anger issues." She scratches him by his ear. "And short temper or not, you're part of the family now, right everyone?"

Scraps kicks his feet in the air. "Yeah!"

Persimmon looks around for Derpoke. She realizes he hasn't said a word in a long while. He is lying in a ball by a tree. She steps over to him and notices tears on his snout. "Did the barking frighten you, my friend? He was just defending himself."

Derpoke shakes his head. "It's not that." He sniffles. "Calvin, Gilby... they never had a chance. No matter what we did. They were doomed."

She rests her paw on his back. "Maybe I shouldn't have told you all the details. I just... I felt like you should know the truth."

"Yes, I'd rather know the truth. It just hurts my heart to think of them in so much pain."

Gory images of Gilby, Berry and the others flash through Persimmon's mind. "I know. That day will haunt me forever. But their deaths will not be in vain. I have a plan."

16

DERPOKE, SCRAPS AND Bruiser stand at attention facing Persimmon, who is perched on top of a boulder. The squirrel couple, Chloe and Tucker, are in attendance as well, but they're listening from a tree—Persimmon has vouched for Bruiser, but they've had one too many close calls with dogs in the past to make them feel totally safe.

Persimmon has just finished laying out her grand plan to rescue other animals. As she concludes, she adds a few last words of inspiration. "So, my friends, I am incredibly pleased that you've agreed to join me on this journey. Together, we are going to save a lot of lives and alleviate a lot of suffering. I admire you for being brave enough to put your own lives at risk to save those who cannot save themselves."

Derpoke speaks up. "But we're going to be as safe as possible about all this, right?"

Persimmon smirks, knowing her ever-prudent friend would ask this, and she answers warmly. "Yes, of course. If I learned anything from the tragic slaughter of the calves it's that the only way to do this is to be prepared. We must understand the full story of why the creatures we are saving have been imprisoned or are being harmed in order to know how to help them."

Persimmon makes eye contact with each of her companions. "I could not be more honored to have each of you by my side on this quest. Each and every one of you has unique talents and abilities that will make our mission successful. And our mission is simple: Wherever we travel, if we see any creature in harm's way, we do everything we can to save him or her. Do we agree?"

They all call out emphatically. "Yes!"

"Fantastic! Now, there is just one more order of business I wanted to mention before we start our adventure. If we are dedicating ourselves to saving the life of any animal we come across, it only makes sense that we not take other animals' lives while we do this. As a team, we must make a pact not to eat any living creature."

Persimmon hears audible gasps and groans from the group. "So no more fish?" Scraps asks.

"To put it plainly, Scraps. I feel like we'd be hypocrites if we go around calling ourselves heroes, rescuing some animals while taking the lives of others."

Scraps is still confused. "So, no more fish... ever?"

Persimmon steps off of the boulder and over to the group. Along the way, she picks up a black beetle. She holds the beetle up for everyone to see.

"Do you see how his little legs flail? Do you see how he's trying to bite at me? He's fighting to survive. He wants to live. And I know you think, 'But he's just a beetle,' but that's how the humans view you." She points at Scraps. "You're just a raccoon." She points at Tucker, "You're just a squirrel." Tucker looks around, surprised she is referring to him.

Persimmon continues. "Who are we to go around deciding, 'Today is the last day this fish will ever see his mother? I would be heartbroken if some human came into the forest and shot you, Derpoke. It would crush me. That's how the fish feels about his friends. That's how this beetle feels."

She puts the beetle down and he dashes away, ecstatic to live another day. "When I saw Berry's throat slit—the blood gushing out, him bellowing in pain—and not one of those humans even winced, something clicked in me. It changed me forever, for the better. I haven't eaten one living creature since then. Not a bug, not a fish, nothing. No creature deserves to suffer. That's why I'm doing this."

Her friends stare at her silently. She wonders anxiously, *Are they with me? Did I just lose them?*

"I'm in, Persimmon." Bruiser nods affirmatively. "Whatever you say goes."

Derpoke sighs. "It's a logical argument, Persimmon. I don't know why I never thought of it that way. I can't say that I'm not going to miss the delicious taste of fish, but if they really feel the same fear that Calvin must have felt when he was killed, I'd be a monster to continue doing it. Bravo! You are a persuasive orator."

Persimmon playfully bows to him. Then she turns to her little brother. "Scraps?"

Scraps kicks the dirt. "Forever?" Persimmon nods. Scraps gets an idea. "What if the animal is already dead in the trash? You know like sometimes there will be leftover chicken meat or hunks of flesh—I don't even know what animal it is, but it tastes good. What do you think about eating that stuff?"

Persimmon ponders this. "I'd say it's up to you to decide what you do and do not want to eat. However, there are so many delicious options that don't involve harming other creatures that I'd hope at some point you'd lose your appetite for eating animals."

"Okay, deal. I'll work on it." He seems satisfied with her response.

Persimmon looks up at Chloe and Tucker. Before Persimmon can even say a word, Chloe pronounces, "No need to worry about us. Give us some nuts or berries and we are good. Oh, and maybe some apples. Mushrooms are tasty, too."

"Perfect," Persimmon replies. "Well then, I think we're good to go."

Scraps cuts in, but this time it's not about fish. "Wait, we have to come up with a name for our team."

"Oh, right." Persimmon scans the group. "Does anyone have any suggestions?"

Scraps immediately blurts out, "Savvy Saviors!"

"I'm proud of you for using the word *savvy*, Scraps," Persimmon commends him. "But let's keep brainstorming."

Scraps shouts again, "Rascal Raiders! Hairy Heroes!"

Derpoke jumps in. "What is it with you and alliteration? Do you really think anyone is going to take us seriously with names like that? 'Hi, we're here to save your life. We're called the Hairy Heroes.'"

Scraps pouts and challenges the opossum. "Okay, know-it-all, do you have anything better?"

"Well..." Derpoke hesitates for fear of being shot down. "I did come up with one possibility. What about Critter Manumitters?"

The other team members stare at him quizzically.

Scraps bursts into laughter over this silly-sounding word. "Oh, that's much better, Mr. Vocabulary."

Due to Scraps' mockery of his suggestion, Derpoke decides to keep his other team name to himself, figuring that the Recalcitrant Rescuers is possibly even worse—he is correct.

Persimmon quiets her little brother. "Scraps, teasing is not permitted. If we're going to have a successful brainstorming session, everyone needs to feel comfortable sharing their ideas."

Scraps nods apologetically. Persimmon turns to her opossum friend. "I'm not sure what manumitter means exactly, Derpoke, but Critter Manumitters is a bit of a mouthful."

"To manumit means to free from slavery and servitude," Derpoke explains to the group. "But never mind."

"That's okay, everyone," Persimmon states. "It's not vital for us to come up with a name immediately. Let's ruminate on it for a bit. I do think it's a wonderful idea, though, for us to name our team eventually. It will bond us together."

Chloe crawls down the trunk of the tree, closer to the rest of the team. "Persimmon? As I mentioned before, the humans are already raising new calves to eat, so is our first mission going to be to save them?"

"I'd like to," Persimmon looks at the ground, discouraged. "But there are so many reasons why we're not ready right now. For starters, there aren't enough of us. And the calves are so weak and sick that we need to figure out a better way to get them out of there. Carry them, maybe? But who is big and strong enough to lift those heavy calves? I haven't figured it out yet. They are also so large, it's hard to hide them. The humans would probably hunt us down in a few days and we'd all be right out in the open." Persimmon lets out a deep sigh. "One day we will absolutely go back and save those calves. I owe that to Gilby and the rest of them. But I just don't know how to make it work at the moment."

"So where are we going instead?" Derpoke asks.

"I've already spoken to the crows," Persimmon replies, perking up at the thought of their second major rescue attempt—one with a much higher chance of success. "And they will guide us to our next mission. We need to free creatures who are smaller, who can run fast and hide really well. Animals we have a better chance of saving while we're still mastering our skills at rescuing."

"What type of animal is that?" Scraps inquires.

Persimmon smiles.

17

THE CROWS FLY high above the forest canopy, periodically looking down to make sure the furry team is still following them. Persimmon and Derpoke trek side by side along the forest floor with the rest of the gang trailing them. Chloe and Tucker are not far behind, darting through the tree branches above.

Derpoke pants as he tries to keep up with his swift raccoon friend; his tongue slightly dangles from his mouth from feeling overheated. He looks up at the scorching sun and squints at its brightness, unable to hide his discomfort any longer. "You know, I hate to complain, but…"

"Derpoke, you love to complain." Persimmon grins slyly.

"Okay, I won't deny that. Nonetheless, I want to point out that I have great night vision for a reason. At this time of day, I'm supposed to be snugly curled up in a tree."

"Believe me, my friend, I'd rather be traveling at night too, but we are dependent on the crows to get us to our destination and they need to travel during the day."

Derpoke scratches his stomach. There's not really much more to say on the subject, but he felt the need to at least vocalize his frustration.

Meanwhile, Scraps laughs as he roughhouses with Bruiser a few feet back. Ever since the team began its journey, the two have had a marvelous time playing games with each other. Sometimes Scraps will jump on the Doberman's back to hitch a ride, only to have Bruiser playfully shake him off. After, Scraps will run around Bruiser's legs, trying to trip the dog, but Bruiser doesn't miss a beat, pretending to bite at the rascally raccoon as he darts around.

As Derpoke watches them, he whispers to Persimmon. "Aren't you concerned about Scraps' safety? Bruiser seems calm now, but what if something triggers his temper? He could easily thrash the little guy into pieces in seconds."

Persimmon had actually been enjoying their spirited playing. "What? No. Look at them. They're having so much fun. I can't tell you how much it warms my heart to see Bruiser so happy. You should have seen him when I met him. I was truly worried he might not survive."

"I know he had a really rough time. I'm just looking out for Scraps. I mean, what if the little guy bites Bruiser playfully, but something snaps in Bruiser's mind from when he was abused?"

Persimmon pats Derpoke's fur reassuringly. "It's sweet of you to look out for my little brother, but to be honest, I actually feel safer with Bruiser around."

"Cause he's all big and strong?" Derpoke grumbles.

Persimmon teasingly flicks his ear. "What's that you say, Mumbles?"

Derpoke laughs and pushes her paw away. "Stop." He scratches at his side again. "What is..." Instantly, he ceases laughing. "Wait." He picks through the fur under his right front leg and lets out an audible gasp. "Ah! It's a tick! Get him off! Get him off of me!"

Persimmon calmly scrounges through his fur. "Okay, hold still or I can't get him."

Derpoke gets more frantic. "Hurry! Get him off. I can feel him sucking my blood!"

Bruiser comes bounding over. "Everything okay?"

"He's fine," Persimmon explains. "He just has a tick."

Bruiser guffaws. "Ha, try havin' dozens of maggots eatin' at yer skin."

Derpoke is unamused. "Yes, yes, I'm glad you all are having so much fun. Now please remove him."

Persimmon picks at the tiny arachnid, and finally pries him from Derpoke's skin. He lets out a sigh of relief as Persimmon places the tick in the nearby brush. Derpoke sees that everyone has stopped. Bruiser, Scraps, Chloe and Tucker are staring at him, and a few crows have even flown down to see what the hubbub is all about.

"What's the hold up?" a crow calls down.

"He just had a tick." Persimmon explains. "Everything is fine."

The crows fly back up into the sky. "My, my, my."

Derpoke scurries ahead, embarrassed and muttering. "Let's see how you all act when you find some parasite feasting on you. Not so much fun when…" His voice trails off as he moves away.

Bruiser keeps pace with Persimmon. "Fragile feller, eh?"

Persimmon watches Derpoke. "He can certainly be a bit finicky, but he's the most loyal friend you'll ever have."

"I don't doubt it." Bruiser lowers his voice. "I wanted to bring somethin' to your attention. Don't look back, but we're bein' followed."

Persimmon almost looks back, but catches herself. "Really? By whom?"

"That hot-tempered raccoon, Rawly. I smelled him a while ago, but I was waitin' for a chance to tell you discreetly. Do ya want me to chase 'im off?"

"Hmm. No, he's following us for a reason. I think he wants to see what we're up to, but he's too proud to admit that he was wrong about how he treated you."

"Thanks again for stickin' up for me. I had a feelin' that some of your friends might not accept me. Heck, I can't say I blame 'em. I'm sure he's met a few snarlin' dogs in his day."

"Yeah, well, we all need to learn to be more accepting. I mean, look how sweet you are with Scraps. I bet you never thought you'd be buddying up to a feisty raccoon."

Bruiser looks back at Scraps fondly. "No ma'am. He's a great kid." The Doberman pauses and looks around at the lush forest—the tall trees, the red and yellow flowers sprinkled throughout the brush. He takes in a deep breath, savoring the fresh air. "I never thought I'd ever see beyond that backyard, but thanks to you, I'm enjoyin' a stroll through the woods, I have a full belly, and I'm surrounded by some new friends. This is good livin'."

Scraps motions for Bruiser to come play with him again. Bruiser nods. "Looks like I'm bein' summoned."

Before Bruiser darts off, Persimmon stops him. "Hey Bruiser. Keep the Rawly thing between us. The truth is, even though he can be a pest, he's pretty crafty. If we're really going to make a difference as a team, we're going to need all the help we can get."

As Bruiser trots away, he calls back, "If you won me over, Persimmon, I'm convinced you can win anyone over."

Persimmon smiles to herself. *Maybe Rawly's not a lost cause after all.*

*   *   *

Chloe and Tucker hop from one tree to the next, playfully racing each other. Tucker stops and waits for Chloe to make a long leap to the tree he's perched on. She jumps high in the air and sticks her landing with grace.

Tucker applauds. "Impressive, Sweet Pea."

"Why thank you, Pupsy."

Chloe starts to move to the next tree, but Tucker blurts out, "Can I ask you a question?" Chloe halts and looks at him, waiting. He hesitates, then decides to just say it. "Are you sure about this?"

"You mean going on this rescue mission? You're asking me this now?"

"Well... I said yes before, because I didn't want to disappoint you. I just... I mean, Persimmon had her tail shot off. What if one of us gets hurt?"

Chloe bounds to the next tree. "Tucker, we'll be fine. Persimmon learned from her mistakes on the last mission, and she already said that on this rescue, we'll thoroughly plan out every second." She hops onto a branch and scurries toward the trunk.

Tucker follows her. "I just don't want to lose you."

Chloe stops. She turns back around to face Tucker and cuddles up to him, wrapping her tail around his torso. "Pupsy, you're not going to lose me. Okay!"

He nods, still unsure.

Chloe continues. "The thing is, the whole time I was growing up, and then when you moved into that tree with me, I listened to those poor calves cry day and night—and I did nothing."

Tucker perks up, having an aha moment. "Okay, we'll move. We won't live by the veal farm any longer."

"Tucker, you're missing the point. If we moved away that wouldn't stop them from bellowing in pain, it would just stop us from having to listen to it. What they're being put through is wrong, and I don't want to sit by any longer. I want to make a difference." She looks him in the eyes, earnestly. "Persimmon, Scraps, all of them, they're really brave, and I think they're going to save lots of animals' lives, but they need help. That's where we come in. We're fast and agile—we can climb anything. Right?"

"Yes, but… I want to help, too. But I thought we were going to start a family in the spring."

Chloe laughs. "Pupsy. Is that what you're worried about?"

"Well, that and getting my tail shot off."

Chloe licks Tucker's furry face affectionately. "We will absolutely start a family together. But don't you want our pups to be proud of their parents for standing by their convictions? We can do this—together. Come on, be excited with me."

Tucker ponders this for a second. "Okay. Only if you… beat me there!" He darts off across a branch and makes a giant, arcing leap to the next tree. Chloe chases after him. She is not one to lose a race.

*   *   *

Persimmon, Derpoke, Scraps and the rest of the team drag their feet as they walk. Fatigue has won for the day. The night envelops the sky rapidly, and it couldn't come a moment too soon—they are all ready to sleep. The crows keep charging ahead, though, and the team hasn't been successful in getting their attention to ask them to stop for the night.

Suddenly, the crows start cawing in unison. Two crows fly down below the treetops and call out excitedly.

"We're here!"

"We made it!"

The news invigorates the team. They quicken their pace to follow the birds. Very soon, a familiar stench hits their noses—a mixture of excrement and urine.

Derpoke coughs. "Ugh. It smells like the building where the calves were forced to live."

Persimmon nods as a queasy feeling comes over her. This is the smell of animals suffering.

The team comes upon a tall wire fence with barbed wire on top. Beyond are rows upon rows of metal cages stacked side-by-side—more than a thousand in all. The cages are propped up on wooden planks with tin roofs overhead. Creatures stir inside but although the cages are out in the open, they are just far enough away that the team can't clearly see the animals.

Scraps whispers, "So this is where the humans kill these animals to steal their fur?"

Persimmon peers at the vast fenced-in area that is filled with imprisoned furry critters. "This is it. Our whole lives, we've heard stories that places like this might exist, so it's the perfect location to start our rescue missions as a team."

"Those stories about humans killing other animals just to wear their fur always sounded so gruesome—so callous—I hoped they weren't real," Derpoke states, sickened.

"I know," Persimmon replies solemnly. "Now we're going to find out the truth."

18

THE CROWS HAVE quieted down and are settled for the night in the surrounding trees. They will wait until morning to get whatever fruits and berries the group can gather as their tasty reward for guiding the team, and then they will be on their way.

Persimmon, Derpoke, Scraps, Bruiser, Chloe and Tucker lean up against the fence and squint to get a look at the creatures locked in the cages.

"So, what do minks look like again?" Scraps asks.

"The crows said they look like weasels—long and slender, with short legs," Persimmon responds.

Derpoke cuts in. "I hope they're not as tricky as weasels. You can't trust those pesky vermin."

Persimmon looks surprised. "I never knew you had such strong opinions about weasels."

"He has strong opinions about everything," Scraps quips.

The others laugh. Derpoke does not. He glares off into the distance trying to think of a witty comeback. Nothing comes fast enough, though. Just at that moment, through the fence, he spots two powerful figures darting straight for them.

"Dogs!" Derpoke cries out.

Sure enough, two Rottweilers are bolting toward them at full force. The team steps back from the fence just as the two furious dogs slam their paws against it, barking out threats. "Get outta here! We'll rip you to pieces!"

Derpoke, Chloe and Tucker cower behind a tree. Persimmon and Scraps hold their ground, but they are definitely intimidated. Bruiser barks right back at the other dogs.

For a moment, the Rottweilers are taken aback by the sight before them: two raccoons, two squirrels, an opossum and a Doberman all together?! Never have they seen such an odd mix of animals. But that doesn't trip them up for long and they resume their ferocious barking.

Bruiser gets right up against the fence and tries to bite at one of the Rottweilers. The Rottweiler is so seething mad that white froth sprays out of his mouth as he tries to bite at Bruiser. Persimmon knows she can't let this go on or Bruiser might get hurt. She inches her way closer without putting herself in harm's way. "Bruiser, it's alright. They're on the other side of the fence."

The frothing Rottweiler teases the Doberman. "Yeah, Bruiser. You might get hurt."

The second Rottweiler joins in on the fun. "What kinda wimpy dog lets a raccoon break up his fights?"

Bruiser snarls. "If this fence wasn't here, the two a ya'd be a pile of bloody bones already!"

The one Rottweiler motions toward Bruiser's wounded neck and body. "Looks to me like you already lost a few fights. Maybe your little raccoon friend wasn't around to save you."

Bruiser lashes out at the fence, biting into the metal. Persimmon is worried he'll chip a tooth. That's when Scraps tugs at her back. "Humans!"

Scraps points to a white house adjacent to the fur farm, where lights are being turned on. The team was so focused on the cages they hadn't even noticed the house.

"Hide!" Persimmon calls to her friends.

She and Scraps dash behind the nearest tree, while Bruiser continues to bark at the other dogs.

"Bruiser, the humans will see you," Persimmon calls out. "It will ruin everything!"

More froth sprays out of the Rottweiler's mouth as he celebrates his victory. "That's right. Run away! I knew you were too afraid to stay and fight!"

Bruiser is too smart to let the dogs goad him any longer. He joins the others behind the brush and trees.

The second dog notices the lights in the house as well. "Mando, you woke the Petersons," he sheepishly points out.

Mando rears and snarls. "Shut up, Diablo. We're protecting the property. That's what we're here to do, right?"

Two humans come charging out of the house with shotguns and flashlights, just as worked up as the Rottweilers. The first, Russell Peterson, is a portly twenty-year-old who looks as though he has downed one too many burgers with one too many beers. He wheezes as he runs, and seems genuinely delighted to be wielding a deadly weapon. The second, Jackson Peterson, is Russell's younger brother by a year. Jackson has one of those patchy beards found on young men—the kind where he's so proud he can grow any facial hair at all, he doesn't notice how ridiculous it looks. Jackson isn't wearing a shirt, exposing a painful-looking sunburn on his back and chest.

The Peterson boys make their way over to the barking dogs. Russell excitedly shouts over the barking. "What is it, fellas? You catch some sons a bitches tryin' to steal our minks? Huh?"

The dogs bark in the direction of a tall oak tree. Russell and Jackson aim their guns into the woods, waiting for some movement. Persimmon and the others remain still. She and Scraps are perched on a low-hanging branch, Chloe and Tucker are high up in the tree, and Derpoke and Bruiser sit quietly below. Persimmon can see Tucker shaking with fear, and she looks into the eyes of the frightened and frozen Derpoke. She's worried one of the team may get so scared they'll try to run away. She has to do something.

Russell taunts the rescue team. "Come out, come out, wherever you are. We'll only shoot your face off."

The Rottweilers are still barking. Russell swats at them with the butt of his gun. "Shut up, idiots! Let me listen!" The dogs continue to bark. "I said, shut up!" Russell kicks Mando in the ribs. Mando yelps and ceases barking.

Persimmon gives Scraps a surprised look: Did Russell really just kick his dog?

Russell and Jackson shine their flashlights into the dark woods. Tucker looks like he's about to leap to the next tree in fear, so Persimmon makes a calculated decision and calls out to the team. "Everyone, stay absolutely still."

She then hollers to the brothers, "I'm right here, fools!" To the humans it sounds like the usual raccoon squeaking. Jackson aims his flashlight at the tree and Russell cocks his gun. Persimmon yells again. "Right here, nitwits!" She crawls down onto the trunk, away from Scraps, and pokes her head out.

Russell lowers his gun, disappointed. "A raccoon?! A frickin' raccoon?!"

Russell kicks at Mando again, but Mando jumps away. "Idiot dogs! You wake us up at two in the mornin' for a frickin' raccoon? I should shoot *you*!"

Jackson cuts in. "Russell, ain't their fault. You got 'em so riled up, they'd bark at a leaf hittin' the ground."

Russell kicks and shakes the fence to scare Persimmon away. "Get outta here, raccoon!" Persimmon runs down the tree, pretending that Russell succeeded in scaring her away. She calls out to her friends as she runs off. "I'll be back. Stay here."

Russell yells at Jackson. "You think you can train 'em better? You gotta get 'em mean. You gotta get 'em angry, so if some sons a bitches try sneaking onto our land to mess with our property, they'll bite their damn balls off."

Russell scolds the Rottweilers. "Commando, Diablo, get your asses over here!" The dogs timidly step toward Russell, hoping they aren't going to get another beating. Both have their ears lowered and they hunker down to a crawl as they near Russell, fearing they're about to get a sharp kick.

Russell gives each dog a swift swat to the top of the head. "You attack *human* intruders, not raccoons. Got it? I don't want no more two a.m. wake-up calls for a goddamn raccoon."

Jackson smirks. "They don't know what the hell yer sayin', man."

Russell stands up and starts heading back toward the house. "They'll figure it out next time when I put my boot up their asses." Jackson bursts out laughing and follows Russell.

Mando and Diablo don't move. They stay low to the ground. Mando hears Persimmon trot through the leaves to meet back up with her friends. The Rottweiler makes eye contact with her, then quickly looks away. He went from fearsome to humiliated in a matter of minutes and doesn't want her to see him this way. Persimmon ponders, *It looks like we may have just added two more to our rescue mission.*

19

PERSIMMON, DERPOKE, SCRAPS, Bruiser, Chloe and Tucker set up a base camp about fifty trees from the fur farm, far enough to make the Rottweilers think they've moved on.

Scraps is flabbergasted. "How did the humans know we were coming for the minks?"

"They didn't," Persimmon replies. "They were talking about *humans* stealing the minks, but that begs the question—why would other humans want those minks?"

"Do humans eat minks?" Chloe wonders aloud from up in a tree. "Or maybe they want the fur, too?"

"I don't know," Persimmon responds. "But they take the threat seriously enough that they have a high fence and two menacing guard dogs."

Derpoke butts in. "If I might interject for a moment. Persimmon, I am quite concerned about your propensity to put your life in danger—even if you have good intentions." He looks directly at Tucker. "I saw Tucker position himself to run away, and if he wants to do so, you should let him."

"Are you calling me a coward?" Tucker calls down angrily. "At least I didn't freeze up the moment those dogs started barking."

"Enough," Persimmon interrupts. "Everyone was scared, and for good reason—the humans had guns pointed in our direction. Tucker—and this goes for everyone, really—if humans are waving guns around and you're hidden, it's best not to startle them by dashing off."

Tucker speaks up. "I could have made it. *You* made it."

Persimmon continues calmly. "Yes, I did make it, but I also alerted them to my presence so they wouldn't be caught off guard. A frightened human shoots first and thinks later. That said…" She turns to Derpoke. "The humans reacted the way I knew they would. I could tell that they weren't looking for us, and if they realized the dogs were barking up a storm over a raccoon, they'd simply be annoyed."

Bruiser steps into the mix. "Annoyed? That don't seem to fit how they were treatin' those dogs. I'm not defending those Rottweilers' nasty attitudes, but that cold-hearted man hittin' 'em sure brought back some hurtful memories."

"True, the humans should not have hit them, but before anybody forgets, if that fence hadn't been there, those beasts would have chewed our legs off," Derpoke counters.

"I'm with Bruiser," Persimmon declares. "Mando and Diablo are just being loyal and acting the way they've been taught to act—or should I say, the way they've been beaten into acting."

Derpoke presses on. "Okay, yes, I agree. Those humans are despicable, and they have no right to treat those dogs that way. That still leaves us with two dogs foaming at the mouth, trying to eat us. How are we supposed to get past them?"

"Perhaps *I* have a solution," a deep, almost intoxicating voice interjects from a dark burrow in the ground. The entire team swings around. At first, they only see two glowing eyes. Then, from out of the burrow struts a long and slender creature with short legs—very similar to how the crows described minks. In fact, exactly how the crows described minks.

20

THE STORY OF VINCENT THE MINK
(April – More Than a Year Ago)

MARGEAUX HEAVES AND strains, and, with one last exhausting push, delivers her sixth and final kit—Vincent. Vincent squirms around in the dark nest with his four brothers and one sister. They are all deaf and blind, and have no concept of the world into which they have just been born.

Margeaux licks her little ones clean and strokes their silver-white fur. This is supposed to be one of the most joyous days of a mother's life, but for Margeaux, it is tainted by the sorrow of what is to come. For three years now, she has given birth to litters of lovable fur balls, and for three years, humans have snatched them away to eventually kill them for their precious fur—the mink curse: to naturally possess something humans deem valuable.

Heartbreaking thoughts cross her mind. *Should I end their misery now? It only gets worse from here. But how can I kill them? They're my sweet little kits. Yet how can I knowingly allow them to live a caged life?* She gazes lovingly at the tiny kits suckling on her teats, instinctively drinking to live. *I can't. I can't harm them.*

She lies back in the cut-up pieces of newspaper in her human-made nest, which is tucked in the corner of her barren cage. Her heart is heavy. How can she save them?

*   *   *

Vincent is the first of the litter to venture out of the nest. His sight and hearing are sharpening, and he is eager to explore the world. He crawls out of the tiny box and plops down onto the wire floor. He squints, shielding his eyes from the blinding sun, and looks every which way at the world around him. He can see the blue sky and the ground below, but, to his surprise, he is surrounded on all sides by the walls of a minuscule wire cage—creating severe claustrophobia. He can only walk two or three paces either way before a see-through gate stops him. He bites on the metal, but it doesn't bend. He looks back at the small hole leading into the nest and sees his mother peering out at him. "Mother, I want to be down there." He points to the dirt below with his blackish-pink nose.

"I know, my son," his mother responds. "Play in here for now. We'll have a discussion about that soon."

Vincent's brother, Frestin, is the next to pop out of the nest. He lands with a thud on the wire floor. "Ow, this hurts," he complains. "I'm going back in the nest."

Vincent bounds over to his brother and nudges him with his head, encouraging him to play. Frestin kicks at Vincent. "Stop, Vincent! This ground hurts."

"Don't be such a wimp," Vincent taunts. He leans in and whispers, "Come with me. When mother isn't looking, we'll bite through these walls."

Vincent looks up at the hole to the nest to check if the coast is clear. Sure enough, his mother has gone back into the birdhouse-like enclosure where the rest of the kits are sleeping. Vincent and Frestin dart to the far side of the cage. They notice that right next to their cage is another one full of minks, and then another beyond that. In fact, their cage is just one in a row of cages, all filled with mother minks and their litters.

Frestin is surprised by what he sees before him. "Everywhere you look it's more kits with their mommies. There are so many, and they're all trapped just like us."

"Not for long," Vincent declares. He begins nibbling on the metal.

Frestin grimaces. "It's too hard. You'll crack all your teeth, and then you'll look even uglier."

"And with busted teeth, I'll still look better than you," Vincent smirks. "Now step back and behold my immense power." He chomps down on the wire with even more gusto.

Unbeknownst to the disobedient duo, their mother has peeked her head out of the nest and is watching as they bite away. Just then, she has a revelation. *That's it! My kits are too clever to spend their lives in captivity.*

*   *   *

The six kits sit in a group facing their mother. Vincent, Frestin and their sister, Alia, sit quietly, waiting for their mother to speak, but Trenton (the most unruly), Marcel and Wren bite at one another playfully. Margeaux shushes them. "Quiet, everyone. Pay attention. Trenton, stop pestering your brother." Trenton bites Marcel one last time before reluctantly facing his mother.

An unsettling chill comes over the children as they see Margeaux's grave expression. "My kits, what I am about to tell you is going to be difficult to hear. You are so young, you should be free to play, but that is not our life. You must listen to me carefully and take this very seriously. It may save your lives."

The little minks stare at her, confused, not sure what to make of her somber mood.

Margeaux continues. "In about three weeks, the humans are going to open that cage door and take you away from me." Each kit stops breathing as the horrifying news rushes over them like a tsunami. "They are then going to split you up and put you in other cages with other young minks. You may never see me again."

Frestin and Alia start to sob.

"Mommy, they'll take us away? Forever?" Vincent asks.

Margeaux starts to get emotional. She tries to compose herself. "Yes. But..."

"I'll bite them. We'll scratch them," Trenton angrily blurts out.

Margeaux struggles to hold back her despair. "Yes, Trenton, I want you to fight—viciously—but first I must teach you how to escape, how to always look for a way out of here. I have to prepare you for life beyond this cage."

Vincent, Alia and Marcel rush up to their mother and cling to her. "But Mommy, how can we fight back?" Frestin asks. "The humans are so big."

Margeaux comforts him. "You'll use your teeth and your nails, and, most importantly, you'll use your minds. The humans may be bigger, but you are craftier."

Vincent feels sick to his stomach. He looks over at his brother Wren, who seems frozen. "Wren, are you okay?"

"What will we do without Mommy?" Wren asks softly.

Vincent doesn't hesitate. "Don't worry. We're going to escape—as a family."

*　　*　　*

The next three weeks are stressful and hectic. Margeaux tries to focus on training her kits to escape this hellish life, but the knowledge that they will soon be torn away weighs heavily on her. She teaches them every trick she can think of to give them the best chance to escape. She tells them to look for defects in their cages, like rotting wire, since she's seen other minks bite through the metal and squeeze their way to freedom. She teaches them to use any opportunity when the cage door is opened to swiftly jump out. She does her best to prepare them for life outside the cage, if they are lucky enough to break free. She has little to no knowledge of the forest beyond the fur farm, but she believes in her heart that it must be safer than where they are now. She warns them that she has seen large creatures sneak up to the cages, hoping to devour the minks that lie inside, so she insists that if they do escape, they spend most of their time hidden—either underground or up in the trees that she's seen and always hoped to one day climb. She discusses every possible aspect of their escape while trying to avoid the one explanation that she doesn't quite know how to break to them. Then, one day, the always-inquisitive Vincent asks the dreaded question. "Mommy, why are the humans taking us away?"

Margeaux's not sure if the truth will send her little ones into a panic, derailing her efforts to train them, but she must prepare them for everything—even their own gruesome deaths. "My dear Vincent. You know how snug and comfortable it is to cuddle up to your brothers and sister as you sleep?"

"Yes," Vincent replies.

"Well, the humans think our fur is soft, too. And they want to take it for themselves."

Trenton, Frestin and the others turn to listen as well. Margeaux is on the spot—it's now or never. "My kits, there is a reason I want you to escape this dreadful place so badly. In order to take our fur—in order to *steal* our fur—the humans kill us."

The six mink siblings gasp and ask in unison, "Kill us?! How?"

Margeaux shakes her head. "I don't want to talk about that specifically. They will just kill you."

Vincent pushes for an answer. "But how?"

Margeaux starts to shake from anxiety. "It is dreadful. I can't say. The important thing is that you need to use the tools I have taught you as soon as possible. Once the cold sets in and your fur thickens, they will begin the massacre."

"But why don't they grow their own fur?" Vincent inquires.

"Humans don't grow fur like we do," Margeaux responds.

Trenton grits his teeth. "So they think they can just take *ours*? Our eyes aren't as big as theirs, maybe we should take their eyes out and use them as our own."

Alia, Wren and Marcel cheer.

Frestin hides under his mother's fuzzy belly. "I don't want to die, Mommy."

Margeaux strokes his back. "I know, my sweet Frestin. You must be strong. You must be savvy."

Vincent, mature beyond his years, replies confidently, "Don't worry, Mommy. We'll protect ourselves." He looks over at Trenton, who's feeling equally tough. The two nod in agreement—no one is going to break apart their family.

∗   ∗   ∗

A few days pass. The kits have outgrown the nest and are sleeping huddled up with their mother on the harsh floor of the wire cage. Suddenly, they hear a panicked chatter break out among the other minks. Then, off in the distance, there is the sound of minks hissing and screeching. The animals sound terrified. The noise grows louder and louder until it's completely deafening.

Vincent jolts awake. "It's happening!"

The other kits and Margeaux pop awake as well and jump to the edge of the cage to witness the fracas. They can see nothing, though, other than their row of cages and the row across from them. All of the mother minks and kits in the surrounding cages climb frantically around their tiny prisons, trying to see what's causing the frenzy and dreading what's coming. Most of the mothers have lived through this before, and they know that the time has come for their innocent kits to be ripped from them forever.

Frestin, Wren and Marcel grab tightly onto their mother's fur, weeping.

"Mommy, no! Don't let them take me!" Frestin pleads between sobs.

Vincent, Trenton and Alia attempt to remain calm. The time has come to act. They have an escape plan, and getting hysterical is not part of that plan.

Vincent keeps his eyes focused down the row of cages. Just then, he sees Russell and Jackson step around the corner. Jackson looks sweaty and ill-tempered, but Russell grins as if he's enjoying himself.

"They're coming! Get ready!" Vincent warns.

Vincent's brothers and sister crowd around the edge of the cage to get a glimpse. They have seen the humans briefly before, but today the men are even more menacing and ugly. The Peterson brothers are wearing thick leather gloves and holding long metal rods with tongs at the end. Russell opens a cage and sticks the metal rod inside. There is fierce hissing as a helpless kit is yanked out of the cage, the tongs grasped firmly around his neck. He thrashes around but it is no use— the tongs are too tight and the human is too strong.

Vincent turns to his brothers and sister. "It's okay. Follow the plan. Fight, bite, scratch. No matter what."

Margeaux opens her arms. "My kits, hug me. I know we have a plan, but let me just hold you one more time."

The six kits crowd around Margeaux, squeezing her tightly. Her legs are shaking from fear but she speaks through her distress. "No matter what happens, I love you, and I am proud of you—each of you. Remember this moment. If you ever get scared, remember my embrace."

Vincent tries to comfort her. "It's okay, Mommy. You trained us well. We're all breaking free today."

Russell and Jackson go from cage to cage, dragging the small kits out by their necks. The mothers and kits hiss and scream, bite and shake, to no avail—the humans are too powerful.

Jackson approaches the cage where Vincent and his family are confined. Frestin, Wren and Marcel grab tightly onto their mother.

Vincent spits out orders. "Places! Focus!"

Jackson flips open the cage door. Margeaux immediately lunges at the tongs. Vincent is taken aback. This wasn't part of the plan.

"Run, kits! Run!" Margeaux screams.

Trenton leaps into action. He runs up Jackson's arm and scratches at the man's exposed neck. Jackson falls back. Marcel sees his chance and jumps out of the cage. He climbs stealthily down a wooden plank to the ground and runs full speed along the dirt toward the woods— just like they planned.

Jackson grabs at Trenton with his leather glove and tosses him over the row of cages. Vincent can't see where Trenton lands, but he knows there is no time to wait. He turns to Wren. "Go!" he yells.

Vincent lunges toward Jackson, landing on the man's leg and chomping through his pants into his flesh. Jackson hollers at the top of his lungs. Wren is just crawling out of the cage when Russell comes bounding up and slams the door right onto the mink's fragile body. Wren squeals in pain. He starts to fall back into the cage as Russell slams the cage door again, this time onto Wren's right front leg. There is a loud crack and Wren screeches in agony before tumbling back into the cage.

Jackson clasps tightly onto Vincent's back with his left glove. He shakes Vincent violently and lifts him high above his head. Just as Jackson is about to slam Vincent against the ground, Russell grabs Jackson's arm, stopping him.

"What the hell are you doing, idiot?! That's expensive property," Russell barks.

"The goddamn thing bit the hell outta my leg," Jackson snaps.

Russell snaps right back. "That's your own damn fault, takin' them outta there all half assed. Each one of these things is worth money. Money you don't got." Russell points to Wren, who is whimpering in the cage. "Look at what you made me do to that one. He's all busted up. Waste a damn money!" Russell squeezes the arm Jackson is using to hold Vincent. "Now put this one in another cage!"

Vincent thrashes around in Jackson's grasp, biting at his glove. Jackson glares at Vincent. "One day, you little shit. You're gonna get yours."

Jackson carries Vincent toward a separate set of cages. Vincent looks back at his family, who are still in their cage. "Mommy! I'm sorry. I tried!"

Margeaux calls out, "Vincent, never give up. You were so brave! Never..." Vincent is carried out of earshot.

Margeaux looks down at Wren, who is writhing in pain on the wire floor. "Mommy! Mommy!" he cries out.

"I know, my little kit. I know," she says, trying to comfort him.

Margeaux looks through the bottom of the cage and is relieved to see Trenton on the ground a few feet below, uninjured.

Trenton calls up to her. "Mom! I can help you."

"Trenton, no," Margeaux demands. "Run! Get away from here. The humans will be back soon. Run as fast as you can and never come back."

Trenton protests. "But Mom..."

Margeaux lets out a guttural yell. "Run! Save yourself or I will never forgive you!"

Trenton looks hurt, conflicted. How can he leave his family in that cage? He looks up at Frestin and Alia, who are quivering in terror, then at his emotionally spent mother as she leans over his dying brother, Wren. Trenton closes his eyes briefly and then darts toward the woods, not looking back. With a second kit having escaped to freedom, Margeaux feels a fleeting moment of relief. Then she looks down at Wren, and the moment ends. She has a pained look in her eyes. She is breathing heavily. "Frestin, Alia, I want you to go into the nest. Don't look out here. You understand?"

"Why, Mommy?" Frestin asks.

"Just go!" she commands.

Frestin and Alia crawl into the dark nest and hide.

Margeaux looks down at the battered Wren. Blood is dripping from his mouth. He is alive but in immense pain.

Margeaux speaks softly to her injured kit. "Wren, I know you are hurting very badly. The humans are going to leave you like this, and you will suffer for hours. I don't know how long." Her heart is pounding. "Wren, my gentle kit, I love you."

Margeaux gazes up through the wire cage at the sky, which is a beautiful, light blue. Such a gorgeous day for such a horrific tragedy. She looks at the nest door to make sure her other kits aren't watching. They are not.

Margeaux looks back down at her anguished son. *If there was only another way.* She then rips into his flesh as quickly and painlessly as she knows how.

✳   ✳   ✳

Jackson tosses Vincent into a cage with three other young males. Vincent's face smacks against the wire. Jackson punches the side of the cage. "I shoulda crushed your skull, you little shit! You got lucky today."

Jackson storms away, limping on his sore leg. Vincent watches through the wire, glad the human seems to be in pain. Once Jackson is out of view, though, Vincent crumbles onto the cage floor. He feels as if his heart has been crushed into pieces. His whole family has been torn apart. What he doesn't know is that the greatest heartbreak of his life is yet to come.

21

PERSIMMON, DERPOKE AND the rest of the team sit silently in awe of the mysterious mink standing before them. His soft fur is a striking black with an underlying hint of blue. He seems calm and collected, despite being surrounded by much larger creatures, and there is a certain cunning air about him. They can also tell he carries a weight on his shoulders—a deep sadness stained with anger—although from what, they are not sure. The mink gazes back at each of the animals surveying him, as intrigued by them as they are by him.

The mink speaks. "My name is Vincent. I overheard you say that you were planning on freeing my fellow minks. Any creature with such a noble plan is a friend of mine."

"We're the Champions of Courageousness!" Scraps calls out spiritedly.

The tiny raccoon looks around at his team members to see if they like his latest suggestion, but their disgruntled expressions make it clear that they do not.

Persimmon grins. "I'm so happy to meet you, Vincent. I am Persimmon, and as my younger brother, Scraps, pointed out so enthusiastically, my friends and I have joined together to go on a mission—to save the lives of any animals who are suffering. Our official name is actually still a work in progress, but that does not reflect on our professionalism as a team. We take this mission very seriously. We heard that minks were being held captive and killed for their impressive fur, which is why we made the journey here."

Vincent's expression lightens and the corners of his mouth turn up slightly—not quite a full smile, though. It's been a long time since he truly smiled. "Really? How fortuitous that I ran into you. I escaped that prison last winter, and I have spent many hours since trying to figure out how to free my family and friends. We have until this coming winter before the humans massacre the next round of minks, but the sooner we get them out of there, the better. In fact, I already have a plan. I just needed more dexterous paws than my own in order to open the cages, and you," he motions to Persimmon and Scraps, "are perfect. Just so you know, though, there are around five-thousand minks imprisoned in more than a thousand cages on that fur farm."

Persimmon is blown away. "Wow. A thousand cages?"

Derpoke speaks up. "Vincent, my name is Derpoke." The opossum turns to the team. "I'd like to point out to the group that with the calves, there were about a hundred stalls, and it took almost all night to get the doors open. If we are going to open a thousand cages, we must recruit more team members—and it sounds like more raccoons specifically."

"Yes, I agree we need more help," Persimmon remarks. "But don't forget, we had to chew through all those ropes. That's what held us up the most. Vincent, are the minks tied up in any way?"

"No. What are calves?" Vincent inquires.

"They are a type of creature humans eat," Derpoke answers with a sigh. "We tried to save them before the humans could slaughter them. In fact, from what I've seen—and smelled—of the minks' cages so far, you all are treated in much the same way. Or, should I say, *mistreated* in much the same way?"

Vincent looks concerned. "You *tried*? You were unsuccessful?"

"We did our best, but we didn't understand how injured the calves were," Persimmon replies, ashamed. "When we attempted to free them, they could barely walk. That's why we need to learn as much as possible from you about how this farm works, and then scope it out before we make our official rescue plan. We want to make sure that once we free the minks, they'll actually be able to run away."

Vincent lets out a sigh of relief. "Ah, well. No need to worry about that. We minks are quite speedy. And don't worry about a plan, either. I have one all figured out. The first step of which is dealing with Mando and Diablo." Vincent examines the group to make sure he has everyone's attention.

"When I first escaped, I had no idea what to eat. I had been trapped in those cages for almost a year, and they always fed us the same dreary slop—later I found out it was a mixture of rotten meats. Not very appetizing, I can assure you. So, I foraged in the forest for anything that seemed edible. Berries, fruits, bugs, fish, you name it. A few of these things made me sick, one of which was an orange mushroom. I will spare you the details, but let's just say I was emptied of anything I had recently ingested and felt quite ill for some time. But that gave me an idea. I know I can't free the other minks with those Rottweilers at my heels, but I figure if I feed them these mushrooms, I can open all the cages while they're overcome with sickness."

Persimmon is aghast. "You mean poison them?"

"It's not going to harm them other than to make them sick," Vincent reassures her. "And they'll be debilitated long enough for us to conduct our rescue. It's the most sensible of all the plans I've devised."

Persimmon isn't convinced. "Well, it may seem sensible, but it's cruel. They didn't ask to be locked up in that fur farm any more than you and your family did. I know it seems hard to believe, but I think I can persuade them to help us."

Vincent scoffs, dumbfounded by her naïveté. "Help us? Persimmon, I admire your optimism. I even understand how these dogs could be considered victims, given the way the Peterson brothers treat them, but that doesn't outweigh the fact that they are trained killers. I've seen it with my own eyes. If you set even one paw on that side of the fence, they will devour you faster than you can scream 'Stop!'"

Persimmon isn't swayed. "Vincent, you haven't met Bruiser yet, have you?" Bruiser nods at Vincent. "When I first ran into Bruiser, he was ready to tear *me* to pieces, but after one conversation, he completely changed his mind about raccoons. Now I trust him with my life. And he's here today to help rescue your friends and family. If *he* can change, any dog can."

Vincent clenches his jaw. He licks a chipped tooth in the front of his mouth, trying to remain calm, but he is becoming increasingly frustrated. "I suppose you can spend days attempting to win over these dogs, but know that every minute you waste talking to them is another minute the minks suffer horrendously. I know. I was in there. Sitting in the blazing sun, overheating to the point where you think your fur is on fire. Trapped forever in a cramped, barren cell, standing on painful mesh wire that digs into your paws. Watching all your friends around you go insane. I could go on, but it is too painful to discuss."

A somber gloom presses down on the team. Vincent is visibly upset. He looks uncomfortable after showing so much emotion to this group of strangers. He tries hard to smother those caustic memories, and being reminded of them drains him.

Bruiser turns to his raccoon friend. "Persimmon, it sounds like those minks are really in a bad way. If makin' Mando and Diablo a little sick will give us time to save 'em, I say we go with it." He pauses, but then quickly blurts out, "I don't wanna sell out my own kind here. I mean, it burns me up seein' those dogs beat up by humans just like I was, but I know how they think. You could spend weeks tryin' a convince 'em that the humans don't care 'bout 'em, but they won't budge. It's a point of pride to keep intruders away."

Vincent peers over at the Doberman, touched. "Thank you, Bruiser. I hope I have not offended you. This is not a slight against dogs. I just want to free my family."

Bruiser nods his head. "I get it, Vincent. We good."

Persimmon looks over at her trustworthy opossum buddy. "Derpoke, what is your opinion?"

Derpoke shifts uncomfortably. "Well, uh... Persimmon, you know I greatly respect you."

"Yes, it's okay. You can be honest," Persimmon assures him.

Derpoke continues. "I guess I have two points then. One, although I am embarrassed to admit it, I was once foolish enough to try those orange mushrooms, and though they did make me very sick, after a day or so I was fine. Which is more than enough time to get in and out of there. Of course, that first attempt is just to scope out the farm. Who knows if they'll get wise to the smell of the mushrooms for the second attempt?"

Derpoke looks at Persimmon to make sure she isn't annoyed by what he is saying. She doesn't look perturbed, so he goes on. "Two, my biggest concern with trying to convince these Rottweilers to come to our side is actually a tactical one—it ruins the element of surprise. The moment you talk to those dogs, we lose the upper hand, and that might jeopardize any hope we have of saving the minks."

Persimmon looks at the ground, letting all of their comments sink in. She then looks up into the tree at Chloe and Tucker, who are listening in, and at Scraps, who is by her side. "Does anyone else have any suggestions? Any input?"

Scraps chimes in. "What if we dug a hole and tricked the dogs to fall into it by making them chase us? Then they'd be trapped while we raided the farm."

"That's a good idea…" Vincent pauses, having forgotten the little raccoon's name.

Scraps fills him in. "It's Scraps."

Vincent continues. "Yes. That's a good idea, Scraps. I thought of that myself, but it would be quite an effort to dig a hole deep enough so that they can't jump out. Plus, that doesn't solve the problem of them barking, which will wake the Peterson family."

Persimmon pats Scraps on the head. "Thanks for the idea, Scraps, but Vincent is right."

Persimmon struggles to keep her eyes open. She and her friends haven't slept for almost a full day. She is weary, and tired of thinking. "My friends, it has been a long day. Here is a solution that will hopefully alleviate all of our concerns, and then we can sleep." She takes a deep breath before she begins. She's in the minority on this one, and needs to work her magic if she's going to persuade them.

"I appreciate all of your input. It makes me all the more confident that as long as we stick together, we can solve any problem. When I originally gathered this team it was because I saw that there were animals out there who needed help—who needed saving: the calves, the minks. Mando and Diablo fall into that category, too." Persimmon makes sure to look at each team member to drive her point home. "They don't deserve this life. I know it makes the rescue more difficult, but our mission is to save *any* animal who is suffering—no matter how much trouble it causes us. I'm not saying that it's going to be easy to convince them, but I believe it's absolutely possible. Bruiser is proof of that."

Persimmon pauses, making sure she still has everyone's attention. She does.

"Vincent, I completely agree that every second counts, so I will talk to them once, and only once. I think that's all it will take anyway. And I want you to know that helping Mando and Diablo does not detract from our goal to help your mink brethren. It sounds like they are trapped in deplorable and hideous conditions, and we are going to do everything we can to save them. I promise you that." She turns to her opossum friend. "Derpoke, as for the element of surprise: Whether or not I talk to them, I don't think they'll expect us to poison their food, so if these mushrooms work the way you and Vincent say they do, they'll be too busy vomiting to be concerned with anything else."

She addresses the group again. "Does that work for everyone?"

Everyone looks around to see if there are any objections. They all end up looking at Vincent to see what he will say.

Vincent feels the weight of their gazes and gathers his emotions before speaking. "Persimmon, you have assembled a thoughtful and brave group. I appreciate any help I can get to rescue my friends and family, and if I must acquiesce on this point to have your help, then so be it."

Persimmon is relieved. "Thank you, Vincent. We won't let you down." She turns to the team. "Okay, everyone, let's rest."

The team collapses into various spots to get some much-needed shut-eye. Persimmon, Scraps, Derpoke and Bruiser curl up by a fallen tree trunk. Chloe and Tucker nest together in the tree above. And Vincent crawls back into his dark burrow. He cannot sleep, though— not now. This is the closest he has ever come to rescuing his tormented fellow minks. He has dreamed of this moment for so long—the aspiration of liberating them has kept him alive through some of his darkest moments. And now, with the help of this daring and compassionate team, he may finally see his dream become a reality. His family and friends have been tortured by the Petersons long enough. There will not be another massacre this winter. It stops now! He *will* save them this time—or die trying.

22

The Story of Vincent the Mink, Part 2

The Massacre

THE AIR IS filled with the deafening sound of weeping baby minks who have just been torn away from their mothers. This is the sound of despair. Vincent looks down at the rows and rows of cages—they go as far as the eye can see, across from him, on either side of him—filled with sobbing kits. Each enclosure appears to contain five or six minks. He had no idea there were so many other minks at the fur farm. *Are all of us going to die? Are they really going to kill every last one of us for our fur? I don't want to die. I just want to be with Mommy, Frestin, Trenton... Is Trenton okay? I saw him thrown over the cages, but did he get hurt when he landed? Did anyone else get out while I was being carried away? I know for sure Marcel got away.* Vincent smiles to himself. *He got away!... I'm going to join him one day. I'm going to get out of here. They're not taking* my *fur.*

Vincent observes the three other male minks stuck in the cage with him. They are all crying, "Mommy! Mommy!" One is pressed up against the side of the cage, scratching feverishly at the metal, futilely trying to claw through the wire.

Vincent tries to speak over the sound of the wailing. "It's okay. We're going to get out of here." The three minks continue howling, not noticing him at all. They are too overcome by their own sorrow.

Just then, Vincent sees Jackson coming toward his cage. He braces himself. *Is he coming back to continue our fight?... I'm not afraid. I'll take him on again.* But then Vincent sees that Jackson is holding a bag with something wriggling around inside. *He has another mink. Perfect! The moment he opens the latch, I'm out of here.* Vincent prepares to flee. Jackson reaches into the bag and starts to pull out the thrashing mink. With his other hand he begins to open the latch. Vincent stands at attention, ready to leap. Jackson opens the latch and pushes the mink from the bag toward the cage door.

"Frestin!" Vincent yells, his heart sinking. Jackson tosses Frestin into the cage and quickly closes it again, and walks away.

Vincent and Frestin hug, but the reunion is bittersweet. "I was hoping you had escaped, my brother," Vincent says, disappointed.

"I thrashed around as much as I could," Frestin explains. "But it was no use. By the time they opened the cage after you left, they were wise to our plan. They took me out as cautiously as possible."

Vincent pats his brother on the back. "If we're going to be trapped in here, I'm glad we're together at least. I thought we'd never see each other again."

"Me, too." Frestin lets out a sigh of relief. "It's good to see you, my brother."

"Where are the others? Is Trenton okay?"

"Yes, Trenton ran free. He made it!"

Vincent is relieved. "He did?! Yay! So both he *and* Marcel escaped."

"Yes. Two of us made it out!" Frestin and Vincent stomp their paws on the mesh floor in celebration. It feels truly comforting to have some good news on such a horrendous day.

"Did anyone else make it?" Vincent inquires. "Did you see where they put Wren and Alia? Is Mommy okay?"

Frestin looks away, his joyful demeanor changing immediately. He can't look Vincent in the eyes for this news. "Wren was badly hurt when they closed the cage door on him. He couldn't really move."

"Is he..." Vincent doesn't want to ask. "Is he... did he die?"

Frestin starts to cry. He can't bear to tell Vincent what happened. He doesn't want to think of the sound Wren made when he died. He doesn't want to think of the last image he has of his mother, standing in the cage, devastated, with the blood of their brother—her son—staining her face. Although he knows she acted out of mercy, the memory still disturbs him to the core.

Vincent cuddles up to Frestin. "It's okay. At least we're together."

Vincent wants to cry, too, but he must stay strong for his disconsolate brother. He looks around the cage and examines his new surroundings. Before him are three bawling minks who he does not know but with whom he must now share a suffocating cell. This cage is much like his old one but this one has scattered patches of fur strewn about. *Whose fur is this? Where are these minks now? Dead? Surely dead.*

In the cages on either side of him, the kits are either crying or frantically biting at the wire, looking for a way out. *Did their mothers warn them of this day? Did they prepare these kits for how to survive until they escape? If they escape... How can I get both Frestin and me out of this cage? Only one of us getting out is just as bad as neither of us getting out. Today was shattering. We can never separate again.*

Vincent looks through the wire floor at the dirt below. There is a small pile of feces under his cage. In fact, there is a pile of excrement below each cage. The stench turns his stomach. The noise of the kits crying reverberates through the air. *When will they stop? It's unbearable.* This is his new home: filth, misery, hopelessness.

*   *   *

"What are your names?" Vincent addresses the other three minks in his cage. They have finally quieted down and are huddled in a pile at the opposite end of the enclosure.

One of the minks stirs. He has a black tint to his fur, similar to the few black hairs that are starting to show up in Vincent's still silver-white coat. "I'm Emmett." The gravelly tone of his voice makes it sound as if the air coming out of his lungs is scraping against sandpaper. "What's yours?"

"I'm Vincent, and this is my brother Frestin." Vincent motions to Frestin, who nods hello.

The mink sitting next to Emmett speaks up. "My name is Bailey." His voice is softer, almost fragile, and his fur is a brilliant white. "You're lucky to be locked up with your brother."

"Very lucky," Vincent agrees. "But since we're stuck in here together, I consider us all brothers. And we need to work together if we're going to escape."

Emmett can't believe what he just heard. "Escape?! How? I've pulled and chewed on every piece of wire in this pen."

"We're not going that way," Vincent responds. "See that cage door? We're going right through there."

The third mink in the cage, who sports cinnamon fur, harrumphs. He wears a sour expression. He doesn't say anything, just grumbles and turns away.

"You don't have to believe us," Frestin snaps. "But two of our brothers escaped that way already. It's our best bet. With teamwork and planning, we can do it."

The brownish mink challenges sullenly without turning around. "You're fools. I bet you don't even know why we're in here."

"We do," Vincent fires back. "And that's why it's imperative that we plan our escape."

Emmett cuts in, his voice quivering. "What do you mean? Why *are* we in here?"

Vincent shoots Frestin a look. If the minks were bawling uncontrollably about being taken away from their mothers, how will they react to hearing that they've been sentenced to die?

"Your mothers didn't tell you?" Vincent asks.

Emmett and Bailey have blank, frightened expressions.

"Well..." Vincent treads lightly. "They're going to take our fur. I..."

The brownish mink cuts in. "They're going to murder us for our fur."

Emmett and Bailey start shaking out of fear. "What?! When? How?"

Vincent speaks up quickly to explain his plan. "Yes, it's true. They plan to kill us when the cold sets in. I don't know how they're going to kill us, but we..."

The brownish mink twists around to face the others. "They're going to snap our necks. Then they're going to skin us, ripping our fur from our dead bodies just so they can wear it over their own skin. We're all going to die—slow, horrible deaths."

Bailey starts sniffling again, ready to burst into tears at any moment. Emmett begins to hyperventilate. The minks in the cages on either side sit in stunned silence as well. Even Vincent and Frestin are unable to speak. Somehow, their imminent demise seems more real now. Vincent gets lost in thought. *They're going to break our necks? How? Twist our heads around? Stomp on us?* A terrified shudder shoots down his spine. *What did we do to deserve this?*

The brownish mink glares at Vincent—angry at the world, angry at being doomed to this horrid fate, angry with Vincent for spreading false hope. Vincent pops out of his stupefied haze. Even if his own confidence has diminished, he knows he has to stand his ground or he'll lose the group forever. He glares back. "You may already be resigned, but not me. Not my brother. And not anyone else who dares to fight back. When the time comes to make our escape, we'll be ready, and those of you who did not prepare will die in this place. It's your choice."

Vincent looks at Frestin for reassurance. Frestin nods. He believes in his brother. If the rest of these minks want to perish in this death factory, that's their problem.

✳   ✳   ✳

A month has passed. The sun beats down on the rows of cages. The tin roofs over the pens barely offer any shade from the baking rays, and the minks are boiling in the heat. Emmett and the surly brown mink (who Vincent and Frestin have nicknamed Grumbles) pace back and forth incessantly. The cage is tiny, so they only go two paces before having to turn around. They constantly bang into one another in the cramped space, but they keep going. They can't help it. Emmett keeps repeating the same thing over and over. "Get out. Get out. Gotta get out."

"Those guys are losing it," Frestin whispers to Vincent.

Vincent whispers back. "I know. Being trapped in here is making them crazy."

"Being trapped in here is making us *all* crazy," replies Frestin. "But they're going to get hurt—or hurt someone—if they keep racing around the cage like that."

"Ignore them," Vincent counsels. "Every time you tell them to stop, it just causes problems."

Vincent catches Bailey slurping on the water bottle. "Bailey, I told you. Don't drink all the water."

"I'm not. I'm just thirsty," Bailey whines.

"We all are, but we have to ration it," Vincent reminds him. "You know that the Petersons rarely refill the bottles, and the last time ours was empty, I thought we were all going to die from dehydration."

Bailey plods over to where Vincent and Frestin are sitting, continuing to complain. "It's so hot and I'm so itchy." Bailey scratches his eyes, his neck, his underbelly. "Bugs are crawling all over me."

Vincent tries to comfort him. "I know. Mites, fleas, lice—we're infested, but there's no way to pry them all off, so we just have to pretend they're not there or think about other things."

Frestin tries to lighten the tense mood. "Did you see that hole the minks are ripping open in the cage next to us?"

Vincent and Bailey get excited. "Really?!"

"Yeah, look." Frestin points into the adjacent cage. "You see that brown part of the wire at the back of their cage?"

Vincent and Bailey examine the back of the cage, and sure enough, a few wires have been pulled apart. The hole isn't big enough for a mink to crawl through yet, but it's a start.

Vincent is impressed. "Wow! That's so great."

"I think some of the cages are older," Frestin explains. "So it's easier to chew through the wire."

Just then, Emmett and Grumbles bang into one another again, pushing Grumbles onto Vincent's back.

"Watch it!" Frestin hollers.

Grumbles hisses back. "Shut up! Shut up! I'll scratch your eyes out."

Frestin steps toward Grumbles, but Vincent bounces in between the heated minks. "Frestin, calm down. It's fine." Vincent holds Frestin back and whispers quietly so that Grumbles can't hear him. "Be patient. He's crazy. He doesn't know what he's doing."

Frestin speaks loudly so that Grumbles *can* hear him. "Yeah well, he better watch out or he's going to find out really quickly who's the toughest one in here."

Grumbles isn't listening, though. He has already gone back to his nervous pacing. Emmett has stopped at least. He sits in a far corner, biting at something that is clearly bothering him on his back.

Vincent tries to reason with Frestin. "You can't let him get to you. He's obviously falling apart being trapped in here. What do you gain by antagonizing him?"

"It will shut him up." Frestin starts chewing on his right hind paw. Vincent looks at his brother disapprovingly. Frestin snaps defensively, "What?"

"You know what. You're chewing on your paw again."

"Maybe I like clean paws," Frestin remarks indignantly.

"Oh yeah?" Vincent challenges. "I'm pretty sure you licked off any hint of impurity the last eight times that you chewed on them today."

"So what?" Frestin counters. "It comforts me."

Vincent delivers his winning blow. "Well, maybe it comforts Grumbles to pace back and forth."

Frestin thinks about that. He can't argue his way out of this one. Vincent grins. "Victory is mine?"

"Victory is yours," Frestin acquiesces, before pausing and adding with a smirk, "This time."

✳   ✳   ✳

A few more weeks go by. It is dusk, and there is a blue haze in the air. Vincent opens his eyes. His black fur still feels warm from roasting in the sun all day. He can hear other minks in nearby cages shuffling back and forth, and he knows they are succumbing to despair over being trapped. Vincent peers around his own cage. Most of the others are still asleep except Emmett, who is nibbling on his own tail. Vincent looks closer and notices blood on Emmett's face.

Vincent hops up. "Emmett, are you all right?"

Emmett jolts out of his trance and drops his tail. It falls to the floor of the cage. He has completely severed it from his body, leaving only a bloody stump on his back.

Vincent is shaken, revolted. "Emmett, what have you done?!"

Emmett is frightened, lost. "I can't get out, Vincent. I can't get out."

Vincent is horrified. The commotion wakes the other minks in the cage.

"What's going on?" Frestin gripes. He notices the severed tail on the cage floor and then sees Emmett's bloody mouth. Queasiness overcomes Frestin. He can taste bile brewing in his mouth. "What happened?!"

All the other minks stare at Emmett, disgusted.

Emmett feels a mixture of shame and agitation. "Don't look at me! Leave me alone!"

The ruckus riles up the unhinged Grumbles, so he starts jumping up and down, and then throws his body against the side of the cage.

This aggravates Emmett even more. "I said, don't look at me!" he hisses at the gawking crowd.

Vincent comes to his defense. "Okay, everyone. Leave him alone. Just let Emmett be." Vincent gathers Frestin and Bailey and motions for them to turn away from Emmett.

Emmett glares at his cagemates, then picks up his tail with his teeth and huddles in a corner of the cage. He starts chewing on the severed appendage again.

Vincent whispers to Frestin and Bailey. "He was always scratching and gnawing on his tail. He definitely seemed a bit disturbed, but I never thought he'd do something like this."

"I wish I could say I'm surprised, but the way he's been acting—he and Grumbles have completely lost it. It's frightening," Frestin remarks. "Is that us next?"

Bailey scratches his itchy eyes. "Do you think so?" he asks nervously. "I don't want to eat my tail."

"We're going to be fine," Vincent assures them. "We need to focus on our escape, and keep our minds sharp—not think about how trapped we are." Vincent looks beyond the wire and into the woods. "Look at those trees. Just imagine what's beyond those trees."

Frestin and Bailey give Vincent a hesitant look, not sure if they're in the mood to play along. Vincent pushes on. "Come on. Dreaming about life beyond this cage is the only thing that will keep us sane." Frestin and Bailey are still quiet, but Vincent won't be deterred. "I'll go first. Mom told us she has no doubt we can climb those trees. That's what I want to do right when I get out of here. Climb to the very top and look around to see everything we can't see from in here."

Frestin joins in. "All right. I want to sleep on something soft instead of this hard wire floor. Maybe that green stuff is soft. What did Mom call it?"

"Grass," Vincent answers. "Yes, I bet that would feel great under our bellies—so soothing." He pictures himself relaxing in the gentle grass. "What about you, Bailey?"

"Well, my mother told me that one of my older brothers escaped, and he came back to see her and said that there was this thing called a stream. It's just water flowing on top of the dirt. You can drink all you want. I want to do that. He said that you can even go in the water to swim. Do you know what swimming is?"

Vincent's and Frestin's interest is piqued. "No. What?"

Bailey explains. "You jump in the water and move your legs and flop around."

Vincent doesn't understand. "Why would you flop your legs around?"

Bailey tries to clarify. "You can move around without touching the ground." Vincent and Frestin look confused, so Bailey gives up. "I don't know how to describe it. I didn't really understand it myself, but he said it was the best feeling ever."

Vincent and Frestin close their eyes and try to imagine floating in water, kicking their legs around, and not standing on the ground. It all seems magical—even surreal, but no more nonsensical than being left to fester in a filthy cage barely bigger than they are.

*   *   *

Vincent is in the middle of a heated conversation with two minks in one of the cages adjacent to his. The minks seem frantic, desperate. "We haven't had water for days. Please. We just need a little water," one of them begs.

"If I turn the bottle your way, it could break off the hinge and dump out all the water," Vincent replies. "Then we're all doomed."

The mink pleads with him. "We're going to die! Lowden isn't moving. Do you see him?" Vincent peers through the cage to see a brown mink collapsed on the floor. "He's dying. He won't respond. He is barely breathing. If you don't give us water, his death is on you."

Vincent is incensed. "I can't help. There's nothing I can do. The Petersons are killing him, not me."

"We'll remember this," the other mink snarls. "If you ever need water, we'll remember."

The minks in the other cage move away toward the one shady corner of their enclosure. Two other minks are already huddled there, so the argumentative critters push to make room for themselves. Lowden remains listless, slowly breathing in and out, baking in the sun and barely alive.

Vincent walks over to Frestin with his ears low. "It isn't my fault. We don't have any water to give."

"There's nothing we can do," Frestin says, validating Vincent's decision. "Hopefully, the Petersons come around with water soon. We're almost out, too. I will say this: Those guys have terrible luck over there. I think that's the same mink who got impaled when he was trying to squeeze through the hole in their cage."

"It's such a shame they can't make use of that hole," Vincent adds. "They're so close to escaping, but the loose wires are just too dangerous. I thought they were gonna poke their eyes out when they were trying to squish through it the other day."

Vincent notices Bailey scratching ferociously at his eyes. "Speaking of eyes. Hold on, Frestin." Vincent moves over to the distressed mink. "Bailey, I warned you not to scratch your eyes."

"I know," he whimpers. "But they itch so badly, Vincent." Bailey's eyes are cloudy and a milky discharge oozes out of them.

"I know they itch," Vincent commiserates. "I'm so sorry you're in such agony, but there's a cut above your eye, and I'm worried you'll make it worse if you keep scratching. Your nails are too long, and they're digging into your skin."

Bailey is quiet for a moment, resisting the urge to touch his swollen eyes. But then he howls, "I can't stop!" He scratches even more vigorously. "Make it end! Please. Help me! If I can just get them out of my head."

Vincent can see that his poor friend is on the brink. "Bailey, you have to calm down. You're..." Vincent stops himself. What more can he say? Bailey has every right to scream. He's in insufferable pain. Anyone in his right mind would go insane living like this.

Vincent runs to the front of the cage and slams his body against it. He shrieks at the top of his lungs. "Russell! Jackson! Help us! We're dying in here. We have no water. Our eyes are burning. Our flesh is melting. You have no right to treat us like this! You have no right to torture us! Let us out of here!" He pounds the cage wall with his paws. "Freedom! Freedom!"

Vincent bangs his paws against the bars a few more times, then falls to floor, spent. No one is coming to save them, and he knows it.

* * *

It's now August, and the sun shines down even more intensely on the fur farm. Only the night is a respite from the hellish heat. But the days are so excruciating, it somehow feels like there are more days than nights.

Grumbles hasn't ceased pacing back and forth in the cage. He goes and goes until his heart feels like it will burst and then he crashes to the rigid floor, panting, "Freedom. Freedom." Ever since hearing Vincent's outburst, he has repeated this mantra continuously.

With Emmett's tail detached, the anxious mink has turned to devouring his paws. Each one is raw and mangled, so sore he struggles to walk. He spends most nights nibbling on his feet or scratching his ears. Sometimes he can be heard murmuring to himself, although it's difficult for the others to make out what he is saying.

Bailey's eye infection has worsened over the past month, rendering him blind. Thick scabs are embedded in the fur around his eyes, the result of his incessant scratching. His pain persists, but he's too worn out to speak up about it any longer. He quietly whimpers to himself on occasion and finds comfort curling up to Vincent when he's sleeping. When Bailey seems dazed, Vincent and Frestin help direct him to the water bottle.

In the cage adjacent to theirs, Lowden's body decomposes in a corner. Jackson came by once to add water to their bottle, but it was too late. Jackson glanced at Lowden's lifeless body and just continued working, unmoved by the gory sight. He also didn't bother to extract the carcass from the pen. The other minks do their best to avoid the area, but it's very difficult to ignore a rotting corpse, especially the corpse of a friend.

On this day, Vincent and Frestin rest at the front of their cage, facing the forest. Neither is sleeping; they're too hot and weary to move. Frestin has his paw in his mouth, licking and chewing on his toes. Vincent opens his eyes and sees that Frestin is indulging his bad habit again. "Frestin," Vincent scolds.

With his paw shoved in his mouth, Frestin looks at his brother. Vincent motions to his brother's paw. Frestin doesn't protest; he just stops chewing.

There is silence for a moment. Vincent looks out into the woods. Frestin sighs, overwhelmed with desperation. "Vincent? I'm trying not to be, but I'm scared. I'm scared we'll end up like everyone else— crazy, bleeding, dying. I'm scared of having my neck snapped, that our plan won't work, that we may really never get out of here."

Vincent doesn't answer immediately. He's frightened as well but doesn't want to discourage his brother.

"Are *you* afraid?" Frestin asks.

Vincent briefly ponders how to answer that question so as not to alarm Frestin. He then replies with sincerity. "I'm concerned. I'm in pain. I feel sick. I feel angry. Frustrated. Filled with hate. I despise the Peterson family. But I'm not afraid. Because I have you. Because we're smarter than those horrible humans. We have a solid plan. And no matter how much they try to stomp us, they will not win. We will escape. I know it."

"But how can you be so sure?" Frestin presses.

"I just feel it," Vincent answers assuredly. "I can even visualize it—us running into that forest—as if it already happened. I'm going to climb the tallest tree and you're going to relax in a field of fluffy grass."

Frestin's mouth turns up into a devilish smile. "I changed my fantasy."

Vincent is surprised. "Oh really? Okay, what do you want to do when you get out of here?"

"Snuggle up to some females," Frestin responds slyly.

Vincent can't believe what he just heard. "What? What do you mean?"

"I don't know exactly," Frestin smirks. "I just want to be close to them. Can't you smell them? Sometimes I get a whiff of them in the air, and I just want to be near them."

Vincent is thoroughly confused. "I honestly don't know what you're talking about. Now I'm concerned you might be losing your mind as well."

"Well, that's the fantasy that's been getting me through the days, so don't knock it."

Vincent looks at his brother quizzically. "Dare I ask what other odd things you daydream about?"

Frestin looks amused by the question. He peers through the bottom of the cage at the excrement below. The mound of feces has risen astronomically over the past few months, since no one has come by to clean it up. "Okay, I came up with the perfect name for those piles of poo."

"What?!" Vincent looks over at his brother, bewildered. "I don't know which is grosser, your comments about females or your fascination with our droppings."

"Come on, aren't you even a little intrigued about what I've named them?"

"You're going to tell me even if I don't ask," Vincent mutters. "So what is it?"

"Slar," Frestin answers proudly.

Vincent looks at the mounds of waste. He tries not to smile, but he can't help it.

Frestin cheers. "I told you! That's the perfect name for it."

Vincent laughs. "That's so stupid."

"But I'm right. It looks like a heaping pile of slar."

At that moment, Vincent and Frestin realize they're both smiling—genuinely smiling. It feels so good. Happiness. There has been none of that for so long—maybe ever really. What a blissful feeling. For a brief moment, they forget the hell around them. But slowly, reality starts to seep back in—Bailey's blindness, the minks' frantic pacing, their own aching, sickly stomachs gnawing at their insides, their fear of the impending massacre. Happiness felt good while it lasted—even if it was fleeting.

A crisp air has set in. It's October. The cooler weather is refreshing after the searing summer, but with it comes the promise of death. Any day now could be their last, and the minks are conflicted about their rapidly approaching demise. If they truly are doomed to spend their lives trapped in these cages, they'd rather be dead sooner than later—at least the suffering would finally be over. But wishing for death means they've given up any hope of escape. They can't help but wonder: *This can't be all that was meant for my life. Will I really never live one day devoid of misery? Will I really never step one foot out of this stifling pen? Never enjoy food that isn't rotten? Never have enough water to actually quench my thirst? Never feel any comfort at all? That can't be. It's not right.* But nothing is right about living in these cages, so they languish and they despair.

All of the minks have become delirious. Of the group, Vincent's and Frestin's faculties were the last to go, as they had tried to keep their minds acute with games and fantasies of life beyond their cage. But the madness crept through them ever so slowly that they didn't even realize it was happening.

Frestin has chewed his paws raw, but Vincent gave up chiding him about it a while ago. What's the point? Frestin almost can't help himself—even when he forces himself to stop, a few seconds later he finds himself unconsciously biting them again. Most of the time, Frestin broods in a corner, munching and licking his paws while obsessing over having his neck broken. *Will it be quick? Will it be painful? Will they twist and twist until my head pops off?*

It's not that he's given up hope of escaping; he just can't shake the fear of being killed.

Vincent has joined Grumbles in pacing back and forth in the cage. At first he tricked himself into believing that it was just a tactic to use while ruminating over their escape plan, but it has since turned into an unyielding compulsion. Fixated on the escape, he replays the plan over and over in his head as he paces. *Then we'll jump. We'll leap so high, right past them. Jackson and Russell won't see it coming. They can't stop us. How could they? We're too fast.*

Bailey's blindness prohibits him from moving much. His loss of appetite and thirst have weakened him further. Though Emmett's paws are deformed from his constant chewing, he still roams around the cage out of frustration. He moans as his sore pads bend around the wire floor, but he keeps going. Something in his brain tells him that he must keep moving or he will wither away.

With the chillier weather, the minks' lush fur grows—becoming the beautiful hair that humans covet so rabidly they're willing to kill for it. Vincent's and Emmett's coats have blossomed into a bold black, but Vincent's boasts a rare blue hue. Frestin and Grumbles are a warm brown. Bailey wears a white as bright as fresh snow, glistening in the sun. Their rich fur has sealed their fate. Any day now. Any day now.

*　　*　　*

Minks shriek in the distance, awakening Vincent with a jolt. *It's happening. The massacre has begun.* He suddenly gets the same sick feeling in his stomach that he had on the day he was torn from his mother. *Mother! Is her death planned for today as well or will they keep her alive to breed more kits? And what about Alia? Is she being rounded up today? Is she even still alive? When Frestin and I escape, how can we leave them here?*

More blood-curdling cries echo through the air—they're getting closer. Vincent rustles awake the other minks in his cage. They had only just slipped into slumber after having been up all night, freezing in the frigid December air. Snow blankets the ground and snowflakes sprinkle the minks' backs. The water in their bottle has hardened into ice, so they haven't had anything to drink in far too long. The harsh elements batter their unprotected cages. Winter is here, a Grim Reaper at their door.

The minks grouse about having to get up, but then they hear the screams. That jerks them into alert mode immediately. Grumbles resumes racing back and forth in the cage, more frantically than ever. "They're coming! They're coming!"

Vincent addresses his troops. "Okay, everyone. This is it. We've talked about this day—dreaded this day—for a long time, and it's finally here. Stay alert. Keep focused. We have a plan. All we have to do is follow it, and by tonight we'll be sleeping freely in the forest."

Emmett rocks back and forth, grinding his teeth. Vincent steps over to Bailey. "Are you sure you want to do this?"

"Absolutely," Bailey replies. "Even if I somehow hop out of here, I can't run away. I won't have any idea where I'm going."

"But we'll guide you out," Vincent offers.

"Vincent, I'd be a liability to all of you—maybe even more so in the forest. It's okay. Just promise me you'll think of me when you first get to enjoy swimming."

Vincent puts his paw on his friend's back. "Bailey, you are the most noble mink I will ever have the honor of knowing."

Right then, Jackson begins making his way down the row of cages. The minks' hearts jump. Jackson has the same dim-witted grin he always wears on his face—a permanent stupid look that is only heightened by his pathetic patchy beard. He's wearing a thick camouflage jacket and a black wool cap that's long enough to cover his ears, and he is pushing a wooden crate along the ground. Vincent and Frestin press their faces up against the front of the cage to get a better look. Jackson goes from pen to pen, opening the latches and grabbing the minks inside, either with a metal rod that clamps around their necks or by scooping them up in his glove and tossing them into the wooden crate.

Vincent looks at his brother gravely. "If you make it out first, just run. Don't wait for me. I'll be right behind you soon enough."

"Look at you trying to be all heroic." Frestin mimics Vincent's authoritative tone. "Just jump on my back, everyone. I'll carry all of you out of here."

"Frestin, this isn't the time for jokes," Vincent scolds. "I'm serious. Run straight for the forest."

"I'm just anxious. Joking makes me feel better." Frestin puts his paw on his brother's paw and states with bravado, "Besides, I run into that forest with you by my side or I don't run into it at all. That's the plan."

Vincent opens his mouth to argue, but Frestin just shakes his head and stomps the bottom of the cage. "The brothers."

Vincent knows there's no arguing with Frestin on this issue, so he stomps the cage as well. "The brothers!"

Jackson opens the cage beside theirs—the one containing Lowden's dead body—and snatches the squealing minks inside. The ones who hiss and put up a fight, Jackson shakes around and smacks with the metal tongs.

Vincent calls out to his cagemates. "Get in position! We're next!"

Bailey plants himself near the latch, huddling close to the ground. He breathes in slowly, trying to calm his nerves. Vincent, Frestin and Emmett stand at attention, forming a circle and facing counterclockwise. Grumbles is too out of his mind to coordinate with the rest of the group, so he just jumps up and down, chanting, "We're next! We're next!"

Jackson reaches for the latch on their cage. Vincent shouts to Bailey, "Get ready!"

Jackson undoes the latch. The minks are silent, still. Vincent, Frestin, Emmett and Bailey don't move a muscle; only Grumbles continues his jumping. Jackson pulls open the door and pokes the metal rod into the cage toward Bailey who is holding his position next to the door. Just before Jackson clamps the tongs around Bailey's neck, Vincent yells with a might equal to the glory of this moment, "Now!"

Bailey hoists himself up and starts spinning around. In unison, Vincent, Frestin and Emmett begin racing around in circles. The interior of the cage is complete chaos. Jackson drops the metal rod, startled. "What the hell?!"

"Emmett! Go!" Vincent hollers.

With that, Emmett spins out of the circle and leaps through the cage door and onto the snow-covered dirt below. He lands on his chest and skids on the slick ground but quickly props himself back up. He struggles to run with his mangled paws, but pushes forward—fueled by the taste of freedom—fast enough to sneak under the next row of cages and out of Jackson's reach.

Jackson slips on the wet snow and snarls. "Damn it!" He hops to his feet and rushes for the cage to stop any other minks from breaking loose, but he's too late. Frestin is just about to leap from the cage door himself. Just at that moment, though, Grumbles sees the cage door open and springs for it. Before Frestin can hop out, Grumbles rams Frestin from behind, knocking him off balance and throwing Frestin straight into the wooden crate.

"No!" Vincent cries out.

Grumbles, seemingly oblivious to what he has done, hurls himself at the ground. He lands with a thud, rolls over, and sprints down the snowy dirt path toward the forest. Jackson bolts after him, but Grumbles is too quick.

Vincent knows this is his moment. The cage door is open. Jackson is distracted. With one bound, Vincent can leap to freedom. Instead, he leans out of the cage door, presses his paws against the outside of the cage and plunges into the wooden crate. Another mink, crawling out of the crate at just that moment, looks stunned at Vincent's foolish nosedive. The mink scurries away on top of the row of cages toward the trees, laughing hysterically at his unexpected luck.

Jackson has regained his balance and promptly slams the crate lid shut, infuriated. "Bastards! You little bastards!"

Inside the crate, Vincent crawls on top of yelping minks, searching for Frestin. The air is musty and filled with the sounds of more than forty frantic minks. They kick and whip around, trying to crawl to the top of the heap of writhing bodies—both to escape and to avoid being crushed to death on the bottom of the pile.

Frestin sees Vincent coming toward him through the darkness and is absolutely flummoxed, even angry. "What are you doing?! You fool! You could have jumped to freedom!"

Vincent hollers back over all the noise around them. "I'm not leaving without you!"

Frestin wants to scream. He's moved that his brother risked his life to save him, yet he's furious that now they both may die. Vincent wasted a perfect chance to escape, but Frestin knows he would have done the same if the tables had been turned.

"Stupid Grumbles." Frestin mutters, hoping to make peace.

Vincent nods. "Stupid Grumbles."

Just then, Jackson opens the crate lid. Vincent and Frestin look up to see Bailey being tossed on top of the pile as Jackson swiftly slams the lid shut again. Vincent and Frestin try to crawl to Bailey, but the other minks clamber over him to reach the top.

Vincent shouts into the darkness. "Bailey!"

Bailey responds, his voice quivering. "Vincent? Vincent!"

Vincent tries to reach Bailey, but the blind mink is banged around and toppled over by the other frenzied minks.

Vincent pushes his way toward Bailey but keeps getting thrown back. Frestin grabs onto Vincent's tail. "Vincent, come on! We have to get out of here. You can't help him."

Vincent stops climbing. He feels terrible, but there's nothing he can do. Bailey's body disappears under a mountain of minks. Vincent looks away, pauses, then collects himself. They have to get out of here! "Jackson is going to open the lid again, and when he does, we need to be up there." Vincent motions toward the top of the crate.

Frestin nods. The brothers claw their way through the squirming mass of minks, all fighting for their lives. The minks step on one another, biting and hissing. If they want to survive, they have to battle their way to freedom.

The lid opens. It's now or never. Vincent and Frestin haul themselves toward the open air, digging through the struggling minks. Jackson tosses another squealing mink down into the pit, then closes the lid. Vincent and Frestin hold their ground at the top of the pile, scratching and gnashing their teeth at anyone who challenges them. They must escape.

The lid opens again. Sunlight fills the box. Frestin sees no other way—they can't maintain their position much longer. He pushes himself underneath Vincent's body to prop his brother up and out, over the side of the box. Vincent falls onto the snow below. Frestin goes to leap out, too, but Jackson catches him and tosses him back into the crate.

Vincent gasps. Right then, Jackson twists around toward Vincent. He grabs at the mink, but Vincent sneaks under the crate. Jackson pushes the box aside, but Vincent is nowhere to be found.

Jackson curses. "Damn it! Russell's gonna kick my ass!"

Vincent clings to the bottom of the crate. He sees Jackson turn back toward a cage, so he scurries in between two mounds of frozen excrement and under a row of cages. Vincent watches with rapt attention as Jackson lifts a thrashing mink over to the crate, opens the wood top and tosses the mink in. "Come on, Frestin. Jump out," Vincent murmurs. Frestin does not jump out, though. Vincent watches again as Jackson opens the lid to throw in another mink. He waits and waits for Frestin to come popping out, but nothing.

Vincent kicks at the snow in frustration. *Come on, Frestin! Where are you?!*

He watches as Jackson fiddles with the wooden lid. Then the human pushes the crate back down the dirt path in between the row of cages. *Where is he going?* Vincent stealthily follows Jackson, hidden underneath the rows of cages so as not to alert Jackson to his whereabouts.

Jackson pushes the crate into an open area behind the rows of cages. The snow isn't as deep here and the ground is an icy sludge. Vincent quietly creeps up to the edge of the cages, far enough to see into the open area but still hidden in the shadows. Vincent is taken aback by what he sees before him. *Why is the sludge crimson?* He looks up to see a pile of bloody corpses, a towering mound of dead minks stripped of their skin. All that's left on each carcass is exposed muscle—dripping with blood—and two black, lifeless eyes.

Vincent lets out a shrill yelp, as if all the air had been kicked out of him. The massacre is more horrifying than he could even have imagined during all those long nights stuck in that cage. *Do I know any of these minks? Is one of them Alia… or Mom?! I can't even tell. They're just a mangled mess of flesh and blood.*

Russell tosses another bloody body onto the gory pile. His camouflage jacket is stained red, as are his boots. He has been at this all morning—killing, cutting, tearing, tossing.

Vincent's reaction is visceral. He can barely breathe.

Jackson rolls the wooden crate past Russell. "Got another batch, bro."

"Gas 'em up," Russell barks. "We don't got all day."

"What you think I'm doin'? Damn. What's got into you?"

"This damn blood's soakin' through my jacket and my shoes! I'm freezin' my nuts off here," Russell roars.

Jackson stops pushing the cart and heads toward Russell. "All right, we'll switch if ya want."

"No, idiot. You can't cut fer shit. You ruin every pelt you cut. Just keep 'em bitches comin'. Let a man do the cuttin'."

Jackson rolls his eyes but doesn't say anything. Vincent can see Jackson attaching a large hose to the wooden crate, but he's not quite sure what's going on. To the right of the crate, Vincent notices another pile of minks. They still have their fur intact, but they're not moving. *Are their necks already broken? Maybe Jackson breaks their necks as he takes them out of the crate… Okay, new plan. The moment Jackson opens that crate I'll run up and attack his legs. That'll give Frestin just enough time to run away.*

Jackson pulls a tiny mask over his mouth and flips a switch on a separate machine. A loud mechanical whirring fills the air. The hose vibrates along with the machine. Vincent makes sure neither Jackson nor Russell is looking and quickly darts under another row of cages closer to the crate. As Vincent gets closer, he can faintly hear screeching, gasping. *What is that?!* Vincent listens more closely. The screaming is coming from inside the box. *What is happening?! Are they breaking their necks in there? How?*

Vincent's legs are shaking. He's trying to maintain his composure so he can rush Jackson, but his nerves are giving way. *Please be okay, Frestin. Please be okay.*

Jackson turns off the machine. Vincent braces himself, but instead of opening the lid, Jackson carts the crate closer to Russell and out of Vincent's view. *Darn!* Vincent dashes back to his original hiding spot under the other row of cages. He sees that Jackson has already begun pulling out handfuls of minks, but to his relief, Jackson is not snapping their necks. Jackson tosses mink after mink into a pile near Russell. Vincent surveys each batch coming out of the box, looking for Frestin. Nothing. Nothing. Then, finally, Jackson pulls out an armful of minks and Frestin is among them.

"Frestin! I'm here!" Vincent calls out, more hopeful now that he sees his brother again.

Frestin slides down the pile of minks, not moving.

Vincent calls out again. "Frestin, I'm over here! Come on. Run!"

Frestin still doesn't move. "Frestin, this is no time to be afraid!" Vincent scolds, but there is still no response. Vincent becomes agitated, worried. *Why isn't he moving? Is he knocked out?! Did he get trampled in the box? Is he dead? No, please. Please don't be dead.*

At last, Frestin breathes! Vincent's heart skips a beat. *He's alive!* Frestin's chest rises ever so slightly, and his mouth is open, but why isn't he running away? He seems dazed. *Maybe he got shaken around in the box and he's trying to catch his breath.* Some of the other minks beside Frestin are not moving, but Frestin is definitely alive.

Russell adjusts his blue latex gloves with a snap and picks up a white mink from the pile near Frestin. He drops the limp body onto a metal table in front of him. Russell picks up a sharp blade and swiftly hacks off all four of the mink's paws. Vincent watches in horror. Russell then opens the mink's mouth and starts cutting along the gum line. He chops off the nose and starts peeling back the skin, exposing the bloody muscle below. Vincent looks away, aghast. He feels queasy, knowing what's coming next—Russell will mercilessly strip away all of the mink's fur, leaving behind only the mess of muscle, maze of veins, and once-beating heart without a casing to enclose them.

"Frestin!" Vincent twists back around, trying to avert his eyes from the sickly sight. "Frestin! You have to run now! They're going to skin you!"

Frestin doesn't move. He slowly breathes in and out, in and out.

Out of the corner of his eye, Vincent can see that Russell has shoved the half-skinned mink's head through a metal loop and is tearing the fur down over his lower legs. With one last heave, Russell rips the fur off of the mink's body completely. Vincent is sobbing. "Frestin, please. *Now*, I'm scared. I can't live without you. Please, run!"

Russell tosses the fur in one direction onto a pile of pelts and throws the white mink's carcass in the other direction on top of the pile of dead bodies. He reaches indiscriminately for the next mink. Vincent's heart is pounding. Is Frestin next? Vincent can't take it any longer. He runs full throttle toward the pile of minks where his brother lies. "Frestin! Run! Run!"

Vincent sprints up to Russell and clasps his leg. Russell screeches in pain. He grabs at Vincent, who is now biting through Russell's jeans and into his flesh. Jackson darts over and starts kicking at Russell's leg, trying to swat Vincent off. Vincent digs his nails in deeper.

Russell hollers at Jackson. "Stop! Stop!" Russell grabs Vincent by the back of his neck and punches his back three times with his other hand. Vincent has the wind knocked out of him and loses his grip. Russell hobbles over to a cage, opens the latch, and tosses Vincent inside.

Russell sucks in cold air and coughs. "This little fucker's got some balls on 'im! Damn!"

Jackson rushes over to Russell. "Why didn't you crush 'im?"

Russell hacks as he tries to catch his breath. "You see that blue tint to his coat? He's gonna be worth a lotta money, idiot."

Jackson looks over at Vincent, who hisses at him from the cage. "So what? That's the one that bit me earlier in the summer. He deserves to die."

"I don't care what he done. You don't see me cryin' 'bout my leg like a wuss." Russell holds up the leg that Vincent just sank his teeth into. "We can breed 'im. I finally got me a blue male mink, and you just wanna kill 'im? And you wonder why pop wants to pass the farm onto me, not you."

"Whatever, dick," Jackson snaps.

Vincent calls out to his brother. "Frestin, they're distracted. Run! This is it! Get out of here!"

Russell steps up into Jackson's face. "What'd you say?"

Jackson is overshadowed by Russell's girth. He's not winning this argument. "Nuthin."

Russell steps back over to his butcher bench. He picks up Frestin's body from the pile. Vincent pleads desperately. "Wait, don't! Please! Don't hurt him!"

Russell lays Frestin's body out on the table and hacks off his paws, one by one. Vincent angrily slams his body against the side of the cage.

Jackson peers into the cage at Vincent thrashing around. "Damn, look at the little bastard go. He's pissed."

Russell pries open Frestin's mouth, cuts the gum line and chops his nose off. Vincent screams and cries from his wire prison. "Frestin! No! Please! Stop!"

Russell slashes off Frestin's ears and starts to peel back his fur from his face and neck. Vincent is so ferociously upset that he's begun to foam at the mouth. He bites so hard into the metal cage that one of his front teeth chips in half, but he keeps whipping his body about the enclosure.

Jackson laughs. "Look at 'im go! He's goin' nuts!" Jackson barks at Vincent like a dog, taunting him. "Rrrrr! You're the angriest little mink I've ever seen. Rrrrr. Not so tough behind that cage, eh?"

Russell yells at Jackson. "Get back to work, jerk off! My damn hands are freezin' out here and you're playin' around. The longer you act a fool, the longer we gotta be out here doin' this."

Jackson grabs his crotch in Russell's direction. "Bite me, bitch."

Russell throws one of Frestin's paws at Jackson, who dodges it. "Missed!" Jackson grabs the wooden crate and pushes it through the snow, on his way to gather more minks.

Russell puts Frestin's head through the metal loop. Vincent looks away. He can't watch any longer. It's too much. *When will it end? When will it end?* Russell tugs at Frestin's brown fur. The membrane tears away from the muscle and severs from the body. Russell tosses the fur with the rest of the pelts and lobs Frestin's blood-drenched body onto the pile of cadavers.

Vincent feels like his chest is being crushed in. Something inexplicable compels him to turn back around. His eyes fall on the dead minks. One of them is Frestin, but which one? They all look the same.

What does it matter? Why is he looking at them? He can't turn away. Vincent locks eyes with one of the slain minks. He knows those loving eyes. It's Frestin. He's still breathing. His brother is still alive.

No. Oh, no. Vincent's heart sinks even farther. *The horrendous pain he must be in.* "Frestin," Vincent gently calls out. "I am so sorry. It's all going to be over soon. No more pain. I love you, Frestin. I'm right here. I didn't leave you. I'm right here, my brother."

Vincent sees Frestin's unsheathed torso rise and fall, ever so slowly. His eyelids have been sliced off, and his unblinking black eyes stare up at Vincent. After nearly a year of wishing for freedom, Frestin wishes for nothing more than an end to it all.

"I'm right here, Frestin. I will never leave you. You are not alone."

Frestin's breathing comes to a halt. He is dead. Vincent collapses onto the cage floor, numb. He thought he knew what heartbreak was when he was torn from his family so many months ago, but seeing his brother die—skinned alive—*this* is heartbreak.

Everything has changed. The confidence he once had that he would one day escape is gone, evaporated. He has no idea what will happen to him now. He doesn't care. He is sure of only two things: One, his own escape is no longer enough. After the horror he witnessed today, he will never be truly free until all of his brethren are free as well.

Two, he will never laugh again. Never. That type of unbridled joy died along with Frestin.

23

PERSIMMON SHAKES THE wire fence with her paws. It's night. She is sitting by herself at the far perimeter of the fur farm, looking out over the grassy field that lies between her and the minks' cages. *Come on, Mando and Diablo. Don't be stupid. These poor minks need your help. You get one chance at freedom and that's it. If we have to go the route of the mushrooms, you're going to feel pretty foolish when you stop vomiting long enough to realize the minks are gone—and worse, that you've been left behind.*

She waits for Mando and Diablo to come bounding across the field to the fence, but sees nothing yet.

She shakes the fence again. "Mando! Diablo! Come out and play!"

There! The Rottweilers bolt straight toward her, barking. They slam into the fence, pounding their paws against the metal and biting into the wire next to her. Persimmon steps back out of instinct, but she isn't intimidated. Despite the fact that the ferocious beasts tower over her and want nothing more than to tear into her flesh, she has come to make peace—to usher them to freedom. It's just a question of whether or not they're smart enough to let her.

"We'll eat you alive, raccoon! Get outta here!" Mando snarls.

Persimmon speaks in a composed manner. "Boys, I would keep it down if I were you or else you might wake your humans." The dogs continue to growl and chomp at her. She presses on. "Do you really want to get hit again for waking the humans up over a silly raccoon?"

Mando lowers his growl. "That don't hurt me. I've had worse than that and I'm still fightin'. Now why don't you jump over this fence and see how tough we really are?"

Persimmon remains calm. "Exactly. You've had worse beatings. Don't you see? They don't care about you. Jackson and Russell have no right to treat you like this. Why don't you join us? We'll set you free."

Diablo jumps in. "Waddya mean? We *are* free."

"Are you?" Persimmon asks, pleased that he has given her such a perfect setup. "Then why are we talking through a fence?"

Diablo is at a loss for words. He never thought about it that way.

"They need us," Mando retorts indignantly. "We have a job to do. We protect this farm from intruders like you."

"I'm not an intruder," Persimmon replies. "I don't want to get *into* this horrible place. I want to get everyone *out*, including you."

"Aha! I knew it," Mando scoffs. "You're tryin' ta steal our minks!"

"I told you she was up to somethin'. Can't trust no raccoon!" Diablo adds.

"No, we're trying to free you as well. The Peterson family mistreats all of you. They verbally abuse and beat you. As for the minks, they have it much worse than you. They suffer in cramped cages their entire lives until they're slaughtered."

Mando is dumbfounded. "Waddya care about the minks? They're stupid. They just run around in circles all day. Sometimes they chew their own tails off. And they even sleep in their own shit."

"They don't do all that stuff because they're unintelligent." Persimmon is incensed. "How do you think you would act if you were trapped in a tiny cage all the time? It makes them insane. As for them sleeping in their own feces, let me guess, you've never seen the Petersons clean their cages, have you?"

The dogs think about that for a second. Has she finally gotten through to them?

"So what," Mando snaps back. "We got a job to do, and ain't you or nobody gonna steal those minks."

"Steal them?!" Persimmon mutters under her breath, "Thick-headed buffoons." She looks directly at the Rottweilers with a stern expression. "Listen to me very carefully. I want to help you, but there are two of you and thousands of minks, and they're suffering immensely. I've heard horrible things about what they're forced to endure. Right now some of them have open wounds. Some don't have any water. And some are going slowly insane because they're trapped in stifling, barren cages. It's unbearably cruel, and we're here to put a stop to it. You're either with us or against us."

Mando gets right up to the fence. He's so close that Persimmon can smell his rotten breath. "You can bring back your dogs, raccoons, opossums and human friends. We don't care. We'll tear all youse to shreds and enjoy every delicious moment. Maybe 'fore we kill you, we'll eat those two squirrels right in front of ya—just for fun."

In her typical unflappable fashion, Persimmon is unconcerned with his threat, but she does find one thing he said very intriguing. "*Human* friends? What is that supposed to mean?"

"We know it was you," Diablo retorts. "Now it all makes sense. You and those humans raided the farm up the road, tryin' ta steal the minks, but the critters all got away so now you're tryin' ta steal our minks." He leans into the fence. A wad of froth drips down the mesh wire. "Just try it."

Persimmon shakes her head in disappointment. "So be it. You're both fools. Heartless fools." With that, she turns and heads back into the woods.

24

"YES, I MET some minks who said humans had freed them," Vincent explains to a spellbound Persimmon, Derpoke, Bruiser, Scraps, Chloe and Tucker back at their base camp deep in the forest. "That's why the Petersons built that giant fence and got Mando and Diablo as guard dogs. None of those security measures were on the farm when I was trapped there. But why are you so interested in humans freeing the minks?"

Persimmon is flummoxed. "Because it's amazing. Not only is there someone out there doing exactly what we're doing, but they're *humans*. Humans who actually risk their lives to save suffering animals. That's a revelation. Surely you can admit that after your experience with the Petersons, you didn't think it was possible."

"Well, yes, I was surprised—even skeptical," Vincent concedes. "But they assured me that the masked humans went from cage to cage opening them up and just letting the minks hop out. That did restore my faith in humans a bit, but it's not like we're going to find these humans to help us."

Chloe calls down from a nearby tree, excited. "Do you really think humans would help us? We could save all kinds of animals then."

Scraps joins in with glee. "Wow, first a dog joins our team, and now maybe a human, too?! I've never been close to a human. Do you think they'll give us their fresh food? Even straight from the table like they do dogs?"

"Okay, hold on," Derpoke cuts in. "A Doberman is one thing, but humans? We know what they did to the calves, and now look what they're doing to the minks. They cannot be trusted."

Persimmon puts her paws up to halt the commotion. "Alright, everyone. Nobody's recruiting humans to our team. I don't think all humans are evil, but that doesn't mean we can trust them just yet. I simply think it's interesting that there are humans out there who even care to save other animals."

A familiar voice booms out from behind a nearby bush. "You kick *me* off the team, but you're planning on letting *humans* in? I'm offended." The team swings around to see Rawly looking as smug as ever.

Everybody except Persimmon and Bruiser looks shocked.

"Well, well, well. Look who got lonely without us," Persimmon retorts.

"You didn't think you could conduct a grand rescue without me, did you?" Rawly quips.

"Perhaps he has a conscience after all," Persimmon says snidely.

Bruiser seems tense. "Who are your friends?"

"Ah, impressive olfactory skills, Bruiser." Rawly beckons. "My friends! Your presence is requested." Out from behind a tree saunter five young raccoons—four males and one female. Rawly goes down the line, introducing them. "This is Drig, Linder, Fisher, Dusty and…" Rawly nuzzles up to the female raccoon and exclaims proudly, "This is my beautiful Claudette."

Claudette smiles bashfully.

Persimmon and Derpoke glance at one another quickly, as if to say, *Wait, Rawly was able to trick some female into falling for him? Amazing!*

The new gang of raccoons nods and waves hello. They seem like a sturdy, athletic lot. "They're going to help free the minks," Rawly declares.

The rest of the team murmurs enthusiastically. "Wow, really?" Persimmon asks.

"Yep, I figured you all would appreciate it." Rawly is pleased with himself. "I overheard you all talking about needing more raccoons to open the cages, so I took it upon myself to gather some trustworthy companions."

"We're delighted that you've agreed to join us," Persimmon says to the new recruits. "It really is kind and brave of you." She switches to a more serious tone. "I need to make sure you know what you're getting into, though. Did Rawly explain the dangers involved? I don't want to deter you from helping, but I want you to understand that this is a very risky mission. It could even be a life-threatening one."

Claudette steps forward. "Yes, Persimmon, we're aware of the dangers. I have to say, it's so lovely finally meeting you in person. Rawly speaks very highly of you."

"He must save his compliments for when I'm not around, then." Persimmon says dryly. The team laughs.

"Well, I don't want you to get too full of yourself, you know," Rawly shoots back good-naturedly.

Claudette surveys the entire team. "In fact, we've heard stories about many of you." She looks at Scraps. "You're adorable, so you're Scraps, right?" He giggles nervously over having a pretty raccoon compliment him. "And I'm guessing you're Derpoke and Bruiser." Derpoke blushes and Bruiser grins. "And you two up there must be Chloe and Tucker."

Chloe responds with an animated wave of her bushy tail. "Hello!"

Claudette looks at Vincent blankly. "I'm sorry. I'm not sure of your name."

"My name is Vincent. I escaped from the farm last year, and I cannot begin to thank you enough for joining us. The only flaw in our escape plan was that we needed more creatures with dexterous paws to help—and then all of you raccoons arrived. It's kismet."

"Happy to help," Claudette responds. "I'm glad you escaped. Rawly said that this team is risking their lives to save other animals in trouble, and we wanted to be part of that mission. Some of us have had bad run-ins with humans before. Linder lost his father to a hunter and Drig lost his brother. I've lost family, too. We want to help other animals in the same predicament."

"Thank you, Claudette. Thank you all so much." Persimmon is glowing. "I don't know how tired you are from your journey, but we have the escape plan all set and we can share it with you whenever you're ready."

"Let's hear it now," Rawly blurts out. "We're ready to save some minks."

"I appreciate your enthusiasm, Rawly," Vincent exclaims. "You make quite the first impression."

Persimmon and Derpoke shoot one another a mocking look, as if to say, *Just wait 'til Vincent gets to know him better.*

*   *   *

Vincent has just finished going over the rescue plan with the team. They've worked out a few details with the new raccoons and everyone seems confident that they'll be able to pull it off. Vincent still hasn't cracked a smile but he does seem a little less intense. It's hard for him to feel any joy after what he's been through, but now that the rescue planning is coming along so well he feels more hopeful than he has in a long time.

As the team members disperse, Rawly steps over to Bruiser. "Bruiser. Wait up."

Bruiser stops to listen.

"I owe you an apology," Rawly states. "When we first met, I was not very welcoming. Until I encountered you, I had only had negative experiences with dogs, so I was prejudiced, I admit. But when I was hiding in the trees the other night, I saw how you stood up for Persimmon and the others against those Rottweilers, and... well, I misjudged you."

"We good," Bruiser replies. "If you're willing to risk your life along with the rest of us, that's good by me."

A few feet away, Persimmon approaches Vincent before he crawls into his burrow. "Vincent, can we talk privately?"

Vincent nods and they step away from the base camp into the forest, out of earshot of anyone else.

"I didn't want to say this around the others," Persimmon whispers. "But I can't help but feel that you're still not telling us the whole story about how the humans freed the minks."

"No, I just didn't think you all would be interested. It seems..." Vincent stops himself. He gets a nagging, guilty feeling. He doesn't want to lie to Persimmon. She and her team are risking their lives for him and the other minks. The least he can do is be honest.

He subtly licks the tooth he chipped when Frestln died; it has become a nervous tick. "I didn't intend to lie to you." He pauses, trying to figure out the best way to tell her. Might as well not beat around the bush. "Not all of the minks that the humans freed survived. In fact, a lot of them died—from the harsh winter, from starvation, from being run over by cars. They weren't prepared for life outside the cage. You have no idea what it's like to be trapped in a tiny cell your entire life and then suddenly be freed."

He takes a deep breath. He doesn't like to talk about his life. "I almost died when I first got out—more than once. I was even attacked by wild minks who thought I was trying to take their territory or steal their mates. I just wanted a friend. I just needed someone to show me how to survive in the forest. Then, luckily, I met a mink who showed me how to forage for food and how to find a burrow in the winter. That's why, as I mentioned, the final stage of my plan is to be a guide for all the minks we're going to free. I'll teach them everything they need to know."

Persimmon sighs. "Why didn't you just tell me that in the beginning?"

"I did tell you about my plan to show them how to survive in the wild," Vincent answers. "I just didn't explain why it was so important. I was worried that if you knew a lot of the freed minks didn't make it, you wouldn't want to help us at all. You were already so cautious, wanting to spend time scoping the place out before proceeding with the rescue mission."

Persimmon cuts in. "Well, I already said that when we first scope out the farm, if the minks are healthy enough to break free, we'll go ahead with the mission that night. I just want to ensure that we're not going to free five-thousand minks to have them just collapse to the ground like the calves did and then immediately get thrown back in their cages when the humans find them."

"Don't worry about them being able to get away. They'll most likely be disoriented, and some will have hurt paws or wounds, but the majority will be able to run for their lives." Vincent pauses. He doesn't want to get emotional. "I apologize for not being forthcoming earlier—I was scared you'd give up on us. You are my best hope to save them. I already tried going back to the farm with a group of minks to attempt a rescue mission." He clenches his teeth. "I failed—badly. I was the only survivor. Those two murderous Rottweilers got to everyone else."

A dark cloud has come over Vincent as he speaks, and Persimmon tries to comfort him. "I'm so sorry. You were right about Mando and Diablo. We'll handle them your way. And thank you for being honest. We're going to get your friends and family out of there. I promise you."

Vincent looks at the ground. His heart is heavy. *She has no idea what it's like being trapped in that farm. No one does except the other minks. I cannot fail again or they will be massacred. And Mom is still in there. I know she is. She has to be. I need her to be.* He feels a sharp pain in his chest, as if someone were tightening their grip on his heart. *They're all still stuck in there, suffering every day, and I'm out here—free. They deserve to be free. They have a right to be free. And I'm not going to give up until they are—all of them.*

25

THE STORY OF VINCENT THE MINK, PART 3

FREEDOM

VINCENT IS CHOKING. He wakes up abruptly, unable to breathe. Jackson has the metal tongs tightly clasped around his neck and is squeezing so firmly that the exhausted mink begins to black out.

"Gotcha, bastard! You ain't gettin' away this time," Jackson threatens.

Jackson is transporting Vincent to a different cage. He thinks he's being clever, attacking Vincent while he is sleeping, but he doesn't realize that Vincent is completely spent and in no mood to fight. The massacre has ended and the Peterson brothers have gathered all the pelts and discarded all of the bloody carcasses. Vincent finally passed out after thrashing around so furiously when Frestin was being killed, and now Jackson is moving Vincent to the area where they keep the minks for breeding.

Jackson tosses Vincent into an empty cage and taunts him. "Have a nice winter, sucka. Come spring, you're gonna get some sweet mink tail."

Vincent crawls into a corner and curls into a ball. He's glad that he's alone in the cage. He doesn't want to interact with anyone else. He doesn't want some nosy mink asking why he's so sullen. He doesn't want to talk about Frestin's death with anyone—ever. Vincent spends the next few freezing cold days lying on the hard metal floor feeling heartsick with the image of Frestin being skinned alive on a constant loop in his head. He tries to forget it but there's no forgetting that kind of trauma. You just hope the details eventually fade with time.

Vincent lies nearly motionless for a week, wishing he didn't exist. He longs for the aching sorrow to go away. It does not.

Finally, Vincent rolls over and notices the most miraculous thing he has ever seen. At the back of the cage, some of the wire has turned reddish brown. He quickly hops up and darts over to inspect it. Sure enough, the wire is rotting. *Yes. Yes! It's rusted just like the cage near Frestin and me where the minks peeled back a hole. Only their hole was pulled toward them, leaving dangerous spikes that stabbed into their flesh when they tried to crawl out. If I push these wires outward, I can squeeze through this. I can escape!*

Vincent rushes to the front of the cage and peers out to make sure neither Jackson nor Russell is around. Nope, the coast is clear! He dashes back to the rusted section and begins biting at it, pushing on it, ramming it. It's working! Slowly but surely he's able to break a wire here, a spoke there.

Vincent's heart is pounding. He may actually break free. Even better, he may finally break his mother free. And Alia, if she's still alive. What a wonderful day! The Peterson brothers have not won. They did not crush him. They *cannot* crush him.

✳   ✳   ✳

Vincent labors day and night pushing, chewing, tearing at the rusty wires. He has to work fast before the Petersons discover what he's up to.

The minks on either side of him notice what he's doing and watch gleefully. "Hey, you. You're gonna break outta here! That's amazing! Break me out too, will ya?"

Vincent ignores them. He doesn't have time for chitchat.

"Hey, mink. I'm talking to you. When you get outta there, just open my cage. You don't gotta talk to me. Just open my cage."

Vincent finally addresses them. "Quiet. You're breaking my concentration. I need to focus."

"I'll leave ya alone. Just promise you'll help me out. I'm gonna die in here if you don't."

Vincent keeps ripping away at the wire. He doesn't respond. He can't be responsible for getting all of these other minks out of the fur farm at the moment. First he has to get himself out, and then he has to find his family. If he can locate his mother and Alia, he'll try to figure out a plan to break the other minks free, but he doesn't have time to think about that right now.

∗   ∗   ∗

A week goes by, then two. The winter keeps getting colder and colder, but Vincent barely notices. He is obsessed with cracking through his cage. Then one day he looks at the hole he has created. Is it big enough for his body? Should he attempt to squeeze through or keep biting? His mouth is sore, raw, bleeding. More of his teeth are cracked. His paws are no better. He's exhausted. *Maybe I can fit.*

Vincent takes a few sips of his water. He takes a deep breath. *Yes, this is it. Now is the time.*

Vincent pushes his head through the hole. No problem. He inches his neck and torso through, but the space isn't wide enough for his front legs. *Maybe I should have put my front legs through first, but it seemed better to slide through.* He tries to pull his body back to readjust, but he isn't going anywhere. He has gone too far already. He has to keep moving forward.

His lungs are being crushed. His breathing is labored. Will he be squeezed to death in the corner of his cage? He almost laughs at how absurd and tragic that would be. He pushes harder with his hind legs. *Come on!*

The minks in the cages beside his see that he's struggling. They cheer him on. "You can do it. Just push. You got it."

Vincent keeps straining with his hind legs. The minks continue to encourage him. "Let out all your air. Make yourself thinner and then push really hard."

Vincent listens to their advice. He breathes out all the air in his lungs and wiggles his body back and forth. He begins to feel light-headed, and then kicks as hard as he can with his back legs and then... freedom! Vincent falls to the ground. It takes him a second to catch his breath. He's a little dazed.

The other minks yell excitedly. "You did it! You're free!"

Vincent hops up. "I did it! I did it!"

A sense of elation shoots through him. He's never felt so exhilarated. "Freedom! Freedom!"

He looks up at the minks still trapped in cages. How can he leave them? Vincent looks at the blue sky. It's morning, and the Peterson brothers will most likely be out any minute milling about the fur farm. He can't risk getting caught again, and he still has to look for his mother and Alia.

Vincent crawls up the wood plank leading to the back of the cages. He runs to the front side of the first one. The mink inside praises him profusely. "Thank you! Thank you!"

Vincent pushes on the latch at the front of the cage. It doesn't budge.

"It's not moving," Vincent exclaims, his heart racing.

The mink inside the cage directs him. "Try pulling it out and then pushing it up."

"I did. I thought I knew how to open these things, but it's not moving." Vincent keeps prying and prodding at the latch. It doesn't move at all. "How do the humans open this darn thing?!"

Vincent looks up at the sky again. The sun is completely out and he is right out in the open. He stops pulling at the latch. "I can't get it. I'm sorry."

"Wait, just push it up," the mink pleads. "You gotta keep trying. I'm gonna die in here."

Vincent looks at him. He licks his chipped tooth nervously. "My friend, I am sorry. I have to look for my mother and sister. I'll come back. I promise."

The mink becomes hysterical and grabs at Vincent through the cage. "Wait, don't leave. I don't want to die. Please, I don't want to die!"

Vincent feels terrible, but he can't spend any more time trying to open this cage. He climbs down the wood beam, reassuring the mink as he does. "I'll come back. I promise."

The minks plead as Vincent disappears behind a row of cages. "Don't leave us! We're going to die!"

Vincent runs through the pile of snow in between the cages. He scurries underneath another row of pens. "Mom! Mom! Alia!"

Vincent goes from row to row, shouting their names, but all of the rows look the same—just lines of cages filled with frantic, miserable minks. *How am I ever going to find them?!*

Vincent runs out into a row and, to his horror, sees Jackson walking down the pathway. Luckily, Jackson is walking away from Vincent or he surely would have seen him. Vincent slides to a halt and darts underneath a row of cages, where he hides behind a pile of excrement.

Come on! Where are they? Maybe I can just find Mom. I don't even know if Alia is still alive. Vincent carefully peers down the row to see if Jackson is still there. He is. *What am I going to do?! I can't let them catch me like they did last time. I'll never have this chance again.*

Vincent feels sick, hopeless, guilty. *I'm so sorry, Mom. Please forgive me. I'll come back. I'll come back for you.*

He weaves in and out of the piles of excrement underneath the cages. Other minks notice him scurrying about and they cheer him on. "You did it! Run! Keep going!"

Vincent gets more and more excited as he nears the field between the cages and the forest. Freedom is so close.

He stops underneath the last cage in the row and looks out over the snowy field. He searches all around for any signs of the Peterson brothers. He didn't come this far just to get caught—or worse, killed. No sign of them. It's now or never.

Vincent takes a deep breath and runs faster than he ever has before. The snow is deep enough that he is practically running blind, cutting a path through the icy substance. He runs and runs with snow shooting out behind him. He feels unstoppable. He feels invincible. He feels alive.

Vincent gets to the forest's edge and keeps going. He races deep into the woods, not looking back. He wants to get as far as possible from that filthy fur farm—from the grasp of those violent, appalling humans.

After a few minutes, he starts to slow down. He can barely breathe. He walks a couple more paces and then stops. He turns around. He has run so far, he can't even see the edge of the forest any longer. He lies down in the snow, panting vigorously. His tongue dangles from his mouth. His chest is pounding as he sucks in the chilly air. He closes his eyes. He wants to cry. He wants to laugh. He wants to yell at the top of his lungs in victory. He did it. After so much pain. After so much heartache. He is free. He is finally free.

*   *   *

The air is so fresh! Vincent is in awe of his new surroundings. No putrid smell of excrement burns his nose and eyes. No harsh wire floor cuts into his paws. The snow is so soft to the touch; it feels like he imagines it must to walk on the fluffy clouds he used to gaze at from inside his cage. And best of all, there are no walls. He can run anywhere he pleases. Vincent sprints in between trees, over plants and through the white snow. Freedom is more thrilling than he ever imagined.

I only wish I could share all this with Mom and Frestin. Frestin and I spent so many nights talking about doing what I am doing right now, and he'll never get to appreciate how wonderful it is.

Vincent remembers Frestin's dream of rolling in the grass if they ever escaped. He looks around, but all the grass is covered by snow. *Hmm. I guess I'll have to wait before I can roll around like Frestin wanted. But that's okay. I'm free now. I have all kinds of time.* Another idea pops into Vincent's head as he is reminded of his own dream. He scopes out the trees around him and picks the tallest one in sight. He climbs as high as he can before the branches begin to bend under his weight. It feels so gratifying to exercise his muscles and climb without any restrictions.

He surveys the treetops as far as he can see. There's so much to explore. He climbs back down, just as quickly as he had ascended, and hops onto the frosty forest floor.

He looks around the woods. It's quiet. For the first time in his life, he is completely alone. It feels liberating and overwhelming all at once. *Okay, enough fun for now. I need to implement Mom's training for life outside the cage. First, I need to find food, water and shelter.*

*   *   *

A few days go by. Vincent's exhilaration over his newfound freedom has turned into a slight panic. He has had difficulty finding sustenance and shelter. He has eaten a few bugs—all of which tasted gross—and an orange mushroom, which made him severely ill. Then he spent two days vomiting up the little food he had been able to find. As for a safe location in which to hide, he has slept anywhere dark and dry that he could find—inside fallen tree stumps, under thick brush—but he hasn't slept well. He wakes at the slightest noise, fearing some ravenous giant beast will come and devour him. He has seen so few wild animals in his life that his imagination has gotten the better of him. One recurring nightmare is a monster with talons like a bird and a circle of teeth jutting out of its neck instead of a head. However, no animal has even come near him yet.

Vincent treks through the snow, continuing his search for food, when he hears a trickling noise that sounds both familiar and foreign at the same time. *What is that?* He trudges through the snow toward the sound. He would run, but he's a bit weak.

The curious mink steps down an embankment and there before him is water. And not just water, but a long stream, flowing over the ground just like Bailey described.

"Hooray!" Vincent cheers. He runs to the water and dips his head completely in. He slurps down a massive wave of liquid. It's so refreshing, so revitalizing. He pulls his head out of the water and shakes himself dry. *I can do this. I can survive out here. All the water I could ever want to drink. Bailey would be so pleased. Dare I jump in and give swimming a go?* He ponders this for a bit but decides he's exhausted from foraging all night. *I'll sleep near the stream today and then go for a swim tomorrow.*

Vincent walks along the stream, almost giddy from his discovery. *That sound I heard reminds me of the few times Jackson or Russell would pour water into our bottles. That's why it sounded so familiar. Only now*

I will never run out. As he walks, he notices a dark hole midway up the embankment. *Aha, I believe I just found my burrow for the day.* He crawls up the hill and peers in. "Hello? Any beasties in here?" No response. *Perfect.* Vincent begins to crawl into the darkness when he hears a menacing growl. Two piercing eyes appear about a foot in front of him. Vincent stops abruptly.

"I don't mean any harm. I was just…" Before he can finish, the creature lashes out at him. Vincent crawls backward as fast as his legs will take him and falls out onto the snow.

The creature pokes his head out of the dark hole, hissing. "Get out of my burrow! Get out!"

It's another mink! Vincent is relieved and excited to see a fellow mink. "I'm sorry. I was just looking for…"

"Get out of my territory!"

"Wait, I just escaped from the fur farm. I'm so glad to see another mink. I've been…"

The mink rushes down the hill toward Vincent, gnashing his teeth and hissing violently. Vincent turns and jumps into the water. He splashes through the surface, surprising himself when he glides effortlessly through the liquid. The water may be chilly but his thick coat keeps him nice and snug. He twirls around and pushes himself swiftly away from the mink hissing on the bank. *Wow, without a doubt, this I was meant to do!*

Vincent swims down the stream a bit, and when he can no longer see the hissing mink, he pops up for air. *After all that time in the fur farm, surviving the massacre, surviving the cage. I finally get free, and I almost get killed by a mink. Life is odd, to say the least.*

"I'd keep moving if I were you," a voice threatens from the riverbank.

Vincent looks around, annoyed. "Oh, come on. Seriously? You minks can't call this entire stream your territory. I have a right…" He abruptly stops talking and stares in disbelief at the brown mink before him. The mink stares right back at him. They recognize one another, but from where?

Vincent's mouth is agape. He gets a sick, sad feeling in his heart. This mink looks exactly like… "Frestin?!"

The brown mink smiles widely. "Vincent?! Is it really you?! It's me, Trenton."

Vincent leaps out of the water, effervescent with joy. "Trenton?!" They stomp the ground and hit their paws together. "My brother!"

Vincent and Trenton hop up and down, merrily celebrating their miraculous reunion.

Vincent is still stunned. "You look so much like Frestin. I can't…" Vincent looks closer at Trenton. "Now I see the white on your chin and your belly, but you two look so much alike it's uncanny. My brain knew you looked familiar, but I couldn't place you. Trenton, my brother, it is so good to see you!"

Trenton pats Vincent with his paws gleefully. "Yippity dippity doo! I can't believe it! My very own brother. You look like Mom with that blue in your fur." Before Vincent can respond, Trenton continues. "Mom. Oh, wow. I've dreamed about seeing you, seeing the whole family every night since I escaped. I can't believe it's finally happening. Where is everyone else?"

The smile fades from Vincent's face. He sighs. "They…"

Trenton looks concerned. "None of them made it?"

"No… Well, I don't know. Everyone except Mom is gone, I think. It makes me sick to say it, but Frestin and Wren I know for sure. Alia most likely didn't make it through the massacre."

"But you think Mom is still alive?"

"I don't know. She was in a different area. They use her to breed other minks. Maybe I just want her to be alive so much that I still think she must be." Vincent licks his chipped tooth. "It was awful,

Trenton. The humans are so cruel. Every day in those cages we suffered so much. The massacre was even worse."

Trenton pats Vincent's back. "I'm so sorry. I have felt guilty every
day since I escaped. When I first got out, Marcel and I..."

Vincent lights up. "Oh, Marcel. Where is he?"

Trenton looks away, saddened. "He... the cold, the lack of food...
soon after we got out—it was too much for him."

Vincent sighs heavily. "All of our brothers are gone... and most
likely our sister and mother, too."

Vincent and Trenton stare blankly at the calm stream, watching
the water trickle over the rocks. Their excitement has been soured by
the devastation of their losses. They had both hoped for so long that
their family members might still be alive, and in a matter of moments
their hopes have been crushed. It's as if they all died in that instant.

"You look tired, my brother," Trenton says finally. "And I bet you're
hungry. Why don't you come inside and we'll chat more in there."

"You have a burrow?" Vincent inquires.

Trenton grins. "Just you wait and see."

✳   ✳   ✳

Vincent sleeps for a full day and night. He's never been so snug. Trenton
doesn't just have a burrow—he has a whole set of tunnels leading to a
cozy nest. For the first time in Vincent's dismal life, he sleeps soundly,
curled up on a soft bed of brush that is a far cry from the hard wire
floor on which he slept for so long. No nightmares. No being jolted
awake to the sound of minks crying or screaming out in pain.

Trenton sets out some fish for Vincent when he awakens and the
starving mink devours it in no time, never having eaten fresh fish before. With that in mind, Trenton takes Vincent out to the stream and
teaches him how to catch fish. It takes a few days for him to master,

but Vincent is a natural—like swimming, fishing is a talent he never knew he had.

Trenton spends weeks teaching Vincent skills that he'll need to survive in the wild. They bond as if they had never been apart. Trenton starts to fill the hole in Vincent's heart left by the loss of Frestin—not completely, for he'll never heal completely from Frestin's death, but there's a camaraderie, a joyful spirit he never thought he'd feel again. They catch up on the lives they led during the time they were separated. Vincent doesn't hold back about life in the cage. He wants Trenton to understand the gory truth about what the other minks are going through. He's laying the groundwork for this: "Trenton, we have to go back. We have to save the other minks."

Trenton rolls around in the nest, uncomfortable. "I knew you were going to say that one day."

"So you'll join me?" Vincent presses.

Trenton pauses, trying to figure out how to respond. "I... I told you I went back to the edge of the forest with Marcel when we first escaped. We wanted to rescue you all, but we were too afraid. We couldn't bear to get caught again. It's no excuse for leaving you there, but it's the truth."

"I don't hold it against you, Trenton. I understand. But we can do this. Those minks need us. *Mom* needs us. We should round up a group of minks and rush in there, saving every last one of our caged brethren."

Trenton starts to fidget with the dry grass in the nest. "You said yourself you couldn't open the latch."

"I was exhausted from days of biting through the wire. I was malnourished. I was nervous I'd be seen in the daylight. If we get a whole team in there one night—a whole team of prepared and well-rested minks—I bet we can rescue every last one of our trapped friends. How great would that feel?"

"It would be amazing, but it seems impossible." Trenton picks at the dry grass more vigorously. "Also, what if we're caught? You told me what it's like to live in those cages. I'm not as strong as you. I wouldn't survive one frickita week in there. And I'm afraid of the massacre. We're free out here. Are we really ready to give this up?"

Trenton is pacing around the nest. Vincent tries to look him in the eyes to get his undivided attention. "We're not free. Not as long as they're in those cages." Vincent holds up his paw to stop Trenton's pacing. "What happened to you, brother? You used to be so brave—ready to take on the giant, vicious humans."

"Frickita." Trenton cusses and kicks at the dirt. "Vincent, I just don't know how we can pull it off."

"Leave that to me. I just need you to show up and work fast."

"You haven't even seen the wild when it's warm out, my brother." Trenton daydreams. "The females. Oh, the females are so cuddly. It's the best."

"You and Frestin. I'll never get this talk about females. I don't have time for such nonsense."

Now Trenton looks Vincent in the eyes. "But Smickety Smoo, it's bliss."

"I can't be truly happy until Mom's out of there, and I don't know how you could be either."

Trenton huffs. He lies on the grass, exasperated. "Look, let's just wait 'til the cold air goes away and the snow melts. The humans will be able to track us in the snow. Once it's warm, we'll figure out a plan to rescue everyone. I don't want them to be in there any more than you do. I just don't want to end up back there myself. Now, can we please talk about something else, Smickety? Feeling guilty is weighing me down."

Vincent nods. "Done." He adds mockingly, "Smiggity Smoo."

"No, it's *Smickety* Smoo. Get it right, my brother."

Vincent is disappointed about his brother's frivolity. Freedom has softened Trenton. It's easy to put the suffering of the other minks out of your mind when you're living so comfortably. Even Vincent finds this gentle, privileged life intoxicating. Living like this makes it easy to forget how horribly the others are living. Vincent vows to himself to never get so complacent that he ceases thinking about the misery of the other minks. They don't deserve what they're enduring, and he's their only hope. No one else seems to care.

$*$　$*$　$*$

For the rest of the winter, Trenton continues to teach Vincent how to survive in the wild. For example, he warns Vincent to never drink the stream water too close to the fur farm. It's tainted with run-off excrement and urine.

They also survey the land around them, so Vincent can get to know his surroundings. While they do this, Vincent strategically buddies up to any minks he meets, knowing that one day he will ask them to join his rescue mission. He even brings them food to endear himself to them. Although he thinks that as fellow minks they should want to help free the others, Vincent knows it will be a hard sell to ask them to risk their lives and possibly give up this idyllic lifestyle.

Trenton spends most of their walks chatting jovially about his favorite foods (fish and frogs), his favorite place to play (a serene spot along the stream near his burrow), and his favorite pastime (females). "The snow is starting to melt, my brother, which means that soon the females are going to be hippity hopping around looking for us."

Vincent isn't all that interested in talking about females, but he humors his brother. "Uh huh. So which do you enjoy more: eating fish or spending time with females?"

Trenton stops in his tracks. "Are you kidding?!"

Vincent is amused by how seriously Trenton is taking this conversation. "Saving the other minks, I can't get you passionate about. But talking about females? You lose your mind."

"I would give up all the fish in the stream for the rest of my life if females would pay attention to me from the cold season through the warm and back through the cold season again."

"That should be your line to win over the next female," Vincent jests.

Trenton thinks about it for a moment and smiles widely. "Yes. Yes, you are wise, Smickety Smoo."

Just then, Vincent and Trenton hear a moaning noise. It sounds like a creature in distress. The brothers look at one another and Vincent rushes toward the crying animal, with Trenton close behind.

As they get closer, they hear the creature mumbling. "Run. Water. Trees." More moaning. "Water. Ants. Water." Vincent shudders. He knows that voice. He was haunted by that nonsensical, incessant chattering for so many nights.

"Grumbles," Vincent whispers furiously.

"What?" Trenton asks.

Vincent moves forward and sure enough, there in the half-melted snow is Grumbles, looking sickly and emaciated. Vincent glares at the dying mink. Grumbles notices Vincent and stops mumbling. The frightened mink smiles. He remembers Vincent and is relieved to see a familiar face in this lonely forest full of creatures who are indifferent, or even worse, dangerous.

Vincent does not smile back. He is seething. Trenton starts walking toward the sickly mink. "Don't touch him," Vincent orders.

"He's scared," Trenton replies. "He's not going to hurt me."

"I know this mink," Vincent explains. "Do you remember how I told you that a mink knocked Frestin into that wooden crate—the crate that carried Frestin to his death?"

Trenton nods.

"This is that mink. Grumbles. He killed Frestin."

Trenton steps back and examines Grumbles. He appears to be crazed and is thin with torn fur. "He looks sick."

"Good," Vincent says spitefully. "I hope he's in a lot of pain."

"Vincent. He can hear you."

"I want him to. You hear that, Grumbles? I'm glad you're in pain." Vincent charges at Grumbles, gnashing his teeth. "Do you remember me? How you killed my brother?"

Grumbles hides his face. He doesn't run away, though. He is too weak to run.

Trenton grabs Vincent to hold him back. "Vincent, he's frightened. Look at him."

"Don't tell me you feel bad for him. He murdered our brother."

"You said he banged into Frestin when he was trying to jump out. It doesn't sound like it was intentional. He was trying to break free, too."

"I don't care if it was an accident," Vincent counters. "If this disturbed fool hadn't been so rash, our brother would be here with us right now. Instead, he was skinned right in front of me. Do you know how much pain he must have been in? How petrified he must have been? And you're defending the mink who put him there?"

"The *Petersons* killed Frestin. Grumbles just looks..." Trenton motions for Vincent to talk to him a few feet away, where Grumbles can't hear them. Vincent reluctantly follows.

Once the two minks are out of Grumble's hearing range, Trenton continues. "Vincent, he's dying. I bet he hasn't eaten in weeks. We'll just get him some food, and maybe..."

"You want to help him?! After what he did to our brother?!"

Trenton doesn't back down. "It was an accident. I'm going to get some food."

"Trenton," Vincent says authoritatively. "We're leaving him here."

Trenton turns around. "He'll die of starvation. Or worse, he'll get eaten."

"That's not our problem."

Trenton is shocked. "You've changed, Vincent. Your heart has hardened. It's cruel to leave him out here."

Vincent is eerily calm. "No, cruel would be going with my first instinct and ripping his throat out. We're just giving him freedom. If it was so important for him to be free that he had to push Frestin to his death, then let him be free."

Trenton doesn't know what else to say. He turns away from Vincent and starts to walk off to look for food.

"Trenton, you better not bring food back for him."

Trenton keeps walking, not bothering to turn around. "Or what?"

"Or our journey together ends here," Vincent threatens.

Trenton stops. Very slowly, he turns around. His mouth is quivering. He looks ready to cry. "How could you? We finally found one another. I thought about you every day and missed you so much. You're my brother." Trenton closes his eyes. "You say you want to save all those minks suffering in those cages, but you have a mink right here, in pain, and you want to leave him to die or be eaten? You're asking me to kill him. I can't. I can't do that. Don't make me choose between you."

Vincent starts to breathe heavily. He grits his teeth. He looks like a volcano is boiling inside of him and it's about to erupt. Vincent screams angrily and then rushes toward a tree. He stabs his nails into the bark, scraping and shredding the base of the tree. Bark splinters all around him.

"I hate them! I hate those humans!" Vincent falls to the ground and rips through the snow to the dead grass and dirt below. He thrashes about, screaming. "Frestin! Why can't you be alive? How could they kill you?" Trenton watches Vincent fall apart, not sure what to do.

Vincent looks up at Trenton and then gets right in his face. "How can you forgive him? Explain to me how you can forgive Grumbles for sending our brother to his death?"

Trenton is intimidated, but stands his ground. "Vincent, I understand..."

"No," Vincent yells. "Tell me how you can forgive Grumbles."

"Grumbles is out of his mind, and you know why? Because of that cage. He didn't ask for that life, just like you didn't ask for it. Only you're stronger than he is. You both escaped, but only one of you made it out with your sanity. Blame the Petersons. This is their fault. Blame the humans who want to wear our fur. They killed Frestin. Grumbles was just running for his life. I can't punish him for that."

Vincent kneels in the snow, spent. "I'm going to make those humans regret what they did to Frestin. I'll show them what suffering is."

Trenton rests his paw on his brother's back. "And I will help you." Vincent looks up at Trenton, surprised and pleased. Trenton asks, "Now, can I trust you here with Grumbles while I go get him some food?"

Vincent nods. He knows there's no justice in killing the disturbed mink. He will save his ire for the Petersons.

∗   ∗   ∗

Vincent and Trenton sit near Grumbles. A trail of ants leads up to the sickly mink. The brothers try to swat the insects away but there are hundreds of them.

Grumbles is near death. He didn't eat the food Trenton brought him. He just lies there, muttering to himself. But he seems less fearful with the two brothers keeping him company. Trenton holds Grumbles' paw in his own. At first, Trenton wasn't sure if Grumbles even noticed his presence, but when Trenton went to move, Grumbles held firmly onto his paw. It comforts him. So Trenton stays.

And then after a long day and night, Grumbles stops mumbling. He stops twitching. He stops breathing.

Trenton looks over at Vincent with a grave expression. Neither says a word—there's nothing more to be said. Grumbles lived a terrible life, and he died a terrible death.

The brothers stand and head back to their burrow. Both feel empty. So many minks who escape die. There must be a way to help them. Vincent starts brainstorming. It's not enough to save the minks—he must help them become acclimated to the wild as well.

*   *   *

Soon, the frigid winter air floats away, replaced by a warm, soothing breeze. It's March. Vincent and Trenton are gearing up for the momentous escape. They have recruited a dozen other minks to help them. They'd prefer to have more help, but twelve will have to do. They will just have to work fast and coordinate impeccably.

Throughout the winter, Vincent kept an eye out for Emmett. After seeing Grumbles in such bad shape, he wondered if Emmett might be curled up somewhere, dying, but his former cagemate is nowhere to be found. *Perhaps he ran off and kept going beyond these woods*, Vincent speculates. That's the best-case scenario, but he fears the worst. Emmett's paws were badly mangled and he could barely walk. He would have been an easy target for some larger animal to prey upon, just one more example of a mink who desperately needed help after escaping the fur farm. But Vincent has concocted a plan for training them to survive in the forest. He will use many of the methods Trenton taught him when he first escaped.

Surprisingly, some of the wild minks have griped about the potential influx of new minks in the woods. They don't want competition for resources or mates, but Vincent has assured them that he'll encourage any newly freed minks to spread out once they've learned basic survival skills. What Vincent doesn't say is how disappointing it is for these minks to be so unwelcoming. *How can they be so territorial over such a vast area when all of us caged minks are forced to live for so long with multiple other minks in a cramped pen? These wild minks truly have no idea how good they have it out here, and those who were previously caged have conveniently forgotten their life before they lived in the woods. Well, it's my job to make sure that no one outside the fur farm ever forgets about all the minks trapped there.*

It's not all work for Vincent, though. Whenever he can, he tries to appreciate his newfound freedom. He does so to honor Frestin, his mother and the other minks who cannot enjoy the glories of life outside of a cage. The most rewarding experience is when Vincent finally rolls around and rests in soft green grass, just like Frestin had dreamed about doing. He makes a point to do so whenever he's not preparing for the rescue mission. With the gentle grass caressing his back, Vincent feels closer to Frestin. It's one of the only times he feels a sense of calm.

Trenton has only one request about the rescue: that Vincent wait until after mating season. Vincent doesn't bother cuddling up to any females—he has too many other things on his mind—but Trenton wants to make sure he doesn't miss out, especially if things go awry.

The day finally comes, though, and when it does, they are ready.

Vincent, Trenton and their twelve brave companions make their way to the fur farm. It's farther away than they remember and takes more than a day to reach, but soon the familiar rancid smell of excrement and urine fills their noses.

Vincent turns to his brother. "We're close."

When they reach a giant wire fence, they stop abruptly, taken aback.

Trenton surveys the obtrusive wall. "When did they build this?"

"That's odd," Vincent answers. "It wasn't here when I escaped. Perhaps they put it up to keep other minks from breaking out."

"I guess," Trenton responds. "Although that seems like poor planning since we can just dig a hole underneath."

Vincent pushes on the taut wire. He hasn't been around metal barriers in a long time and it instantly brings back horrifying memories. "True. But if this fence had been here when I was escaping, it definitely would have slowed me down. By the time I dug a hole, the humans very well might have caught me."

"Hmm. Well, let's dig a few holes so all the freed minks can run out more easily."

"Exactly what I was thinking, my brother," Vincent commends him.

"Looks like I'm more strategic than you thought, Smickety Smoo."

The fourteen minks begin digging three holes. The night is still and the moon is barely visible giving them advantageous cover. They are energized and exhilarated. It's a perfect night to pull off their raid.

Everything appears ready to go, according to their plan. If only Mando and Diablo weren't secretly watching from across the field.

26

PERSIMMON AND THE rest of the team have assembled. It's dusk. Each member mills about the base camp that's been set up deep in the woods away from the fur farm, preparing for the rescue. The original team—Persimmon, Derpoke, Scraps, Bruiser, Chloe and Tucker—are chatting and going over last-minute details. Rawly is huddled with his gang of raccoons—Drig, Linder, Dusty, Fisher, and Claudette—chanting in unison to pump themselves up. Vincent is off by himself, peering into the forest. Persimmon sees the blue-tinted mink all alone, staring intently into the darkness, so she walks over to check on him.

"You okay?" Persimmon inquires.

Vincent keeps focused on the shadowy woods. "Yes, just waiting for my forces to get here."

"You have a lot of friends and family in there, so I know how much this means to you," Persimmon persists, trying to get him to open up. "We're going to do everything we can to get them out of there."

Vincent turns to her. They barely know one another, and yet she's so warm with him—a warmth he hasn't known since he was torn from his mother. "Thank you. Thank you for everything you're doing."

Vincent places his paw on top of hers, which catches her off guard. He always seems so cold, so distant. "I say this with all sincerity,

Persimmon. Tonight, you may save thousands of lives. You don't have to, but you are trying. And you're doing it out of kindness. That's admirable."

Vincent lets go of her paw. "This is the most important night of my life. I'm ready." He looks back into the woods. "I may even see my mother again."

Persimmon goes to say something, but she's interrupted by a rustling of leaves nearby. As she and Vincent perk up their ears, six minks appear from out of the darkness.

Vincent smiles. "My reinforcements!"

The minks greet Vincent and he introduces them to Persimmon. "My fellow minks, this is Persimmon. Without her, tonight would not be possible."

The minks stomp their feet on the dirt and cheer. "Persimmon!"

Persimmon is moved by the flattery. "Welcome, friends. Let's get started."

Persimmon crawls up onto a fallen tree stump and faces the team. "Okay, listen up." Everyone quiets down except Rawly, who is still encouraging his troops. "Rawly, I need your attention."

"Sorry." Rawly stops his merrymaking, but he adds with zest, "We're invigorated. Motivated! Let's save some minks!"

"Yes, that's the plan," Persimmon replies, ignoring his unruly demeanor. "First, the most important thing. I will reiterate this one more time to make sure we are perfectly clear: Until I give the order, no one releases any minks—not one cage is opened until I am positive we can release them safely. If we do it too soon, they could all die. *We* could all die. We need to make sure they are capable of running out of those cages on their own. I don't want a repeat of what happened with the calves."

"What are calves?" one of the new minks asks.

"They're other creatures that humans mistreat—just like the way the humans mistreat minks. Their inability to walk derailed our previous rescue mission." She addresses the group again. "Does everyone understand that they wait for my order?"

The group calls out as one. "Yes!"

Persimmon continues. "Now, I know the team leaders have gone over the plan many times with you all, but one last time, is there anyone who is unclear about his or her assignment or partners?"

No one speaks up. "Good. Then I just have one last order of business. I've come up with what I believe is a suitable name for the team. Our mission is to unfetter all creatures imprisoned and abused by humans, and I think that anyone else who shares that goal should automatically be welcomed to join this team. Therefore, from this point forward, we should call ourselves The Uncaged Alliance."

Murmuring passes through the group—Persimmon's team, Rawly's troops, the minks.

"I love it!" Chloe calls out.

Persimmon surveys the rest of the crowd. Everyone is nodding in agreement—except Rawly.

"Can't we be called something tougher, like The Raging Rebels?" he complains.

The rest of the team yells at him for being so negative.

"Hush up!"

"Don't be such a naysayer!"

"Okay, okay," Rawly caves. "Fine. The Uncaged Alliance it is. But if anyone asks, I'm referring to us as Uncagers. That sounds way more fierce."

"Wonderful!" Persimmon taps her front paws on the ground in celebration. "Then everyone get in here."

The original team members gather in and the new members follow their lead. Persimmon starts the charge. "Uncaged Alliance. To no more cages!"

The other team members kick their paws together with their neighbors and call out: "No more cages!"

* * *

Persimmon shakes the fence at the far edge of the fur farm. She stands alone. She's been here before, but this time Mando and Diablo are about to get a very big surprise.

"Mando! Diablo!" Persimmon calls out in a singsong manner. "My old friends! Where are you?"

Like clockwork, the Rottweilers dash across the grassy field. This time, though, they don't bark loudly. They know this trick and they're not going to fall for her ploy.

"You just won't go away, will ya, raccoon?" Mando growls. "Step a little closer. I got somethin' to tell ya."

"Nah," Persimmon states calmly. "You two bore me. I'd rather you speak to my friend."

Persimmon doesn't take her eyes off the furious dogs. She just calls back into the woods, "Bruiser!"

Bruiser struts out from behind a tree, confident in his own impressive strength.

Diablo laughs. "Look who it is—the coward dog who hides behind his raccoon."

"Yeah, so afraid, he's willing to take on *both* of you," Persimmon teases.

Mando's and Diablo's ears perk up. They're intrigued. "He's gonna brawl wid us? Please," Mando hisses.

"Yep," Persimmon exclaims. "If you win, we leave here forever."

Diablo cackles. "Ha! We win, you ain't walkin' away nowhere."

Mando joins in. "Ain't no way he can beat us both."

Persimmon ignores their taunts. "And if he wins—scratch that, *when* he wins—we get to free any minks we want."

Diablo scoffs. "Git outta here. Ain't no minks gettin' free, nohow. Git back in dose woods where ya came from."

Mando shuts down his companion. "Hold on, Diablo. Ain't no worry they gettin' past us." Mando looks beyond Persimmon and glares straight at Bruiser. "We good by those terms. I wanna chew on this toy since I first seen 'im."

Off in the distance, close to the Peterson house, Jackson beckons the dogs. "Mando! Diablo! Come 'n' get it!"

The Rottweilers turn their ears in his direction.

Diablo perks up. "Food! We settle dis later."

Persimmon quickly speaks up. "Seriously? You're going to walk away just like that?" She turns to Bruiser with a smile. "Looks like somebody wants their din-din from their master." Bruiser laughs mockingly.

Diablo barks at Persimmon. That stung.

Meanwhile, Jackson taps on the dog food can. "Mando! Diablo!" He swats at a buzzing mosquito and murmurs angrily to himself. "Come on, you idiot dogs. I'm gettin' eaten alive out here."

Unbeknownst to Jackson, Vincent and Tucker are hiding beside a shed just out of his view. Right beside them is a pile of bright orange mushrooms. They wait anxiously, hoping the dogs don't come running over to get their dinner.

Back by the fence, Persimmon continues her ploy. "So, are you gonna eat your little snack or are you gonna protect your farm?"

Mando lashes at the fence. "Come on in, raccoon! See what happens!"

Jackson slaps a mosquito against his neck. He looks at his fingers. There's a tiny splatter of blood—*his* blood sucked out by the vampiric insect. "Screw this. Dumb dogs can eat whenever the hell they want." He storms off toward the house, leaving the dog dishes unattended.

Vincent and Tucker look at one another and grin. They quickly pick up a pawful of orange mushrooms.

Back near the woods, Persimmon and Bruiser are starting to dig a hole under the fence. Discreetly, they give one another a concerned look. They're waiting for a signal from Chloe that Vincent and Tucker are finished tampering with the dogs' food. Until then, they have to stall Mando and Diablo—or the whole plan is ruined.

Bruiser acts quickly. "So, which of you two dogs am I fighting first?"

"Hold up," Mando argues. "You said you was fightin' both a us at the same time."

"I *am* fighting both of you," Bruiser counters. "First, I'll tear you up, and then I'll tear up your friend."

Mando moves closer to the fence and bares his teeth. "Naw. Ain't no changin' the rules."

Bruiser continues to provoke him. "You're too scared to take me on by yourself?"

Mando slams his face right up against the fence. "We ain't scared. You ain't got no honor changin' the plan."

Over at the dog food dishes, Vincent and Tucker madly rip up the orange mushrooms into tiny particles and mash them into the dog slop. Chloe calls down as quietly as she can. "Hurry up!"

"Sweet Pea, we're going as fast as we can," Tucker responds. "It has to be mixed in well or they'll detect it."

"Persimmon and Bruiser can only hold them for so long. You..."

"Chloe, enough," Tucker whisper-shouts.

Chloe mumbles to herself. "Don't 'enough' me! How long does it take to rip up some mushrooms?" She sits back on the roof of the shed, squinting to see the brawl brewing between Persimmon, Bruiser and the Rottweilers.

Bruiser stops digging and steps back from the hole he and Persimmon are creating. Persimmon scolds, "Bruiser, what are you doing? Get back here and help me."

"I didn't agree to fight both at the same time," Bruiser whines.

"But you told me you could. To quote, you said, 'I could knock 'em both down with one bite.' Did you not?"

"Don't tell me what I said," Bruiser barks. "Anyway, I *can* take 'em both on. But with two of 'em on me, I know they'll get at least a few good bites in, and I don't feel like gettin' bit tonight."

Diablo snorts with laughter. "You don't feel like gettin' bit?"

Both Diablo and Mando fall to the ground, cracking up as if that was the funniest thing they have ever heard. Bruiser grits his teeth.

While the Rottweilers are distracted, Persimmon glances at the shed to see if Chloe is giving the signal, but she is just sitting on the roof, waiting. Persimmon starts to worry. *How much longer can we keep this up? Soon we'll either have to fight or give up. We're clearly not fighting, and the moment we give up, they'll rush over to that food. What is taking Vincent and Tucker so long?*

Mando and Diablo stand back up, still chuckling. Diablo can barely catch his breath. "Oh, wow. That was good. I almost don't wanna kill ya just cuz ya made me laugh so hard."

Mando steps back over to the fence and slobbers through the wire. "We fightin' or not? This game's gettin' borin'."

Persimmon doesn't want to lose the Rottweilers' attention, so she improvises. She rushes at Bruiser and hits his legs. "Get in there and fight them!"

Bruiser steps back, surprised. Persimmon again scratches at his legs, this time more fiercely. "I said, get in there and fight them. All these minks are counting on you to save their lives, you coward!"

Bruiser bares his teeth at Persimmon. "Don't scratch me, ya hear? Or you're gonna regret it."

Mando and Diablo watch with glee. They love a good fight.

Persimmon jabs her nails into Bruiser's leg and the Doberman knocks her to the ground with his head. "I'm tellin' ya, Persimmon. Back down. This is your last warnin'."

Mando gives Diablo a devilish smile. "This is almost as much fun as fightin' that dog ourselves."

Persimmon charges at Bruiser, and just before she hits his legs, the dog chomps down on her body with his powerful jaws. He picks Persimmon up, shakes her around, and tosses her onto the dirt. The raccoon's body hits the ground with a thud. Mando and Diablo cheer at the wild turn of events.

Persimmon rolls around on the ground, moaning. Worried, Bruiser darts over to his dear friend. "Persimmon, I'm so sorry. What have I done?" Bruiser looks up at the snickering Rottweilers and then rushes up to the fence. "Look what you made me do! I'll tear your limbs off! Fight me now!"

"Pathetic," Mando snickers. "Come on, Diablo, we have some supper to eat."

The Rottweilers start to walk away. Bruiser gets anxious. They haven't received the signal yet from Chloe. He has to keep them there. He yells after them, "I'll fight both of ya at the same time! Cowards!"

Mando and Diablo don't look back. They trot away, victorious.

Bruiser walks over to Persimmon, who is still crawling on the ground, moaning. "You can stop your moanin', faker. They're gone."

Persimmon rolls over onto her back and lets out one more loud fake moan and then smiles widely. "Hooray for me! What did you think of my performance?"

Bruiser smirks. "Average."

Persimmon playfully taps his muscular leg. "Come on, I was magnificent. So, did Chloe give the signal?"

"No," Bruiser states, concerned.

"Goodness, what else could we have done?" Persimmon flips back over onto her stomach and looks through the gate at the fading silhouettes of the dogs. "What a fiasco. The rescue could fall apart before it's even begun."

Over at the shed, Vincent and Tucker rush to mix the dog food and mushrooms together. Tucker complains frantically, "You can still see little pieces of orange. Why did we have to pick the brightest, most noticeable mushroom in the forest?"

"Just keep mixing," Vincent rebukes.

Chloe squints and, to her shock, sees Mando and Diablo trotting across the grass straight toward them. "They're coming!"

"What?!" Vincent squishes the dog food faster. "We didn't give the signal."

"Too late. Get out of there!" Chloe yells.

Vincent stops mixing the food. "Good enough." He puts a slab of rotting meat that he had pulled out of the Peterson's garbage on top of the concoction. "Let's go," he says to Tucker as he runs behind the shed.

Tucker continues to fiddle with the dog food. "It's not mixing. They're gonna find out."

Chloe calls down to him. "Tucker! Get out of there!"

As Mando approaches the shed, he notices Tucker tinkering with their dog dishes. "Hey, some squirrel's messin' with our food!"

Mando and Diablo jump into high gear and dart toward the shed, barking.

Chloe screams. "Run, Tucker!"

Tucker tries to toss his slab of rotting meat onto the food but misses. He sees the dogs rushing toward him and darts behind the fence and past Vincent. Vincent knows the dogs will chase after the frantic squirrel in that very direction, so he follows Tucker under the fence and into the woods.

The dogs dash behind the shed, but the squirrel has disappeared. On the roof, Chloe crouches down, hoping she won't be discovered.

"Stupid squirrels!" Diablo gripes. "I told ya somethin' was eatin' our food lately. Didn't I?"

"Hmph. We'll get that vermin next time." Mando inspects his food. "Look at that. They gave us some meat. It's about time we get some respect 'round here."

"Yeah!" Diablo bites into the hunk of rotting flesh. "Just wish all our food tasted this good. I'm gettin' tired of this canned crud."

Chloe listens, grinding her teeth, waiting nervously to see if they'll eat the mushroom mixture.

"Shut up," Mando snaps. "You're lucky you get fed at all. You remember bein' at the Maxwells' house? Ain't feed us nuthin'. Make us fight all the time. You wanna go back to that?"

Diablo puts his ears down. "No."

"Then eat what yer given," Mando barks.

Diablo sulks as he bites into the canned food and mushroom mixture, followed by Mando chomping into it. Chloe hears them chowing down and can barely contain her excitement. Quietly, she puts her tail up in the air and begins to twirl it around.

At the outer fence, Persimmon sees Chloe's signal. "They're eating the food!" Persimmon hugs Bruiser's legs. "Success!"

Bruiser crouches down to let Persimmon crawl onto his back. Once on top, the eager raccoon shakes her front paws back and forth to signal the waiting teams. (If her tail hadn't been shot off by humans, she would be twirling it around instead, but she has to work with what she's got.) Scraps and Derpoke, Rawly and his troops, and the other minks all start digging holes under the fence. The rescue is moving into phase two.

27

MANDO AND DIABLO have vomited up a mess. The ailing dogs lie on the ground, dry heaving. Vincent and Tucker watch from the side of the shed while Chloe surveys the scene from the roof.

Vincent pats Tucker on the back. "It's working!"

"Is it wrong of me to get a little joy out of seeing those two dogs slightly miserable?" Tucker asks.

"Tucker, I feel the same way." Vincent grins. "Just don't tell Persimmon."

He turns to Tucker and Chloe. "You two know your roles. Chloe, you're lookout on the shed and Tucker, you're lookout over at the cages. If the dogs get up or if you see any commotion from the humans in the house, call out to me immediately. Be safe."

Vincent looks at Chloe. "Okay, we're good to go, my lady. Give the signal."

Vincent starts to run off, then turns back to the two squirrels. "And thank you." He rushes toward the rows of mink cages.

*   *   *

Persimmon sees Chloe twirling her tail again, this time signaling that the dogs are incapacitated. Persimmon's heart skips a beat. "Let's go!"

Bruiser allows Persimmon to crawl onto his back again and she flaps her front paws up and down, signaling the other teams stationed along the fence. Everyone jumps into action. Team One—Persimmon, Scraps, Derpoke and Bruiser—crawls into the two holes they have dug. Team Two—Rawly and his troop of raccoons—crawls into theirs. Team Three—made up of four of the minks Vincent recruited—inches their way through the hole they've dug, while the other two minks that Vincent enlisted head back to the base camp deep in the woods, where they will wait to greet and then organize the freed minks. Water and food have already been set up and a few herbs and other medicinal plants have been gathered for the sickest ones.

The Uncaged Alliance crosses the grassy field. They can't believe they're finally on the other side of the fence. It felt like it was never going to happen and now, suddenly, the moment is here. The moon is almost completely full—exposing them—so they move forward with caution. They didn't come this far just to get caught now.

As the teams near the cages, the rank smell of excrement and urine attacks their noses.

Scraps whispers to his sister. "Do you think the minks will be standing in their own feces just like the calves were?"

"I'm afraid they probably will be," Persimmon replies. "This is getting to be a disturbing trend. And from what Vincent said, we're probably going to see even more upsetting things in the minks' cages than that. Are you going to be okay seeing all this?"

"I can handle it," Scraps nods confidently. "I just want to get them out of here."

"That's my brave little brother."

The three teams are now at the edge of the cages. Once the caged minks are released from their pens, they'll be sent to this spot, where Derpoke will be stationed to direct them to some Team Three minks in the field. Then, those Team Three minks will point the way to the outer fence. There, two other Team Three minks will guide the newly freed critters through the holes under the fence and into the woods. A path has been cleared so the freed minks can follow one another through the woods to the base camp, where those two other Team Three minks will be waiting to take care of them.

The minks in the cages have noticed the diverse group of forest creatures coming toward them. They've never seen anything like it. Some of them call out. "Hey! Help us!"

Persimmon addresses them. "Yes, we're here to help. We just need to check out the cages first."

More minks yell: "Break us free!" "Help us!" "Open my cage! Please!"

Persimmon and Scraps climb onto the end of one row of cages. Rawly and his team split up into pairs and crawl onto their assigned rows. Bruiser stays on the ground, standing guard in case the dogs— or worse, the humans—come rushing at them.

Each team of raccoons examines the minks in the cages, trying to determine if they're fit to run free. Persimmon and Scraps walk on top of the cages, looking inside. Inside each pen is a horrific sight. In the first, Persimmon sees one mink scratching deep gashes into his belly, another with puss oozing from his infected eyes, and yet another gnawing at his already raw tail, which looks ready to drop off at any moment. She winces, appalled at the bloody mess.

In the next cage, maggots consume the carcass of a dead mink as other minks huddle in a corner to avoid the terrifying scene and atrocious smell. Many of the cages have dried bloodstains on the wire—dismal remnants of minks trying futilely to bite their way out.

As Persimmon reaches another cage, a young brown mink begs, "Can you help us? Please." She is alarmed to see that one of his front paws is dangling—limp and broken.

"Yes, sweet one. We're here to save you. We'll be..."

The young mink tries to lick her through the cage. "Thank you. Thank you. I don't want to die in here."

Persimmon rubs his head through the cage to calm him. "Yes, we'll be back. We just need to check the other cages."

She and Scraps move on to another cage. The young mink calls after them. "Don't forget me. Please. My paw—it hurts so much!"

In a cage, two rows down, Rawly and Claudette see four minks covered in their own feces. A few weeks ago, the excrement got blocked up at the bottom of their cage, ceasing to drip through, so now they're walking around in it, sleeping in it, living in it. Claudette gasps. "How could the humans do this to them? It's as if they think minks aren't capable of suffering."

"They know, beautiful. The humans just don't care," Rawly states. "It was the same thing with the calves."

Claudette is clearly shaken. "But look at them. Chewing off their own tails. Pacing back and forth in these tiny pens. I didn't realize the cages would be so small. It's no wonder they go insane."

Persimmon and Scraps continue checking their assigned cages. As they go down the line, minks beg for them to unlatch the enclosures. The siblings attempt to assuage them, but some are hysterical. "Help us! Help us!" The minks pull and bite at the wire. Being so close to freedom has riled them up.

Scraps speaks loudly over the pleading minks. "All this just so humans can wear their fur?! This is awful, Persimmon. We have to set them free. Look at them running back and forth. They can surely sprint through that field and into the woods."

"Yes, yes. Only a few more cages. I think you're right, though."

Persimmon and Scraps quickly scope out the final few cages in their row. More of the same horror: infected eyes, broken limbs, fear, desperation, death.

Rawly hops down from his set of cages and darts over to Persimmon's row. He looks up at her and blurts out before she can say a word. "Persimmon, these minks are desperate to get out of here. I know that we haven't checked all the cages yet, and yes, the minks are very badly bruised and some have broken legs, but the majority of them are running like mad in their cages. I'm sure they can make that fence from here. This is sickening. They're suffering as much as the calves. Some are suffering even more. I really think we should rescue them tonight."

Persimmon replies without hesitation. "I agree."

"You do?!" Rawly is stunned. "I thought you were gonna give me a hard time."

"No, it looks like you got something right for a change." She smiles. "Give your team the signal. We're saving these minks from this infernal place *now*."

Rawly exuberantly gallops off to his team. He shakes his tail around to signal that they're all clear to start freeing the minks.

Persimmon turns to Scraps. "Where's Vincent?"

28

AT THE OTHER end of the fur farm, Vincent runs frantically from cage to cage. He is in the section where the minks are kept for breeding. "Mother! Mother!" Vincent calls up to the cages. *Where is it? I know our cage was here somewhere.* He runs down the dirt path between the two rows of cages. "Mother!"

Vincent stops running. *There! That's the cage.* Something feels very familiar to him. "Mother?!" Vincent runs under the pens, around the piles of excrement, and straight up the wood beam to the cage. He looks inside. There is a black mink inside. "Mother?" The mink turns around.

"Son?" The female mink rejoices and moves closer to the side of the cage where Vincent stands. But Vincent huffs in disappointment. It's not his mother.

"Do you know what happened to my mother?" Vincent inquires. "She was in this cage before you. Her name is Margeaux."

The female mink seems confused. "You're not my son?"

"No, I'm sorry."

She sinks down, dejected.

Vincent asks again. "My mother was in this cage before you. Do you know what happened to her?"

"No. I never met her," the female mink replies morosely.

"Margeaux, you said?" A voice comes from inside the next pen. He recognizes the brown female mink inside.

Vincent's eyes light up. "I remember you! I'm Margeaux's son."

"Yes, you have her blue hue," the brown mink remarks. "Sorry to say, but the humans came for her a while ago. I haven't seen her since. That was back when it was still cold."

Vincent starts to tremble. "Was that before or after the massacre?"

"You mean, when the humans kill all the minks?"

"Yes, yes!" Vincent is getting frantic. "Did they take her before or after that?"

"I don't... It was before. I'm sorry. She was so sweet. I always liked her. I..."

Vincent stops listening. He is hyperventilating. The news cracks his heart. *Be strong. Be strong. You prepared for this. You knew this might happen.* Vincent drops down the wood beam. He walks in between the piles of excrement in a daze. *Keep it together. There are so many other minks who need rescuing tonight. They're counting on you. You must find the fortitude—for them.*

Vincent tries to run down the pathway, but his legs are giving way. Hopelessness is kicking in. Deep sorrow.

"Vincent?" Persimmon rushes down the dirt path to the disconsolate mink, who is hobbling to stay up. "Vincent? What happened? Are you hurt?"

"No, I can do this." Vincent struggles to walk straight. "Let's help get these minks out of their cages. Are we freeing them tonight?"

"Scraps, Rawly and the other raccoons are already opening some cages."

Vincent tries to move forward but his legs are betraying him. "Great, the rescue's already started." He almost collapses but Persimmon catches him. "I'm sorry, Persimmon. I wanted... I couldn't find my mother." Vincent fights back tears. "She's not here." He can't stand up any more on his own. "I always thought I'd come back and save her. I always thought I'd see her again. I wanted so much to see her." Vincent breathes deeply, trying to catch his breath. Persimmon holds onto him. "I thought I could handle it if she wasn't here... I should have escaped sooner. No, I never should have left without her in the first place." Vincent looks at Persimmon. His throat is sore from holding back tears. "I'm sorry. These other minks need my help. I'm sabotaging the plan. It's selfish of me."

"No. It's alright." Persimmon holds his paw to steady and comfort him. "Vincent, you've been through a lot. The mission has already started. Our plan is working. Just take a few moments. It's okay."

Vincent steadies himself. "I just need to breathe."

Persimmon helps him sit on the ground. "Take your time. I'm going to run back and open more cages."

Vincent nods. "I'll be there shortly."

Persimmon dashes off down the dirt path. Vincent is left alone. The minks in the cages above him stare down and call out to him. "Are you breaking us free? Did that raccoon just say you were getting us out of here? Open my cage next. Please!"

Vincent doesn't feel like responding. He needs a moment to let the devastating news of losing his mother sink in.

Right then, a giddy mink runs at lightning speed past Vincent, almost banging into him. Vincent is startled. Then out of nowhere, another mink rushes by yelling, "We're free! We're free!"

Vincent calls after him. "Wait, you're going the wrong way! There are no holes under the fence on that side!"

The exuberant mink keeps going. Vincent sits up, worried, *What are they doing? That's not the way out. We had a path set up for them. They're just going to get stuck that way.*

Vincent hops up and races down the path in the same direction Persimmon ran. He has no time to feel sorry for himself. This night is bigger than reuniting with his family. Thousands of minks are relying on him to save their lives, and he will not let them down—not after all he's been through to get to this moment.

29

CHAOS. FREED MINKS are running every which way. Vincent can't believe his eyes. The fur farm is crawling with jubilant and crazed critters. It's encouraging to see them so happy, but the mayhem could derail everything. Any minute, the noise could rouse the sleeping dogs and the nasty Petersons.

Vincent sprints to the grassy field. He sees Derpoke trying to wrangle hordes of disorderly minks. Derpoke, panting and clearly overwhelmed, sees Vincent and hollers, "They won't listen! They're gonna wake the humans!"

Vincent joins in on attempting to corral the frenzied animals who are running down the path toward them. "This way! This way!" Vincent starts pushing minks in the direction of the fence where the holes are. He even stops a few, grabbing them as they rush past. "Whoa! Run to the fence that way and tell any mink you see to follow you."

A few rows down, Persimmon darts through a mass of delirious minks, calling out, "Wrong way! Go back down the path the other way! There are holes under the fence that way!" Some minks turn around and follow her directions, but others keep running the wrong way.

Persimmon reaches Rawly, who is speedily unlatching cage after cage. Without noticing the exasperated raccoon, Rawly peers down into the cage he's about to open and orders, "Run down this path and the opossum and minks will direct you under the fence."

"Rawly, stop! Stop opening cages!" Persimmon commands.

Rawly ceases and looks at her quizzically. "Why?!"

"Look around you. The minks are running wild."

"So round 'em up. Whose job is that?"

"You're opening the cages too fast. Derpoke and the mink team can't control so many unruly creatures. We need your help sending the freed minks in the right direction. They're running everywhere."

"We're never gonna get through all these cages if we don't keep going," Rawly counters.

"If the Petersons wake up, *no one's* getting out of here," Persimmon yells. "They're all going to die." She stares at him, brow furrowed. "Now stop arguing and help me direct these minks. Immediately!"

Rawly is impressed by her forcefulness. He jumps off of the cage and starts rounding up disorderly minks. "That way! Down that path! Go!"

All the minks in Rawly's row begin to head down the path, finally going in the right direction. Persimmon crawls down the front of a cage and drops to the ground. She corrals a young brown mink who is running by.

"You, stop!" The mink screeches to a halt and Persimmon continues. "I need your help. We have to get you and your friends out of here safely, and the only way to do that is for everyone to run directly down this path. At the end of the path, an opossum will guide everyone through the field and under some holes that my team dug below the fence. You'll follow a path through the woods and then you're free. It's as easy as that. We have food and water for everyone. Can I count on you to help out?"

The mink looks confused. Persimmon asks, "Do you understand what I'm saying?"

The young mink stares at her in awe. "What are you?"

"I'm a raccoon."

"Wow!" His mouth is agape. "You're so big. And you have stripes. Well, *you* don't, because you don't have a tail, but your friends do. My name's Nibbin, by the way. Raccoons are so…"

"I need you to focus, Nibbin," she commands impatiently. "Can you help me or not?"

"Yes, raccoon. Sorry, raccoon. Okay. All the minks run down this path and through the field. Food and water are in the woods for us. Got it."

"Good. Also, round up other minks to guide everyone while you're at it. We need as much help as we can get."

"Yes, raccoon. You can count on me."

Nibbin stands there, staring at Persimmon. She motions for him to get going.

"Oh, yes." He twists around. "Going. Going."

The young mink rushes off, rounding up his fellow minks and guiding them toward the field. Persimmon smiles to herself. Order is slowly being restored.

*   *   *

Near the last row of cages, Bruiser runs frantically to head off a horde of minks who are running straight for the shed where the dogs are lying, and just beyond that… the house. Bruiser would normally bark to get their attention, but he has to be extra quiet so he doesn't wake the Rottweilers or the humans.

Chloe, who is atop the shed as lookout, sees the minks running straight toward her. She looks down at Mando and Diablo, who are finally sleeping after having vomited uncontrollably for almost half an hour. She's hesitant to run past them even though they look like they're asleep, because one swift move from either of them and she's as good as dead. Chloe glances back at the crazed minks. They're racing closer and closer. She'll have to risk it. If they get anywhere near those dogs or that house, the Petersons will be outside in no time.

Chloe climbs down from the shed. About thirty feet away, Tucker, who is stationed on the roof of one of the rows of cages, sees his loved one leave her post. He watches anxiously as she runs around the dogs and straight for the group of minks coming her way.

Chloe calls out to the minks. "Turn around! Stop!"

From the opposite direction, Bruiser runs past the wall of minks, flips around and bares his teeth at them. He growls in their direction and whispers as threateningly as he can muster, "Get back! Go the other way! Now!"

The minks slow down when they see the menacing dog. Bruiser moves forward, growling more intensely. A few minks run past him, but since he sees Chloe coming up behind him, he decides to let her handle those minks while he focuses on the group in front of him. Bruiser pretends he's in attack mode and keeps charging at them, hoping to frighten them into turning around. "Go back! There's an opening in the fence through the field. Run!"

The minks realize that Bruiser is actually trying to help, so they turn around and run in the direction of the fence.

Meanwhile, Chloe catches up to the three minks who made it past Bruiser, blocking their path. "Go back! You'll wake the dogs."

The minks stop. They stare at Chloe and get a murderous look in their eyes. One mink bares his teeth. They crouch down, ready to pounce. Before Chloe can react, they are on top of her—biting, scratching, eating her. Chloe screams.

Bruiser twists around and sprints toward her. Tucker shrieks and jumps down from the roof, darting toward his loved one.

Chloe scratches at her attackers, fighting for her life. Bruiser bites down into the back of one of the minks, crushing his spine. The mink squeals and Bruiser tosses him away. Bruiser then bites down into the back of another mink. The mink shakes around and digs his nails into Bruiser's face. Bruiser chomps down harder, smashing the mink's insides. The mink squeaks out one last breath and goes limp. Bruiser spits out the body.

The third mink suddenly realizes that he's the only one left and retreats into the field. Bruiser kneels down next to his squirrel friend. "Chloe! Are you okay?"

Chloe moans. There are bite and scratch marks all over her body. Blood drips from the gashes. "I'm hurt, Bruiser. I think I'm hurt badly."

Tucker rushes over and curls up to his Sweet Pea. He starts licking her wounds. "Chloe, are you okay? Please be okay."

Chloe gasps. "They were eating me, Tucker. They were biting into my flesh and chewing it. I don't understand."

Bruiser looks around at all the freed minks still running around the fur farm. "Come on, we need to get both of you out of here. It's not safe. Chloe, can you climb up onto my back?"

Chloe rolls over. "I can walk." She tries but staggers.

Bruiser kneels down. "Just hop on my back. I'll carry ya." The Doberman turns to Tucker. "You, too, little buddy. I'm not takin' any chances."

Both squirrels climb onto the large dog's back.

✳   ✳   ✳

Persimmon is on top of a cage, talking to the minks inside. "Okay, you got all that? I need you to help us guide your fellow minks out of here. Can I trust you to do that when I open this cage?"

The four minks inside call out in unison. "Yes!"

Persimmon undoes the latch on their cage. One goes running out without stopping, but the others hop down and immediately start guiding minks down the pathway to the field. In fact, Persimmon has recruited a large team of minks to help organize the rescue mission. The minks have formed lines down the dirt paths in between the rows of cages, through the field, and even out beyond the fence in the woods. Finally, Persimmon feels like the mission is back on track until…

"Persimmon!" Bruiser calls out her name, so she looks around and sees the Doberman carrying Tucker and Chloe. They look distressed, so she rushes over.

When Persimmon steps up to the trio, she notices blood smeared all over Chloe's fur. "What happened to her?!"

"She got attacked by some of the minks," Tucker replies, upset.

Persimmon's mouth drops open. "What?! Why?"

"She says they were trying to eat her," Bruiser answers.

"Really?" Persimmon is flummoxed. "Do minks eat squirrels?"

Tucker points to a gaping wound on Chloe's back and yells, "Those blasted creatures pounced on her like famished beasts. She's out here risking her life for them, and they try to eat her!"

Persimmon peers at the bloody bite marks covering Chloe's body.

"Do you believe us now?" Tucker asks heatedly.

"Tucker, I believe you," Persimmon says sincerely. "I'm just surprised. Vincent warned that you two should stay up high, but I didn't realize it was because the minks might try to eat you. We have to get you out of here."

"No," Chloe responds. "Carrying me out of here will slow things down. Don't worry about me. Can you help me get to higher ground, though?"

Tucker chimes in. "Sweet Pea, they could attack again. It's too dangerous."

Chloe takes Tucker's paw into hers. "Pupsy, it'll be more dangerous carrying us through all these crazed minks. It's safer up higher for the time being. Now let Persimmon and the team get back to the rescue."

Tucker concedes without saying a word.

Bruiser kneels down and Persimmon wraps her mouth around the back of Chloe's neck and gently lifts her up. The injured squirrel moans in pain. The raccoon climbs a wood beam to the metal roof and softly places Chloe down. Tucker is right behind and curls up next to his wounded mate.

"Once things quiet down with the rescue, we'll come back and carry you to the base camp," Persimmon assures them.

Tucker nods. Chloe closes her eyes, shaking slightly from the pain. Tucker licks the wounds on her back and belly.

Right then, out of the corner of Persimmon's eye, she notices a mink dragging himself along the pathway below. "I'll be back later," she says quickly.

Persimmon speeds down the beam and over to the afflicted mink. She sees that his two back legs look broken. Despite his grave injury, he continues pulling himself toward the fence in a desperate attempt to escape. Persimmon is dismayed but keeps calm so she doesn't alarm him. "It's okay, sweet one. We'll help you out of here. Just wait. We'll get someone to carry you."

"No," he argues. "I need to get free. I can't be left behind."

"We're opening as many cages as possible to free the minks who can run first, and then we'll come back for you."

The injured mink ignores her and keeps hoisting his body forward through the dirt, panting from exhaustion as he goes.

Persimmon goes to say something to Bruiser, but then she sees two, three, a whole mess of injured minks throwing themselves out of the cages onto the hard ground below. Because of their broken limbs, missing eyes, and other wounds, some can't climb out properly. In fact, pretty much every cage in the fur farm has at least one or two minks too injured to escape on their own safely. Persimmon had planned for this, though. She and the team were set to come back and rescue them after all of the cages had been opened, but these minks are so desperate to escape, so afraid to be left behind, that they're risking more bodily harm by jumping out. Persimmon even witnesses one mink fall out of his cage and land on his neck. She hears a ghastly crack and sees the mink convulsing in pain.

Persimmon runs down the row of cages, calling up to the minks, "We're not leaving you! Do not jump out of your cages. Please. You'll just get hurt even worse. We'll be carrying all of you out of here."

Most of them ignore her and continue to toss themselves onto the solid ground below. Persimmon yells out for her faithful dog friend. "Bruiser!"

Bruiser bounds over to her and Persimmon asks urgently, "Can you start picking up minks and carrying them on your back? I need these minks to see that we're not leaving them. They're going to kill themselves trying to break free."

Bruiser nods and jumps into action. He starts picking up the injured minks with his mouth and placing them on his back. "Hold on tight, my friends!"

Persimmon finds this predicament incredibly frustrating. *We need more dogs. Why couldn't stupid Mando and Diablo have been more helpful?*

Persimmon hightails down a few rows where the other raccoons are still opening cages. "Drig, I need your help transporting some injured minks."

Drig stops what he's doing and stares at Persimmon, not following her request. She stares right back at him, displeased with his insubordination. But she knows exactly why he's hesitating and doesn't have time to get into a dispute. She knows what she needs to do. "Rawly asked me to come find you. Do you want me to get him and have him bark the order at you or do you feel like saving some lives?"

Drig looks questioningly at Claudette, who is opening cages in the next row over. Claudette says impatiently, "What are you waiting for? Help her out."

With that, Drig hops down from the cage. Persimmon nods at Claudette in appreciation and then leads Drig down the row parallel to where Bruiser was collecting minks. Debilitated minks litter the ground. Some are hobbling and dragging their bodies—others are too broken to walk on their own. They call out to the raccoons, "Help! Please don't leave me!"

Persimmon weaves around the flailing minks. "Stay here. We're not leaving you. Drig will be coming to take you all to safety. No more jumping out of cages!"

Persimmon has better luck with this group of minks, who are comforted when they see Drig lifting up their brethren and hoisting them onto his back. They realize they're not being left behind after all.

Persimmon jogs back to where Bruiser had been collecting minks. She sees the mink with the broken neck squealing in pain and unable to move but still very much alive. Persimmon looks around to see if anyone is watching. A mink lying on the ground nearby pleads with her. "Take me next!"

"Yes," Persimmon responds. "Bruiser the dog will be coming back shortly. Let me help your friend first. He's gravely injured."

Persimmon picks up the writhing mink as best she can without touching his cracked neck. She carries him into the darkest depths beneath the cages, out of view of the other minks. She glances around again to make sure no one is watching. She looks down at the shaking mink. He is making wheezing sounds as he moans. Persimmon whispers softly to him. "I'm so sorry, sweet one. I wish there was another way." She bares her claws.

*   *   *

A few minutes later, Persimmon steps out from underneath the enclosures in the opposite row. She breathes solemnly and tells herself, *You did the right thing. There was nothing you could do to save him. He was in such agony.*

"Do you need my help with anything?" Vincent asks, startling her. She was so caught up with guilt that she didn't even notice him walk up to her. *Did Vincent see me?* She doesn't want anyone to know what she just did, even if it was out of mercy.

"Sorry, didn't mean to frighten you," Vincent apologizes.

"I'm fine." Persimmon collects herself. "I was just deep in thought. All these injured minks keep jumping out of their cages because they're afraid we'll leave them. I was thinking about the best way to get them all out of here."

"I saw Bruiser and Drig carrying some of them to the fence. Great idea. Do you need my help with that?"

"Actually, I saw you wrangling the freed minks at the end of the rows," Persimmon replies. "That seemed to be working very well. I think you can just continue to do that. You're doing a great job, Vincent."

"Thank you. I think…"

"Vincent?" He hears a soft and weary voice from a cage above him. He stops talking immediately and looks up. A black mink with a blue tint to her fur is staring down at him with eyes that are at once amazed, bewildered and full of love.

"Mother?!" he blurts out.

Vincent darts under the enclosures and scurries up the wood beam to the front of the cage. He frantically pushes his body through the door and hops inside. Vincent and his mother embrace, smelling one another. Margeaux is shaking with joy. "My kit! Oh, my sweet kit!" She licks his face. "It's you! It's really you."

Vincent starts sobbing in her embrace. He wanted so much just to be near her again. "I thought you were gone, Mother. I thought I lost you."

Margeaux caresses Vincent's face with wet kisses. "It's okay, my kit. I'm right here."

Persimmon looks up into the cage, teary-eyed. *This* is why she's risking her life to save all of these other animals—to give them a new life; to give them some semblance of happiness.

Vincent quivers as he speaks. "Mother, I escaped when it was cold. I wanted to come rescue you, but I was too afraid of being caught. I'm so sorry. I should have rescued you, too."

Margeaux runs her paws through her son's fur. "Vincent, there's no need for apologies. I wanted you to escape. That's all I ever wanted. Besides, you were always here in my heart. You never left me." She licks his tears, then asks earnestly, "Are your brothers and sisters here, too?"

Vincent closes his eyes and turns away from her. He can't bear to break the news.

Persimmon is still peering into the cage. She can't really hear what they're saying, but she sees Margeaux's heartbroken expression. This is a mother learning the tragic fate of her babies.

Vincent embraces his mother again and calls down to Persimmon. "Can we get my mother out of here?"

Persimmon nods. She crawls up to the cage. Margeaux is the last mink left in her cage. She's weak, more worn down than when Vincent last saw her. This bleak life has not been kind to her. Persimmon has to put Margeaux on her back and carry her to the ground, as she cannot walk on her own.

Margeaux suddenly tenses up when she sees Bruiser heading toward them. "Watch out! Dog!"

Vincent calms her. "Mom, it's okay. He's with us. Actually, is it okay if he carries you out of here? Persimmon and I have to continue freeing the other minks, and the sun will be up sooner than we'd like. I promise, I'll meet with you later."

"If you trust him, then I trust him. Although I never would have believed you if you had told me before today that I would be riding out of here on a dog."

Bruiser steps over to Persimmon, Vincent and Margeaux. He kneels down and Persimmon helps the physically beaten but emotionally resilient mink onto his back. Bruiser then carries Margeaux to the next row over to pick up more injured minks.

"Vincent, you're not going with your mother to the base camp?" Persimmon asks. "I'll understand if you want to spend time with her after being apart for so long."

"No, no," Vincent replies. "This is where I belong. I'm not leaving here until every mink is free."

With that, Persimmon and Vincent get back to work. The team is very close to having their first major success, but they can't ease up now—they're not clear of danger just yet.

30

EMPTY! EMPTY! ALL of the cages are empty! Vincent races down the rows, marveling at seeing so many cages devoid of his fellow minks. *They're free! We're doing it!* He is overjoyed. *No more suffering. No more fear of the massacre. No more metal bars blocking them from the beautiful forest. They'll learn to swim, sleep in comfortable burrows, play. And the vile Petersons never saw it coming!*

Vincent can barely contain his excitement, but he doesn't want to get too far ahead of himself. The fur farm isn't completely cleared out yet. The cages may be empty, but Bruiser, Derpoke, Scraps, Rawly and his team of raccoons are still picking up injured minks and carrying them to the base camp. Unfortunately, it's slow going since there are so many ailing minks and not very many animals big enough to carry them, but they still have time before morning comes, and the most promising news is that they haven't heard a thing from either the Rottweilers or the humans.

Vincent decides to check on Mando and Diablo. He climbs on top of the roof of the last row of cages. From that vantage point, he sees Tucker sitting beside Chloe on a nearby roof. Vincent calls over to them. "Are you two okay?"

Tucker, who is clearly distressed, snaps at Vincent. "Chloe was attacked by your bloodthirsty relatives."

Vincent is taken aback by his vitriol. "What? Why did they attack
her?"

Tucker is furious, heartsick. "She was trying to stop them from
waking the humans. Foolish, crazed minks were running straight for
the house. And then when she got to them, they just pounced on her.
They tried to eat her, Vincent."

Vincent is stunned. "What?! Tucker, I had…"

Tucker yells over him. "Why didn't you tell us that minks eat
squirrels? She could die!"

Vincent moves to the edge of the roof. "I told you two to stay up
high. That's why I stationed you on lookout."

"So you *knew* there was danger," Tucker counters.

"Well yes, but I warned you about that," Vincent says, flustered. "That said, I mean,… I certainly didn't think they'd try to
eat you."

Tucker stops paying attention to Vincent. He gazes at his sleeping,
wounded Sweet Pea. She looks battered, torn up. The thought of losing her gnaws at him.

Persimmon crawls onto the roof beside Vincent. She calls to the
dispirited squirrel, "Tucker, I'll come over there next. We'll get Bruiser
to carry Chloe out of here. Has the bleeding stopped?"

"Yes," Tucker responds. "She's sleeping now, which is comforting—she's not in so much pain." Tucker glares at Vincent and then
goes back to tending to his loved one.

Persimmon sits beside Vincent and whispers, "Don't take it personally. He's just worried about Chloe."

Vincent whispers back. "Persimmon, I knew there was some possibility it might be dangerous—that's why I suggested we position them

up high—but I had no idea something like this would happen. Do you think she'll be okay?"

"I hope so. Maybe I should have erred on the side of caution and not had them be part of this particular mission."

"They were so eager to help, though," Vincent responds. "Plus, they're incredibly fast. They're perfect lookouts. But I guess I underestimated how crazed the minks would be—and how famished. When we're stuck in those cages, we're rarely fed, and as I mentioned before, the food we are given is unappetizing rotten meat." Vincent moves around a bit, seeming uncomfortable. "It's true that some minks eat animals like muskrats and squirrels, but I thought the ones here would realize Chloe and Tucker were helping them. We're all part of a team. That's how I see it. Chloe and Tucker aren't food; they're friends."

"I understand," Persimmon responds. "There's nothing we can do about it now other than learn from our mistake." She peers over to where Mando and Diablo are sleeping. "How are our sickly friends doing?"

"That's actually why I came up here." Vincent and Persimmon squint to get a better view of the dogs. Mando's leg twitches as he sleeps.

"He's probably having terrible nightmares," Vincent remarks. "That's what happened to me when I ate those orange mushrooms."

"I saw them vomiting earlier. They seemed miserable."

"Good." Vincent clenches his jaw. "I hope they feel terrible."

Persimmon turns to him. "You really hate them, don't you?"

"Yes. They're murderers, and they've callously helped keep my fellow minks captive all this time. I hope they wake up and still feel sick, and then when they see that all the minks are gone, they're humiliated. My only concern, as I said, is how soon they and the Petersons come looking for us."

"Yes well, you and the other minks are running far away from here, right?"

"That's the plan." Vincent surveys the grassy field, watching Derpoke, Claudette and Linder carry injured minks under the fence. "We're going to go downriver and start a new life as far away from this place as possible. But first, after we finish here at the fur farm, I'm going to get a team together to search for all of the minks who went running haphazardly into the woods."

"Right, of course." Persimmon taps her paw on the metal roof, cursing her oversight. "We didn't factor that into our plan."

"The minks were much more frenzied than we expected. I can't blame them, though. I was ecstatic when I escaped, too. But they'll die out there if we don't find them."

"So you're going to start doing that right after we finish here, Vincent? Aren't you exhausted? I agree it's vital to get them sooner rather than later, but don't you need some rest?"

"I'll rest once all of the minks are safe." Vincent continues to watch as injured minks are carried out of the fur farm on the backs of the team members. He is anxious. Not all of the minks are free yet. They're so close, but every single mink must escape before they can consider the mission a victory. "I remember what it was like when I first got out of this place. I had no idea what to eat, where to sleep, how to survive. The longer we wait, the farther away they'll get. And once the sun comes up, who knows how long it will be before the stupid Petersons discover what happened and start searching for us."

"You should go, then," Persimmon urges. "We have things under control here, and you're right—the minks will be running all over the forest."

Vincent turns to Persimmon, surprised. "Are you sure? I feel like it's my duty to be here until every mink is freed and of all the team members are safe."

"We'll be fine. You can't exactly carry the injured minks out of here, and you know these woods better than any of us. If I had thought of it, I would have suggested you go sooner."

Vincent mulls over this for a moment. "Hmm. Alright, but if those Rottweilers or the humans wake up, run, okay? If any minks are left in here, we'll find a way to save them. The Petersons won't kill the minks. They want them alive so they can steal their winter coats."

Persimmon smirks. "Me, risk my life? What makes you think I'd do anything that reckless?"

"Just be safe. Persimmon, you did a remarkable job tonight. I commend you."

She smiles. "Likewise."

Vincent dashes down the wood beam and races across the field. At just that moment, Bruiser crawls back under the fence to pick up more injured minks.

Vincent calls out to the Doberman as he runs by. "Great job to-night, Bruiser! I'm going to look for lost minks."

"Good luck!" Bruiser calls back.

Vincent slides under the fence and down the pathway toward the base camp, with a skip in his step. He's feeling energized, victorious. Suddenly, a burly mink slams into Vincent, knocking him off balance into the brush.

"Vincent," he hisses. "I've been waiting for you."

Vincent hops up. "What are you doing, Nat? Someone might see us talking."

Nat hisses louder. "I don't care. That dog killed my friends. You know that?! Chewed them up!"

Vincent is calm, calculated. He steps into the woods away from the path, motioning for Nat to follow. Once they're out of earshot of anyone that may pass by, Vincent turns to the seething mink. "They'd still be alive if you had done what I asked you to do correctly. I told you to distract Chloe, not attack her."

"Oh, is that the little squirrel's name? Chloe? Well, we decided to improvise. We wanted a little snack."

Vincent looks at Nat with disgust. "You're such a fool. That squirrel—Chloe—risked her life tonight to save thousands of minks. You don't eat a squirrel like that. You show her respect."

Nat gets in Vincent's face. "I'm the fool?! She's just a squirrel. I eat them all the time. Next you're gonna tell me I should respect that murderous dog who tore up Clev and Ronsey."

Vincent stands up to Nat. "You mean Bruiser? Who also risked his life to save thousands of minks? They both helped more tonight than you did. You *are* a fool. You almost blew the whole plan."

Nat bares his teeth. "They're gonna pay for what they did."

Vincent licks his chipped tooth, annoyed. "I don't have time to chat with you right now, Nat. Other minks are counting on me."

Nat grabs a pawful of Vincent's fur. "You'll make time. And you're gonna help me get that dog and squirrel."

Vincent nods. Then without warning, he lunges at Nat. He sinks his teeth into Nat's throat and tears and tears until he rips a gaping hole. Nat tries to protect himself but barely has time to react. Blood spews from his neck, and he falls face-forward to the ground—not moving.

Vincent wipes his mouth and spits out blood. He quickly digs a hole behind some plants and drags Nat's lifeless body into it. Just as speedily, he kicks dirt into the hole to cover him up.

Vincent sprints deep into the woods. He races around trees, through thick brush, faster and faster. Finally, he comes to a clearing. He looks up at the giant white house before him. He made it. His eyes are filled with fury. He utters a violent, hateful snarl: "The Petersons."

31

VINCENT SNEAKS OVER to the side of the house that faces away from the fur farm. It's dark there. He's hidden. He looks up and sees that a window on the first floor is open. The sneaky mink latches his claws into the side of the house and hoists himself up. There's a screen. As quietly as possible, he rips a hole in the screen just big enough for him to push through.

Vincent drops onto the living room floor with a thud. He stands as still as a statue to make sure no one has heard him. Nothing stirs in the house. It's completely quiet. He hasn't been detected.

Vincent scurries over to the staircase and peers up. It's a long way to travel without any cover, but there's no other way to the second floor. His heart is pounding. This is the moment he's been waiting for all night—the part of the plan he didn't dare reveal to Persimmon.

He looks around. No movement in the house. He dashes up the stairs as fast as his short legs will take him. One step, two steps. He hops higher and higher, hoping no one will come creeping around the corner. Eleven steps, twelve steps. No one yet. He's nearly there. Vincent feels almost lightheaded from adrenaline. He's not scared, though—he's exhilarated.

Vincent reaches the top of the stairs and stops to rest, breathing deeply, *This is it. Everything changes after this.* He finally catches his breath and surveys the hallway. *Who sleeps in what room?*

All but one of the doors are open. Vincent slinks along the thick carpet toward the room on the far left. The carpet masks the sound of his footsteps.

He peeks into the bedroom—darkness fills the room except for a little moonlight seeping in through the window. Vincent can see a human in the bed. *Who is it?* He can't quite see up that high, but he sees dark splotches on the ground beside the bed. He moves in closer. It's blood.

Vincent's heart skips a beat. He quickly climbs onto the bed, full of nervous excitement. There before him is Jackson—blood splattered all around his head, the flesh of his throat torn to shreds, his eyes scratched to mush. Dead. Jackson is dead.

Vincent lets out a guttural sigh. He rips at the bed sheets in victory.

A voice calls out from the doorway. "Smickety?"

Vincent twists around. "Trenton!" He jumps off the bed and rushes over to his brother, embracing him. "You did it! You killed him! What about the other humans?"

"They're all dead. Russell, the dad, their mother. All dead."

Vincent scratches at the doorframe. He's so emotional, he doesn't know what to do with himself. Vincent sees that Trenton's brown fur is covered with blood. "Are you okay? Are the other minks okay?"

"It's not my blood, Matta and Bilton were thrown against a wall when they were getting Russell. They're hurt, but they were able to run out of the house on their own, so I think they'll be okay."

"So all of the other minks are out of the house except you?"

"Yes. I waited here like you asked." Trenton sits down. He seems exhausted... disturbed.

Vincent crouches down beside him. "What's wrong, my brother?"

Trenton stares off into the dark hallway. One of his eyes is missing from when Mando and Diablo attacked him during their first rescue attempt at the fur farm. His left ear was also torn to shreds. Scars line his face. He looks embattled. "It was a long night, my brother. I felt sick with anxiety all day, and then tonight…" He trails off for a second. "It was brutal. There was so much blood. I took Jackson out with the help of some other minks. He had this look in his eyes when he realized what was happening. He urinated on the spot. And then he was dead."

Vincent moves closer to his brother. "You don't feel sorry for them, do you?" He makes eye contact with Trenton. "Remember that Jackson, Russell, their father—that whole family has murdered thousands and thousands of our friends and family, mercilessly hacked them apart. They skinned Frestin alive. And if we hadn't killed them tonight, they would have killed thousands more. I promise you that. They had to be stopped."

"I know. They were killers—callous murderers. I just feel sick."

"You kill fish. The fish didn't kill your family and friends."

"Well, true. I just…" Trenton stumbles over his words. "I was in here with Jackson. The other minks were spread out between the parents' room and Russell's room next door. Russell's door was closed, so the minks had to crawl along the outside of the house to get in. After my team and I finished with Jackson, I could hear Russell putting up a fight in there. I thought he was killing all our friends and that he might run out of the room and out to the farm. Maybe attack all of you. I was just so scared. I understand that the Petersons needed to be stopped. I wanted them to be stopped. I just wish I didn't have to be the one to do it."

Vincent puts his paws on his brother reassuringly. "Trenton, I'm sorry. I wish I could have been here, but I had to help free the other minks, and I couldn't let Persimmon and her team know about this part of our plan. You know that if we had waited until tomorrow, the Petersons would have come looking for all of the minks and trapped them again, only to kill them. It had to be tonight. I'm sorry you had to be the one to do this. If I could have done it myself, believe me, I would have. You're the only one I trusted to do it right. And you did. You stopped the massacres. They'll never kill another mink again."

Trenton looks hopeful. "So the minks all got away? You freed them?"

"Yes. *We* freed them."

"But how do you know Persimmon and her team won't find out about the Petersons?"

"Everyone wants to get as far away from here as possible," Vincent explains. "They're fearful of what will happen when the humans wake up. She already said they're leaving immediately for their next mission." Vincent looks at his weary brother and suddenly remembers. "Trenton, Mother's alive."

"What?!" Trenton sits up and grabs his brother with glee. He finally seems happy. "How? Where is she?"

"She's back at the base camp by now. I told her you'd meet her there."

Trenton sits back against the wall. He closes his eyes. He smiles. "That's the greatest news I've ever heard. Mother's alive." Trenton's blissful gaze turns to concern. "Wait, you didn't tell her about what I did tonight, did you?"

"No, no," Vincent reassures him. "If you don't want her knowing your part, I won't reveal it. I may not tell her we killed them at all. I don't know how she'd react. And just so you know, if you still feel sick over taking the Petersons' lives, they planned to kill her. Mom told me that this last mating season she refused to breed with the male mink they put in the cage with her. He fought with her and tore her up pretty badly, but she staved him off. Since she wouldn't produce any more kits, those savages decided to murder her during the next massacre." Vincent pats his fatigued brother lovingly. "Trenton, go wash off that blood in the stream, and then go see her. You've done enough for one night. Oh, and do not let anything slip about the Petersons to anyone on Persimmon's team."

"Aren't you coming back?" Trenton inquires.

Vincent sighs. "No, I have much to do this morning before we can leave this part of the forest forever. I need to get a team together to look for the minks who ran into the woods. But first, I need to deal with those Rottweilers."

"I thought you said they'd die from eating those poisonous mushrooms."

"They will. They're probably dead already. That part of the plan worked fine. As I suspected, the raccoons and the rest of the team have no idea of the difference between the orange mushrooms that make you sick and the ones that kill you. But humans are going to find the dogs' bodies and that's not the story I want to tell." Vincent has a gleam in his eye. He's proud of himself. "I'm going to cover up all the vomit and scratch apart those dogs just like you did with the Petersons. Because here's the thing—when the family and the dogs are found dead, the humans who discover them are going to assume it was other humans who freed our fellow minks and that they killed the dogs and the Petersons, but I want to send a very clear message that it was minks who did it. That's why I told you to scratch the humans so obviously. I don't want there to be any misunderstanding. When they look back on this night, I want the humans to know that we fought back. I want humans to live in fear of us."

Trenton stares at his brother. He doesn't like this side of Vincent. He had the same malicious expression—the same vicious tone—when he suggested leaving Grumbles to die in the snow and when he came up with the plan to kill the Petersons in the first place. Is Vincent enjoying this?

Vincent can sense that his brother is uncomfortable. He helps Trenton up and declares warmly, "I know you don't want to kill anymore. That's just not the type of mink you are. And I know doing what you did to these humans greatly upset you. I won't ever ask you to do anything like this again."

"You won't have to," Trenton replies, confused. "The Petersons are dead. It's over."

Vincent looks up at the dead human on the bed. He grins. "No, my brother. For me, it's only just begun."

32

THEY'RE ALL SO happy! Persimmon beams with pride as she watches the joyful reunions between baby minks and their mothers at the base camp. "Mommy!" The young minks run into their mothers' embrace. "My kit!" The blissful looks on their faces are enough to melt her heart. Brothers and sisters also reunite after thinking they'd never see one another again. Families are coming back together and Persimmon couldn't be more proud to have helped make this jubilant day finally happen.

Derpoke saunters over to the pleased raccoon, who hugs him cheerfully. "Look at this, Derpoke! Isn't it wonderful?"

"It really is," Derpoke agrees. "It almost makes me want to run back to Oak Tree Forest to give my own mother a hug."

Persimmon scratches his head affectionately. "Sometimes I feel like *I'm* your mother. I certainly feel protective of you like a momma opossum."

Derpoke smiles on the outside but frowns on the inside. *My mother? Ugh.* He changes the subject before she catches on to his disappointment. "You did an amazing job tonight, Persimmon. You handled every problem masterfully. As for me, I wanted to apologize for losing control of the minks. They were just coming so fast. I got in over my head. I'm sorry."

Persimmon pats him on the back. "Derpoke, my friend, don't be silly. You're always such a worry bug but you were fantastic tonight. Besides, we can talk strategy later. This is a time for celebration. Look how happy they are. They're free, and we helped achieve that."

Derpoke peers out at the sea of cheerful minks. He makes a concerted effort to cast aside his usual anxieties and share in their merriment. And it works. A sense of elation fills him. The team really did accomplish something remarkable. Why not let himself revel in that?

Meanwhile, fifty trees away, Tucker and Chloe are snuggled high up in the trunk of a tree. Bruiser and Drig stand guard at the base of the trunk in case any stray minks decide to start trouble. Tucker huddles close to his loved one as she sleeps. Every now and then she awakes from a nightmare, but Tucker is right there to comfort her. She groans in pain before she drifts back to slumber. With every groan, Tucker becomes more and more resentful of the minks. *How dare they attack my Sweet Pea after all that we did for them? Not only are these rescue missions dangerous, but the creatures we save don't even appreciate it!*

He sits there stewing. He's exhausted but can't sleep—not with Chloe so badly damaged. *She's going to make it. She has to make it. There are still so many things we have planned together.*

Back at the base camp, Rawly weaves through the mass of minks. The little critters all seem in awe of him, and they thank him as he passes by. Rawly nods, stopping every now and then to see if anyone needs assistance. If they do, he waves over one of the other raccoons or one of the minks from the rescue team to tend to the injured animal. Rawly loves this—the gratitude, the prestige, the celebrity of it all. *All these minks were going to be killed, and we saved them. Amazing. I don't know why I gave Persimmon such a hard time about helping with these rescue missions; I was made for this! What a thrill!*

"Rawly." A familiar voice calls out to the proud raccoon. He looks around at the minks milling about. There are so many of them but none seem to be beckoning him.

"Rawly." There it is again. Rawly realizes the voice is coming from the darkness of the forest around the base camp.

He moves closer to the sound. "Who is that? Come out into the clearing."

Without revealing himself, Vincent whispers softly from behind a tree. "It's me, Vincent. I want to speak with you. Come into the woods, but try to be discreet."

Rawly hesitates for a moment. *What is this little mink up to? Why's he being so secretive?* The raccoon is intrigued, though, so he surveys the base camp to make sure that no one is watching, and after deciding that the coast is clear, sneaks into the woods.

The dark closes around Rawly. A few feet away, Vincent reveals himself from behind a large tree. His fur is wet, giving his already shadowy appearance a sleeker sheen. A musty smell emanates from his damp body. Rawly is disconcerted by the mink's demeanor. There's a nefarious air about him that Rawly never noticed before. Vincent continues to speak in hushed tones. "Follow me. I don't want anyone hearing our conversation."

Rawly becomes even more alarmed. *Is this a trap? Why is he drawing me farther into the forest?... Oh, don't be ridiculous. Why would it be a trap? We just saved all of his mink friends... He's definitely up to something, though.* Rawly is concerned, but he knows he'll look weak if he refuses. He's not about to let a minuscule mink think he intimidated a raccoon.

Rawly follows Vincent deeper into the forest, keeping his guard up in case he is suddenly surrounded by ravenous minks.

After trekking far enough away that the chatter from the base camp is a mere murmur, Vincent stops and turns to the tense raccoon. "Thank you for meeting with me, Rawly." Vincent reaches out to pat the raccoon on the back. Rawly flinches and immediately regrets revealing that his nerves are on end. Vincent notices but decides to ignore it so as not to embarrass the proud raccoon. Vincent does, however, find it interesting that this brawny creature, who is three times his size, feels threatened by him. The savvy mink decides to put Rawly at ease.

"Rawly, I wanted to commend you on your impressive leadership skills. I see how loyal your troops are to you, and tonight you proved why."

Rawly stands up straighter. He lets out a soft sigh. It's remarkable how well flattery can ease someone's tension.

Vincent continues. "Tonight you saved the lives of thousands of minks. We will be forever grateful to you."

Rawly eats up the ego-boost. "No need to thank us. It was the right thing to do. I can't stand to see the way those humans were mistreating you all. I'd storm that place again in a heartbeat."

Vincent's ears perk up. "I'm very pleased to hear you say that. In fact, that's what I wanted to discuss with you. I feel a kinship with you, Rawly. I can tell that you dislike the humans as much as I do. Am I correct in that assumption?"

Rawly scowls. "Can't stand them."

Vincent grins and slides in closer. He looks exhausted but focused. "We've saved my fellow minks here, but there are many other fur farms in the area with thousands of other minks trapped and awaiting death. I would never be able to forgive myself if I just ran away, leaving them to die. So I'm getting together a crew to raid those farms and free all these other minks as soon as possible."

Rawly is surprised. "I thought you were taking the freed minks downriver."

"Yes, that is still happening. I assigned a few trusty companions to lead them as far away from here as possible. And the minks who are too injured to make the journey will be set up along the riverbank. But that's just part of the plan. I also have some brave recruits who are willing to join me in rescuing other captive minks at these nearby fur farms."

"And that's the part you neglected to mention to Persimmon," Rawly challenges.

"Not completely true. You're right that she doesn't know I'm actually following through with these other rescues, but I did tell her I was hoping to do them. Instead of offering to help, though, she gave me a big lecture about all the risks involved. She thinks the humans will be on alert after the mission we just pulled off here, and that it's too dangerous if they know we're coming." Vincent grits his teeth. "Too dangerous?! Rawly, I won't allow thousands of minks to perish just because a few humans might try to fight back." Vincent digs his claws into the ground, crushing the dirt below. "I'm breaking my fellow minks out of those cages no matter what. I dare humans to get in the way."

Rawly's eyes pop open. He's never heard another creature—especially such a small one—be so bold, so confident in the face of human tyranny. *If only Persimmon talked like that, we'd be unstoppable.*

Rawly replies, invigorated. "Whew! You've got moxie, Vincent. I like it. But why are you telling *me* all of this?"

"I'm glad you asked," Vincent says coolly. This conversation is flowing just as he had intended. "Since Persimmon won't help me, I thought I could turn to you... and more specifically, your troops. I know you are loyal to her, so I would never ask you to leave The Uncaged Alliance yourself. That said, without tipping off Persimmon, do you think you could spare maybe two or three of your raccoon troops to help me finish the job we started here?"

Rawly's hurt that Vincent didn't invite him to join his crew. He wouldn't abandon Persimmon, but he would like to at least be asked. Vincent knows this, but he can't risk the possibility that Rawly would try to join his team. Rawly's strong and motivated, but he's also a loose cannon who's under the mistaken impression that he is an effective leader. Vincent doesn't need a raccoon with bloated ambitions; he needs raccoons who will follow orders and get the job done. Rawly's troops are malleable and trained—the perfect combination.

"Hmm. Your enthusiasm is almost enough to make me want to join your crew myself." Rawly pauses, hoping Vincent will take the bait and beg him to join his crew. Vincent does not. He stares at Rawly silently, calling his bluff. Rawly is annoyed—his ego bruised—so he decides to muddy things up a bit. "You're right. I couldn't desert The Uncaged Alliance. I'm too important to the operation. And not just me, *all* raccoons are invaluable to these missions. It would really hinder our next rescue to lose any."

Vincent expected Rawly to play hardball, which is why he prepared a rousing speech for just this moment. "Rawly, I know you're in a tight spot here. Both Persimmon and I can't succeed without you. On my end, I need clever raccoons with dexterous paws—like yourself—to rescue the minks in these other fur farms. And because you're a fearless visionary, I know that the threat of humans fighting back isn't enough to deter you from doing the right thing by saving these other minks. That said, because you're an invaluable warrior, you're absolutely right, Persimmon can't pull off her future rescues without you, either. Ultimately, you're torn between two sides that desperately need your help."

Rawly nods to himself. He's eating up every word of this, as Vincent knew he would. Rawly could listen all day to someone complimenting his great qualities.

Vincent licks his chipped tooth. He gets a kick out of this scheming. "But… here's the thing. If you lend me some of your troops, you're the hero for both of us. For my side, you can continue your legacy of bravery vicariously through your raccoons, who will help me free more minks. And for Persimmon, she gets to have you by her side directly to help free other creatures elsewhere. It's a win-win."

Rawly's eyes light up. He salivates. "You make some excellent points. I *am* a fearless visionary, but I am also an indispensable warrior. Huh." He ponders this for a moment, then says, "I've made my decision. I will allow you to have two of my troops. But if we're being honest here, you're going to need more than two raccoons to free thousands of minks at multiple locations."

"Yes, I am aware of that. My intention is to recruit more raccoons along the way. And we'll have much more luck doing so if we already have some on our side."

Rawly nods, impressed. "Wow, looks like you got every angle figured out." Rawly is inspired by Vincent's talent for scheming so he wants to show off that he can do some of his own. "Don't worry about Persimmon. I'll get you those raccoons without her knowing the wiser."

Vincent nods. "I knew you were the raccoon for the job."

Rawly rushes off, but before he has gone too far, he halts and turns around. "Hey, one last thing. Why are you all wet?"

Vincent conjures up a quick lie. "Long night. I've been looking everywhere for escaped minks who ran astray. All through the woods, in the river, wherever I thought they might be. I found a few and sent them to the base camp. It actually felt great to take a dip in the water after the stressful night we've had."

Satisfied, Rawly turns and darts back to the base camp. Vincent sits for a moment. *If Rawly knew the truth, how would he react?* A half hour ago, Vincent was splattered with the blood of Mando and Diablo. *Would he think it barbaric or would he be impressed?* Vincent contemplates that for a second before deciding. *He'd be impressed. Because he understands. You can't reason with these humans; they have to be stopped. How do you reason with an animal who feels no remorse for hacking apart thousands of other innocent animals simply to wear their fur? You can't...* Vincent shakes his head in disgust. *You don't.*

33

"CHLOE, YOU ALMOST died!" Tucker is frantic. He paces back and forth on a tree branch as the couple argues.

Chloe stumbles to get up. Her wounds have closed slightly, but in the daylight it's all the more obvious how many deep bite marks cover her body. "Tucker, just because I got hurt doesn't mean I should quit."

"Hurt? You were almost eaten." Tucker stops in front of his companion. "Sweet Pea, be reasonable. We can stay in this tree until you've healed. The Petersons won't be looking for us. We'll be safe here."

Chloe caresses Tucker's ear. "Pupsy, I'm all right. I..."

"Are you? You can barely stand."

"Okay, yes, I'm badly injured. But Bruiser said I could rest on his back during the journey for as long as I needed to. By the time we are ready to attempt our next rescue I'll be as good as new."

Tucker groans loudly. He's not getting through to her. "What am I supposed to do if next time you're actually killed? Is this really worth it to you? One of us dying?"

Chloe looks Tucker in the eyes, warmly. "Pupsy, I would be devastated if I lost you. You know that. Yes, these missions are dangerous, but it's absolutely worth the risk to help these animals."

Tucker scoffs. "You think this is thrilling. You should have seen the excited look on your face leading up to the rescue. I'm not cut out for this. I was scared and anxious the whole time. If it's not dogs running after me, it's minks trying to eat you. I don't want to live this life. I want to run around in trees and eat nuts and berries with you."

Chloe sighs. She starts crawling slowly down the tree trunk, trying to hide the pain as she moves her aching limbs. "These animals need our help. How could you enjoy that type of carefree life knowing that all of these other animals are out there suffering?"

Tucker hops onto the branch adjacent to her and then crawls down below to monitor her climbing. He can tell she's fighting through the pain to act tough and he doesn't want her losing her balance. "But animals are probably suffering everywhere. This feels like just the beginning. Who knows what other horrible things we'll find humans doing to other beings—are we going to save them all?"

Chloe stops descending and looks down at him. "We can try."

Tucker climbs to her level. "This is too risky. I won't watch you die."

"What are you saying? You're going to quit?"

"Maybe," Tucker threatens.

Chloe lowers herself onto the nearest branch. She motions for Tucker to come closer. He's reluctant, so she moves nearer to him instead. "Pupsy, I want to spend my life with you. I want us to do this together."

"You want me to follow you no matter how much it puts our lives at risk."

"No, I want you to *want* to help these other animals. That's the kind of squirrel I fell in love with."

Tucker's mouth gapes open. That tore at his heart. He glares at her. "I'm sorry to disappoint you." Tucker calls down to Drig on the ground below. "Can you guide Chloe down the tree? She's having some trouble." Tucker turns to Chloe and grits his teeth. "I'm not quite strong enough to catch you if you fall either. Just one more way I'm inadequate."

Tucker races off into the treetops before Chloe can say anything. She'd rush after him if she weren't hurt so badly. She feels terrible. She does love him, so very much. That last remark just came out wrong. *Should I quit? Is this really too hazardous for us?... But these animals need our help. Why can't Tucker see that? Why doesn't he care more?*

Drig makes his way up to the branch on which Chloe is perched. "You need my help getting down?"

"I'm fine. Just stay close in case I start to lose my grip."

Chloe starts lowering herself down the tree. She is in pain and her muscles shake as she attempts to climb down.

Drig speaks up. "Chloe, I can tell you're independent and I respect that. But in the interest of time, can you just let me carry you down?"

Chloe sighs. She knows he's right. She latches onto his back and Drig rappels down the tree trunk toward Bruiser, who is waiting at the bottom.

Once they reach the ground, Drig says, "I'm going to check and see if the others are ready to get going."

Bruiser nods and Drig rushes off toward the base camp. Bruiser turns to the sullen squirrel. "How ya feelin'?"

Chloe is in low spirits. "I'll heal."

Bruiser can see that she's not her usual peppy self. "You know, usually your smile shines so bright I can barely look straight at ya."

Chloe breaks into a slight smile at the compliment. "Sorry to be so down. I just said something truly insensitive to Tucker, and I feel awful about it." She pauses for a moment, then asks, "Bruiser, do you think it's too dangerous for us to try to save these animals' lives?"

"Are you askin' 'cause you got all bit up?"

"I'm asking because I don't want to lose the love of my life. Tucker thinks that we should quit the team."

"Hmm. Seems more dangerous for me to get in between a feudin' couple." Bruiser grins. "To be honest, I'm a bit biased, due to my past and all. I thought I had it bad, but then I saw what humans did to these minks. Shameful. If there are more animals out there suffering like this—and I know there are—then I don't know nuthin' more important than to find 'em and free 'em."

"I feel the exact same way. But Tucker just wants us to go off and eat acorns all day. I don't know how to get him to care more."

Bruiser sits down beside Chloe. "I don't know if ya can make someone care more, but I know he cares 'bout you. Maybe that'll be enough. And I know he's worried 'bout your safety. From the moment you got attacked, he didn't let go of ya. Made me wish I had my own Sweet Pea."

Chloe looks up into the trees where Tucker ran off. She ponders this for a moment. "Thanks for listening, Bruiser."

"You bet."

∗   ∗   ∗

The minks at the base camp are getting restless. The sun is up and they're ready to move on. This is their first taste of freedom and they don't want to hang around a boring clearing in the woods that's overflowing with other agitated minks. Some have even begun stepping away in small packs. Persimmon is doing her best to keep them in line, but the minks are tired, hungry, thirsty—and anxious to begin their new lives.

Persimmon hurries over to a group that is just beginning to move into the forest. "Excuse me. Hello?" The minks turn toward her. "You all should stay around the base camp until Vincent returns. He's going to lead you to your new home."

"We're starving," one of the minks responds. "The food ran out here, so we're heading down to the river."

"I understand that you're hungry, but we need to keep everyone in this area so that no one gets left behind."

Rawly comes bounding over to Persimmon and the minks. "Persimmon, can I talk with you for a moment?"

Persimmon looks at the minks. She doesn't want them to leave.

"It's urgent," Rawly insists.

Persimmon addresses the minks. "Please just stay here a little longer. Vincent should be back any time now." She walks a few paces away with Rawly.

"Our team really should get going," Rawly insists. "The sun is up and you know as well as I do that the Petersons have most likely discovered that their prized creatures are all missing. We do not want to be here when they come looking for them."

"We can't just leave them here all disorganized," Persimmon counters. "We need to wait until Vincent arrives and leads them downriver. We didn't go through all that trouble to rescue them just to..."

Before she can finish, Linder and Dusty come walking up.

Linder interrupts her. "Persimmon? Rawly? May we have a word with you?"

"We're kind of in the middle of something," Persimmon replies impatiently. "Can it wait?"

"It's important," Dusty urges.

Persimmon laughs to herself, feeling a little overwhelmed. "Goodness, never a dull moment around here. Is everything alright?"

"Well, I don't know how to say this, but..." Linder pauses, filled with trepidation. "I know The Uncaged Alliance is heading off beyond Oak Tree Forest, and well, this is our home. It was a real honor going on this mission with you and we're glad we saved all these animals, but..."

Rawly cuts him off. "Hold on. Are you quitting?"

Linder stammers. "We... it's just..."

Rawly doesn't let him finish. "I can't believe you two. We're a team. You don't just quit on your team."

Dusty's ears flop down in fright. "Rawly, we didn't join the team thinking we'd be doing this for the rest of our lives. We like it here in the forest. We're not quitting, we're..."

Rawly gets in Dusty's face, standing on his hind legs and hovering as close as he can to intimidate him. "You *are* quitting. You saw how these humans treated the minks. That kind of thing is going on everywhere, and you're just going to let it happen? I can't stand..."

Persimmon puts her paw on Rawly's chest, pushing him back. "Rawly, it's fine. They did a remarkable job helping out. I don't expect anyone to leave his or her home to join our team forever." She turns to the two cowering raccoons. "We were lucky to have you two for this mission. I thank you for all you did tonight."

"You're going to let them off just like that?" Rawly snaps.

"Let them off?" Persimmon retorts. "They did us a favor."

Rawly hisses at them. "Cowards."

Now Persimmon gets in Rawly's face. "Enough! Every member of The Uncaged Alliance is free to leave whenever he or she would like, and they surely will not be berated after putting their lives on the line like these two did."

"Thank you, Persimmon," Dusty replies humbly. He looks at Rawly. "Rawly, I'm sorry. We're exhausted."

Rawly doesn't even look at the two exiting raccoons. He walks away, disgusted.

Dusty calls after him, "Oak Tree Forest is our home. Our families are here."

Rawly is too far away to hear.

Persimmon addresses the two raccoons. "Don't pay any attention to him. He's the grumpiest raccoon I know. If you ever change your minds, you are free to look for us. I don't know where we'll be, but I can assure you that we'll be happy to have you as part of the team again. Until then, good luck." She pauses and then quickly adds, "Can you two do me one last favor?"

Dusty and Linder nod.

"We have to get going, so can you try to keep all the minks in order until Vincent gets here? He should be arriving soon."

"You can count on us," Dusty exclaims.

Persimmon smiles and then quickly cuts her way through the minks milling about the base camp. She looks around, searching for someone. She catches the eye of Margeaux and heads straight for her. "Margeaux, hello again."

Margeaux cheers up at the sight of the friendly raccoon. "My dear Persimmon. I thought you had gone."

"Soon. Actually, that's why I wanted to talk with you. Vincent hasn't shown up at the base camp yet. I was hoping to make sure everyone got off safely and to say goodbye to him, but it looks like I won't get the chance."

"I'd be happy to pass the message along to him." Margeaux leans in and asks with apprehension. "Do you think he's all right?"

"Yes, I wouldn't worry." Persimmon pats Margeaux's paw. "I'm sure he's fine. He's out rounding up minks who ran astray. Knowing him, he won't give up until every last one is accounted for."

"Oh, that's what Trenton was just doing as well. Have you met my other son Trenton?"

Margeaux gently pulls on the tail of a mink who is standing next to her, chatting with another mink, and facing away from the two ladies. Trenton turns around, freezing when he realizes he's face-to-face with Persimmon—the one animal in the forest he's supposed to avoid. He tries his best to act natural, but his paws begin to shake. *Oh no. Don't say anything stupid. Just keep calm.* His first instinct is to run away, but he holds his ground, trying not to look suspicious—which makes him feel all the more so.

Persimmon is surprised. "No, I haven't met him yet. That's incredible. You have another son who survived the fur farm. I had no idea." She turns her attention to Trenton. "Very nice to meet you." She looks at Trenton for a moment with a quizzical expression. Trenton knows she's going to ask why Vincent never mentioned having a brother. He has to head her off before she does.

Trenton blurts out, "You're probably wondering where I got all these scars."

"No, no. I would never be so rude. I was actually wondering..."

Trenton cuts her off. "It's all right. I know that's what everyone thinks when they look at me. Vincent and I went back to try and rescue our mother and the other minks, but Mando and Diablo ambushed us."

"Oh, really." Persimmon looks confused. "Vincent said that everyone except him was killed on that mission."

Trenton's paws begin to shake more intensely. His breathing quickens. *Please don't figure me out. Please don't figure me out.* He presses his paws to the ground, hoping to mask the trembling. "Yes, on that mission none of the minks survived except Vincent. Sorry I'm tired, so I'm not quite clear-headed. What I meant was that Vincent and I both went on rescue missions to the farm separately. I went once long before he did with other minks to try and save Vincent and my family." Trenton rambles on nervously. "The way Vincent is, even after he saw what those Rottweilers did to me, he still went back to try and free the other minks. I'm ashamed to say that I didn't go with him that time. My reflexes are slower since the attack, and, as you can see, I'm blind in one eye."

Persimmon rests her paw on Trenton's back, reassuring him. "You shouldn't be ashamed at all. It was brave of you to go back in the first place."

"I guess bravery runs in the family," Trenton remarks good-naturedly, trying to keep things light. He wants nothing more than to get away from Persimmon before he slips up again. He gazes up at the sky. "Wow, the sun's shining pretty brightly. We should probably get going, right?"

Persimmon agrees. "Yes, my team needs to move on and you minks need to start your journey down the river. We all have to get out of here to avoid any run-ins with the Petersons." Trenton cringes at hearing the name. He bites his tongue so he doesn't make the mistake of mentioning the Petersons' gory demise.

Persimmon embraces Margeaux, bidding her farewell. Trenton is relieved that this chance meeting is finally ending. His jaw is clenched and his stomach is in knots.

Persimmon turns to Trenton and pats him on the back. "Please say goodbye to Vincent for me, and congratulate him on a job well done."

Trenton relaxes. He has averted disaster.

At that very moment, Vincent is watching Persimmon talk with Trenton and his mother, far enough away that he can't be detected and hidden in the shadow of a fallen tree trunk. Dusty and Linder stand at attention, covered by the same shadow. Vincent is speaking with them, but he doesn't take his eyes off of Persimmon.

"Did Persimmon catch on that Rawly was in on it?" Vincent inquires.

"No," Dusty responds. "Rawly played it off really well. I almost thought he was actually upset with us."

"Good." Vincent lays out the plan. "Dusty, round up the first group. Once you see Persimmon exit the area, start leading them to the river." Dusty nods and rushes out into the open toward the minks. "Linder, round up the second group and follow right after Dusty."

Linder nods and heads off in the same direction as Dusty.

Vincent sees the conversation between Persimmon and his family ending. Persimmon walks away, and once she's a few feet from them, Trenton hobbles in the opposite direction and surreptitiously enters the woods.

Trenton meekly tiptoes over to Vincent. His paws are still shaking. "Did you see the whole thing?"

"Yes," Vincent replies sourly.

"Are you angry with me?"

Vincent turns and looks at his brother tensely. "Did you tell her anything?"

"No. She was really suspicious, but I just lied my way out of it. It wasn't my fault. Mom introduced us. I had no idea Persimmon was around or I would have gotten out of there."

Vincent lets that sink in for a moment, then finally says, "It's fine, Smickety. I'm not angry."

Trenton sighs in relief. The last thing he wants is to upset his brother.

Vincent observes Persimmon as she walks over to Derpoke, Scraps and Claudette, while he continues his conversation with Trenton. "What did she want?"

"She was looking for you, actually. She wanted to say goodbye. Are you avoiding her because you're worried about slipping up as well?"

"No," Vincent answers bluntly. He does not elaborate.

Trenton explains. "She seemed pretty disappointed that she might never see you again."

"If she knew what we had been up to, what we were about to do, I have a feeling she'd be perfectly happy never seeing me again." The way Vincent says this, he seems hurt by the notion.

Trenton sees his chance to talk his brother out of all the sordid plans he has hinted at involving the other fur farm owners. "Do you think maybe we're going too far?"

Vincent shoots his brother a disdainful look. "No. There's only one way to stop these humans. You know that, Trenton. They're just going to keep mercilessly killing thousands and thousands of minks until we put an end to it... an end to *them*. How many times do I have to keep making that same point?"

Vincent stares at his brother, waiting for a response. Trenton replies timidly, "I'm sorry. I know."

"I need your help on this, Trenton," Vincent states. "More importantly, your support. I'm trying to save our fellow minks' lives, and we're the only ones willing to do what it takes to put an end to these massacres forever." Vincent is clearly upset. He looks back at Persimmon and her team as they disappear behind a tree. "I just wish she understood all that," he whispers, almost to himself.

Vincent checks to see if he can glimpse Persimmon and her friends one more time. No, she's gone. And he will most likely never see her again. It's now up to him to lead these rescue missions—to free his brethren from this torture. He's their only hope, and he knows that all too well.

Vincent snaps out of his dour mood and jumps into gear. "Come on, we have a lot of work to do."

34

A WEEK HAS gone by. The team ventured far enough away from the Petersons' fur farm that they'd be safe, but eventually their weary little legs would take them no farther, so they found a quiet spot, deep in the woods, in which to rest. And goodness, did they ever need the rest. The excitement and stress of the rescue mission took such a toll on them that once they finally stopped moving, they practically collapsed. Everyone slept through the entire first day and night.

After catching up on their sleep, they spent the rest of the week relaxing, eating and chatting. Bruiser and Scraps had the most fun. Scraps is endlessly thrilled about getting to play with a dog—an animal he had been taught to be so cautious of growing up—and now he takes rides on the "ferocious" beast's back, nips at his legs, and plays hide-and-seek with him among the trees. Likewise, Bruiser couldn't be happier to buddy up to the little guy. He was so lonely chained up in that backyard, hoping Aidan would come out to play, and now he has a friend who never tires of his company.

Sadly, Chloe and Tucker didn't speak the entire week. Tucker spent most of the time high up in a tree, heartbroken. He didn't feel like interacting with anyone, especially Chloe. She could tell that he needed some time to himself, so she left him alone, but she wanted very much to go snuggle up to him. Since they first got together, they have barely spent a moment apart, and it worries her that she doesn't know how to resolve this issue. *If I stay with The Uncaged Alliance, he won't forgive me. If I leave the team and go off with him, I won't be able to forgive* myself.

Chloe's health, at least, has been gradually improving. She has made a point to exercise her muscles and be as active as possible in order to regain her strength. She was incredibly fit before the mink attack and wants to be in optimal condition for the next rescue mission.

The high point of the week for Persimmon was Claudette agreeing to join the team's vow not to eat any animals. As the team was chowing down together one day, Claudette exclaimed how excited she was about her decision. "You know, I've always felt guilty about devouring crayfish, frogs, all living creatures. Every time I was about to bite into one of them, they seemed so frightened. Poor critters. And now I feel so relieved—I won't have to feel guilty whenever I have a meal." Claudette pops a blackberry in her mouth with delight. She talks with her mouth full. "What's interesting is that it never occurred to me that it was an option *not* to eat other animals. When I was growing up, everyone around me had no problem doing it, so I just followed their lead. I'm glad I met you, Persimmon. You gave me that extra nudge I needed to make the change."

"Claudette, you're my new favorite raccoon," Persimmon beams.

"Hey, I thought *I* was your favorite raccoon," Scraps pretend-gripes.

"Looks like you're going to have to do something spectacular to win me over again, little brother," Persimmon teases.

Rawly saunters over and pats Persimmon and Claudette on the back condescendingly. "I'm ecstatic that you two are getting along so well. My old friend, Persimmon, and my irresistible love, Claudette." Rawly showers his girlfriend's face with kisses but she closes her eyes and pulls away, knowing from the tone of his voice that he's about to deliver a snide remark. "You two females can eat your little berries. That leaves more fish for us males."

Derpoke, Scraps and Bruiser shoot Rawly a nasty look. He smirks, "Well, us *real* males."

Drig and Fisher scratch at the ground cheerfully. To add insult to injury, Rawly picks up one of the dead fish that he had gathered for himself and his two raccoon goons and swallows it. He slurps loudly to be extra annoying.

Persimmon rolls her eyes. "Right. Because snatching a scrawny crayfish from the water and ripping his little body apart makes you so tough."

"That's what raccoons do," Rawly counters. "We eat crayfish and water creatures. In case you forgot, that's how Fisher got his name. Oh, wait, let me guess: Next you're going to suggest Fisher change his name to Raspberry."

Drig and Fisher laugh way too hard for such an unfunny comment and Rawly guffaws, pleased with his own wit.

Persimmon calmly waits for them to cease their laughing fit, then remarks, "It's a choice, Rawly. Raccoons, opossums, dogs, humans and some other creatures can choose whether or not they want to eat other animals or eat vegetables, fruits and nuts. So, if it's a choice, why would you *choose* to kill another living creature?"

"Because they taste good," Rawly snaps back thoughtlessly.

"Thank you," Persimmon responds confidently. "You have just proven a very important point in front of everyone." Bruiser, Scraps, Derpoke, Claudette and Chloe listen intently. Persimmon seems poised to give Rawly a much-needed tongue lashing, and they can't wait to watch.

Persimmon's eyes are ablaze. She's fed up with Rawly's attitude. "You're so arrogant about your leadership skills, but here's the problem: You can't tell your team to risk their lives to save a group of animals one minute and then the next minute, in celebration, scarf down a different animal. It's hypocritical. And it's cruel."

Persimmon stares at Rawly, unafraid of anything he might throw at her. Rawly grits his teeth. He's seething and yet her logic is spot on. He asks sourly, "So, what are you going to do, kick me out again?"

"Kick you out? I've never kicked you out. You keep quitting, because you don't like to be told what to do. Rawly, I want your help. We *need* your help. You are a vital member of this team, but I can't have you questioning my decisions at every turn. During the planning stages of these missions, I have asked for everyone's input multiple times, but if we're in the middle of a rescue and I ask you to stop opening cages, do not fight me on it." Persimmon stomps her paw on the ground to drive her point home. Before Rawly can respond, she turns to Drig. "The same goes for you, Drig."

Drig looks stunned. "What? What did I do?"

Persimmon continues her diatribe. "You know what I'm talking about, Drig. When I come to you during a mission asking for your assistance, you do not need Rawly's permission. The fact that I'm instructing you to do something is reason enough to follow. Innocent minks could have died from you hesitating like that."

Persimmon makes eye contact with Rawly, Drig and Fisher. "I can't make any of you more compassionate. Ideally, everyone on this team should care enough about the suffering of other creatures that they wouldn't want to eat them, but I can't force you to stop. There's a little part of me that believes that one day you'll just get it. But listen closely." She pauses to make sure they're paying attention; at this point, all of the team's jaws have dropped open. "I will not stand for insubordination. When we're out on our missions, what I say goes. There are too many lives at stake for me to waste time arguing with you. Got it?"

Rawly, Drig and Fisher are momentarily shocked into silence. They were not expecting such a forceful lecture. The other team members assume Rawly will lash out with a hostile speech of his own, but instead, remarkably, he nods in agreement. "Got it." Persimmon stares at Drig and Fisher, making it clear that she expects a verbal confirmation from them as well. They say simultaneously, "Got it."

The team stands quietly. No one moves. The mood is tense. Derpoke, Bruiser, Claudette, Scraps and Chloe try to keep from smiling. They have immensely enjoyed seeing the three macho raccoons thoroughly and rightfully embarrassed.

35

PERSIMMON AND DERPOKE relax on a bed of grass. A soothing breeze gently caresses their fur. Their legs rest by their sides as they lie on their backs, enjoying the sunny day and gorgeous blue sky. Their paws and mouth are stained with sweet blackberry juice. This is comfort at its best.

Derpoke turns to Persimmon. He looks like he's about to say something, but he just gazes back up at the sky and sighs. He looks back at Persimmon, but still doesn't speak. Persimmon can tell there's something on her best friend's mind. "Yes?"

"I was… I don't want to bother you if you're resting."

Persimmon keeps her eyes closed, soaking up the warm sun. "What's on your mind, my friend?"

"Do you ever think about Gilby?" Derpoke asks sullenly.

Persimmon is taken off guard by his bringing up such a painful memory during such a peaceful moment. "Um… yes, I do." She seems hesitant to divulge any more than that.

Derpoke can tell she isn't exactly in the mood to discuss something so heavy. "Never mind. I know it's a depressing subject."

"No, it's alright." She reaches over to him and pats him on the stomach. "We can talk about it if you'd like. What makes you ask?"

"I just... I want to feel happy. It's such a lovely day. Cool breeze. Soft grass. Fresh air. I'm here with you. But just when I think I'm enjoying myself, I feel sick in my heart that Calvin never got to enjoy anything so grand."

"Ah." Persimmon understands. She lets out a solemn sigh. "I know how you feel. Gilby, Calvin, Berry—all the calves are never far from my thoughts. Sometimes I even wish I could stop thinking about them, but then I feel guilty about wanting to forget them. And, of course, I don't really want to forget them. What I want is to find a way to forgive myself for not saving them."

Derpoke slumps over on his side, dejected. "I think back on that situation with the calves and I don't know what we could have done differently to save them. Even if we had freed them earlier, where would they have hidden?" Derpoke huffs into the grass beside him. "It feels hopeless. And now there are more innocent, gentle calves locked in those filthy stalls waiting to be slaughtered." Derpoke looks as though he is carrying the weight of the world on his back, pressing him down, crushing him.

"I know. It eats at me, too." Persimmon sighs, burdened by the same crippling weight. "With all the horror we've seen inflicted on these poor creatures, I feel ashamed I didn't start trying to save them sooner. How many years did I frivolously play in the forest while countless creatures were being massacred?"

"Do you think we're terrible for leading such idle lives while they were suffering?" Derpoke's fuzzy face is riddled with guilt.

"No, my friend. And I'll explain why." Persimmon rolls onto her side to face her distressed companion. She takes hold of one of his paws. "We are not terrible, because the moment we found out what these creatures were going through, we did something about it. If we had just gone back to playing, *that* would make us terrible. I think our elders thought they were keeping us safe by sheltering us from human cruelty, but really that ignorance was just another form of apathy. So here's the key: The thing that keeps me from crumbling into a despondent gloom is our rescue missions. We just saved thousands of lives at the mink farm. And we're going to save thousands more wherever we end up next. Just focus on that. One day we'll figure out how to go back and save those calves, but for now, we're saving other animals. That's all we can ask of ourselves."

That thought comforts Derpoke—or maybe it's the fact that Persimmon is holding his paw.

Persimmon sits up. "Seeing as how the joyful mood is already ruined, there's something that's been nagging at me for a while, and I wasn't sure how to bring it up."

Derpoke sits up as well. "If it's depressing, you've come to the right opossum."

Persimmon lets out a quiet laugh. "Fantastic." She takes a moment to ponder how to explain her quandary and then begins. "Seeing how the humans treated the calves was awful, and finding Bruiser in such a sickening state was heartbreaking, but it wasn't until I saw how those people treated the minks that my fears were solidified. Do you think humans really don't care about how much these animals suffer, or do you think they're oblivious to it?"

Derpoke ruminates for a bit, thinking back to all of the horrors they've seen perpetrated by humans, and then answers resolutely. "There's no doubt the humans know they are causing overwhelming suffering for these animals. The calves cried endlessly day and night. The minks even chewed off their own tails, they had gone so insane. And from everything I've heard about the way the calves and minks were slaughtered, the humans seemed to be unmoved by the animals' wailing appeals as they cut them up. You can't be oblivious to that."

"Yes," Persimmon responds. "I know the humans that are imprisoning and killing the animals are heartless, but I'm talking about the humans who want to eat calves and wear minks' fur. Do they know these animals suffer so extensively their entire lives?"

"Hmm," Derpoke thinks deeply. "I can't say for sure, but how else do they think the calves are housed and killed? Clearly, they're babies, so they don't die of old age. As for the minks, even the humans who don't actually kill the minks themselves know that they are being killed just for their fur. That is obviously a selfish and silly reason to take an animal's life. Why punish the minks just because your body is incapable of producing adequate amounts of hair to keep you warm? Or worse, because you think it's soft and looks fancy?"

Persimmon bites her lip. "So you seem pretty convinced that humans are consciously cruel."

"Yes," Derpoke answers without hesitation.

Persimmon grabs at the grass around her, fidgeting anxiously. "But then what about those humans who rescued the minks? Even if most humans are cruel, not all of them are."

"True." Derpoke seems more confident now, as if being forced to answer these questions has deepened his own beliefs about humans. "But do those same humans still eat other animals? Why save one creature and not the other?" Derpoke sits up straighter and animatedly makes his case. "I've seen humans be cuddly and loving with their dogs and cats, but then in the trash cans of those very same humans, I've found the flesh of other animals." Derpoke whips his tail on the ground. "Honestly, the more I think about your suggestion that we shouldn't eat animals, the more ashamed I am that I ever did."

"But that's part of the problem," Persimmon says, leaning in to Derpoke. "You didn't know. And you had never thought about it before. That's how our parents raised us, so we thought it was okay. Maybe it's the same for humans. Maybe once they find out what's really happening, they'll stop just like we did."

Derpoke shakes his head and crinkles his pink nose. "Persimmon, you give them too much credit. I think they know, and even if they didn't, how are *we* supposed to teach them?" Before Persimmon can answer, Derpoke continues. "Because I know you too well. You don't just want to save these animals; you want to teach the humans that what they're doing is wrong. Just like you educated everyone in The Uncaged Alliance."

Persimmon doesn't respond immediately. She scratches an itch in her grayish-brown fur, thinking. *He's right. I didn't even realize it, but that's what I really want to do. No matter how many minks we rescue, no matter how many calves we set free, humans are just going to keep shoving more animals into cages and killing them unless we change their minds about how very wrong it is. But how can our small band of idealists ever change the minds of millions—if not billions—of humans?*

Just then, Persimmon and Derpoke hear rustling in the bushes beside them and their ears perk up. Derpoke freezes and Persimmon steps in between him and the noise to protect her friend.

From the nearby brush, out pops a wobbly, tiny brown mink. It's Nibbin. His face lights up when he sees her. "Raccoon!"

Persimmon recognizes the little guy. "Well, hello. You helped me during the fur farm rescue. You're Nibbin, right?"

The minuscule mink hops over and excitedly hugs Persimmon's leg. "I found you! I've been searching forever, but I finally found you!" He taps his brownish-pink nose. "And I have this to thank."

Persimmon is perplexed. "What are you doing here? Is everything okay with the other minks?"

"Oh yes, they're all fine. Some went downriver. Some stayed by the river. And some went with Vincent. But I didn't want to go with them. I want to go with you."

Persimmon is alarmed. "What do you mean, some went with Vincent? He didn't lead the other minks downriver?"

The young mink answers innocently. "No, he went deeper into the woods with a group of minks... oh, and two raccoons from your team. I don't know where they went, though."

Persimmon looks over at Derpoke. "Interesting." She focuses back on the young mink with a friendly smile. "Nibbin, I very much appreciate you wanting to come with us, but I think you should be with your fellow minks. You're so young. You should be with your mother."

"She was killed by the Petersons." Persimmon's and Derpoke's hearts sink. One of the many tragedies of the Petersons' massacre: orphans. Nibbin continues. "That's why I want to join your team. I want to help other kits like me. I bet they're just as scared as I was, so I want to save them just like you saved me. I want to be brave."

"I'm very sorry about your mother," Persimmon replies tenderly. "What about the other minks, though? Can they take care of you?"

"I can take care of myself," Nibbin exclaims zestfully. "Remember, I helped round up all my fellow minks. Didn't I do a good job?"

"Well, yes, you did. You were very helpful. But you're practically a baby, and I don't know anything about minks."

"That's okay. Neither do I. I've been trapped in a cage all my life, so I have no idea what minks do in the wild. We can learn together."

Persimmon can't help but love the little guy. How can she say no to such an eager recruit? "Alright, fine."

Nibbin runs circles around their legs. "Yay! Yay!"

Derpoke seems amused and slightly uncomfortable. Persimmon tries to slow the hyper mink down. "Okay, okay. Calm yourself." Nibbin stops and looks up at Persimmon earnestly. "You can join the team, but you're in a training period. Which means you can witness our next rescue mission, but not actively participate in it. I can't have you getting hurt. How does that sound?"

Nibbin again starts running circles around their legs. "Yay!"

Derpoke grimaces at the peppy mink's victory dance. Persimmon scratches Derpoke's head fondly. "I guess we have a new team member. Come on, it's about time we started our new mission anyway."

36

IT'S DAYTIME, SO the team is resting in various trees and bushes. They have been journeying for about a week since they decided to resume their adventures. As usual, Derpoke and Scraps are curled up in the same den with Persimmon, but now Nibbin has joined the slumber party.

Nibbin begins to shake in his sleep and whimper unintelligibly. He's cuddled up to Persimmon, who wakes at the commotion. She looks down at the tiny brown mink, making sure he's safe.

"Everything okay?" Derpoke whispers.

Persimmon nods. "Yes, he's just having nightmares again. Poor little guy. Life in those cages was traumatizing for him." Persimmon softly caresses Nibbin's brown fur and he quiets down.

"I'm sure it's going to be a long time before any of those poor minks are able to overcome what was done to them in that fur farm—if ever," Derpoke remarks. "That's why I'm torn about the idea that Vincent's out there conducting other rescue missions. Do you really think that's why he's leading a group of minks into the forest?"

"I have no doubt," Persimmon replies. "At one point, Vincent asked me if The Uncaged Alliance could help him release the minks in the other farms, but after I made a case for how dangerous it would be, he agreed to only focus on the minks at the Peterson farm. Clearly that was a ruse to throw me off the trail."

"It *is* too dangerous," Derpoke agrees. "The humans will be on high alert now that we conducted this rescue. Why would he do something so risky?"

"He knows firsthand how horrendous life is in those cages," Persimmon answers. "He doesn't want his fellow minks to suffer even one more day, which of course, I understand. I want to help them, too. But it just isn't strategic. The only reason we succeeded in our mission at the Peterson fur farm was because the humans had no idea we were coming." Persimmon sighs. "I hope they are all okay. I fear they will not be."

"He even stole two of our team members to pull off this stunt," Derpoke adds.

Persimmon nods. "It would seem our mink friend is as wily as you had anticipated he might be. Speaking of that, I forgot to mention, I met Vincent's brother Trenton."

Derpoke looks confused. "I didn't even know he had a brother."

"Exactly. Vincent never said a word about it. And Trenton acted very odd during our encounter. I got this strange feeling he and Vincent were up to something. Now we know what."

Derpoke shakes his head disapprovingly. "Goodness me, minks are sneaky."

"Shh." Persimmon points to Nibbin. "He's part of the team now. You don't want to offend him."

"I'll change subjects then," Derpoke concedes. "I'd like to share my concern one more time about going into the city."

"Duly noted… again. However, I think it's our best bet to find our next rescue mission," Persimmon states. "As has been proven quite often lately, where there are humans, there are sure to be creatures being harmed."

Derpoke rests his head on his front paws. "Never was there a truer statement."

*   *   *

The team ventures through the forest at a steady pace—all excited to start a new rescue mission. Rawly, Claudette, Drig and Fisher are ahead, jogging to enhance their stamina. The others prefer chatting and playing as they stroll along. Bruiser and Scraps roughhouse as they always do on their walks in the woods, but this time Nibbin joins in. Small and remarkably swift, Nibbin weaves in and out of Bruiser's legs with Scraps chasing after him, tripping the large canine on occasion but all in good fun. Persimmon, Derpoke and Chloe walk along together, watching the merriment and making small talk.

The only team member not with them is Tucker, who has been following along up in the trees and avoiding interacting with anyone. Persimmon asks Chloe if Tucker is alright, but instead of divulging the true reason for his distance, Chloe just says that he needs some space.

Just then, Tucker comes bounding down a tree and lands next to Persimmon, Derpoke and Chloe. He butts into their conversation as if he has been practicing his speech in advance—which he has. "Persimmon, before we get to our next destination, I think it's important that I voice my concern about the newest addition to our team."

"You mean Nibbin?" Persimmon asks, perplexed. She peers over at the tiny brown mink, who is hopping onto Scraps' back and laughing joyfully.

"Yes, *him*." Tucker glares at Nibbin and continues. "As you know, minks viciously attacked and tried to eat my love Chloe."

Chloe cuts in. "So you still love me, then? Because you've been avoiding me for days."

"My love for you was never in question," Tucker snaps. "Just your lack of good judgment."

The other team members get quiet, realizing they're in the middle of a lover's spat.

Before Chloe can comment, Tucker charges on. "Simply put, that mink is dangerous to have around."

Tucker is now speaking loud enough for Bruiser, Scraps and Nibbin to hear, so the three playmates slow their pace and listen in.

Persimmon responds carefully, knowing that she has an audience. "Tucker, the attack on Chloe was absolutely horrendous, but Nibbin would never do such a thing. You should get to know him. He's as sweet as can be."

"He's as sweet as can be—*now*." Tucker paces alongside the others, adamant about making his point. "But when he gets older and larger he will develop a taste for squirrels."

The other team members tense up and everyone stops.

Chloe replies, almost embarrassed for her love. "Tucker, be reasonable. It's…"

Tucker stands on his hind legs to give himself some height, his tail flaring up in the air. "Oh, you think it's such a silly notion? His ilk clearly eat other animals. Next you're going to have a fox join the team."

"Tucker, The Uncaged Alliance is an inclusive team," Persimmon explains. "As long as the members agree to work together to save other animals in need, we welcome them openly."

Tucker strikes back. "First you let team members join who still eat other animals. Now you're letting team members join who specifically eat other team members."

That stings Persimmon. *We can save more lives if we accept all willing participants, but does it make me look weak as a leader to bend on my moral stance?* She doesn't have the answer at the moment, so she replies with, "Our ultimate goal is to save as many lives as we can. The bigger our team, the better our chance for success. Rawly and the other raccoons are a work in progress, but I can assure you that Nibbin does not pose a threat to you."

Chloe chimes in. "Tucker, we can be a good influence on him. He's young. Those other minks just saw us as food. He'll see us as friends. If you were to kick him out, it would surely sour him on squirrels."

"Please don't kick me out," Nibbin begs. He crawls over to Tucker, keeping low to appear as nonthreatening as possible. "I won't eat anyone, Mr. Tucker squirrel. Honest."

Tucker notices everyone staring at him, judging him for seeming to harass an innocent child. He lashes out. "Sure. *I'm* the rotten one. Those minks try to eat my loved one, but *I'm* the barbarian? Maybe I should just quit the team. I bet you all would prefer that, wouldn't you?"

Tucker darts to the closest tree and rushes up the trunk at lightning speed, so fast that no one has time to even react.

The team members turn their attention to Chloe, who looks down at the ground, dejected. *What has happened to my Pupsy?*

The team peers back up into the trees, trying to spot Tucker. Did he just quit?

At that moment, Rawly, who is ahead fifteen trees away with his raccoon troops, calls out from atop a stump. "Hello, snails! What is taking you so long? The city's just up ahead. We made it!" He hops back onto the leaf-covered forest floor and mumbles to himself, "Without me, this team just stands around staring up into trees. Get it together, lazy bugs!"

37

THE CITY: CARS zoom down the streets. There are lots of lights and few trees and bushes to provide protection. Humans mill about. The team has to be careful. It's nighttime, so luckily most of the citizens are fast asleep, but it would be silly to survive all that they've been through just to be hit by a car.

It has been a while since the team was near a city, so as a treat, they decide to rummage through some trash cans for whatever delicious leftovers they can find. They come across a house where the trash cans are sufficiently hidden in the shadows and get to work sorting through the garbage. Persimmon uses her back legs to steady herself as she sifts through a bin with her front paws. She smiles when she comes across a sandwich and tosses it to Bruiser and Scraps. They pick out the rotting meat, which Rawly quickly snatches up for his raccoon troops. Tucker keeps to himself in a tree on the side of the house, not in the mood to eat. There is still an awkward tension between him and the rest of the group.

Derpoke sits comfortably on the concrete, delightedly munching a stalk of corn, dropping yellow kernel shavings all over his fuzzy cheeks. Suddenly, he feels like he's being watched. Sure enough, when he looks up, he sees an orange tabby cat peering at him from atop a green fence. Derpoke freezes without swallowing the corn in his mouth.

"Enjoying your trash?" the cat remarks disdainfully.

Derpoke remains still, slightly embarrassed to be called out for devouring someone's discarded food.

Bruiser hops over and growls at the tabby. "Get outta here, cat."

The cat licks her arm casually and admires her dark orange stripes shining in the moonlight. "I believe you are mistaken, *dog*. You see, you are intruding on *my* home, and at any time I could start whining up a storm to wake my humans. Although I haven't yet, so perhaps you should be thanking me instead of threatening me." The feline goes back to leisurely grooming herself.

Persimmon hops off of the trash can to intercede. "Excuse us, cat. We don't mean to intrude. We're happy to move on to another home if we're bothering you."

The cat sits up straight. "What's bothering me is everyone calling me 'cat.' My name is Apricot, thank you very much."

Scraps perks up. "Oh, like Persimmon."

"No, like A-p-r-i-c-o-t," she enunciates, assuming that Scraps is a little dim.

Persimmon interjects. "What he means is that *my* name is Persimmon. You and I are both named after fruits."

"How fascinating," Apricot replies sarcastically. "We must be long-lost twins."

The rest of the team has gathered around to check out the sassy feline. Apricot surveys the team—six raccoons, two squirrels, one dog, one opossum and one mink—with a grin. "You have quite the troop here. I've rarely seen such a motley crew. Are you all friends?"

That's Scraps' cue to proudly declare their moniker. "We're The Uncaged Alliance!"

"You've actually given yourselves a name!" Apricot laughs. "If I didn't know better, I might say you banded together just to amuse me."

Chloe, who is on the ground, bangs on the bottom of the fence where Apricot is perched and shakes her bushy tail defiantly. "No, we've banded together to help save other animals in trouble."

"Don't let her get to you, Chloe," Bruiser urges. "Cats couldn't care less about anybody but themselves."

"Au contraire, kind sir," Apricot replies. "I care very much about... on second thought, no, you are correct with that assessment." Apricot's pupils widen as she focuses on the tiny Nibbin, who is crouched beside Persimmon. "You remind me of a rat, only longer. Are you very fast?"

Nibbin hides in Persimmon's grayish-brown fur as she protectively places her paw on his back. Persimmon scolds, "Some of us have taken a pledge not to harm or eat other animals."

"How noble of you." Apricot yawns. "Anyway, I don't want to eat him. I just want to play with him for a bit."

Persimmon has had enough. She turns to the team. "Come on, everyone. This is a waste of time. We have more important things to do."

They pick up their food and walk down the concrete path, glaring at Apricot as they pass.

Apricot watches them go and waves them off with a flick of her tail. Just as Tucker, the last member of the team, walks by her, she casually states, "It's a pity. I do happen to know of a group of animals that could use some saving, but enjoy your night on the town, Uncaged Alliance."

Apricot stretches and then saunters along the top of the fence. Persimmon stops in her tracks. How can she not be intrigued?

"Persimmon, it's just stupid cat games," Bruiser warns. "Now that we're not paying attention to her, she's trying to reel us back in."

Persimmon ponders for a second, then bounds back over to the fence. She calls up to the cunning cat. "Okay Apricot, you've piqued my interest. Where are these animals who need our help?"

Apricot stops and pivots to look down at Persimmon. "Hello again." The cat grins, pleased with her power of persuasion. "To be honest, I don't think you'll be able to save them. Even if you could break them free, which is virtually impossible, they're not exactly..." Apricot pauses to find the right word. "How should I put this? They're not exactly inconspicuous."

"Leave the rescue plan to us," Persimmon replies confidently. "We've pulled off some impossible feats before."

"I don't doubt that," Apricot licks her lips. "And that's why I'll take you to them. I do love a good show."

With that, Apricot gracefully leaps off the fence and past the other team members.

Bruiser turns to Derpoke and whispers. "I think we just found someone even more unlikable than Rawly."

38

THE TEAM—PERSIMMON, DERPOKE, Scraps, Bruiser, Rawly, Claudette, Drig, Fisher, Nibbin, Chloe and Tucker—follows Apricot through the streets, deeper into the city. They try to stay in the shadows and hide whenever they see cars and hear human voices, but as they travel farther from the safety of the forest, they begin to worry about not having an escape plan in case they are spotted. Still, the intrigue surrounding the mysterious creatures that Apricot has promised to show them keeps the team moving forward.

As they stroll along, Bruiser looks down at Chloe, who is walking beside him. Most of her wounds have healed, but the bite marks on her back and neck have left scars where the fur hasn't grown back. Bruiser inquires, "Chloe, do you need me to carry ya on my back?"

"That's very kind of you, Bruiser, but I'm actually doing better. I think I look worse than I feel. I guess all these marks will just give me some character."

"Looks like we're twins," Bruiser quips, referring to his own scars. "If your injuries start actin' up, though, I'm here for ya."

Chloe looks up at the dog towering over her and feels a massive sense of awe that this strong, foreboding creature, who would normally chase her up a tree, is offering to assist her. She can't help herself;

she reaches out and hugs his leg, her tiny body barely reaching past his elbow. Bruiser blushes, not used to this type of affection, and licks the top of her head in appreciation.

Tucker sees this and rolls his eyes. *Hmph. Already flirting with other males.*

The team presses on, and just when Derpoke is about to suggest that they turn back for safety, Bruiser sniffs the air. "What is that smell?"

Nibbin puts his snout up and breathes in a gulp of air as well. "Ohh, I smell it too! It smells sweet and salty at the same time. Yummy!"

Without turning around, Apricot announces nonchalantly, "Yes, it's just around the corner. I told you this place was interesting."

Persimmon takes a whiff with her tiny black nose. "It smells delicious." She turns to Derpoke, who is walking beside her. "That's odd. Normally when we're nearing animals who are in trouble, there is a foul odor. I can definitely sense other animals, but that sweet and salty odor overpowers their smell."

"Maybe the humans feed them that food to fatten them up for eating," Derpoke suggests.

"Interesting hypothesis," Persimmon replies, considering the idea as she moves forward.

The team turns a corner and there beyond a vast parking lot is a very large circular building. They stare at it, amazed.

"Wow," Claudette remarks. "I had no idea humans created such large buildings. Do humans live here?"

Apricot rolls her eyes at Claudette's lack of knowledge. "It's called an arena. Humans hold events here: basketball games, hockey games, concerts, et cetera, et cetera."

The team looks quizzically at the haughty cat. "Oh, come on," Apricot scoffs. "Please don't tell me you have no idea what any of those things are."

"We live in the forest," Rawly snaps back. "You interact with humans all the time. Why would we know anything about human games?"

"Because everyone knows what basketball is," Apricot replies impudently.

"Is basketball what makes the arena smell so delicious?" Scraps chimes in.

Apricot stares at Scraps in disbelief. "You forest dwellers really need to get to the city more. No, basketballs are made of cow skin and rubber, so I can say with all assurance that that is not what makes the arena smell so sweet."

The entire team gasps. "Eww! Skin?!"

Derpoke speaks up. "*Cow* skin? Do they kill cows here?" He can't believe his ears. Thoughts of poor Calvin and the other calves flash through his head. He turns to Persimmon and Scraps, slightly frenzied. "Cows are the calves' mothers, remember? Maybe this is where humans keep them."

Persimmon's heart starts to pound faster. "Is that true, Apricot?"

Apricot puts her paws out to quiet them down. "Hush up! I don't know why you're getting so frantic, but there are no cows in that building. Basketball is a game. The humans put the cow skin around the balls and they throw the balls in hoops. I'm not going to explain the whole game to you because it's boring, but they seem to enjoy it a great deal."

Rawly harrumphs, disgusted. "How sick. They play a game with the skin?"

Apricot claws the pavement in frustration, throwing a petty temper tantrum. "Yes, but that's not what I'm here to show you. Get over the whole basketball thing. Now, follow me."

Apricot storms off across the parking lot. The team scurries to catch up to the aggravated cat. She motions for them to slow down once they reach two large semi-trailer trucks that are parked back to back. Trash is scattered all over the ground: bags with kernels of popcorn spilling out, used napkins, red plastic cups with drops of soda in them, paper sticks with sugary cotton candy wrapped around them. The team members inhale: *That's* where the sweet and salty smells are emanating from. Up close, though, the food doesn't seem so appetizing.

The team hides in the shadow of one of the semis. There are no humans in sight, but they know they still must be careful. Looking underneath the trailer, they glimpse the long, strong legs of a few creatures standing in a row on the other side. Each team member is slightly anxious, but mostly they are excited about seeing these creatures for the first time.

Persimmon looks over at her younger brother and sees that his eyes are wide with glee. He wears the biggest smile she's seen on him in a long while. He's in awe.

Apricot whispers, "Now don't get too close to their legs. These creatures spook easily."

"Who's there?!" They hear a booming voice from the other side of the trailer. Derpoke and most of the other team members freeze but Nibbin is so exhilarated that he's hopping up and down.

None of the team members says a word.

"I said, who is there?" the voice calls out again, agitated.

Persimmon peers underneath the semi-trailer. All she can see are the animals' legs, all of which are taut and at attention. "We're friendly," she assures. "We've come here to help you."

The voice replies, surprised. "Help us? Reveal yourselves and explain how."

Persimmon looks over at Derpoke, who unfreezes only to shake his head "no." Persimmon pats him on the back encouragingly and crawls over between the semi-trailers. Bruiser follows in case she needs assistance.

"Make sure they can see you or they might trample you," Apricot warns.

Persimmon's heart is pounding. In front of her, she can see two large pens enclosed by metal fences off in the distance. Before she can make out what type of animals they contain, however, she is confronted by a group of the largest mammals she's ever seen. They are taller than humans and they stand on four legs. They look kind of like the calves, but they seem much prouder and are far more muscular. Some are pure white and others are brown, and they all have very short hair except for the row of flowing locks on the backs of their long necks. They are all tied to the semi-trailers with short brown ropes. To Persimmon's right, four creatures are tied in a row and another four are tied to the truck on her left.

The brown creature nearest to Persimmon bends his long neck down, his nostrils blowing hot air toward her. She steps back in fear. The creature remarks, "Don't be afraid. You're the one sneaking up on me. So, what do you mean you came here to help us?"

Persimmon is momentarily speechless. The creatures are so intimidating. She just stares up at the breathtaking animal before her.

"What's with the perplexed look, tiny raccoon?" he asks. "Haven't you ever seen a horse before?"

One of the white horses jokes, "Maybe she's been rendered speechless by your bad breath, Charlemagne."

The other horses laugh.

"Quiet, Ramses!" Charlemagne chides. "Nobody cares to hear your wisecracks now. I think she's afraid I might eat her. Tiny raccoon, we don't eat other animals. We eat hay."

"We'd eat apples and carrots, too, if these repugnant humans would ever give us any," Ramses remarks.

The other horses murmur in agreement. One of them moans, "What I wouldn't give for an apple. Just one."

Persimmon finally finds her voice. "Forgive me. None of us except Apricot—she's the cat on the other side of the truck—has ever seen a horse before. You are quite handsome creatures. How do you know what raccoons are, though?"

"Raccoons are everywhere," Charlemagne says. "In many of the cities we've been to, raccoons come around to nibble on the food left by wasteful humans. That's what I was assuming you and your friends were doing snooping around our truck."

"No, no," Persimmon explains. "We were told by our friend Apricot that there were animals here who needed our help."

Apricot pricks her ears in disdain over hearing Persimmon refer to her as a friend.

"You see, my companions and I,"—Persimmon points to the team members who have begun assembling behind her—"we created a team to save any animals in trouble. It looks like all of you are tied so tightly to this truck that you have barely any room to move. And I'm assuming that little bit of grass on the ground is hay, which means you are only given a meager amount of food, and I don't see any water. We'd like to find a way to free you, if possible."

The horses rustle back and forth, invigorated by this astonishing revelation. Their hooves make clopping sounds on the pavement. Excitement shimmers through their bodies.

Charlemagne, who is normally quite reserved, can barely contain his enthusiasm. "You really came here to help us escape?"

Rawly steps forward and sits up on his hind legs. "Absolutely we're here to help you," he states authoritatively. "I'm Rawly, one of the team leaders." Persimmon cringes, but Rawly doesn't notice and continues. "We've seen how humans mistreat all kinds of animals and we want to put an end to it. We're here to save you from your captors."

The horses whinny cheerfully.

Ramses neighs. "When can you get us out of here? Tonight?"

Persimmon feels awful ruining the jubilation, but she doesn't want to give them false hope. "Before we get ahead of ourselves, I want to make it clear that although we are definitely here to rescue you, we have only just arrived and haven't even explored the premises fully yet. First, we need to meet all of the animals and then we can discuss the safest and quickest way to get you all out of here."

Charlemagne replies calmly. "I understand." He takes in a deep breath and pulls at the halter clamped around his face. "It's just so comforting to think of actually escaping. They hit us across the face and whip us constantly. It's an abysmal life. I never thought we'd get out of this place."

"What is this place, by the way?" Persimmon inquires.

Charlemagne clenches his jaw in anger. "The circus."

39

THE TEAM STEPS past the semi-trailers and walks toward one of the fenced-in pens. As they move along, Scraps looks behind him and perks up when he sees two horses who are much shorter than the rest. "Oh look! Baby horses!"

One of the tiny horses snaps at him. "Excuse me, we are *not* children. We are full-grown adults."

"He don't mean no harm," Bruiser replies humbly. "Just curious." Bruiser motions to Scraps. "Do you think you might want to apologize, little feller?"

Scraps lowers his ears and looks at the ground. "Sorry, Mr. Horses."

The other tiny horse reprimands, "And I'm a female!" She looks at her fellow miniature companion and shakes her head with distaste. "Raccoons have no manners."

Bruiser scoots Scraps along with his snout. The horse at the far end of the second semi-trailer explains as they pass by. "Humans have bred them to be smaller. Some of the miniature horses have lots of health issues because of it, so it's a sensitive subject."

"Sorry 'bout that," Bruiser replies. "Just learnin' as we go."

At the front of the team, Persimmon catches up to Rawly and speaks softly. "Rawly, before we get to these next animals, I want to mention one thing. We really…"

Rawly interjects. "I know what you're going to say: I shouldn't guarantee their escape when we have no idea if we really will be able to save them."

Persimmon is surprised and impressed that he understands his mistake. "Yes. Exactly. But if you get that concept, why would you fill them with false hope?"

Rawly stops abruptly. The other team members walk past him and Persimmon, seeing that they're having another tense debate. Rawly looks at his raccoon friend with an unexpectedly genuine expression. "Persimmon, they're tied to the back of trucks. Maybe it's nice for them to get a small taste of hope. You saw his expression. He was about to cry."

Persimmon is impressed by his sincerity. "Rawly, I know you mean well, but we have no idea what we're getting into here. Look around. The animals we have seen so far are huge. They're nothing like the minks, who can just disappear into the forest. If we…"

Rawly walks away from Persimmon without letting her finish. "Okay, Persimmon. Whatever you say."

Persimmon sighs. She'll have to let this one go for now. Something tells her, though, that it will not be the last time they spar over this issue.

Nibbin stands by the metal fence where the next creatures are trapped. It's a circular enclosure with metal bars that have holes big enough for minks and raccoons to crawl through. Nibbin is so ecstatic to meet all of these extraordinary new animals that he speaks at a rapid pace. "You're all so colorful and have such fancy patterns. It's wonderful. Look at your black hooves. You're just like the horses, only more decorative. What type of animal are you?"

One of the black-and-white-striped creatures bends down to look directly at the squeaking, diminutive Nibbin. His head is more than twice the size of Nibbin's entire body. "We're zebras. My name is Somersault. And what type of animal are you? An extra-long rat?"

"I'm a mink!" Nibbin declares enthusiastically.

Claudette, who is standing near Nibbin, chimes in. "Oh my, you're gorgeous creatures. I hope we're not bothering you. We're actually here to help—maybe get you all outta here."

The other four zebras quickly gallop over. They crowd tightly together, pushing one another aside to get closer to the team. Another zebra speaks up. "What was that? You want to help us escape?!"

Somersault jumps back in. "Please, you have to help us. The humans whip us all the time, squeeze our throats. I got kicked in the side today because I missed a jump in the show."

"That's terrible," Claudette cringes. "What is a show, though?"

Somersault is perplexed. "You don't know?"

Another zebra interrupts him. "That's what the circus is. They make us run around and perform ridiculous tricks while other humans watch and laugh and clap. When we're not performing, they have training sessions where they hit us and whip us until we get the maneuvers just right."

"Ha. It doesn't matter if we get the maneuvers right," Somersault adds, getting more upset. "They hit us regardless."

"It's true," the other zebras agree in unison.

"Well, that's just terrible," Chloe chimes in. "We feared as much. That's why we came to free you. We just don't know how yet."

"I know how," Somersault blurts out exuberantly. "Let me show you!"

The other zebras follow Somersault to the enclosure's gate. "It's over here. Come on!"

The team scampers along the pavement outside the enclosure. They stop at the gate entrance where Somersault is leaning his head over the fence. He knocks the lock on the latch with his nose. "You open this lock. The goats have the same thing on their gate over there." Somersault motions his head toward the enclosure beside them, where five goats have gathered to see what all the hubbub is about. Somersault continues. "You just need the keys to open the lock."

"What are keys?" Persimmon asks.

Apricot shares her insight from having lived with humans for so many years. "My humans have keys for everything: their car, front door, shed. They're tiny metal objects. I could point them out if I see them."

Persimmon follows up. "So where do we get these keys?"

"The humans have them," Somersault explains. "They keep them on their belts."

Persimmon scratches her head nervously and asks out loud to no one in particular, "How are we going to get them off their belts?"

Somersault gets overexcited and kicks the fence, making a loud, reverberating clanking sound. "Steal them! When one of the humans comes to open the gate, knock the keys out of his hand!"

The other zebras concur. "Yeah! Bite his hand!" They prance around boisterously, energized at the thought of escape.

Persimmon shushes them. "Please. You'll wake the humans. They'll see us and then no one will be saved."

Somersault quiets the other zebras. "Shh, my friends." He leans his head back over the fence. "Sorry, you don't know how terrible it is in here. We're stuck in this pen all day with barely any room to run. We get antsy. It makes us crazy. But we'll be quiet."

Persimmon addresses the eager zebras. "I understand it must be maddening to be stuck here all day and night. Once we've explored the whole arena, we'll brainstorm a way to get you all out of here."

"We appreciate it so much," Somersault says. "Don't forget about us!"

The team quickly scurries over to the next enclosure, where the goats wait impatiently. Derpoke, the slowest of the bunch, begrudgingly watches the others pass him by.

"Need help?" asks Drig, who is quite fit and large for a raccoon.

Derpoke is incensed by the question. "I am perfectly fine, thank you. Some of us prefer to pace ourselves."

"And maybe some of us shouldn't have scarfed down so much corn." Drig grins and quickens his gait.

"Corn is healthy for you," Derpoke mutters under his breath. "Maybe some of us shouldn't be so judgmental."

"Shut up over there!" A wrathful human voice hollers from the other side of the zebra pen.

Rawly cries out, alarmed. "Humans! Hide!"

The team scatters as quickly as possible. The humans haven't seen them yet, but they're approaching quickly. Derpoke, Scraps, Bruiser, Rawly and Claudette run for the closest cover—under the trucks to which the horses are attached. The horses, spooked by all of the small critters running toward them, start to neigh and trot nervously. Derpoke nearly gets clobbered by a hoof but ducks out of the way just in time.

Persimmon, Drig, Fisher, Nibbin, Chloe and Tucker see the horses panicking and veer toward the goat enclosure instead.

A human yells at the horses. "Shut up, you idiots! What has gotten into you?"

"If you keep yelling, Lorenzo, you're just gonna spook them more," the other human warns.

Lorenzo lifts the menacing metal rod in his hand. It's a bullhook—a long pole with a sharp hook at the end that closely resembles a fireplace poker. The very sight of it sends shivers down the animals' spines. Lorenzo glares at his coworker and then slams the bullhook against the zebra enclosure threateningly. "That's gonna be your head, if *you* don't shut up."

The other human grimaces at Lorenzo but doesn't say a word. He's not sure how the hotheaded Lorenzo will react to someone standing up to him. Lorenzo has an unkempt black, braided beard, a worn-in black leather vest, and a tattoo of a glaring red bull on his right bicep. He thinks all this makes him look tough, but he looks more like a five-year-old in a biker-pirate Halloween costume.

Lorenzo smiles devilishly. "Nah, I'm just messing with you, Nutsack." Lorenzo playfully pokes his coworker's rear end with the metal stick. "You like that? Huh? You like it right there?"

"Stop, man." His coworker inches away from Lorenzo. The zebras have huddled in the far section of their pen, away from the humans, as have the goats. They're quite familiar with Lorenzo's unpredictable outbursts.

While the humans are distracted, Persimmon and her group rush under a semi-trailer they haven't yet explored. On one side of the truck, four creatures are tied up—a species they've never seen before. They're even taller than the horses, with huge humps on their backs and bushy, matted fur.

Lorenzo makes his way over to the horses who are unfortunately tied up with nowhere to run. They whinny helplessly as they see the menacing Lorenzo nearing them.

"You mothertruckers wanna keep us up at all hours of the morning? You think it's funny?" Lorenzo shouts. He holds up his bullhook and jabs Charlemagne in the side. Charlemagne neighs loudly in pain. The team members hiding under the trucks wince.

Rawly turns to Scraps, Derpoke, Bruiser and Claudette. "We have to help them."

"Not now, Rawly," Bruiser chides. "Won't do no good runnin' out there now, blowin' our cover. There's a time and a place. We'll get these creatures outta here soon enough."

Rawly huffs but stays put.

The horses quiet down, fearing more retribution from Lorenzo.

Lorenzo surveys the area and sees that all of the animals are cowering nervously. He fiddles with one of the braids in his beard, proud of his ability to leave all those in his wake trembling. "Now that my work here is done, Nutsack, I'm…"

"It's Daniel," the skinny man stands up taller, trying to assert himself. "Stop calling me Nutsack."

"Oh, I'm sorry." Lorenzo starts sniffling, pretending to cry. "Did I hurt your precious feelings? Do you need a hug? Maybe you want me to hold your balls while I'm at it." Lorenzo reaches for Daniel's crotch.

Daniel steps back and swats Lorenzo's hand away. "Chill, man."

Lorenzo lets out a deep laugh. "Oh, that was great! Classic! Well, how about this?" The smile suddenly fades from Lorenzo's face, twisting into a vicious snarl. "You wanna keep your job? Cause this isn't even my gig working with these animals. But you're too inept to keep them quiet and you're always sleeping through your shift, so I have to come out here and crack down on their asses—and yours."

Lorenzo jabs Charlemagne in the side again without any warning. Charlemagne trips to the side and whinnies. Lorenzo licks his lips and puffs up his chest. "This horse wouldn't be getting hit if it wasn't for you, Nutsack, so do you have anything else to say?"

Daniel keeps his mouth shut and looks away from Lorenzo, who is standing uncomfortably close to him.

"That's what I thought," Lorenzo says, twirling the metal weapon in his hand. "Now, as I was saying. Since my work here is done, I'm gonna go check on my girls. Can I trust you to keep these mother-truckers in line?"

"Yes," Daniel replies, resigned.

"Good." Lorenzo marches off toward the arena. Persimmon, Drig, Fisher, Nibbin, Chloe and Tucker watch him disappear around the corner of the building.

Persimmon glances at her companions underneath the truck. All of them have looks of pure disgust on their faces.

"Worst human yet," Chloe remarks.

"Definitely," Persimmon agrees. "I hope that's the last we see of him."

40

WITH DANIEL WATCHING over the animals in the parking lot, the team has reconvened at the back entrance to the arena. It's a gigantic double door, substantial enough for trucks to drive through to unload equipment, stages, and whatever else is needed for the shows.

Apricot addresses the group. Being the only orange animal among them, she stands out, something she enjoys very much. "There are more creatures inside who I'm sure you'll want to see, but even though I know it's going to be an emotional strain on this fearsome team to part ways, there's no way everyone can come into the basement at the same time. The humans are mostly asleep right now, but we'd be too conspicuous with everyone scurrying down the hallways. And although it was fun running for our lives a moment ago, I'd prefer to make it home safely tonight."

"That makes sense," Persimmon concedes. "I'd like to be one of the few who go in this first time. Is there anyone else who really wants to go inside?"

"It only makes sense that I go as well," Rawly declares.

Scraps rushes up to Persimmon. "Please, can I go? Please. I promise I'll be quiet."

Persimmon puts her paw on his back. "I understand your gusto, little brother—these animals are awe-inspiring—but being trapped here isn't fun for them at all. Can you keep that in mind when we meet them?"

"Yes, definitely. I just…" Scraps squeezes his paw, attempting to restrain his enthusiasm. "They're just so amazing. None of the other animals in the forest look anything like them."

"I agree. Of course you can come." Persimmon turns to the rest of the group. "I think humans feel the same way Scraps does and that's why they attend the circus—to see these enchanting creatures. Unfortunately, they don't take into account that these creatures are being held against their will."

"Held against their will *and* beaten—all because humans find it entertaining to watch these poor creatures perform tricks." Rawly scoffs. "Selfish." The exasperated raccoon heads toward the double doors. He's so worked up he doesn't want to wait any longer to begin this jailbreak.

Chloe steps front and center. "Persimmon, I'd like to stay out here, actually. I want to examine this outdoor area more closely to see if there is a quiet and stealthy way to cut these animals loose."

"That's a great idea, Chloe." Persimmon is thrilled by the squirrel's initiative. "Can the rest of you help her?"

Bruiser, Drig, Claudette, Nibbin, Fisher and Tucker nod in agreement, so Persimmon, Scraps and Rawly follow Apricot toward the massive double doors. As Persimmon steps away, she sees Derpoke lagging behind Chloe's group, looking a bit despondent. She calls out to him. "Derpoke, are you okay?"

"Yeah," the opossum mumbles sullenly. Clearly, he is not okay.

Persimmon knows her dear friend too well. "You want to come inside the arena with us, don't you?"

Derpoke glances at her with his ears perked up, trying not to look too eager. He doesn't like to be far away from her. Persimmon laughs at his sheepishness. "Come on, caterpillar. Inch on over here."

Derpoke trots over merrily and joins Persimmon's group as they disappear into the darkness of the basement.

41

THE BASEMENT HALLS are lined with brightly colored, strange contraptions that are unfamiliar to the team—basketball hoops, motorbikes, miniature clown cars, green and gold stands, glow sticks and sparkly metallic stages of all shapes and sizes. All of these items are tinted yellow from the hall lights.

With Persimmon, Derpoke and Rawly behind her, Apricot leads the way, weaving in and out of the props and equipment to keep hidden from any humans. So far no people have been spotted—it is still very early in the morning—but the group doesn't want to take any chances after seeing how volatile Lorenzo was.

"What is all this stuff?" Derpoke inquires.

"The humans use it for the shows," Apricot answers. "These are the items the goats climb on, the horses run around in, and so on."

"Have you seen the shows before?" Persimmon asks as she crawls under a hot pink clown car.

"I stepped in and out of one or two just to see what all the noise was," Apricot replies as she stealthily slides her way out from under the other side of the pink clown car. "I didn't stay for long, though. Watching those animals run around foolishly, following every command given by the humans—it was humiliating to witness."

Just then, they hear a ferocious roar from down the hallway. It's a sound so powerful, so terrifying that it makes everyone's fur stand on end.

Derpoke freezes, paralyzed with fear.

"Silly me, I forgot to mention," Apricot sneers. "All the other animals outside are harmless. But these ones..." She pauses to draw out the tension. "They'll eat you alive." Apricot turns to look at the group with the most devious smile she can muster. "Come on, follow me." The feline marches forward at a quicker pace.

Derpoke holds his ground and whispers to Persimmon. "I think I'll stay here."

Persimmon nudges him with her nose. "Oh, come on. She's just being overly dramatic, as is her nature."

"Did you see that smile?" Derpoke counters. "She might try to eat us herself."

"But if *you* don't come, who's going to protect Persimmon?" Rawly razzes Derpoke.

He moves past Derpoke, hurrying to catch up with Apricot. Derpoke takes a reluctant step forward—he's not going to let that arrogant raccoon get the best of him.

✳   ✳   ✳

Chloe eyes Daniel, who is lying down on a bale of hay near the miniature horses. His baseball cap is laid over his eyes and he's snoring loudly.

One of the miniature horses also peers at Daniel and then clops his hooves on the pavement next to the man. Daniel doesn't stir. The horse looks over at Chloe, who is hiding in some of the bushes that line the arena, and nods his head. Yep, the human is fast asleep.

Chloe gives Bruiser a celebratory pat on the leg. "Good thing for us, this guy is lazy."

"Humans: Either up to no good or up to nuthin'," Bruiser quips.

Claudette, Drig, Fisher, Nibbin and Tucker are also hiding in the bushes. They survey the parking lot for any signs of humans who might be monitoring the area. No one in sight. They're clear to continue their expedition.

They start with the animals closest to them—the ones with the large humps on their backs.

The team scampers over to the animals, who are tied to semi-trailers. As the team nears, one of the creatures warns, "That's far enough, ruffians."

"Ruffians?!" Chloe asks, surprised. "No, we're here to help."

"Yeah, here to help yourself to our hay," another one of the creatures curtly replies.

The other creatures murmur in agreement and eye Chloe with disapproval.

Nibbin hops over to the tall, grumpy animals with pep in his step. "No, silly heads. We don't eat hay. We…"

Without warning, one of the creatures hacks a slimy ball of crud out of his mouth right onto Nibbin's back. Nibbin squeals and rolls on the ground, trying to clean off the mushy, smelly substance. "Eww! You're mean."

Bruiser growls and Drig stomps over to the creatures. Despite the fact that they are at least ten times Drig's height, he yells, "What did you spit on him? Is that venom?"

"Relax," the creature calmly states. "It's my dinner from earlier and if you come any closer, I have some of my lunch bubbling up just for *you*."

"You're going to threaten us after we said we're here to save you?" Fisher is incensed. "Talk about ungrateful."

Just then, a goat with graying red wool calls over from her pen a few feet away. "Don't waste your time on those camels. They're perpetually ill-tempered."

"Ha! Easy for you to say," one of the camels exclaims sourly. "You get fed tasty pellets all day by human children. Try spending even one day having those obese brats ride on your back, screaming, kicking you, pulling at your fur. Then tell me what kind of mood you're in."

"Oh please," the goat snaps back. "Do the humans make you climb up steep staircases and balance on metal bars? Do they punch you and whip you when you trip?"

Chloe hops onto Bruiser's back and shakes her tail furiously. She's much smaller than any of these creatures, but she knows how to get someone's attention. "Quiet! Quiet! All of you have it bad. And none of you should be subjected to this cruel treatment. That's why we're here—to rescue you from this horrible place."

"Rescue us?" One of the camels laughs. "I'll believe it when I see it."

The same sensible goat speaks up. "Stop being so rude, Gregor. She just said she came here to rescue us. That's very noble, if you ask me. You can at least be respectful."

"Oh, come on." Gregor chews on his cud, bored of this idle chatter. "How are some tiny squirrels, raccoons, a dog, and a..." The camel looks at Nibbin quizzically. "I don't even know what this one is. How are these minuscule creatures going to get us out of here? There aren't even that many of them, and they're going to take on all these humans who have bullhooks, whips... guns? They're delusional."

"Gregor, I'm very sorry the humans subject you to this horrendous abuse," Chloe states. "It is absolutely unacceptable. And yes, our team may seem small, but I can assure you: You're going to be mighty disappointed you weren't more helpful when you see the horses, goats and zebras gallop away while you're still here tied to this truck."

For the first time, the cantankerous camels are silent. Chloe is quite convincing. She looks over at the goat and nods in appreciation. "What's your name, madam?"

"Mirabel. What's yours?"

"Chloe," she beams.

"Well, Chloe. Consider me persuaded. What can we do to help?"

Everyone is looking at Chloe with deference. She suddenly realizes they're waiting for her to make the next call, and she likes it.

Tucker notes the significance of the moment as well, and despite his reservations about the safety of these missions, he can't help but feel proud of her.

42

"AND THESE, UNCAGED Alliance, are tigers," Apricot declares with delight, as if she had discovered them herself.

Persimmon, Derpoke, Scraps and Rawly huddle against the wall, as far away from the big cats as they can manage in the cluttered hallway. Derpoke is hiding his head behind Persimmon, pretending that if he can't see them, they're not really there.

Eight tigers pace back and forth in narrow iron cages, barely big enough for them to turn around. With two tigers in each cage, the team is reminded of the cramped confines in which the calves and minks were trapped. The cages are just as barren—no toys, food, water or soft grass on which to lie down. Persimmon, Derpoke, Scraps and Rawly remember the calves' and minks' sad mental state, so they can only imagine what these poor creatures must be feeling. Although one thing they can tell for sure from the tigers' demeanor is that they are furious over their predicament. Even after seeing the team, the tigers don't utter a word; they just pace and glare.

Despite the tension of the moment, Scraps has a spark of wonder in his eyes. He then notices an interesting similarity between the tigers, with their orange fur and black stripes, and Apricot, with her orange fur and darker orange stripes.

"Hey, Apricot, they look like you," he exclaims cheerfully. "Only they're giant, more ferocious versions of you." Then a thought hits him and his eyes pop open even wider. He yanks at his sister's fur. "Persimmon, do you think there are also giant, more ferocious *raccoons* out there?!"

Persimmon pauses to contemplate this for a second. The thought had not occurred to her before. "With all the remarkable creatures we've seen so far today, I wouldn't be surprised if there were."

"Silence!" one of the tigers, Yarick, roars angrily.

The team cowers against the wall and Derpoke pushes his way farther behind Persimmon's back.

"Listen very carefully," the irritated tiger warns. "Leave now or the next time I see a raccoon, I will rip his head from his body and devour his flesh as punishment for you bothering us. Now go!"

Without hesitation, Persimmon, Scraps, Rawly and Derpoke scurry away as fast as they can. As far as they're concerned, their paws can't take them fast enough. Apricot, though, stays behind for a brief moment, staring into Yarick's piercing eyes. She's not challenging him. She's having an existential crisis looking at these creatures who resemble her so strikingly. She's seen them before, but only from afar and in passing. She never realized how similar they looked to her. And there was something in his voice that disturbed her. Not the anger. It was something deeper than that—something sadder. It was desperation.

Her initial thought was to view these creatures as pathetic—so mighty and yet enfeebled by their cages. She wants to be an outsider gazing upon someone else's horrid life, reassured that she doesn't have to live it. Instead, though, she feels empathy—an emotion she considers reserved for the weak.

Apricot quickly turns away from the tigers. She doesn't want to see them any longer. She quietly retreats down the hallway, not looking back, trying to forget what she just felt but fearing she may never be able to.

43

CHARLEMAGNE BENDS DOWN to allow Chloe to crawl up his snout and onto his mane so she can inspect his halter. She examines the firm nylon straps closely and then bites on one as a test. She grimaces. "Hmm. These are thicker than I had anticipated."

"Maybe someone can untie the knot holding the rope to the truck," Charlemagne suggests.

"I'll check that next," Chloe says as she continues investigating the headpiece for weaknesses.

Charlemagne chats as the small squirrel works. He likes the company. "You're so much lighter than those oversized humans, Chloe. I can barely feel you crawling around."

"Why, thank you. I'm light on my feet. Although I wouldn't mind having even a quarter of the amount of muscle you have on your legs. My goodness, I bet you're fast."

"Indeed," Charlemagne neighs proudly. "Unfortunately, the humans never give me a chance to run free. But if you set me loose, I will race away so swiftly that even their cars wouldn't be able to catch me."

Chloe pats him warmly on the side of the head. "That's what we're counting on." Just then she notices the buckle on one of the straps. She thinks back to the latches on the minks' cages and wonders if they work the same way. Her ears perk up in excitement. She peers around the parking lot, looking for Drig. The team members are scrutinizing the various animals' enclosures to figure out ways to set them free. Claudette and Fisher are talking with the goats; Bruiser and Nibbin are meeting with the zebras; and Tucker is scanning the outer perimeter of the parking lot. Chloe finally spots Drig, who is probing the ropes that are tethering the horses to the truck opposite her.

"Drig!" Chloe calls out, excited. "I think I may be onto something. I need your help, please."

While Drig steps over to Chloe and Charlemagne, Fisher is at the goat enclosure analyzing every inch of the gate to see if there is a loose screw or a crack in the metal. Two of the goats, who have black wool with a few white spots, follow along to help.

"The humans force us to climb stairs to balance on top of metal beams," explains Coby, one of the young goats. "And if we even look like we're going to trip or we hesitate to catch our breath, they'll give us a swift kick to the stomach."

"Don't worry," Fisher says, leaning closer to Coby and reaching under the fence to pat his hoof. "I'll bite a human for ya!" Fisher makes the meanest face he can muster to show off his threatening, spiky teeth. The two young goats bleat gleefully.

At the other end of the goat pen, Claudette is sitting on top of the front gate with Mirabel, who is watching as Claudette works. Mirabel is much older than the other goats. Her matted red wool is graying in sections and her once glorious horns are chipped. Her legs are slightly bowed from years of standing on unrelenting pavement and being forced to perform tricks. The gray around her face, however, gives her a distinguished appearance, which is well suited for her infinite wisdom.

As Claudette fiddles with the frustratingly unbreakable lock, Mirabel speaks up. "I've lived my share of disappointment here in the circus, Claudette, so you can be honest." The old goat takes a breath and then looks up at the raccoon. "Do you really think you can get us out of here?"

Claudette stops examining the lock and looks at the weary goat. "I promise you, we will do everything we can to free you. You deserve so much better than this appalling life in the circus."

"I truly hope so." Mirabel's chin quivers. "I don't want to die in here."

Claudette tries not to show it, but a wave of sickening dread sweeps over her. *These poor creatures are so miserable, and we're their only chance at freedom. How are we ever going to get them all out of here?*

44

PERSIMMON, DERPOKE, SCRAPS, Rawly and Apricot are startled by a deafening sound that resembles an out-of-tune trumpet. It came from the other end of the hallway, away from where the tigers are caged. The trumpeting continues, and from the unsettling sound, it quickly becomes apparent that these are calls of distress.

Persimmon gets a lump in her throat. "Come on. These creatures need our help."

She takes off, weaving in and out of the circus props. Derpoke struggles to keep up. "That is a very loud sound, which means these creatures must be very big. Apricot, are we in any danger if we help them?"

Apricot rolls her eyes. "No, foolish opossum. They are gentle giants. They don't eat other animals."

"Good," Derpoke replies as he waddles along. "After those sinister tigers, I'm not sure how much more my fragile heart can handle."

A red curtain blocks the team's view of the "gentle giants," and a security guard sits in a chair in front of the barrier. The team is given a fright as Lorenzo steps out from behind the curtain, bullhook in hand. He twirls it around playfully, seeming oblivious to the fact that he's brandishing a terrifying weapon.

Lorenzo slaps the security guard on the shoulder and gives him a sadistic grin. "One of 'em was getting lippy, so I had to remind her to be respectful. You don't mess up a maneuver in my circus and get away with it."

"Cool." The security guard yawns, uninterested. "I'm bored. You wanna catch a smoke with me?"

"You don't have to ask me twice." They walk down the hallway away from the group and exit the arena through two oversized doors.

"This is our chance," Apricot exclaims as she darts toward the curtain. The team follows with trepidation—they're a little nervous about what they're about to encounter.

Apricot, Persimmon, Scraps and Rawly crawl under the curtain, but Derpoke holds back and takes a deep breath. "Everything's going to be okay. Everything's going to be okay."

Derpoke dips his head under the curtain and stops, awed by the gigantic creatures before him—elephants. There are six of them lined up side by side with their backs to the wall. Out of all the seemingly magical beings that he's seen so far tonight, these are by far the most breathtaking.

Derpoke sees his friends step into the middle of the room and he feels like they are dwarfed to the size of tiny ants compared to these impressive animals. He nearly calls to his companions to warn them not to get trampled, but then he notices the chains wound around the elephants' right front and left back legs. The chains in back are tautly secured to bars in the wall behind them, and the chains in front are attached to metal rings screwed into the concrete floor. The great beasts are completely incapacitated.

Derpoke wonders, disturbed. *These are the largest animals we've seen so far, yet they are the most restricted. And they're secluded in some dark basement as if they've been forgotten. Why would anyone treat them this way?*

The elephants' sorrow is palpable. Each wears a forlorn expression, and the despondent mood is only worsened by the fact that one of the elephants, Padma, is weeping. Her tender skin is still raw from Lorenzo's ruthless beating and a stream of blood trickles out of one of her wounds. Kusum, the largest and oldest elephant in the room, softly rubs her trunk on Padma's head. There are similar scars covering Kusum's left side, especially her left ear, from years of beatings. She looks overworked, yet somehow still dignified.

From the center of the room, the team stares up at the enormous elephants uncomfortably. They want to introduce themselves, but it seems like terribly inappropriate timing. Persimmon considers walking away to let this poor animal cry without interrupting her but the courageous raccoon feels compelled to act. She clears her throat.

"I am so sorry to bother you," she says sincerely. The elephants all turn their attention to Persimmon, stunned by her intrusion. Persimmon stutters fearfully. "I... we're here... I really am sorry... we..."

"Raccoon, please leave us be," Kusum implores. "It has been a very hard night. We cannot have visitors now."

Persimmon stretches her neck and looks up at the towering figure before her. She has one chance to plead her case. "We're The Uncaged Alliance. We've helped many animals who were suffering just like you. We're here to rescue you."

The elephants shift in their chains. Silence fills the room. Even Padma ceases her sniffling. Rescue? Every minute of every terrible day, these elephants wish for a way to escape this soul-crushing life, and now help has come in the form of a ragtag crew of forest dwellers who they could lift with one sweep of their trunks?

"You came here to rescue us?" Kusum asks, perplexed. "Three raccoons, a cat and an opossum? But how?"

Five of the elephants listen intently. The sixth, standing on the far right near the wall, just sways back and forth. She seems troubled and in her own world.

"There are more of us outside," Persimmon explains. "We have vowed to help any animals we see suffering. On our journey, we met Apricot." Persimmon motions to the tabby cat. "She was kind enough to guide us to this circus. From what we've seen so far, you and the other animals are being horrendously mistreated by these humans."

"This is true." Tears stream down Padma's gray cheeks. "The zebras, horses, goats—all of us suffer here at the hands of humans. They hit us constantly. I've never known a day when a human didn't strike me."

Kusum's eyes fill with hatred. "Do you want to know why that brute Lorenzo just spent twenty minutes pummeling Padma with that weapon?" Anger burns in Kusum's eyes, but she remains controlled as always. "During the grand finale of tonight's show, she was supposed to twirl four times just like the rest of us, but she accidentally twirled only three times." Kusum flares her ears in frustration. "She missed *one* twirl, which the audience didn't even notice, and that vile monster beat her mercilessly. He only stopped because his arms got tired."

The team cringes.

Scraps steps forward and calls up to the colossal creatures. "But you're so much bigger than these humans. How can they control you like this? Can't you just squash them with one foot? That's what I would do."

Kusum shakes her head. "Tiny raccoon. If it were only that simple. From the time we're little babies they crush our spirits. We fight at first, but the beating never ceases, so finally we break. Plus, they keep us chained up our entire lives. Little Chatura here…" Kusum taps her trunk on the smaller elephant to her left. "He only arrived recently and hasn't spoken a word since he got here, he's so traumatized by the unimaginable horrors he endured at the breeding facility and training ground."

"What are breeding facilities and training grounds?" Scraps asks.

"Perhaps there will be time to discuss that later," Kusum remarks. "But now, please tell us more about your rescue plan."

"We don't have a plan just yet," Persimmon says, slightly embarrassed. "We're scoping out the situation tonight, and then we'll figure out the safest way to get everyone out of here. I'm open to any ideas you might have."

"It's easy," Lakmini, the elephant to the right of Padma, states animatedly. "You just undo these chains by opening the lock."

Persimmon tries not to show it, but Lakmini's eagerness makes her more anxious because she doesn't have a sound plan to save them yet. "It sounds like the locks on your chains are similar to the ones at the goat and zebra enclosures, so it's all the more imperative we find these keys they were telling us about."

"The humans have them!" Lakmini exclaims earnestly. "The guard outside, Lorenzo, other humans."

"Very helpful," Persimmon replies thoughtfully. "Then we need to figure out how to get the keys from the humans without drawing attention to ourselves. After that, the escape itself will be complicated by your size. If we were to unchain you now, humans would spot you the moment you walked beyond that red curtain. And even if you did miraculously make it past the humans in here, others would surely recapture you out on the streets. You don't exactly blend in with your surroundings."

"Agreed," chimes in Yaso, the elephant closest to the curtain on the left. She's the most high-strung of the bunch and has a shrill voice. "It's too risky. We're going to get caught and beaten."

"Be quiet, Yaso," Kusum chides. "If you want to be stuck in here for the rest of your life, then fine, but don't speak for the rest of us."

"You'll never get out of here," Yaso continues, undeterred. "Where are you going to hide? They'll recapture you like the raccoon said, and then they'll beat us all for your foolish behavior."

"Shut up, Yaso!" Lakmini rustles the chains on her feet, straining to move. That she can't even move an inch only makes her more agitated. She flares her ears. "I can't take it anymore. I have to get out of here! I'm going crazy chained up all the time. I can't breathe!" Lakmini shakes around, trying to break free of the chains, knowing her effort is futile but unwilling to admit defeat. "I can't breathe!"

"Okay, Lakmini," Kusum says softly to calm her down. "I know you feel trapped. I do too, but you must remain quiet or else the humans will come storming in here and quiet you themselves." Lakmini stops her protest. There is no need to remind her twice about the humans' wrath. Kusum continues, "I agree with this raccoon. No need to rush into things. We've survived this long; we can last one more night." Kusum focuses her attention on the diminutive team gathered on the ground below her. "What is your name, raccoon?"

"Persimmon."

"Persimmon, I am Kusum, matriarch of these beautiful ladies." Kusum looks to her right and left, acknowledging her elephant family. "Tomorrow is our last full day in this city. The day after that they'll cram us onto the trains to ship us off to another town far away. If you're going to rescue us, tomorrow is the last night to do it."

A rush of anxiety shoots through Persimmon. *That's not much time to concoct such a complicated undertaking.*

"In the meantime, I urge you to watch one of the shows tomorrow," Kusum adds. "There is one in the afternoon and one in the evening. See what the humans do to us firsthand. And know that for every time an elephant stands on top of a tiny platform, for every time a tiger twirls around, he or she took many beatings to learn how to do it."

Lakmini cuts in, determined to make one last point. She leans forward. "I know I seem intense—erratic, even—but the torment of being chained for hours on end, of being beaten every day of your life with no defense, is unbearable. I'd rather die than stay here one more day."

Padma tears up again. She can't bear this hell either. None of them can.

Up until now, Persimmon has been trying to protect these creatures from crippling disappointment by setting reasonable expectations for their escape, but this sorrowful plea shakes her to her core. She steps under Lakmini's enormous head. The bulky elephant looms over the petite raccoon. Persimmon stretches her paw high into the air. Lakmini lowers her trunk to where Persimmon can reach her. The tiny raccoon feels the elephant's coarse yet warm skin, so different from her own. "It won't come to that, Lakmini. We came here to save you and that's what we're going to do. Don't forget: The humans may be powerful, but we are smarter than they'll ever be."

Persimmon holds her paw affectionately on Lakmini's trunk and smiles confidently. Lakmini's demeanor changes, a calm comes over her. Maybe this team of tiny animals can save them after all.

Rawly is happy to hear Persimmon finally showing some gusto for this mission. He steps forward for the first time. He's been watching the elephant farthest from the door, who has been swaying back and forth during the entire conversation, seemingly unaware that anyone else is even in the room with her. There's a dark cloud hovering over her. "Is she okay?" he inquires.

"You mean Nayana?" Kusum's expression turns mournful. "Poor thing. She hasn't been the same since what happened to Shey. Those two were inseparable."

Rawly asks, concerned. "What happened to Shey?"

45

The Eternal Friendship of Nayana & Shey, Part 1

Unbreakable

(Summer – 23 Years Ago)

"YOU CAN'T BREAK me, humans!" two-year-old Nayana trumpets defiantly. "I know what you're doing. Mommy told me. And you will never break me! Never!" Her blaring declaration echoes off the cold walls. Unfortunately, the dimly lit room feels all the more empty now with her own voice bouncing back to her—a harsh reminder that she is the only living creature in this large warehouse.

Nayana rubs her right ankle with her trunk. Her legs sting from the rope burns. All four of her legs are tightly tethered with ropes that hold her firmly in place, and all four ropes are tied tautly to the metal bars in front of and behind her. There's also a thick chain tightly wrapped around her right front leg that is attached to a metal ring in the floor. She can't move—not forward, not backward, not sideways. She's stuck standing on a hard concrete floor, immobile, in the dark, alone. And she's been like this for eight days.

Mommy said to be strong. The humans are trying to crush your spirits. Make you think they can control you by chaining you. She shakes her right front leg, tugging at the steel chain and rope that are ripping at her flesh. *But it won't work, because you know their devious plan. No human's forcing you to stand on your head. You're too smart for that.*

Nayana's heart sinks as she thinks of her mother. *Those vicious humans. If they hadn't chained her to a wall, she never would have let me be yanked away. And they had to tie me to another elephant just to drag me from her. Savages!* The heart-wrenching memories from eight days ago flash through her mind. An irreparable hole was slashed in Nayana's heart as she heard her mother crying out for her. *Those brutes could have cared less as we screamed.* Anger boils inside the young elephant. It's hard enough to sleep with your legs chained up, but it's impossible when you can't stop thinking about your mother weeping and screaming your name. *Will I ever see her again?* She dares not answer that question. She needs something to keep her going.

Mommy said not to fight back, but how could I not? They were tearing us apart. And now those humans think they can just leave me here to suffer? Nayana bellows mightily. "Absolutely not! If they want a fight, they got one!"

Immediately she winces, though, realizing it was a mistake to exert so much energy. She has to relieve herself, but she's trying to hold it. She's already standing in a puddle of her own urine, which is splattered on the ground around her. She doesn't want to exacerbate the problem. As it is, the putrid smell fills her trunk every time she takes a breath.

Just then, Nayana hears the clanking sounds of metal on metal as the humans open the warehouse door. Her heart skips a beat. *They're coming.*

Twice a day, a group of humans force Nayana to walk around the inside of the warehouse for twenty minutes. For the other twenty-three-plus hours, she's trapped in place. She hasn't seen the warming sun since they locked her up. She craves it.

Nayana guards herself. She wants to ram them all with her head, but she knows better. There are too many of them, and they're taller than she is... for now.

"Grab the ropes." Randy, the group's leader, orders his six subordinates to restrain Nayana. He is clothed in cargo shorts, a tan short-sleeved button down shirt, and a brown cotton safari hat. He thinks the safari hunter getup makes him look like a rugged adventurer, but the eerie implications of the ensemble are completely lost on him.

Some of the workers untether the ropes holding Nayana to the wall, while the others grab hold of the ropes around her legs and tug so hard that the young elephant can't move unless they let her.

Nayana shakes her body. "Don't touch me!"

Randy raises his bullhook and points it menacingly at her face. The weapon casts a threatening shadow on Nayana's forehead. "Settle down, Abby. We can do this the easy way or the hard way. It's up to you."

Nayana glares at Randy and grunts. "My name is Nayana, brute! You can't just name me whatever you please!"

Randy lays the sharp end of the poker on Nayana's trunk. "Feel that? You want that in your skull? Don't matter to me."

Nayana wants to ram this sadistic human into the metal bars behind him, but she wouldn't win that fight. No use in wasting her energy. *His day will come.*

The humans use another larger female elephant as an anchor to help pull Nayana around the room. They put collars around each elephant's neck and then attach the two elephants with a rope. Simultaneously, the humans yank at Nayana with the ropes gripping her ankles. This isn't a walk; it's a tug of war with her body.

Nayana bears it, trying to stifle her revulsion for these humans. It's a humiliating and painful experience, but she's not going to let them see her strain. She mostly can't believe that every one of these humans is completely unsympathetic to her incredible discomfort. They just make friendly chit chat with one another while Nayana struggles to walk.

After the twenty minutes are up, the humans retie all of the ropes to the metal bars behind and in front of her. Three of the humans pull the anchor elephant out of the room, whacking her with the bullhook to keep her moving. She lets out a loud yelp, but it does nothing to cease the sharp jabs to her tender skin. Just like with Nayana, the trainers make a point of targeting the most sensitive areas of the elephants' body—her ears, mouth, anus and feet— because they know she'll be more likely to follow their orders if she fears such severe retribution.

Nayana is securely tied up, so the humans lumber out of the room. Before Randy leaves, he turns around and smacks the bullhook right into her forehead. She's stunned. A searing pain reverberates through her cranium. She doesn't even make a sound, she's so taken aback.

"Disobey me again! See what happens!" Randy threatens. He jabs the bullhook into the soft flesh of her ear. This time Nayana lets out a pained cry. Randy cracks a sinister smile. "That's right. I'm in charge, Abby. I'm in charge."

Randy switches off the light, leaving Nayana in a pitch-black cavern. She fights back the tears welling in her eyes. *Be strong. Mommy said to be strong.*

*   *   *

"Lie down, you dumb animal!" Randy smacks the bullhook into Nayana's back. She squeals, her trunk flailing in the air. Five other trainers pull tightly on the ropes tied around her legs. They hold

Nayana on the ground for almost a minute. "That's right! Keep her down. These animals may be stupid, but they catch on eventually."

Nayana struggles to break free, but the workers hold their grip. "Let me go, brutes! You have no right to do this to me!"

"And release!" Randy orders. The workers give the young elephant just enough slack to sit up.

Nayana breathes heavily, exhausted. They've been at this for an hour. Hitting, yanking, pulling, prodding and forcing her into various wrenching positions, making her learn absurd tricks for her upcoming circus routines.

It's been more than a year since Nayana was first trapped in the warehouse. She spent five months locked in that empty room all alone, chained to the walls for hours upon hours. She stayed strong, though. She didn't let those intolerable walks crush her—despite the jabbing bullhooks, despite the inflamed sores around her ankles where the ropes chafed her skin. She didn't let those abuses break her. But that was nothing compared to what she's enduring now. The isolation was just a method to wear her down, to break her spirit. Now she's on to the actual training, and it is pure hell.

Twice a day, in two-hour training sessions, Nayana is yanked around and beaten to force her to learn tricks completely unnatural to elephants—many of them dangerous for an animal of her size. Lie down! Sit up! Balance on pedestals, do headstands, spin around! These sessions occur in a hidden, fenced-in area so that no one can look in and see the baby elephant struggling for her life. Loud classic rock music is played to drown out Nayana's cries. There is no relief, no escape. Only a dozen people in the world know that she is here now, and the circus trainers want to keep it that way.

Randy, still donning his laughable safari getup, lords over the sessions. He orders the five trainers around, teaching them to dominate the young elephant.

"She ain't learned yet!" he hollers. "I wanna see her bow down to me just when I show her this bullhook." He hoists the jagged metal stick above his head. "Break her right! Do it again!"

The other trainers grab hold of the ropes attached to Nayana's legs and belly and wait for his next command. Nayana tenses up. She knows what's coming.

Like some grotesque medieval torture technique, the trainers pull on their ropes, spreading out all four of Nayana's legs. "Pull!" Randy orders.

The trainer who is holding the rope attached to Nayana's left leg yanks violently on the line, pulling Nayana's leg underneath her and sending her crashing to the dirt—a perilous maneuver since the young elephant's weight could crush her fragile inner organs. Randy swiftly smacks the bullhook down onto Nayana's spine.

Nayana cries out, panicked. "Mommy! I need you!" She desperately wishes her mother would come crashing through the fence to rescue her, but it is hopeless. Her voice is drowned out by the blaring rock music. And even if her mother could hear her, she couldn't remove her own chains to get to her daughter. And where would they go? They are oceans away from the comfort of the South Asian plains and forests.

"Hold her down!" Randy barks. The trainers' arms strain as they attempt to hold Nayana in place, but she thrashes around, terrified.

Randy snarls, "You just won't give up, will you, Abby? You think you're tough?"

He takes his bullhook, lifts it high into the air, and forcefully swings it down, ramming the sharp end of the hook right into Nayana's anus.

Nayana screams. Ripples of anguish shoot through her body.

Randy turns to the other trainers, beaming. "Now she knows who's in charge."

The pain is so intense that Nayana urinates onto the dirt, and unfortunately, some of the liquid splashes onto Randy's boots. The other trainers laugh. One beer-bellied man jests, "Got something on your shoe, boss."

The other trainers laugh harder. Randy grimaces. "Hand me that hot shot, Wes."

Wes tosses Randy a long metal shaft with two prongs at the end. Nayana sees the electrical device and cries out. "No. Please! I didn't mean to. I couldn't hold it. Don't!"

Randy turns on the device. It buzzes menacingly, like a thousand killer bees stuffed in a jar. Randy shoves it against Nayana's sensitive skin. "Get up, you little idiot!" The electricity courses through her body, causing a momentary seizure. She struggles to her feet, hoping he won't stun her again.

"We're doin' the move again!" Randy yells to the trainers. He holds the hot shot to Nayana's face. She stares at it fearfully. "We're gonna keep doing this 'til you get it right." Randy electrocutes Nayana in her side. She squeals as her insides are burned. "I can keep doing this every day for a year, stupid. Don't matter to me. This is my job."

Don't cry, Nayana. Be strong. Don't let them win. She clenches her jaw, but her body is weak—the electrical shocks have exhausted her muscles. *How much longer can I keep fighting? When will this end?*

The trainers tug on their ropes, once again straightening Nayana's legs. She wobbles slightly—the wounds from the rope burns around her ankles haven't been treated, and the pain of the rough ropes rubbing over the open sores is excruciating.

Randy glares at the vulnerable elephant and yells, "Pull!"

*   *   *

"Get up!" "Sit down!" "No! No! Do it again! Now!" Nayana's days are filled with a barrage of furious commands. Over and over she's jabbed with the bullhook, jolted with the hot shot—on the soft pads of her feet, under her trunk, on her spine, on the backs and fronts of her legs. She's pulled this way and that, again and again—only her bruised body knows how many times. On occasion, she even gets confused about what exactly the humans are trying to make her do: Spin around? Stand on her head? They just keep hitting her and yanking at her for hours; it's discombobulating. Mostly, though, it's agonizing.

After another three months, Nayana is nearing her breaking point. Today, Randy and his trainers have been especially vicious. Nayana is being forced to hold herself up with her two front legs on top of a pedestal, putting immense strain on her body. She keeps hesitating, which infuriates Randy.

"Legs up, Abby!" Randy barks. "Legs up!"

"I'll fall!" Nayana protests.

Randy jabs the bullhook into her back legs. "Up, you stupid animal. Don't you get it? Put up your goddamn legs!" Randy turns to his fellow trainers who look baffled. "I told you, they're dumb. Hittin' 'em is the only way to make 'em do anything."

Randy keeps slamming the sharp end of the bullhook into her back legs.

Nayana pleads with him. "Stop! Stop! I know what you want me to do, but it hurts. I'm going to fall!"

Randy takes out his hot shot, so Nayana immediately starts to lift her back legs. Randy smiles. "Thought that would do it. You gotta put a little fear in their hearts."

Nayana teeters on the pedestal. "I can't hold myself up!"

Randy places the bullhook against her back legs to keep her up in the air. "Steady, Abby. Steady."

Nayana sways from side to side and then topples off of the pedestal onto the dirt below. She lands with a loud thud. The air is knocked out of her. She wheezes and lets out a fragile whimper.

Don't cry. Don't cry. Don't let them see you cry. Nayana fights back the tears.

Randy marches over to the fatigued baby elephant, pulls out his hot shot, and stuns her in the side. "Get up!"

Nayana lies there, quivering from the voltage, but she doesn't move to get up.

Randy shocks her again, leaving a burn mark on her sensitive hide. Still, she doesn't get up.

Nayana closes her eyes. *Mommy, Mommy! You warned me to just follow their orders, but I wanted to be strong. To prove they can't control me. To make you proud. But I'm weak. I can't take it anymore. I hurt so much. I just want the beatings to end. I want all this to end.*

Nayana doesn't make a sound. She stumbles to a standing position. She glares at Randy and the other merciless trainers. She glances at the bullhooks dangling from their hands, the ropes littering the ground, the dirt punctured with divots where she struggled helplessly to break free. Then she steps back over to the pedestal and climbs onto it. She lifts up her back legs, performing the perfect handstand.

Randy and the other trainers burst into a triumphant cheer, shaking their bullhooks victoriously in the air.

Randy beams. "And that, boys and girls, is how you train an elephant."

46

THE ETERNAL FRIENDSHIP OF NAYANA & SHEY, PART 2

SHEY

THE MASSIVE BARN door creaks open, revealing an exhausted Nayana flanked by Randy and Wes. Nayana has just gotten off of a semi-trailer truck in which she had been crammed for countless hours, chained in the dark and all alone. She knows one thing for sure: She is now far away from the compound where her mother is locked up.

A heavy odor hits her nose—a nauseating mixture of hay, urine and feces. Randy and Wes hold tightly to ropes attached to Nayana's front legs. In Randy's other hand, he grasps his bullhook firmly, ready to strike Nayana if she gets any ideas about making a break for it. But Nayana is so frightened about where the humans are taking her, she's not thinking of escaping; she just wants to feel some semblance of safety.

"Wake up, lazy bums," Randy hollers. "Looks like you got company." Nayana's heart flutters at the sight of other elephants. For more than a year, she's only seen her own kind in passing as she was dragged from the warehouse where she was imprisoned to the mock circus ring and then back again, so it's incredibly reassuring to be so close to them.

Five elephants are lined up in a row side by side, facing the center of the room. Their right front legs and left back legs are bound by chains connected to the wall behind them and a metal ring in front of them—the same way she had been trapped for so long at the breeding facility, and the same way The Uncaged Alliance would find the herd twenty-two years later.

The two humans march Nayana into the room, parading her past the other elephants. Randy introduces them. "This here's Abby. She's the newest addition to the troupe. Let's give her a Happy World Circus welcome. Ready, trumpets!"

All five of the elephants raise their trunks high in the air and trumpet loudly. Randy applauds them. "Good girls!"

After passing three elephants, Randy tugs on the rope attached to Nayana's left leg. "Stop," he orders. Nayana halts. Randy and Wes use their bullhooks to prod Nayana backward into an open space between two of the other elephants. Nayana is doing her best, but it's difficult to walk backward when you're as large as she is.

Shey, the young elephant to Nayana's right, bravely defends Nayana by reaching out her trunk and tripping Wes.

Wes swats at the elephant. "Peanut!"

The mischievous Shey laughs and trumpets, "Bozos!" She then looks at Nayana to see if her rebellious prank has enlivened the disheartened newcomer.

Nayana can't believe it. An elephant stood up to the humans... and survived. She is equally surprised and encouraged.

Slightly cheered, she squeezes into the space the best she can, hoping to avoid too many more whacks by the bullhooks.

"Thank you," Nayana whispers gratefully.

Shey whispers back playfully. "Any time!"

Randy puts his bullhook against Nayana's head to hold her in place while the other trainer chains her legs to the wall behind her and then to the metal ring in front.

"Welcome to your new home, Abby. At least temporarily." Randy waves the bullhook at her threateningly. "Don't go starting any fights neither. You're lucky I'm sticking you in here with the other elephants on the first night. Don't make me regret it—or I'll make *you* regret it."

Randy and Wes head for the front door. Randy calls out as he strolls along, "Nighty night, ladies. Best rest up good. You've got a long day of training ahead of you tomorrow."

The humans slam the warehouse door shut. The only light is a grating fluorescent bulb behind the troupe. The room falls silent. Nayana is nervous about meeting the new elephants. What if they don't like her?

The elephant nearest the door, Kusum, turns to her sisters and remarks dryly, "Imbeciles."

Nayana smiles. With that sly comment, she knows that she's going to like *them* very much.

"*Ugly* imbeciles, Kusum," Shey quips. "That's even worse."

The others chuckle. At twenty-eight, Kusum has already lived a tough life in the circus, but she still has a glimmer of youthfulness left—a far cry from the worn-down creature she would be years later when The Uncaged Alliance first meets her.

The large elephant to Nayana's left—and at forty-three, the oldest in the room—turns to Nayana and gently caresses the battered little elephant's head. "It's okay, baby child. No need to be scared. We're going to watch over you now."

Nayana lets out a deep sigh. She's overcome with calm; the soothing touch of another elephant is so comforting. No one has been this kind to her since her mother. In fact, over the last year and a half no one has been kind to her at all. It's just been one arduous beating after another. For the first time in so very long, she feels loved.

"My name is Samadara," the affectionate elephant offers. "What's your name, little squoosh? And not the name the humans gave you— the name your momma gave you."

"Nayana," the shy elephant replies.

Samadara continues to caress Nayana with her trunk and smells her to get to know her better. "Why that's a beautiful name. Your mother must have been a very special elephant. And I know that she thinks about you every day. Do you know how I know that?"

Nayana shakes her head.

"Because a day doesn't go by that I don't think about my own baby child." Samadara is quiet for a moment, thinking about her own little one who was torn away. Years ago, Samadara was put in the breeding facility for a while, but when she didn't prove to be fertile enough, they placed her back in the traveling show. It devastates her to think that her child is stuck in another troupe somewhere, so she knows Nayana's mother must be feeling the same way. "She loves you very much. Don't ever question that for a second."

Nayana clears her throat. "Will I ever see her again?" she asks meekly, afraid of the answer.

Samadara glances at Kusum. Since Samadara is the oldest, she is the matriarch and makes all final decisions, but with Kusum being the second oldest and the most matter-of-fact of the bunch, they rely on one another for support. Kusum nods in agreement, so Samadara explains. "We try to be honest with one another no matter how hard the truth is, Nayana. Being forced to perform in the circus is a horrid life, and one of the worst aspects is that we are ripped from our dear mothers at a very young age. I can't tell you for sure that you will never see her again, but I can say that it is unlikely." Samadara takes hold of Nayana's trunk with her own to soften the blow. "However,

I can tell you this: We are your new family and we will defend you, be there for you, love you as if you were our very own babe. Do you understand?"

Nayana doesn't say a word. This brutal truth stings. She needed to hear it, but it cuts deep. She nods but lowers her head to the floor.

"Don't worry, Nayana," Shey pats the forlorn elephant on the back with her trunk. She is only one year older than Nayana, but having experienced the tough life in the breeding center herself, she knows exactly what the newcomer is going through, so she feels protective of her. "If you think my tripping Wes was fun, just wait 'til you see what I do to him next time for taking you away from your mother."

"Oh no you don't, Shey," chides Yaso, who stands at the end of the row, next to Shey. Despite being only twenty-two, Yaso is just as ornery as the day The Uncaged Alliance meets her decades later. "I've had about enough of your shenanigans. Last time you pulled one of your childish pranks, Randy gave me quite the lashing thinking it was my doing. I will not let that happen again."

Shey picks up some hay from the filthy floor and tosses it at Yaso, who swats at it with her trunk. "You little brat!"

Shey giggles, delighted.

"Okay, you two," Samadara intervenes. "You're not making a very good impression on our newest family member." She addresses Nayana. "Don't mind them. Being chained up for so many hours in such smelly, cramped conditions sometimes brings out the worst in us."

"Of course, no matter who Yaso is stuck beside it seems to bring out the worst in her," quips Padma, who is squeezed in between Kusum and Samadara.

Shey giggles even louder and shakes her trunk in celebration of this zinger.

"Padma, that's disrespectful," Samadara scolds.

"What?" Padma defends herself. "How many times has she been moved around because she doesn't get along with her neighbor?"

"Padma," Samadara glares. "Enough."

Padma shuts her mouth. She may only be twelve years old, but she's mature enough to know it's better to keep the peace among the other elephants.

Samadara addresses the entire herd. "Okay, time to rest, everyone. You heard Randy. We have a long day of training again tomorrow, so we better get some shut-eye."

Nayana raises her head, concerned. "I thought they already taught me how to perform in the circus. They made me stand on my head, twirl on pedestals, all kinds of painful tricks. I have to go through more?"

"I'm afraid so, baby child," Samadara sighs. She wishes she didn't have to be the bearer of such bad news but such is the life of the matriarch. "What you went through at the breeding facility—that torment—was only the beginning. Over the next month or so they're going to prepare us to go out on the road as a traveling circus, performing as a troupe. It's going to be very, very hard. But you mustn't forget: We're in this together, and we're going to get through this together." Samadara puts her trunk on Nayana's head. "Now close your eyes, little squoosh. You need your rest."

Samadara leans in closer to Nayana and softly hums a lullaby. Nayana tries to focus on Samadara's humming to ease her anxiety—even imagining that it's her mother lulling her into slumber—but she mostly feels sick. How can she sleep with the fear of more training looming over her? It's been unbearable so far. Will this constant oppression ever end? She just wants to escape into one night of worry-free sleep. Maybe even one full day away from these abusive humans. Is that too much to ask?

*   *   *

"No, Eleanor! No!" Randy hollers at Padma, his voice cracking from frustration. "It's a twirl and *then* you sit on your butt. How many times do we have to go over this?!" Padma is sitting on her bum with her two front legs up in the air. Randy yanks down hard on her left front leg to get her back into the starting position. Padma moans in anguish and then quickly lowers onto all fours to avoid any more jabs from the bullhook.

The other five elephants look on, helpless. It's two weeks into training and they have all been through this same performance hundreds of times, but Padma can't quite remember the order of the steps. This is not out of character for her, unfortunately. She's been in the circus for eight years and every single year, when they go through their new routines during the winter break, she struggles to learn the new moves. She pays for her lack of coordination with constant jabs from the bullhook. Her gray flesh is bruised and covered with hook boils—infected wounds from bullhook beatings.

The six elephants stand on all fours in the practice ring with the trainers brandishing their weapons to force the elephants to memorize the routine—or else. Nayana is doing her best to learn all the new maneuvers, but it is even more complicated to have to coordinate with five other elephants.

The oldest of the bunch, Samadara and Kusum, struggle to catch their breath. They're relieved to stop for a few moments to ease the tension in their aching legs. Their limbs throb with arthritis after decades of standing on pavement. Their bodies were designed to walk on sand and grass, not the hard surfaces found in big cities.

No doors are open in the practice ring, so not a flicker of natural light enters the room—just headache-inducing fluorescent bulbs.

The air is filled with dust from the elephants' shuffling around on the dirty ground for hours on end. A musty odor offends their nostrils. What the elephants wouldn't give to be outside, bathing in the sun, drinking water whenever they please, roaming freely for miles on end over gorgeous plains. But that is not their life. Their life is the circus.

Randy stomps to the center of the room, throwing another tantrum. He berates his human employees. "Happy World Circus is counting on me—on us—to get these animals in working condition. These thickheaded beasts need to know the routines inside and out. They can't be falling all over the place, stepping out of line. It'll make us look like we don't know what we're goddamn doing. Is that what you want, Wes?"

Randy gets in Wes' face. Wes winces but doesn't move, answering like a well-trained soldier. "No, sir!"

"That's right, 'no, sir.'" Randy puffs out his chest. "So if you agree, then why haven't you whipped these stupid elephants into shape in the two weeks we been here? You're gonna make me look bad. And I don't like to look bad." Randy scrunches up his face, trying to look more threatening but really just looking like he ate something sour. "Get it together. The longer you idiots keep screwing up, the longer we're here. And I'm exhausted."

Shey whispers to Nayana. "Did he seriously just say that he's exhausted? We're the ones running around with no breaks. Give me that bullhook and we'll see how fatigued he feels after I smash him over the head with it a few dozen times."

Nayana laughs.

"Focus, Shey," Samadara swiftly warns.

Randy surveys his bedraggled trainers with disdain. "Why do they always give me such losers? Every season I gotta work miracles with a bunch of losers," he whispers, just loud enough for them to hear.

Then he raises his voice again. "I'm doing double duty here. Training baby elephants and full-grown elephants. You know why?"

Randy stares down one of the nervous trainers but before the guy can speak, Randy answers his own question. "Because I'm the best. Ain't no one better than me at training elephants, so you better listen good. I've trained hundreds of elephants over the years." That is a gross exaggeration, but Randy's ego knows no bounds. "I break these wild beasts until they dance on cue. They wow and entertain thousands of people, and bring in billions of dollars." That is actually not an exaggeration. "And it's all thanks to me. They want to see *my* elephants. That's why you better get it right!"

Randy swings his bullhook into the air and rushes toward one of the trainers. The guy covers his head and ducks as his irate supervisor comes charging at him. But then, surprisingly, Randy passes him and slams the bullhook into Padma's ear. "Get it right, stupid animal! Get it right!" Padma squeals in pain.

"You are the stupidest animal I've ever had to work with. Twirl, then sit! Twirl, then sit!" Randy keeps whacking Padma's tender left ear harder and harder.

Shey can't take it any longer. She rushes at Randy from across the room. "Leave her alone!"

"Boss, watch out!" one of the trainers yells.

Randy jumps out of the way just as Shey reaches him. Two of the other trainers slam their bullhooks into Shey's head, but she doesn't even flinch. "Is that all you've got?!"

She raises her trunk and trumpets in their faces defiantly. The men step back from the loud sound. They're startled, but they hold up their bullhooks, ready to strike again if need be.

"That's enough." Randy stands up and brushes the dirt from his safari uniform. He licks his lips. "Good old Peanut. God I love that feisty spirit. You remind me of my ex-wife."

Shey stares Randy down, ready for severe retaliation. She'll take the agonizing onslaught if it saves the more fragile Padma from another beating. But Randy just smirks and claps his hands together. "Back to work, everyone! We're beginning from the top."

The trainers get back into their assigned stations in the ring and slap the elephants with their bullhooks to get them in their starting positions.

Shey looks over at Nayana and smiles. Nayana's mouth is practically dangling open. What an elephant! Nayana remembers when she was brave like that, before the humans crushed her spirit. It's invigorating to see that type of unbridled courage again.

No more being meek for Nayana. These humans may have broken her when she was on her own, but now she has her herd, and she will not be broken again. It's impossible not to feel inspired with a valiant elephant like Shey around.

✳   ✳   ✳

Training is finally over. Two and a half weeks have gone by and it's now time for the circus to hit the road. It couldn't have come at a better time—those few weeks have been brutal. Nayana, Shey, Samadara, Padma, Kusum and Yaso each suffered many painful blows, but they stuck together and protested as much as they could. At night, Nayana would recite the routines with Padma over and over, and Nayana's extra help paid off. Padma made fewer missteps, and while she still isn't a graceful performer, she has improved enough that she has been subjected to fewer beatings.

Nayana is extremely anxious about heading off to her first performance in front of a live audience. First, though, she'll have to endure a grueling train ride to that town—something she hadn't thought of before.

Nayana and the other elephants are being escorted from the barn to the train when the young elephant sees a surprising sight: other animals. And fascinating looking animals at that! She's used to seeing humans all over the place, birds flying in the air, and lizards crawling on the ground, but now for the first time she sees zebras, horses, camels and goats. What is not a surprise is that the humans are also hitting these poor creatures. One circus worker constantly cracks a whip on the horses' rears to get them to move forward to their train cars. Another circus worker tugs hard on the reins connected to a camel's head, jerking him forward.

Nayana is disgusted. She immediately feels a bond with these other animals who are stuck in the same hellish predicament.

As the elephants walk to the train, each is forced to use her trunk to hold the tail of the elephant in front of her. It's an embarrassing, unnatural act, but they'll be whacked if they don't obey. Nayana is in line behind Samadara and in front of Shey. As they move forward, Nayana notices cages off in the distance that contain orange-and-black-striped creatures, furiously growling and pacing back and forth.

Nayana calls back to Shey. "Oh my, what type of animals are those?"

"Tigers," Shey responds. "Stay away from them, though. Other than humans, they're the only other dangerous animals to watch out for in the circus."

"Really?" Nayana is intrigued. "Why are they dangerous to us? We haven't done anything to them."

"Samadara told me that big cats like that attack other animals for food," Shey answers as she keeps moving forward. "I've never seen it happen myself, but you can ask her about it on the train. We have a very long ride ahead of us."

The elephants have reached their boxcar and are forced to walk up the ramp. Nayana and Shey watch as Yaso is sent in first, followed by

Samadara, who struggles the most. The arthritis in her legs makes it difficult for her to walk in general, but the anguish is worsened when she has to bend down to get her head through the short door. Making matters worse, Samadara's back scrapes against the top of the metal doorframe.

"Poor Samadara and Kusum fought through so much pain to survive the training sessions," Nayana remarks to Shey. "Is that going to be us one day?"

Shey grins. "Not if we get out of here first."

Nayana doesn't have time to respond to this wild statement. Just at that moment, a trainer yanks Shey's trunk to turn her around. She has to enter the train backwards so that she faces the middle of the boxcar. Nayana is forced to enter in the same manner. It's a struggle, seeing as how it's her first time, but she has learned to pick up things quickly to avoid as many jabs as possible.

Right before Nayana disappears into the boxcar, she sees Kusum and Padma being forced into the boxcar just behind hers. Their dreary expressions are a foreboding sign of what Nayana is about to experience on this ride.

Once on the train, the humans chain the elephants' front and back legs to the nearest wall.

Nayana complains to the other elephants in her train car. "Is there ever a time when we're *not* chained up? Where do they think we're going to go? We're inside a tiny box."

Samadara looks at Nayana, who is directly across from her and responds somberly. "I know, baby child. I understand why you're upset. The past few weeks, you've asked a lot of questions that I haven't answered. I wanted to focus on getting you through that wretched training first. But we have a long, harrowing journey ahead of us, so it's time that I explained to you what lies ahead of you in the circus."

Nayana's heart beats faster as Samadara continues. "Once the humans leave this boxcar, I'll explain everything. Just be patient a few more moments."

Nayana's heart is pounding in her chest. *I'm about to find out my whole future and I have to wait? Get off this train, stupid humans!*

The trainers finish chaining Shey and then finally walk out, slamming the door shut behind them. The four elephants are left in the cold train car. There is one grated window on either side for ventilation and no heating system. The temperature isn't too chilly at the moment, but as they head up the coast it will be cold. Underneath the elephants' feet is a pile of hay—their only meal for quite some time.

Nayana notices a stream of blood trickling down the side of Samadara's back. "Are you okay? You're bleeding."

Samadara doesn't seem surprised. "Am I? It happens every time I try to step into these blasted train cars. The doorway is too low and it's painful to bend properly with these worn down knees. Don't worry about me, baby child. I've had much worse."

"But will the humans fix you up?" Nayana asks, concerned.

"No," Samadara responds matter-of-factly. "We're on our own, baby child. You can't count on the humans for any help at all, which is actually the perfect place for us to start our talk. You asked about being chained up so much. One of the worst things about being in the circus is that we spend most of our lives in chains. The only times we're not chained up are occasional fifteen-minute walks in the morning, when we're practicing for a show, or when we're performing. The rest of the time we're stuck like this." Samadara shakes the uncomfortable chains around her front left leg. "I have seen it drive many elephants insane and as matriarch I have made it my goal to ensure that doesn't happen to our family."

"And what about these train rides? How long will we be trapped in here?" Nayana asks.

"At least a few hours," Samadara says. "But more likely a few days."

"A few days?!" Nayana can't believe her ears. "Will they at least let us out to move around?"

"Of course not," Yaso huffs. "They could care less if we're uncomfortable in here. Just wait 'til the summer. At least it's cool now, but when the warm air kicks in, it gets so hot in here you think your brain is going to boil."

Nayana takes a deep breath. This a lot for her to digest and they've only just begun the conversation. "We could really be in here for days? But I already have to relieve myself and we haven't even started moving. I was hoping to hold it until we arrived at the first town."

"Good luck with that," Yaso scoffs. "You'll burst. Forget getting to the first town; we may be just sitting here on the tracks for a few hours. Right now the humans are loading all of the other animals and equipment, and then they have to get themselves situated. You're not going to want to hear this, but…" Yaso looks uncomfortable. "We have to…"

"You have to pee and poo where you're standing," Shey blurts out. Nayana is aghast. "What?!"

"You've pooed beside us before," Yaso remarks. "At the training ground, we were stuck in that line all night and most of the day."

"I know," Nayana explains. "But in this boxcar we're in such a tiny space. It's going to smell bad. It may even slosh around. And worse, it will get all over the hay, which we're supposed to eat. I want to hold it."

Samadara, Yaso and Shey look at one another, concerned. Samadara can tell that Nayana is having trouble soaking in all of this upsetting information, so she states in her maternal manner, "Okay, Nayana. Let's discuss the best methods for enduring these long train rides. These boxcars are our main mode of transportation for the next year until we get back to the training grounds. They're filthy and maddening, so we have to keep our minds occupied by chatting, telling stories. We have to…"

"Okay, tell me about tigers." Nayana excitedly interrupts. "Shey said you have stories about them."

Samadara pats Shey on the head with her trunk. "Ah, yes, Shey does enjoy my stories about Ceylon."

Nayana's ears flap open, eager to hear these tales. "What's Ceylon?"

"It's where I come from," Samadara explains. "It's actually where most of us elephants in the circus come from. Right now we are in a place called America, but elephants are not from America, so since the humans figured out that they could make a lot of money by exploiting us, they..."

"What's money?" Nayana interrupts again.

"It's difficult to explain," Samadara attempts to think of a lucid definition. "Basically it's something humans give one another to obtain something." Samadara sees that the young elephant is thoroughly confused, so she gives an example. "Let's say I wanted some of your hay. I would give you money so that you would give me some of your hay."

"But if you asked me for hay, I would just give it to you," Nayana replies, even more confused.

"Yes," Samadara says. "That's very sweet of you, but that's not how humans work. They rarely give one another anything unless they will receive something in return. Anyway, you were asking about Ceylon. It's a far-off land where, for the most part, elephants roam freely. There are humans there called poachers who kill us for our tusks, but I'll tell you about them some other time. So, when I was a child—a little older than you—humans attacked my herd to steal the baby elephants from our mothers." Samadara's face tenses as she remembers this traumatizing day. "The humans murdered my mother right in front of me. They shot her with a gun." Before Nayana can interrupt to ask what guns are, Samadara elaborates. "Guns are weapons like bullhooks that inflict pain on others, but guns are designed to be lethal. They have metal objects inside called bullets that are projected at creatures to pierce their skin and organs, and ultimately kill them."

Nayana looks terrified. "They killed your mommy right in front of you? That's so awful. Being torn away from my mommy was so hard, but… seeing her killed? Humans are so cruel. I'm so sorry you lost your mommy."

"Thank you, baby child." Samadara smiles.

"So how did you get to America?"

"After the humans killed our mothers, they put us on boats," Samadara continues. "Boats are like trains, but they float on water. Some of us died on the long journey, but once we were here they trapped us in circuses. Oh, and zoos."

Another word Nayana has never heard before. "What are zoos?"

"Kusum's actually from a zoo," Yaso says, jumping in to explain this one. "She can tell you about it in more detail at some point, but basically, the poor animals in there are just as miserable as we are in here. Although unlike in circuses, the animals in zoos aren't forced to perform. The humans lock them in small cages all day and night. A lot of the animals go insane from being confined to such cramped quarters without anything interesting to do. This distressed mental state is such a common occurrence, the humans actually named it zoochosis."

The concept of zoos sounds ridiculous to Nayana. "Why would the humans lock them up like that?"

"Because humans are selfish," Yaso utters with disdain. "They're curious about what other animals look like—animals from far-off lands—so they stick them in cages so other humans can come and look at them."

"But what if these animals don't want to be taken from their families and then just stared at?" Nayana asks, anger in her voice. She knows the answer, though.

Samadara steps back into the conversation, shaking her massive head, perturbed. "You just described the greatest grievance that all other animals have with humans. They don't care what we want. They only care what *they* want. If they want to wear another animals' skin or fur, they kill them for it. If they think watching elephants stand on our heads is entertaining, they beat us until we stand on our heads. We suffer because it pleases them."

It's all sinking in for Nayana. She stares down at the hay scattered at her feet. "And they took me from my mother because it's easier than going all the way over to Ceylon to get more elephants."

"That's right, Nayana," Samadara exclaims. "You're a bright young elephant. Now, humans make older female elephants—like your mother and me—get pregnant, and then they take our sweet little babes from us and force them to perform in shows. You, Shey, Yaso, Padma—you're the next generation of elephants. You've never even seen the expansive beauty of Ceylon. I wish so much better for you than a life in captivity."

Nayana's head hangs low. A sorrowful weight squeezes her lungs.

Shey stares at Samadara and Yaso, stunned. "Uh, what happened to that fun talk about ferocious tigers? Way to depress us, Samadara and Yaso. Maybe next you can tell us about that time Randy beat Padma so hard that she was bleeding out of her ear canal."

"Sorry, sorry," Samadara concedes. "You are right, little squoosh. Whenever talk of Ceylon arises, it conjures up a darker side of me. I miss it so." Samadara blows a puff of air out of her powerful trunk, trying to expel the sour feelings. She forces a smile. "Okay, let us talk of tigers."

Nayana's face brightens as she looks back up at Samadara, momentarily distracted from her worries. "Let's!"

*　　*　　*

Nine hours have passed. The elephants have been jostled constantly by the windy movement of the train. They're already worn out, but the ride is far from over. Nayana and the other elephants held off from relieving themselves for as long as they could, but eventually they couldn't wait any longer. Now, after slipping around during the bumpy trip, they're caked in feces.

The train halts for its one stop that day. A trainer yanks open the boxcar door and the nauseating odor of urine and feces hits his nose hard.

"Ugh." He covers his nose and bends forward, dry heaving. "I think I'm gonna be sick."

"Rookie," another trainer mocks him. "One thing you gotta get used to in the circus is that these animals are disgusting. They shit and piss like eighty gallons a day. And then they just stand there in it."

Shey trumpets angrily from inside the boxcar. "We're standing in it because you trapped us in here with nowhere else to go, you tyrants!"

"Shut up!" the trainer yells. "We're giving you water."

He turns on the hose and sprays it at the elephants. "Open wide!"

Nayana, Samadara, Yaso and Shey are all parched. They open their mouths, hoping he'll spray water into them. The trainer sprays water in Yaso's mouth first, then moves on to Nayana.

"Please, more," Yaso begs. "I'm so thirsty. Please!"

"You can't steal all the water for yourself," Shey gripes. "Give someone else a turn."

"Be civilized, ladies," Samadara reminds them. "We're all on the same side."

The elephants feel embarrassed holding their mouths open, begging for water, but it's been so many hours since their last drink that their desperation gets the better of them. It also feels so good to have the clean water sprayed over their dirty backs.

"That's enough." The trainer turns off the hose.

"More! Please!" Yaso pleads, but no luck.

The trainer who gagged tosses in some clean hay and slams the door shut.

The elephants are once again stuck with little fresh air. Nayana is incensed. "They're not going to clean out all this old soiled hay? It's inedible. And all this new hay will just mix in," she yells, getting more agitated. "The smell is unbearable in here!"

Samadara remains calm. "They won't clean the train until we get to our destination."

Revulsion sweeps over Nayana, her anger building like a tornado swirling through her insides. "I hate them! I hate the humans so much! How dare they do this to us?" Nayana shakes the chains wrapped around her legs, trying to pull free. "I need to run around. They can't just leave us in here chained to the wall for so long." Claustrophobia smothers the young elephant. "I can't take it any more! I have to get out of here!"

"Just breathe, baby child," Samadara coos, attempting to quell Nayana's outburst. "Every elephant goes through this in the beginning. It's natural to feel this hatred, but I promise you will gather the fortitude to get through this. We're stronger than we think."

"No," Nayana seethes, pulling at her chains, which are chafing her skin. "I'm not going to just stand here and get used to this. I'm going to get out of here. Out of the circus."

Shey is inspired by Nayana's rant. "I'm getting out of here, too!"

"Not possible," Yaso retorts bluntly.

"Not possible for *you*," Nayana snaps. "We're not putting up with this torture. The humans have no right to put us through this."

Yaso snaps right back. "No elephant has ever escaped the circus. Ever. Just ask Samadara. She'll tell you. And some who tried were killed right on the spot."

Nayana turns her head to the left and stares directly into Yaso's eyes. "At least they tried. That's more than you can say. You just do everything the humans ask you to."

"And I get hit the least out of everyone, too," Yaso replies in the haughtiest tone she can muster.

Samadara cuts in, trying to mollify the dispute. "Yes, Nayana, some have tried to escape. I have seen it with my own eyes." Samadara's distraction plan works. Nayana looks over at her, wanting to hear more. Samadara continues. "This is the story about an elephant named Mammoth. To understand this story, I need to explain something first. Nowadays, circuses generally don't keep male elephants past the age of eight-years-old because around that time they become quite aggressive. Since humans care more about making money than anyone's safety, they used to keep males well into this aggressive stage. Which brings us to Mammoth.

"When I was your age, this large male elephant was at the circus I was in. He drew huge crowds—everyone wanted to see this colossal creature—and even though he became dangerous to keep around—he even broke a trainer's ribs once—the humans' greed got the better of them. One day, Mammoth had just had enough. During the show, he didn't feel like going out into the ring one more time to entertain those heartless humans, so he held his ground backstage. An especially sadistic trainer became furious and beat Mammoth to try to make him move. Mammoth didn't budge, but after the hundredth jab with a sharp bullhook, he finally snapped. He turned around, picked up that nasty human, and threw him straight into the concrete wall. The trainer survived, but he never walked again."

Nayana and Shey listen intently, mesmerized by the thought of an elephant standing up for himself.

Samadara continues. "It was thrilling to watch Mammoth fight back. So many years of being abused by humans and he was finally making them pay. And he didn't stop with just that trainer. He had his first taste of revenge and he wanted more. He ran amok through the arena, smashing the set, ramming into shrieking spectators. The trainers kept hitting him and hitting him, but he just kept right on fighting. And then he finally stormed out of the building. I was so young and naïve, I thought he was free. I cheered and cheered over his escape. But then I heard these loud, thunderous noises. They were the same sounds I heard when my mother was shot. A chill crept through my body. The audience screamed. Then I saw the vicious trainers come back into the arena—relieved, smiling, shaking hands. They looked so happy to have murdered this wonderful creature who was just desperately seeking a life without daily beatings. That was the day I understood for certain that I would never escape from here. There are too many humans and there is nowhere to run."

Nayana and Shey grimace—their enthusiasm over escaping is officially shattered.

Samadara feels awful crushing their spirits, but they need to know the truth. "This is the hardest lesson I will impart to you on this trip, young ones, but there are two types of elephants in the circus. Those who hope they will escape one day, and those who give up hope that they will ever be free. It doesn't matter which one you are, though. You end up at the same place forty years later: Still here."

That stings.

"I am so sorry, my baby children," Samadara says sincerely. "I will do anything for you. Risk my life for you. But I won't lie to you."

Neither Nayana nor Shey says a word. What can they say? They just found out they're doomed.

Samadara reaches her trunk toward Nayana. "Give me your trunk."

Nayana is too depressed to comply.

"Come on, baby child," Samadara insists. "Reach out to me."

Nayana lifts up her trunk limply and Samadara takes hold of it with her own. She caresses the young elephant with maternal warmth. "I want you to be safe. I don't want you doing anything that will get you hurt. We may be trapped here, but I'm going to help you get through this life in the circus." Samadara looks at Shey and Yaso. "We all will."

Shey puts her trunk on top of Samadara's and then Yaso puts her trunk below Nayana's.

As the train starts up again, the four elephants cling to one another. They may not be free, but they have each other.

*   *   *

BOOM! A deafening explosion goes off in the arena.

BOOM! Another explosion reverberates off the walls. The elephants are lined up backstage awaiting their grand entrance, but all the sounds of the bombastic production attack their ears as if they were in the same room. They can hear the ringmaster in the distance, revving up the audience for the spectacle they are about to behold. Nayana stands between Shey and Samadara, as always, wearing a green and gold headpiece and, to her great delight, no chains. It feels so good not having those heavy shackles ripping at her ankles. But she doesn't have time to revel in that too much; she's about to perform for the first time in front of an audience and she is a nervous wreck. She tries to steady her breathing to control her anxiety, but it's not working.

Samadara senses the young elephant's jitters. "Pretend the audience isn't there. Just do the routine the way we practiced and you will be fine."

"What's the first maneuver?" Nayana asks, panicked. "I can't remember. Why can't I remember? We've gone over it so many times."

Samadara pats Nayana's head with her trunk. "It's easy. We circle the exterior of the ring. They parade us around to wow the crowd. Just follow my lead. If you ever get stuck, look at what I'm doing. You're going to be wonderful, baby child."

Out of nowhere, the trainer, Wes, whacks Padma on her tender ears with his bullhook. She squeals as he threatens, "You're in my house now, Eleanor." Wes turns to address all of the elephants. "Listen up, crybabies! Randy may have been the boss during your training sessions, but I'm in charge on the road, and you ain't seen nuthin' 'til you see what happens when you cross *me!*" He slams his bullhook on the ground as he bellows out a pathetic growl. The bullhook bounces off the ground and the tip pokes him in the shoulder. He grits his teeth, trying to pretend it didn't hurt, but it's clear that it did and the elephants are quite pleased.

Wes continues, although he cuts his speech short due to his throbbing shoulder. "These people paid good money for a fun show and you're gonna give them their money's worth... or else."

Samadara whispers to Nayana. "It's his first time running the troupe, so he's trying to exert his dominance over us. Don't let his foolishness throw you off."

Shey remembers being in Nayana's place a year ago—about to perform for the first time. She can't stand seeing her new friend upset, so Shey does what she does best: acts like an imp. She notices that one of the trainers has put down his fancy hat and walked away.

"Nayana, watch this." When no human is looking, Shey reaches for the hat with her trunk.

Samadara cautions, "Shey, don't even think about it."

Shey ignores the older elephant. She stretches out her trunk to pick up the hat and tosses it behind a pile of green and gold pedestals.

A few moments later, the trainer walks back over to the spot where he left his hat. He looks quizzically at the empty bench.

"Don't laugh, Nayana," Shey warns, stifling a guffaw. "He'll know it was me."

The trainer looks around on the ground near the bench. He scratches his head. Two women dressed in sequined leotards walk by, so he asks, "Have either of you seen my hat?"

They shake their heads and keep walking. The trainer continues to look around frantically. His hands are shaking. "Oh god. Oh god."

"This is so good!" Shey looks as though she's about to burst from holding back her laughter. Nayana is smiling and starting to giggle herself.

A man wearing a headset calls into the hallway. "Five minutes to show time! Get in your places, everyone!"

"What am I gonna do?!" The trainer starts to hyperventilate. "Come on, think, Roger. Think! Why do these things always happen to *me*?"

That does it for Shey. She lets out a loud trumpet of laughter, which sets Nayana off, too.

"Shut up! Shut up, you idiots!" Roger hollers. "I'm trying to think."

It suddenly dawns on Roger. He glares at Shey. "Did you take my damn hat, you little brat?"

Roger whips Shey rapidly on her ears. Shey doesn't even wince, she's chortling so hard. "Oh, what an idiot. Classic," she laughs.

The man with the headset yells down the hall angrily. "Elephants! Bring the damn elephants now!"

Wes smacks Kusum and Padma, who are at the front of the line, with his bullhook to get them moving. "Get your act together!" he yells at Roger.

"I lost my hat!" Roger babbles frantically.

"I don't care," Wes barks. "Move 'em!"

Roger whips Samadara, Nayana, Yaso and Shey so they will follow the other elephants toward the arena entrance.

Nayana whispers back to Shey. "Are you okay? He whipped you pretty hard."

"Huh?" Shey responds. "Oh, yeah. I don't even care. That was totally worth it. Did you see his stupid face? 'Where's my hat?!'" She laughs even harder. "Whoo! Humans are such morons. Oh, wow, tell me I'm not more fun than those boring human clowns."

The elephants are shuffled out onto the arena main floor. Nayana was nicely distracted for a minute, but suddenly she's thrust back into the reality of the situation: She's performing in front of thousands of people. Her heart is racing so hard it hurts.

The music swells as the six impressive elephants march around the two circus rings. Nayana follows behind Samadara, but she can't help but be distracted. She's never seen so many humans in one place before and they're all cheering and yelling. The vast number of human kids is the most surprising. She's never seen human children before. They clap and squeal with glee at the sight of the powerful beasts before them.

Nayana feels so exposed. *They're all staring at us—at me. Do they have any idea that just yesterday I was standing in a pile of my own poo on the train? That I was whipped and jabbed with a bullhook just seconds before I came out here? Do they even care?*

Samadara stops in front of Nayana, but since the young elephant is so caught up in the moment, she bangs into Samadara's backside and trips. The audience laughs, thinking it's part of the show.

Roger holds the bullhook near Nayana to guide her back into place, but he doesn't hit her. He doesn't dare commit such a violent act in front of an audience.

Samadara calls out to Nayana. "Focus, baby child. Trumpeting comes next."

Wes lifts his bullhook into the air. "Let's give a Happy World Circus welcome!"

All six elephants raise their trunks to the ceiling and trumpet loudly. A thunderous explosion goes off and fire shoots up around the stage. The audience claps and cheers. Nayana is shaken. So much noise. So much commotion. So much attention.

The female acrobats dance around Samadara and Kusum, who then lift the women onto their backs. The audience applauds again.

Nayana is distracted again by all the bustling, this time missing a cue to sit on her bum. All of the other elephants are sitting, so she sticks out tremendously. She quickly sits down, but just at that moment the other elephants stand back up. The audience laughs at the uncoordinated baby elephant.

Wes isn't so amused, though. He grips his bullhook with all his might, wanting to ram it deep into her flesh but knowing better than to hit the elephants in public. He snarls between his teeth at Nayana, "Get it together you stupid animal, or I'll rip a hole in your goddamn ear."

Nayana feels like crying. She knows this routine so well, but she's discombobulated. Being in front of an audience is nothing like the training grounds. The blaring noise from the explosions and incessant pop music is enough to throw her off, but the audience's overwhelming presence pushes her over the edge.

She does her best to straighten up for the rest of the show but continues to make mistakes. By that point it doesn't matter anyway; the damage is done. She has publicly embarrassed Wes, and he can't take the blow to his self-esteem.

After the show, two handlers chain up the elephants in the basement of the arena. Nayana apologizes profusely to the others. "I'm so sorry. I got nervous. I know the routine. You know I know the routine. I just got overwhelmed."

Yaso harrumphs, but the other elephants are more forgiving.

"It's your first performance, baby child," Samadara comforts Nayana. "You did just fine."

"Don't be sorry," Padma reassures her. "I make mistakes all the time."

The handlers finish chaining the elephants to the wall and leave the room. Right then Wes comes storming in, bullhook ready to strike. He makes a beeline for Nayana and starts whacking her right on the skull. Nayana screams. She tries to cover her head with her trunk, but Wes just stabs her there instead. "Please! No!" Nayana begs.

"You think you're gonna humiliate me in front of all those people?!" Wes yells while hitting Nayana. "Everyone was laughing at me because of you."

Shey tries to intervene by swatting her trunk at Wes. She lands a few smacks to his side, but he mostly just inches out of her reach. Shey trumpets loudly and tries to ram into him, but her chains hold her back.

Wes keeps pummeling Nayana's head, landing blow after blow. Finally Samadara grabs the bullhook out of his hands. Wes jumps up to try and grab it, but Samadara holds it high in the air, far out of his reach.

"Give me my goddamn bullhook back, you bitch!" Wes hollers. "Give it back or you're gonna get it next!"

Samadara stares him down, confident, stern. "Just try and grab it, brute."

Two clowns enter the room to see what all the hubbub is about. When they see Wes hopping up and down trying to reach his bullhook, they bowl over laughing.

"You're kidding!" The clown, who is dressed as a hobo, chuckles and turns to his companion. "We have to add something like this to our act, man. This is hilarious."

"Totally!" the second clown agrees. He calls out to Wes. "You need a ladder, buddy?"

"Even better," the hobo clown gets excited. "Let's get him a trampoline!"

"Shut up, both of you!" Wes snaps. "This is serious. She could do some real damage with that thing."

"Looks more like she's trying to stop you from doing some damage, buddy," the hobo clown quips. "Come on, leave them alone. Let's get our drink on. It's been a long night."

"I can't leave her with the bullhook," Wes complains. "She could poke her eye out or something."

Upon hearing that, Samadara tosses the bullhook high into the rafters above. It catches on a metal beam and dangles from the ceiling.

"Ooohhh!" The two clowns cackle so hard they snort.

Nayana, Shey, Kusum and Padma trumpet joyfully.

"This is better than anything we did in the show tonight." The hobo clown grabs his round belly, trying to catch his breath from laughing so hard. "I think we got a new act: bumbling trainer mocked by sassy elephants."

Two other clowns poke their heads in the door to see what's causing all the merriment. "What's going on? Why are you leaving us out of the fun?"

"We'll tell ya over drinks." The hobo clown motions for Wes to join them. "Buddy, let's get out of here. They can't cause no more trouble with that stick of yours. Let's go blow off some steam."

Wes bites his lip. He's raging mad. No one makes a fool of him. But he's also fatigued from the show and he's not one to turn down a cold drink.

Wes glares at Samadara one more time, hoping to intimidate her before he leaves. She holds her ground, unimpressed.

With that, Wes storms out of the room, flanked on all sides by men in clown costumes.

"Samadara, Shey, you're wonderful!" Nayana beams. Her head throbs, but she couldn't be more proud of her family. How brave of them to stand up to Wes. How generous of them to risk their safety to protect her. She loves them. She *feels* loved.

Nayana has now experienced all of the major aspects of what circus life entails for an elephant. The training may have been brutal, the train ride may have been sickening, and the show may have been debasing, but she knows that as long as she is with these courageous, dignified ladies, she will be okay.

Little does she know, though, that less than ten years later, one of them will no longer be by her side.

47

PERSIMMON, SCRAPS AND Nibbin are snuggled together asleep, high up in the arena's catwalk. They're hiding beside a beam off of the grated walkway so that they won't be discovered while they're resting, and they're close to the wall so that the drop below to the seats isn't too far in case they need to make a quick getaway. Persimmon intentionally grouped up with her little brother and the tiny mink so that she could protect them if an emergency arises.

Most of the rest of The Uncaged Alliance is scattered throughout the catwalk as well. They split up so that if any of them are discovered by humans, the rest of the team could slip away unnoticed.

The team has been sleeping all morning, waiting for the beginning of the show. At the elephants' suggestion, they've decided to see for themselves what the humans are forcing the animals to do in the circus performances. After that, they only have a few hours to concoct a plan for rescuing all of these creatures later tonight. Needless to say, they are overcome with anxiety about being able to pull off this rescue mission in such a short amount of time.

Rawly wanted to be in the middle of the action, so he has taken his group—made up of Claudette and Fisher—all the way out to the center of the arena's catwalk. It's a risky location since the floor is far enough below that the humans look like ants. Raccoons can jump from high up and land on their feet, but this height would push the boundaries of that amazing skill. Rawly doesn't care, though. He is more interested in witnessing the abuse up close than playing it safe.

Rawly and Claudette are curled up together, whispering sweet nothings to each other. Rawly says something in his sweetheart's ear and she giggles.

Fisher, who is resting beside them, grimaces. "Hey, love bugs. Do you really have to do that with me around?"

Rawly grins, proud to be caught getting all cozy with his girl. "If you had Claudette to curl up with, wouldn't you keep her close? Don't worry, my friend. We'll find you a companion soon enough."

"Great," Fisher responds, unamused. "In the meantime, canoodle silently."

Drig and Chloe make up the third group. Chloe insists she's healed to the point where she can make a quick getaway on her own, but just in case her injuries slow her down, she has been paired with Drig, who is husky enough to carry her.

The last group inside the arena is also the oddest pairing: Derpoke, Apricot and Tucker. In fact, Derpoke has awoken from his nap and is looking at his companions thinking the exact same thing. *How did I end up with snarky Apricot and Tucker who's been such a grump for days? Is that how the team thinks of me—as a pest?* Derpoke sighs, resigned to the fact that the others must find him a nuisance. *I should have stayed outside with Bruiser. I'd feel safer that way as well.*

Derpoke's train of thought is disrupted, though, when he sees Apricot begin licking her orange fur. She starts with her back and then licks all the way down to her legs, reveling in her meticulous preening.

"What?!" Apricot snaps at Derpoke without even looking in his direction. "Don't you have better things to do than watch me clean myself, pervert?"

"Pervert?!" Derpoke has never been called such a thing. "I... well, I..."

Before he can think of a reasonable response, Apricot has turned her attention to Tucker. "Hey, squirrel."

Tucker opens his eyes. He had been half asleep, with his head resting on his bushy tail. He looks at the brash cat with a sour expression, not saying a word.

"I've forgotten your name, Mr. Personality," Apricot declares, either unaware of or uninterested in his clear aversion to chatting.

"Tucker," the squirrel replies with little energy, hoping that she'll quickly bore of talking to him.

"Ah, yes, Tucker." Apricot keeps right on pushing. "You know, I think that other squirrel is sweet on you. You should see the way she looks at you."

Tucker is flummoxed. "You mean Chloe? She's my partner."

"Oh, really?!" Apricot is stunned by this revelation. "You two are an item? I had no idea. You've barely said a word to one another since I met you."

Tucker looks away, hoping to hide his sorrow about his absent partner. "I'm not exactly happy with her right now."

"Is that right?" Apricot is thrilled to have stumbled upon this juicy gossip. She prods him for more salacious details. "Did she snuggle up to some other dashing squirrel or something?"

"No," Tucker tsks, disgusted by the thought. He sits up and remarks irritably, "It's complicated, alright?" He moves to a different spot on the catwalk so he can be alone.

Derpoke shakes his head disapprovingly. "You know just how to rub someone the wrong way, don't you?"

"Oh, excuse me." Apricot remarks impudently. "Sorry for trying to make a love connection. I saw how she stares at him longingly and since he didn't seem to notice I thought I'd be of assistance. Not that any of you would appreciate such a selfless gesture. Oh, and by the way, I find it rude that no one has complimented me on not preying upon these little squirrels. I have shown impressive control and deserve accolades for it."

Tucker can hear the cat and opossum arguing. He thinks of his Sweet Pea. *She looks at me longingly?* He misses her—misses talking to her, smelling her, cuddling up to her at night. He's not sure how to make up with her. He's not sure if he *wants* to make up with her. He just knows that he yearns to have her by his side. *What am I going to do? If something bad were to happen to one of us today, would I really want this to be the way that it ends?*

Humans start milling onto the floor below. They're circus workers getting the place ready for the first show of the day. All of the team members hunker down and sit still, hoping to avoid being spotted. Persimmon was leery about having the whole team sneak into the arena in the first place, but she knew that everyone wanted to understand just what they were helping these animals escape from, so she went along with it. As the arena starts to fill up, she begins to regret her decision. It's too late to depart now, though. They'd surely be discovered if they left their spots.

As the day wears on, the same odors that they smelled when they first approached the venue start to fill the air: salty popcorn, sugary cotton candy and all kinds of other treats. The team members' stomachs grumble.

Derpoke moans. "Oh, what I wouldn't give for some corn right about now."

No such luck, though. They won't be eating again for a while.

Another hour rolls by and finally spectators start entering and filling up the seats.

"Okay," Persimmon remarks gravely. "Here we go."

Scraps and Nibbin lean forward to peer down into the arena below.

"There are so many human children," Nibbin notes. "And look how excited they are."

"The kids all have balloons shaped like elephants—and images of tigers on their shirts," Scraps adds. "That's so weird. They act like they love the creatures, but then they come to a place where the creatures are horribly mistreated."

"Hmm." Persimmon contemplates this. "That does seem incongruous."

Outside the arena, Bruiser—who is too conspicuous to hide inside—conceals himself in the bushes alongside the gigantic building. From his vantage point, he can see some of the behind-the-scenes abuse firsthand as he watches the circus workers usher various creatures into the arena. As expected, the humans don't guide the animals gently; instead, they whip them and smack them with their hands.

Charlemagne isn't in the mood to perform another show, so he stands his ground. Bruiser sees one of the circus trainers grab the horse's lips and twist them forcefully. Charlemagne lets out a high-pitched neigh and moves forward. No matter how much he hates prancing around for humans' entertainment, those lip twists are too painful to ignore.

Each time Bruiser sees a circus worker crack a whip onto one of these battered creatures' backs, he so badly wants to rush out and bite the human, but he's grossly outnumbered. He'll have to be patient. If all goes according to plan, later tonight these exotic animals will be running free.

Back inside, the seats are now full and the show is about to begin. The lights go down and the audience cheers with anticipation. The team is nervous as they lie incognito in their various locations throughout the catwalk. They have no idea what a circus show even looks like. All they know is that the creatures involved are miserable and unwilling participants.

One spotlight comes up on a man in the center of the main ring—the ringmaster.

"Ladies and gentlemen!" To the team's surprise, his voice blares throughout the entire arena. "Welcome to Happy World Circus! The most amazing spectacle known to humankind!"

BOOM! A jolting explosion goes off at the entrance to the main ring. Nibbin is so startled that he loses his footing and almost topples over the side of the catwalk. Persimmon grabs onto his fur and pulls him close to her belly. "Hold on, sweet one."

BOOM! Another explosion blasts into the air, followed by green and gold fireworks.

Derpoke covers his sensitive ears. He complains to Apricot. "This is fun to humans? Deafening sounds?"

She shrugs. "Humans are easily amused."

More fireworks go off around the outer two rings of the three-ring circus as the horses trot into the arena with humans on their backs.

"There are Charlemagne, Ramses and the other horses!" Scraps points out to Persimmon.

Then the zebras come galloping out, led by Somersault. They wear sparkly headpieces and do choreographed kicks when they enter one of the smaller rings. The goats and camels are next. The audience cheers the whole time. Kids scream at the top of their lungs.

The final creatures to enter are the elephants, who get the most boisterous applause.

Claudette turns to Rawly. "Those must be the elephants, right? I thought you said there were six, though. I only count five."

"Hmm." Rawly counts the elephants himself. "I swear there were six."

Unbeknownst to the team, deep down in the basement of the arena, Nayana is swaying back and forth in her chains. The kinetic music and explosions from above bounce off the walls and fill the large room in which she's trapped. The noise is ear-splitting, but she doesn't even seem to notice. She's despondent, lost in her own world.

The humans have decided to keep her here because of her so-called "behavioral problems." If they really cared, they'd see that she's severely depressed. But the circus workers have never had any actual behavioral training with animals and don't even think elephants are capable of feeling loss, so a grieving elephant like Nayana is labeled as difficult and kept in isolation until she "comes to her senses." She stews in the basement, locked up all alone. The only good thing is that she gets to avoid a performance.

Back in the arena, the floor has been cleared for the first act: the horses' performance. The team watches as the humans make the horses run in circles around the giant circus rings. Each horse is ridden by a human who goes from sitting to standing and then back to sitting again. The audience oohs and ahhs at the lively presentation, but the horses look thoroughly spooked by all of the noise and flashing lights. The team is disgusted at watching the equines ridden by humans as if they are vehicles.

Luckily, the horses make it through the performance relatively unscathed, so they take their final bows and exit the arena. Next up are the clowns. They pull the old trick where, somehow, tons of clowns crawl out of a tiny automobile. They spray one another with water, toss popcorn at the crowd—much to the children's delight—and conduct all kinds of buffoonery.

That's the general lineup for the show—alternating between human acts and those by non-humans. Humans perform on a trapeze, swinging high up in the air and doing flips onto tiny swings. Then the goats are forced to climb on a jungle gym. Mirabel, who is older than the other goats, cringes at the pain in her joints from years of performing but powers through for fear of retribution later if she does not. After that, motorcyclists come zooming into the arena and spin around inside a metal sphere. Some of the team members close their eyes for fear that they'll see a violent crash, although nothing of the sort occurs. At one point, a man even sets himself on fire and jumps off of a high dive into a tiny pool of water below.

Scraps leans in to his sister. "Some of this stuff the humans are doing seems pretty dangerous. Do you think they are whipped and hit to force them to perform?"

Persimmon shakes her head. "Absolutely not. Look at how they're smiling. And no one is standing over them with a bullhook or a whip keeping them in line. These humans are choosing to perform tricks. The other animals don't have a choice."

Scraps looks perplexed. "Well, that's odd then. The humans are swinging upside down like opossums. They're walking on wires like squirrels. They're doing all these acrobatic maneuvers that I've seen animals do in the forest. So if they can do all that themselves, why beat all these poor creatures to make them do tricks? The humans are entertaining enough."

"That's an astute point, little brother," Persimmon says. "My guess—and I know this sounds awful—is that part of what humans find so amazing about the circus is that the trainers have been able to tame what they consider to be ferocious beasts. It reinforces their belief that humans are the most dominant animal alive."

Scraps surveys the crowd, which applauds with delight as the zebras trot around and dance. It's upsetting, but Persimmon's assessment makes perfect sense—the humans really do seem to get a kick out of watching these other species be debased.

Then come the tigers, and their act only solidifies Persimmon's theory. The lights are dimmed again. The arena floor is pitch black. The team members think for a moment that the show must be over when, suddenly, orange fireworks shoot into the air and cacophonous rock music blasts over the speakers. There, in the middle of the center ring stands a circular black cage and inside the cage are eight tigers and one man wearing a tight, sparkly black leather suit. Just as the spotlight shines on him, the man cracks his whip loudly, ratcheting up the audience's excitement.

Apricot, who has been mostly bored throughout the show, now stares intently at the cage and its inhabitants. What is this man going to do to her distant cousins?

The ostentatiously dressed man with the whip spends the next fifteen minutes or so showing off how he is in complete control of these fearsome man-eaters. With one crack of his whip the wild animals—with teeth so long and sharp that they could rip out his throat with one bite—bow to his every whim.

Apricot is infuriated. She yells, "Eat him! Eat his hideous face off!"

The tabby cat watches, horrified, as her brethren are humiliated. With every crack of the whip, they perform another trick. CRACK! They sit on their bums. CRACK! They roll over on their sides. CRACK! They hop on their hind legs. The audience shouts with gusto at every embarrassing maneuver. They can't get enough of watching these big cats subdued by their master.

Apricot scratches at the catwalk beams in frustration, loudly enough that Derpoke is concerned they'll be detected.

"Shh," he warns. "You're going to get us caught."

Apricot ignores him.

For the final trick, the man kisses one of the tigers on the lips. In disgust, Apricot squeezes the pole next to her. "Bite him now. Just open your mouth and chomp down on his repulsive head!"

The tiger does not, however, chomp down on the man's repulsive head. Instead, the man snaps his whip again and the tiger hops back into a tiny cage. Now that the tigers are stuffed back into their cells, the man holds his arms out in victory for having braved these bloodthirsty beasts. The audience erupts into applause and the lights dim again.

The circus-goers chatter feverishly, astonished by what they just saw.

"That was amazing!"

"He's so brave. I could never get that close to those raging tigers."

"Did you see how he kissed that tiger on the mouth?!"

Apricot sits down on the catwalk, facing away from the arena floor. She can't bear to watch any more. She feels personally offended.

Derpoke steps over to the dejected feline. "There's nothing they could do, Apricot. They've been whipped incessantly their entire lives. You saw how they cringed when that whip got anywhere near them. Imagine what they must go through every day behind the scenes. If they had bitten that man, they would surely have been killed. They're just trying to survive."

Apricot stays silent. She wouldn't admit it to Derpoke, but she feels helpless. To see such indomitable creatures—her own brethren— so thoroughly conquered tears at her heart in a way that she never thought possible.

The lights come back on for the final act of the night: the elephants. They are paraded into the arena, where they're forced to twirl around, stand on pedestals, lift humans onto their backs, and so on. Again, the team watches, disgusted, as the crowd eats up every minute of it. The elephants look so fatigued. They lug themselves around, some limping from arthritis in their legs, but the humans in the crowd seem oblivious to their suffering.

Derpoke is flabbergasted. "These are the most magnificent creatures I have ever seen in my entire life and they're subjected to this demeaning display? And even more despicable, I bet these humans are proud of what they've accomplished here today."

Tucker shakes his head. "Do the humans really think these creatures enjoy this tomfoolery? I mean seriously, the trainers are climbing all over these poor beings like they're inanimate objects."

"I hope Persimmon has a solid plan," Derpoke remarks as he clenches his jaw. "We can't let this go on. Their next performance tonight has to be their last. If no one else is going to stop this, then we must."

In fact, Persimmon does have a plan. She's been racking her brain the entire show. She just hasn't quite figured out all the details yet, and she's not sure how the team is going to react to what she has come up with so far.

BOOM! Fireworks shoot into the air. Confetti sprays down from the rafters. The grand finale has begun. The team holds on tight to the metal bars around them. The arena is filled with piercing noises and commotion. The horses, zebras, camels and goats are marched onto the arena floor with the elephants, and the tiger cages are wheeled out to reveal the big cats one last time.

There is so much movement and racket in the arena that the team members' senses are overloaded. They cover their ears and crouch down, trying to ride out this jarring storm.

Scraps turns to his sister, holding his stomach. "I feel sick."

"I know, little brother." Persimmon caresses his back. "My head is pounding, too. It's over now, though. I'll tell you, if we feel jostled all the way up here, I bet those poor creatures down below are a mess right now."

The performance is done. The team is sufficiently revolted by the humans' cruelty and motivated to do something about it. It's time to discuss how to get these battered animals out of this disgraceful circus.

48

PERSIMMON, DERPOKE, SCRAPS, Bruiser, Rawly, Claudette, Drig, Fisher, Nibbin, Chloe, Tucker and Apricot are crowded together in the bushes surrounding the arena. Persimmon had wanted to convene farther away for safety's sake, but since the show is still letting out, the parking lot is crawling with humans and the team is lucky they've gotten this far without being spotted. It was important for the team to see what the animals go through during performances, but Persimmon didn't quite think through how dangerous it would be to get everyone out of the building afterward. She thought about asking the team to meet up on the roof, but decided that it wouldn't be fair to Bruiser to exclude him from planning the rescue.

They're all a little squashed together inside the bushes, so it makes for an intimate meeting. Everyone feels a mixture of nausea from the overwhelming commotion of the show and excitement about getting the rescue underway, and they chatter energetically.

"One of the things that annoyed me the most was how much those trainers were smiling during the show," Rawly gripes.

Some of the others agree. "Me, too!"

"Behind the scenes we've seen them hit and whip these creatures," Rawly continues. "But out in front of an audience, the humans smile as if they were the friendliest beings ever. What a lie!"

Persimmon adds her two cents. "To that point—and I already know that you're going to give me a hard time for saying this—part of me thinks that some of the humans in the audience have no idea how poorly these creatures are treated."

Most of the team members are shocked by this statement. Drig argues, "Oh, come on. Are you saying those humans think the elephants enjoy twirling in circles with people jumping on their backs?"

Persimmon defends her stance. "I know it seems obvious to us that these animals are miserable, but I think the circuses are purposefully deceiving people by hiding how they really treat these creatures." Fearful of losing everyone completely, Persimmon adds, "That said, I'm sure some of those humans do know that the creatures are beaten and yet they're still going, which is absolutely reprehensible. This injustice must end, and that's why we're freeing these poor animals tonight!"

Persimmon wins back her audience with that declaration. A wave of enthusiasm flows through the group. Now that everyone has had a chance to vent a bit, Persimmon gets down to business. "Ever since we met these creatures last night, I have been ruminating over a workable rescue plan and I think I have one. We can pull this off, but I want to brainstorm some of the details as a team."

The group listens attentively. "I want to commence by warning everyone that this is going to be much trickier than when we rescued the minks. First off, these animals are much larger, which will make them more difficult to sneak away and way more difficult to hide once they're free. Second, there are humans everywhere. And third, we're in the middle of the city, so even if we get these creatures off of the premises, we still have to guide them all the way to the forest. Do not underestimate how truly dangerous each of these complications is."

The team nods.

Persimmon continues. "With that in mind, my best solution for getting everyone out of here quietly is to retrieve the keys. They open up the goat and zebra enclosures, as well as the locks on the elephants' chains. One of the elephants said that the keys can be found on a few different humans, including the guard outside the room. The problem..."

"Oh," Rawly cuts in. "We can poison him like we did the dogs. He won't know what hit him."

"But how do we get him to eat the poisonous mushrooms?" Persimmon asks. "Plus, how are we going to find the time to gather mushrooms in the woods? And most importantly, even if we accomplish all of that, how do we get the keys off of him?"

"Uh..." Rawly thinks about it for a second. He gets quiet, hoping someone will jump in before everyone realizes how flawed his plan is.

"I live with humans," Apricot asserts. "At night they always put their keys somewhere in the house. On a table by their bed. Up on a hook by the door. They don't sleep with them in their hands. You just need to figure out where they keep them and you can easily sneak them out."

"That's smart, Apricot," Persimmon praises, surprised by the cat's helpfulness.

Bruiser chimes in. "Last night I saw these trailers in the parking lot on the other side of the arena. I think the humans might sleep there at night."

"Great!" Persimmon exclaims. "Taking the keys while the humans are sleeping is exactly the type of covert tactic I was thinking about. Keep the ideas coming, everyone!"

Chloe jumps in. "Once we find the keys, the goats and zebras are going to be relatively easy to break free, but the horses and camels are problematic. They're tied to the trucks with thick ropes. Drig and I were able to figure out how to unbuckle their headgear, but it takes a good amount of effort. Raccoons are probably the only ones with digits dexterous enough to undo the buckles with any sense of speed."

"Good luck gittin' near those camels," Bruiser comments. "They spat right on Nibbin."

"They did?" Apricot guffaws heartily. "I missed it? I was so hoping to be there if that happened."

"You knew that would occur and you didn't warn us?" Derpoke scolds.

"And ruin a good laugh?" Apricot can't understand why he's so surprised. "You do realize that I showed you around this circus to amuse myself, right?"

Just when the team thought the tabby cat was being helpful, she's more than happy to crush that delusion.

"Um, excuse me, everyone?" says Tucker. He's a bit shy since he normally doesn't speak up during group discussions. "You mentioned guiding the creatures to the forest. Well, I think I found a reasonable escape route. Last night when we were searching the premises, I noticed that, in the direction of the forest, there's a building with blue lights on top. As long as the creatures head that way, they won't get lost on their trek to the woods."

"Wonderful, Tucker!" Persimmon is impressed. "Everyone has such savvy ideas."

Chloe peers over at her partner. "Good work, Pupsy."

Tucker looks down shyly, smiling to himself.

Persimmon hesitates to bring up the next aspect of her plan, but she knows that it has to be addressed. "About the tigers. I'd like to break them free, but I think it's too dangerous."

The team members nod in agreement, but Apricot gasps. "You're just going to leave them here?! But the humans are abusing them just as much as everyone else."

Scraps defends their stance. "I'm not scared of very much, but the blood-curdling tone in that one tiger's voice… Honestly, I think he would eat as many of us as he could fit in his mouth. And there are eight of them!"

"How dare you," Apricot rebuffs. "You said you were here to save every single creature being mistreated by humans, but then you pick and choose who gets to be free and who stays and suffers?"

Persimmon attempts to assuage her. "I wish we could help them, but our lives would be in jeopardy. Chloe was attacked by minks on our last mission, and they're smaller than we are. Imagine what those tigers could do with their sharp teeth and powerful claws."

"You're not heroes," Apricot hisses. "You're cowards." With that, she storms out of the bushes and through the parking lot, darting past the humans.

"A day ago she didn't care about any of these creatures," Bruiser remarks. "Now she's calling us cowards for not saving *all* of them?" He grunts. "Cats. Ain't no dogs get so emotional."

After Apricot's tirade, Persimmon dreads bringing up the next issue, but it can't be avoided. She gulps. "Speaking of that, I want to discuss the elephants."

The team gets very quiet. Persimmon feels the weight of all the attention pressing down on her. As her plan is currently devised, it may only work if they also do not release the elephants, but she knows that the team will be appalled by that idea. It upsets *her* to consider that possibility. She continues, trying to frame this quandary as delicately as she can. "Ever since we met the elephants I've been racking my brain about how we could release them without being detected. And honestly, I haven't been able to come up with a plan yet. With the horses, zebras, goats and camels, we can surreptitiously slip them out of here since they don't seem to be monitored as closely. But the elephants are guarded at all times by a human, and worse, they're inside the arena."

The team stares at Persimmon. No one wants to broach what he or she really thinks Persimmon is getting at. Finally, the always outspoken Rawly breaks the silence and asks the controversial question. "Are you saying that we shouldn't release the elephants, either?"

"No," Persimmon quickly replies, afraid of the reaction if she were to pause. "I'm saying that I don't know *how* to release them."

Chloe offers a solution. "Maybe once the humans notice that all the other animals are loose, they'll go running after them, conveniently leaving the elephants by themselves and giving us the opportunity to release them."

"That's a possibility, Chloe," Persimmon responds. "But once we get the elephants out of the arena, the circus workers would pounce on them immediately. It would be complete chaos. They could get hurt. We could get hurt. And so could the humans."

"The humans?!" Rawly scoffs. "Who cares if the humans get hurt? They're the ones keeping these poor animals captive."

"I am aware of that, Rawly," Persimmon counters. "But I am also not going to create a reckless plan where someone is going to get hurt. And yes, that includes humans."

Rawly butts in, more heated than before. "So because you're so worried about a few humans getting hurt, you're willing to just leave the elephants here to be beaten for the rest of their lives? That would make us as terrible as these sadistic trainers."

"Let me get this straight," Persimmon retorts, her temper quickly rising. "We prove we're less violent than the humans by intentionally putting them in harm's way? Great logic there, Rawly." Persimmon squeezes her paw, trying to quell her anger. She addresses the group again. "On top of the elephants being so noisy, there's another issue that's just as concerning. If we're able to get the elephants to the forest, what then? These are the largest creatures we've ever seen. It's not like they're just going to disappear into the woods."

She knows her next comment is going to shock the team even more, but as their leader, it's her job to be strategic, even if it seems harsh. She exclaims with certitude, "It's not practical to free creatures who are likely to be recaptured."

"Not practical?!" Rawly paces around looking at the other team members to see if they're as incensed by her words as he is. Everyone tries to avoid making eye contact with him. "How can you be so cold? You promised them you would help!"

"I didn't know what else to say," Persimmon defends herself. "They were so desperate."

Rawly keeps pushing. "You heard those elephants, Persimmon. They'd rather die than be stuck in the circus."

"Of course they would," Persimmon grabs her head with her paws, frustrated with the argumentative raccoon. "It's pure agony for them every day, but that's why—after the disaster with the calf rescue—I said we needed to focus on smaller animals who could easily run away and vanish. We're in over our heads!"

Rawly steps up to Persimmon and glares right into her eyes, ready to stab her with his words. "You know, every time we start a new mission, I feel like you're looking for ways *not* to save these poor animals. Some leader you are."

Persimmon stops breathing. Her jaw quivers. His comment cuts her to the core.

Bruiser growls at Rawly, not liking how close he is to Persimmon with such a hostile tone. "Step back, Rawly, or I'll be forced to step in."

"It's okay, Bruiser," Persimmon assures him. "I can handle Rawly." She addresses him, pain evident in her voice. "Don't you think I feel terrible about this? Those majestic creatures in there are suffering and I don't know how to save them. I feel sick with guilt."

Before Rawly can say another word, Persimmon turns to the rest of the group. "Someone else please talk some sense into this thick-headed raccoon."

No one says a word; they all look away.

Persimmon realizes they may be shy due to the tension. "It's okay. You can speak. Derpoke? Chloe? Claudette?"

Everyone stays silent. Persimmon tries a different tactic. "Chloe, I'd love to hear your input. You've had some clever ideas today."

"I agree that it's dangerous, but…" Chloe hesitates. "I don't know if I'd be able to forgive myself if we just left them behind."

Persimmon tries not to show any emotion in response to Chloe's stance. She turns to her best friend. "Derpoke?"

Derpoke freezes, shaken by being singled out. "Whatever you say. I'll follow your lead."

"Of course *you'd* say that, kiss up," Rawly snipes.

Derpoke ignores him. He will not be shamed for standing by Persimmon.

Persimmon turns to another ally, hoping to sway the group to her line of thinking. "Scraps?"

Her brother sighs. "The thing is… I feel bad leaving them in there too."

Persimmon's heart sinks. She softly asks her trusty dog companion, almost afraid to hear his response. "Bruiser? What about you?"

Bruiser clears his throat. His tail dangles low and his ears flop down. "First of all, I don't appreciate Rawly's disrespectful tone toward you. And second, you know whatever your final decision is, that's what I'm supportin'." He pauses and adjusts the way he's sitting. "But I can say this. When you unhooked that collar from my neck, if you had said, 'Humans are just gonna recapture you. Do you still wanna do this?' I woulda said, 'You bet.' These elephants deserve a chance and it hurts my heart to think they might believe that we just abandoned 'em."

Persimmon sits down. It hits her hard that she's not going to win this one—no matter how sensible her position may be. She looks down at the dirt below her paws, trying to steady her breathing. She then peers back up at the team. Most of them avert their eyes. Others look at her but seem nervous.

"As you know, my goal on these missions is to save as many creatures as we can while keeping our team as safe as possible," Persimmon explains solemnly. "The way my plan works now, we can save quite a few of the animals in this circus—the zebras, goats, horses and camels. They'll be deep into the woods before any human even knows they're missing. That's a major accomplishment. But that hinges on our not releasing the tigers because they're too dangerous. It also means that if we can't come up with a way to quietly release the elephants, we'll have to leave them behind as well.

"Trust me, the idea of abandoning them here crushes me. But if it gives all of these other animals the best chance to be free, then it's the most practical plan. Because the other option is that we free the elephants, a big commotion ensues, and then *none* of the creatures is freed."

Persimmon is pacing back and forth, she's so worked up. "That would be devastating. With that outcome, we let down all of these creatures, not just a few. We'd be setting ourselves up to fail."

Persimmon surveys the team, hoping that her heartfelt plea will have persuaded them. "Are you all really willing to put your lives on the line to free these elephants even though you know that doing so could derail everything?"

Everyone nods without hesitation—except Derpoke, who would jump out of a tree with her if she asked him to. Her speech didn't sway any of them—at all.

Persimmon turns away. She doesn't want them to see her expression. The crestfallen raccoon closes her eyes, shattered. Not because she feels betrayed but because she's afraid for everyone's lives. They're such a noble, courageous crew. It's beautiful and careless all at once. But they're not thinking with their heads. And the only way she can keep them safe is to be the leader that they need her to be.

Persimmon clenches her jaw and composes herself. She turns back around. "I am very concerned about how perilous this plan is, but it seems pretty much everyone else is in agreement. So here's what we're going to do. We will split up into four teams. Two teams are going to sneak into the humans' trailers and look for the keys. A third team, led by Chloe, will head over to the area with the horses, zebras, camels and goats, and tell them that we're freeing them tonight when we find the keys." Persimmon addresses Chloe. "Thoroughly explain the escape route to them and make sure they're ready to go the moment the keys are located."

Persimmon appeals to the rest of the team again. "As Chloe said, once the official rescue begins, all raccoons have to be stationed by the horses and camels to unbuckle their halters. Then while the raccoons are releasing the horses and camels, Chloe and Tucker, since you're extremely fast, you'll take the freed creatures and guide them through the city using the blue-lighted building as your beacon."

Persimmon turns to her Doberman friend. "Bruiser, during all of this, you'll be lookout and, if need be, give a few convincing growls at humans if they somehow discover us and start to close in. That should divert them long enough for the other team members to sprint out of there. Everyone still with me?"

The team nods. Persimmon continues. "While you all are doing that, Derpoke and I will tell the elephants that we're searching for the keys and that we'll release them tonight as well. Now, and this is a very important rule—one that I'm not going to budge on." Persimmon makes eye contact with each member of the team to drive her point home. "Every other animal must be released before we free the elephants. There is no quiet way to get them out of here, so I want to make sure that the others are clear of the premises before the elephants come storming out of the arena. Once all of the other creatures are on their way to the forest, then and only then should whoever has the keys come running into the elephant holding area as fast as they can so that I can unlock them. Is that clear?"

The group agrees, happy with the compromise. "Yes!"

"Uncaged Alliance!" Persimmon puts her paws out, encouraging everyone to join in on the mantra. "No more chains!"

The team members gather in closer and stomp their paws together, revving themselves up for another daring rescue—the riskiest one so far.

49

THE ETERNAL FRIENDSHIP OF NAYANA & SHEY, PART 3

GOODBYE

(14 Years Ago)

NINE YEARS HAVE passed since Nayana first performed in the circus. All of the elephants look like they've aged much more than that, though. Life in the circus has worn them down immensely. When Nayana met the other elephants, the older ones already had scars from years of being jabbed with bullhooks. And now the younger elephants, like Nayana and Shey, are also covered with wounds.

In all that time, Nayana's and Shey's dreams of escaping the circus haven't come to fruition. Ever since Samadara told them the story about Mammoth being killed while attempting to run away, they haven't dared an escape attempt of their own. Over the years, they've had conversations here and there about breaking free and finding a way to Ceylon, but that felt more like wishful thinking to pass the time than a reality. They've traveled all over the country and seen that humans are everywhere, and they know far too well that wherever there are humans, elephants cannot live in peace. Freedom seems impossible.

Despite their dreary circumstances, Nayana and Shey do their best to keep their spirits up by chatting, pulling pranks on the humans and joking around. Their camaraderie is the only thing keeping them from going insane over being chained up all the time. Most of the other elephants find their playfulness amusing, but it bugs Yaso to no end.

It is now mid-summer, well into the circus tour, and at the moment, most of the animals are caged or chained up outside. Before some of the shows, they are put on display outside of the arenas so that the spectators can see them up close. The elephants have mixed feelings about these experiences. It's nice to feel the sun on their backs, but eventually it starts to bake their skin. They also have to deal with the loud, gawking humans. The elephants are placed in electrified pens, chains fastened as always (although bales of hay hide the chains from the spectators' view), so there's nowhere to hide. The poor beasts have to stand there as hundreds of rollicking, rude humans stroll by, staring and yelling.

One day, an obnoxious woman attempts to take a photo of her jaded adolescent son with the elephants in the background.

"Billy, stand there." She holds up her cell phone. The boy steps over to the fence, but the woman corrects him. "No, over to your left. I want to get that elephant in the shot."

The boy rolls his eyes and inches to his left.

The woman calls out to Nayana. "Hey, elephant! Do something. Do one of those headstands or something."

Nayana looks around to see if the woman is really making this discourteous request of her. "Is she serious?"

Shey laughs. "Oh, yes, she's talking to you, Nayana. Come on, you're an elephant. Don't you just love doing headstands?"

"Only if she promises to lie on the ground, so I can do a headstand on her stomach," Nayana scoffs.

Shey and Padma trumpet cheerfully at the thought.

The woman huffs, annoyed that Nayana won't comply. "Come on, you dumb elephant. Do something fun!"

"I dare you to throw some hay at them," Shey quips.

Nayana smirks, contemplating it.

Kusum, who is standing at the far end to the left of Nayana and Shey, calls to them. "Be careful, Nayana. That new trainer, Lorenzo, is watching us right now and you know he'd love an excuse to lay into you tonight."

"Agreed," Yaso interjects. "And with my luck he'll whack me a few times just because I'm standing next to you."

Nayana imagines grabbing a big bale of hay and tossing it at the boy's head. She smiles to herself at the thought, but then assures her concerned herd members. "Don't worry, everyone. It's not my style to pull such an obvious prank. I prefer a more subtle approach."

The irritating woman continues to hold up her phone, waiting for Nayana to do something interesting. Finally, the impatient boy throws his hands up and whines. "Mom, just take the picture already. This is boring."

She snaps the photo and shakes her head. "All right, let's go look at the tigers. Maybe they'll be more interesting than these lame elephants."

Nayana calls out to them as they walk away. "Make sure to frame the shot with Billy right up against the cage. Those cuddly tigers will love that."

"Yeah, why don't you try kissing the tigers?" Shey chuckles. "As their revolting trainer can tell you, they have the most kissable lips out of all the creatures in the circus."

Padma laughs. "You all are too funny. Just when I start to feel sorry for myself over being trapped in this detestable place, you perk me up again."

Shey bows. "Happy to entertain you, Padma!"

"We'd much rather entertain you than these awful humans, Padma." Nayana fiddles with the hay at her feet and laments, "What irks me is that as long as these humans keep paying to bring their kids to see us, circuses will never shut down."

"Ha!" Shey dismisses her friend's naïveté. "Shut the circus down? Please. Humans enjoy watching us be humiliated too much for that to ever happen."

"Baby children," Samadara chimes in. "Don't be so pessimistic. You know as well as I do that over the years we've seen a growing number of humans standing up for us. They hold up signs outside of the arenas; they try to dissuade people from getting tickets; they walk alongside us calling out words of encouragement as we're marched to and from the train. There are humans out there who care about us."

"If they care so much, why are we still here?" Shey grumbles.

"Well," Samadara explains. "I think there are clearly a lot more unscrupulous humans than decent ones. But as I said, the number of compassionate humans seems to be growing every year. I have to believe that one day, somehow, they'll rescue us."

Nayana is flummoxed. "But Samadara, you're the one who always tells us we'll never get out of here. How can you suddenly be so optimistic?"

"What I said was don't be foolish and try to run away," Samadara clarifies. "You'll get hurt that way. But maybe there's hope yet that humans will finally come to their senses and realize it's cruel to keep us trapped in here." Samadara ponders this for a moment, then adds, "And maybe as I get older I just need something to believe in."

Nayana and Shey glance at one another skeptically. They're leaning more toward Samadara's old age being a factor in her newfound
optimism because what's really masked under that optimism is a growing desperation. She's over fifty years old and looks wearier than ever.
She walks with a limp from chronic foot problems brought on by decades of standing on pavement instead of soft dirt. She's not half as
graceful during performances as she once was because of the constant
pain. None of the other elephants would tell her this, but she looks
haggard—like a battle-scarred soldier, who had spent a lifetime at war.

At that moment, a group of humans crowds around Lorenzo as
he discusses the elephants behind him. "All of the tricks you see these
elephants perform in the circus are extensions of natural behaviors you
would see in the wild."

"What?!" Nayana can't believe her ears. "Oh, sure, I bet humans
find elephants on the plains twirling in circles on top of tree stumps
all the time."

"You see, these here are my girls," Lorenzo beams. "I would never
do anything to hurt them. I love 'em like they're my own kids."

"Yuck," Shey feigns gagging. "I guess he beats his own children
with bullhooks, too. On second thought, that wouldn't surprise me."

Nayana shakes her head. "The worst part is that these humans
actually believe his ludicrous lies."

Just then, Nayana sees two teenage boys taunting a tiger. The tigers are stuck in a cage about the size of an SUV and the boys are shaking their hands at the big cats. "Rarrr! Do you see how he's looking at
me? Dude, he so wants to eat me right now."

The second boy snickers. "I wish they'd feed him one of those goats."

"That would be so awesome!" The first boy jumps up and down
energetically. "I bet he'd rip the goat's head off and drink his blood."

"Tiger!" The kid throws popcorn at the cage. "Tiger!"

The tiger sits there, glaring, but instead of lashing out, the feline just yawns and rests his head on his paw.

"Boo!" the first teenager jeers. "These animals suck! What a rip-off. Why don't they make the tigers fight each other?"

The boys storm away, disappointed.

Nayana, who watched the whole ridiculous display, calls out to the tiger. "I admire your patience."

The tiger nods. "I used to growl at them until I realized that's exactly what they want. Now I just ignore them. Every day, though, I wish this cage would suddenly pop open. I'd tear apart those kids' throats in a heartbeat. Then none of us would have to hear their grating voices any longer."

Nayana smiles and says to Shey. "I like those tigers. They have moxie."

"I second that," Shey concurs.

Nayana surveys all the humans roaming around, ogling the creatures in their cages and pens—the aggravated tigers, the frightened goats, the upset zebras. She even sees the poor camels across the way frowning miserably as kids hop up and down on their backs during rides. Nayana sighs. "I am thoroughly convinced that these ignorant humans really think us other animals exist just to entertain them. How egotistical can they be?"

"The answer to that would be *very*," Shey quips.

*   *   *

A few months go by. Winter is here, so the traveling show has come to an end for another season. All the animals are back in their barns and cages for a few weeks, only let out when they're forced to learn new routines for next year's show.

Today, Lorenzo and another trainer, Bernard, are performing tuberculosis tests on the elephants. In order to do this, one trainer uses a giant syringe to spray a saline solution into an elephant's trunk, and then the other trainer covers the trunk with a plastic bag to capture the liquid when the elephant blows it out. Needless to say, the elephants are none-too-pleased with this intrusive procedure.

As the trainers step up to Nayana, Lorenzo stares at Bernard's blue surgical mask and sneers. "You look like a real wuss with that mask on, you know?"

"I'm not messing with no TB," Bernard replies. "Gustav got it and he was sick forever. Hacking up all kinds of crap."

"Well, you can look like a dumbass if you want," Lorenzo remarks as he holds up the syringe in his right hand. He then grabs for Nayana's trunk with his left hand.

Nayana quickly lifts her trunk high into the air so that Lorenzo can't reach it. "Oh, no you don't, you brute."

Samadara warns, "Nayana, just let them do it or he's going to lay into you real hard."

Nayana keeps her trunk in the air as Lorenzo grabs for it. The impatient trainer yells, "Look, you bitch, the longer you fight, the longer this takes. Give me your damn trunk."

Nayana flares her ears and protests. "No, I don't want that foul water shoved up my trunk. It's disgusting and I always spend the rest of the day retching."

Lorenzo grabs for his bullhook and stabs the sharp end into Nayana's sensitive left ear. She squeals.

"You want more of that, Abby?!" Lorenzo threatens. "Now give me your goddamn trunk or I'll beat you so good you'll be coughing up blood."

Shey trumpets at the men. "Leave her alone! She clearly doesn't have TB and even if she did, you stupid humans are to blame for exposing us to it!"

Samadara pleads with Nayana. "Baby child, please just do what he says. I don't want to see you get a beating."

Nayana grimaces. She keeps her trunk up in the air defiantly.

Lorenzo grits his teeth. He holds his bullhook up, ready to hit Nayana again, but instead of whacking her with it, he starts to rub it near her genitals. "Maybe if I tickled you right here, you'd be nicer. Huh?"

Nayana shakes around, but she can't move away because of her chains.

"Hey, leave her alone!" From the other side of the barn an animal handler, Alejandro, hollers at Lorenzo. Alejandro has been sweeping up the barn this entire time but now he can't help but intervene with Lorenzo's lewd violation.

"Excuse me?!" Lorenzo is taken aback. No one challenges him at the circus. "Are you trying to tell me what to do, turd collector?"

"No, I'm telling you not to abuse her," Alejandro retorts. There's a hint of fear in his voice since Lorenzo has been known to bully his co-workers as well as the creatures at the circus. "These are beautiful animals. They don't deserve to be treated like that."

Nayana is stunned. A human is actually defending her? All of the other elephants take notice, too. This is a new phenomenon. They've had a few handlers in the past who were friendly at times (not trainers but the handlers whose job it is to clean up the area around the elephants), but this human isn't just being friendly, he's sticking his neck out for one of them.

"Are you kidding me?" Lorenzo laughs heartily. He pats Bernard on the shoulder. "Do you hear this guy? What does he think he is, a botanist or something?"

"Do you mean a biologist?" Alejandro corrects him.

"Oh, look at Albert Einstein over here." Lorenzo twirls his bull-hook, not so subtly reminding Alejandro that he has a weapon. "Well, if you're so fricking smart, why are you cleaning up shit, Al?"

"It's part of my job to look after the elephants," Alejandro explains sheepishly. He's starting to get nervous about taking on one of the trainers. The last thing he needs is to lose his job, but he can't bear to stand by and watch this vicious lout manhandle the elephants one more time.

"Let's get something straight here, Al," Lorenzo steps toward Alejandro, pointing his bullhook at him. "You clean up these elephants' shit, chain them up and do other menial crap. I, on the other hand, work directly with them on a daily basis and I've been doing this for two years at multiple circuses, so I think I know a little more about elephants than you."

Alejandro thinks for a second. Should he keep this heated exchange going? Will the unpredictable Lorenzo wail on him next? He decides to stand his ground. "All right, so then you must know that elephants are so miraculous that they can communicate through seismic vibrations, right?"

Lorenzo looks at Alejandro, baffled. He doesn't even know what seismic means, much less how complex elephant communication is.

Alejandro grins, victorious. "I didn't think so."

Lorenzo grips his bullhook tighter, fuming, "You think you're smarter than me?! Huh? That you can tell me what to do, turd collector? These are my elephants and I can treat 'em however I please."

Bernard steps back, sensing a nasty brawl brewing. Sure enough, Lorenzo twirls his bullhook around and swings it at Nayana like a baseball bat. The jagged stick smacks into her trunk. Nayana trumpets loudly.

"I can hit 'em all I want and there's nuthin' you can do about it," Lorenzo spews out savagely.

Alejandro tosses down his broom and rushes up to Lorenzo. He grabs the malicious trainer's right arm, preventing him from hitting Nayana again. Lorenzo flips around and knocks Alejandro to the ground.

A supervisor rushes into the barn. "Hey! Hey! What the hell is going on here?"

He pulls the men apart. Lorenzo shakes off the supervisor and growls, "This asshole's trying to stop me from doing my job."

"He's hitting the hell out of these elephants," Alejandro protests. "I'm just trying to stop him from beating them senseless."

The supervisor peers at Lorenzo and then back at Alejandro. "Why don't you just focus on your job, Alejandro, and let him focus on his."

"Wh… wait, but… He was beating the crap outta Abby," Alejandro stammers, shocked.

"Don't be such a softy, Al," the supervisor advises. "These old broads got tough hides. Hitting them with bullhooks is like me flicking you. It don't do nothing to 'em."

Alejandro is speechless.

Lorenzo licks his lips, feeling mighty good. "Hey, Matt, I think this punk is some type of animal activist. We should teach him a lesson about what we do with snitches."

"Let it go, Lorenzo," Matt warns. "Al's just got a big heart is all. I hired the guy myself. He's good people. He's even loaned me a few bucks in a card game here and there. Now get back to work—all of you. Or I'll write you up."

Matt marches out of the barn. Lorenzo stares down Alejandro and licks his tongue at the helpless handler in a sordid manner. Alejandro grimaces and walks back over to his broom to continue sweeping. He feels empty inside, knowing his pathetic protest will have no effect on how these poor elephants are treated.

An hour passes. Lorenzo and Bernard have finished running the tuberculosis tests. Not all of the elephants let the trainers get fluids, so they decided to fudge the samples that they'll later send to the lab.

Before Lorenzo leaves, he makes sure to flip Alejandro off and get in one last insult. "Come on, Bernie. Let's leave Al to hump his girlfriends in peace."

Lorenzo and Bernard exit the barn. Alejandro finishes his work for the night and steps over to Nayana. He looks up at her sorrowfully. "I'm sorry I couldn't do more, Abby. I... I wish..." Alejandro struggles to find the words to convey how horrible he feels.

Nayana notices him stammering and reaches out her trunk to pat him on the shoulder with gratitude.

Alejandro blushes, moved by her friendly gesture. "Thanks, lady. You're too elegant for this place." He surveys the whole line of elephants. "You all are."

Alejandro caresses Nayana's trunk for a few moments and then leaves the barn for the night.

Once Alejandro has left, Shey remarks with surprise. "That Alejandro is the nicest human I've ever met. Can you believe he stood up for you like that? Maybe Samadara's right. Maybe there are some decent humans out there."

Nayana doesn't respond. Shey looks over at her, but Nayana quickly looks away. She's holding back tears and doesn't want Shey to notice.

"Are you crying?" Shey asks. "You don't have to hide it from me, you know."

Samadara affectionately rubs her trunk on Nayana's head to comfort her.

Nayana keeps facing away from Shey. "I'm humiliated that Lorenzo touched me like that. And I feel pitiful for crying again. I'm always crying."

"There is nothing shameful about crying," Shey assures her. "Considering what we're forced to endure, it would be perfectly understandable if you wept every day."

"But you never cry." Nayana looks over at her friend, tears streaming down her face. "I feel so weak compared to you. In all these years I have never seen you cry once. You're so much stronger than I am."

Shey looks at the ground for a moment. "The last time I cried was when they tore me from my mother. I was all alone in that warehouse and I sobbed for days and days. But then one day I stopped. I ran out of tears. And no matter how hard things have been since, nothing has been more excruciating than being taken away from my mother. So I don't cry."

Nayana can certainly relate to that traumatic experience. She contemplates this and then asks, "Would you cry if you lost *me*?"

"What?!" Shey is shocked by even hearing that said out loud. "That's a terrible thing to say."

"I'm just talking hypothetically," Nayana presses. It will comfort her to know. "Would you?"

"Of course," Shey replies, surprised that Nayana even has to ask. "I don't know how I'd get through this without you."

Nayana's face lights up. "I'd cry, too, if I lost you."

Shey glances over at her companion, unimpressed. "No offense, but that doesn't really mean much. You cry when you drop a few pieces of hay in the mud."

Shey playfully pushes Nayana with her trunk.

Nayana cracks a smile. "You know me too well, my friend."

*   *   *

Nayana scratches her right front leg where the chain is digging into her skin. She has learned over the years not to move around too much to avoid chafing from the shackles as much as possible, but having her flesh shredded is all but inevitable. It's early morning and the other elephants are still asleep, but she's restless from the upsetting incident with Lorenzo the night before. Soon the trainers will be coming into the barn to round up all of the elephants to make them practice the new routines, but for now Nayana has a few moments of silence.

Creak! The barn door swings open. *So much for peace and quiet,* Nayana grumbles to herself.

Lorenzo, his underling Bernard and two other trainers enter the barn, waking the other elephants.

"Ugh," Shey gripes. "In between nightmares I was actually having a pleasant dream about drinking fresh water from a river. One of those beautiful rivers we see when we're traveling in the trains."

"Sounds perfectly tranquil," Nayana sighs. "One day, let's do just that."

They smile wistfully at the thought.

The trainers step over to Samadara and start wrapping ropes around her ankles and neck.

"Okay, girl," Lorenzo speaks gently. "Just keep calm."

Samadara instantly knows something is wrong. Lorenzo is never this polite. She shuffles in her chains.

"Easy, girl." Lorenzo tries to keep her relaxed. "The ropes are good," he yells to his trainers. "Now undo the chains. Come on, pull her outta here quick before they get all crazy."

Samadara's heart sinks. She knows exactly what's going on, and she calls out to her herd. "Kusum, Padma, Nayana, Shey, Yaso. I love you. I love you so very much."

"Samadara, what's happening?" Nayana bellows as she bats one of the trainers with her trunk.

"Oh, baby child," Samadara says with despair. "I'm so sorry. They're taking me away—forever."

Nayana and Shey start thrashing around, tugging at the chains around their ankles. "No! NO!" Nayana screams.

As they watch Samadara dragged away, Nayana, Shey and the other elephants begin trumpeting and yanking at their chains, trying to break free so they can rush the humans and stop them from stealing away their beloved matriarch.

Samadara digs her feet into the ground to stop the humans from pulling her away so fast. She wants to say a proper farewell. She wants to look at her herd one last time.

Lorenzo whacks Samadara on her side with his bullhook to keep her moving. "Stop fighting! It'll all be over soon."

"Pull harder, idiots!" he orders his underlings. "Let's make this quick. I haven't had breakfast yet."

Nayana is frantic. "Samadara, no! Samadara!"

Samadara tries to turn around to see her family. "Baby children, I love you. Don't ever forget that."

Nayana pushes so hard on her chains that she trips and falls onto the concrete slab where Samadara had just been standing. That spot had been occupied by Samadara for ten years and now it's suddenly vacant. Ten long years of Samadara guiding Nayana with sage advice, caressing the young elephant with her trunk, comforting her when she needed it most. All of that is being torn away in an instant. Sorrow, from deep inside Nayana, comes crying out, "Mommy!"

Samadara hears this cry and immediately digs her heels into the ground, harder than before, bringing her hefty body to a complete halt. Nayana is so distraught that she doesn't even realize what she has said, but Samadara absolutely does. *She called me Mommy.* It crushes Samadara's heart. So many years ago Samadara's own child was torn away from her, gutting the gentle elephant, but now she hears another sweet babe calling out to her in the same pained tone. It kills Samadara, and yet she feels a warmth come over her. For so long she's been yearning to have someone call her Mommy again, but until this moment she didn't even realize how much it would mean to her.

Samadara shakes furiously and twists around, pulling vigorously at the ropes and dragging the humans across the floor. She looks at Nayana, who is still lying on the ground, devastated.

"Oh, my sweet baby," Samadara whimpers. "How lucky I am to have had you in my life. I hope I did your momma proud. I hope I made you feel the love she never had the chance to give you."

Samadara looks over her herd one last time. Kusum, Padma, Nayana, Shey and Yaso stare at her, tears pouring from their eyes. "You are my baby children and you will always be with me."

Lorenzo rams the bullhook so hard into Samadara's ear that the sharp end gets stuck in her flesh. Samadara screams as Lorenzo yanks and pulls on the bullhook to turn her back around. She reluctantly turns to face the door and is dragged outside of the barn.

Samadara yells the whole way. "I love you! I love you all!" But soon her voice is drowned out as she's shoved into the back of a truck and the door is closed. Lorenzo taps on the side of the truck and the driver revs the engine and rolls down the road. The heartbroken Samadara is stuck inside with no idea where she's headed.

Back in the barn, Kusum, Padma, Shey and Yaso stand, horrified. Nayana is still lying on the ground sobbing uncontrollably. "Samadara! Samadara!" The grief-stricken elephant calls out her name over and over, wishing she could see her one more time but knowing that she never will.

Nayana musters her every last bit of energy to trumpet as loudly as her lungs will let her in defiance of Samadara's abduction. The other elephants join in, creating a cacophony of gloom and anguish.

Lorenzo watches this tragic display and scoffs to his fellow trainers. "What a bunch of crybabies. Let's go get breakfast. I'm starving after that workout."

Lorenzo shuts the barn door so he can't hear the elephants' bellowing, leaving the broken creatures to wallow in the darkness, their misery echoing off the walls.

*   *   *

Nayana lies on the ground in Samadara's vacant spot. She hasn't said a word since Samadara was dragged away yesterday. She just lies there crying on and off, feeling hollow. Shey and the other elephants have left her alone to grieve in her own way. They have also been mourning the loss of their revered matriarch. Late last night, Kusum and Padma discussed how much they admired Samadara's regal demeanor and fortitude despite a lifetime of horrid abuse. They were consoled by talking about their dear friend and knowing that even though she is gone, they'll always have memories of her to cherish.

Shey tries to comfort Nayana by rubbing her trunk on Nayana's legs, but the distraught elephant just pulls her legs away—her chains rattling as she moves—so Shey decides to leave Nayana alone.

Creak! The barn door swings open. "Rise and shine, crybabies!" Lorenzo mocks. "You had your little break. Now it's time to get back to work. We don't pay you to just sit around."

"You don't pay us at all, brute," Shey mutters.

The elephants glare at the heartless human.

Bernard notices Nayana lying on the ground. "Oh, crap. Is she sick?"

Lorenzo rolls his eyes. "No, idiot. I've seen this before. They just get all whiny when they're separated like that. Nuthin' my trusty old friend can't solve." Lorenzo unlatches the bullhook from his belt.

Shey taps Nayana with her trunk. "Nayana, it's time to get up."

Nayana doesn't stir. Her profound depression has rendered her immobile.

Lorenzo pokes Nayana's ear with his bullhook. "Yoo-hoo! Wakey wakey."

Nayana just lies there, not responding. She breathes quietly.

"Get up, dumbass!" Lorenzo kicks Nayana's trunk, but she simply pulls it underneath her chin.

Kusum calls out to the despondent elephant. "Nayana, little one. You have to get up. We all miss Samadara, but this isn't going to bring her back. If she knew that you were getting hit right now, it would break her heart."

Samadara had warned Nayana that she would be taken away some day. At more than fifty years old, the matriarch had lasted more than a decade longer than the average elephant in the circus. If she was in the wild, she could live up to seventy—as long as poachers or other human threats didn't kill her first—but elephants in circuses and zoos normally don't get anywhere near that age. Life in captivity is so stressful and taxing on their bodies that they suffer for years before either dying from chronic health problems or being euthanized because of them.

Samadara was in so much pain from her arthritis, foot abscesses and other physical ailments that she could barely perform tricks any longer. The last thing the circus wants is to bore people by having them watch decrepit animals hobble around. It's bad business. Samadara thought that telling the young elephant she wouldn't be around forever would prepare her emotionally, but it didn't lessen the blow. We all know that one day our loved ones will die, but it still stabs our hearts when that day suddenly comes.

Lorenzo slams the bullhook into Nayana's soft ears. Nayana screams but still doesn't stand up.

"Leave her alone!" Shey trumpets angrily at Lorenzo. "Can't you see that she's grieving?!"

Lorenzo pretends to stand back in fear. "Oh, no, Peanut. I'm so scared." He turns to Bernard. "Hey Bernie, grab that hot shot on the wall. I think a few jolts to the membrane will kickstart her slacking ass. Can't nobody sleep on the job."

Shey frantically taps Nayana with her trunk. "Nayana, get up. Please. I know you're heartsick, but this isn't going to solve anything."

Bernard hands Lorenzo the hot shot. Lorenzo switches on the power. The buzz of electricity fills the air.

All of the elephants chime in and beg. "Nayana, please! Get up!"

Lorenzo zaps Nayana with the electric prod, sending a painful charge through her body. She cries out in agony as her muscles convulse but doesn't budge from her spot. She can't bring herself to get up. Why stand up when there's nothing to live for?

"Get up!" Lorenzo stuns Nayana again. She still doesn't move.

Shey is panicking. Will she lose two of her family members in such a short period of time?

"He'll kill you, Nayana," Shey pleads. "He doesn't care. Please. I can't lose you. Not you, too."

"Leave me alone!" Nayana wails, anguished. "Just let me die!" She is so overwhelmed with sorrow she doesn't want to be bothered with anyone else's feelings.

Lorenzo electrocutes Nayana again and she shrieks from the excruciating pain.

Bernard speaks up sheepishly. "Boss, give her a second. Maybe she'll get up."

"Are you going all soft on me?!" Lorenzo berates Bernard for a few moments, giving Nayana some time to catch her breath.

Shey is sobbing. She can't bear to see her precious companion tortured one more minute. "I'm crying, Nayana. Is that what you wanted? To see me cry?"

"I just want all of this to be over," Nayana says, resigned. "I can't bear to be in the circus one more day."

"And what about me?" Shey fires back angrily. "I lose Samadara and then I lose you? How can you be so selfish? I can't survive this without you. Who am I going to rely on? Yaso? She's uptight and dull. I'd rather play catch with Lorenzo."

"Hey," Yaso remarks, taken aback by the unexpected dig.

Nayana stops moaning. She looks over at Shey. Did she just make a wisecrack in the middle of this catastrophe?

Through her tears, Shey smiles, and immediately, Nayana's gloom lightens. *What am I doing? I'm breaking the heart of the best friend I'll ever have. I am being selfish. She's right.* It suddenly hits Nayana: This has never been about living for herself—it's about living for each other. And she's betraying that bond.

Nayana lifts her head for the first time in twenty-four hours. Bernard, who is still being chewed out by the hot-tempered Lorenzo, sees the battered elephant starting to rise. "Hey look, she's getting up."

Lorenzo turns to see Nayana wobbling to her feet. She is weak from the electrocution and lack of food, but she fights through the throbbing.

"See," Lorenzo grins and holds up the hot shot. "You just gotta give them some incentive."

Nayana is a little lightheaded. She takes a deep breath to steady herself and looks over at her best friend. "Promise me something."

"Anything," Shey sniffles.

"This isn't forever," Nayana says gravely. "One day our entire herd will escape this wretched circus."

"Promise," Shey nods. "I just hope some of these humans step in our path on the way out."

Nayana and Shey grin as they stare down the oblivious Lorenzo. He and the other humans will not continue to control them—to destroy their lives. They will break free from this insufferable life in the circus. They must. The only question is: How?

50

IN THE BASEMENT of the arena, Persimmon and Derpoke crouch down, hidden among the green and gold pedestals. The male security guard is on duty outside the elephant holding area, so the brave raccoon and her loyal best friend anxiously wait for their role in the massive rescue to begin.

The other team members are split up just like Persimmon suggested. Two teams (Rawly, Claudette and Drig on one; Bruiser, Scraps and Fisher on the other) are searching for the keys in the trailer area where the humans sleep, while the third team (Chloe, Tucker and Nibbin) is revealing the rescue plan to the horses, zebras, goats and camels.

Derpoke sees that Persimmon is lost in thought. She's been unusually quiet since they ventured into the arena. At first he thought she was just focusing intently on the plan—there are a lot of moving parts and it will take a great deal of work to make sure it all runs smoothly—but now that they're sitting in silence in the hallway, he notices the anguished expression on her masked face.

"Persimmon, are you okay?" he asks. "Are you upset that no one listened to your warnings about releasing the elephants?"

"No," Persimmon answers, distracted. She stares at the ground as she talks. "I'm proud of them for being so courageous. I would expect nothing less from this team." Persimmon closes her eyes—thinking, thinking. She opens them again as a realization hits her. "These elephants are clearly smart. If we brainstorm together, we surely should be able to come up with a clever plan to sneak them out of here. There has to be a way that's just eluding me right now."

Derpoke nods. "I know you're worried someone is going to get hurt. I am, too."

Persimmon is pressed against the cold floor as if the weight of the world were on her shoulders. Stress causes a sharp pain to shoot through her stomach. She winces and rubs her tummy.

"Derpoke..." She looks at him with such a tortured look in her eyes that he fears what she might say. Her voice cracks as she discloses, "If we can't come up with a safer plan by the time the team brings those keys, I'm not going to release the elephants."

Derpoke freezes. He suddenly gets a sick feeling in his stomach as well. From his expression, Persimmon can tell how shocked he is.

"I know," Persimmon looks at the ground again. "You think I'm terrible."

"No. Never, Persimmon," Derpoke steps over to her. "I just feel so sad for these tormented elephants. The thought that they may never get out of here—how devastating."

"I wish there were another way," Persimmon breathes heavily as if it's a chore to take in air. "But I can't put all of my friends' lives at risk, especially for such a precarious plan that has so little chance of success. I love them too much for that." She grimaces again as another sharp pain attacks her insides. "I hate myself for this. It's the same helpless feeling I had when every single calf was slaughtered right in front of my eyes. I can't save all of the innocent, suffering creatures out there. No matter how much I want to, I can't save them all."

Just then, the security guard pulls out a pack of cigarettes and heads for the back door to exit the arena.

This is it. Whether or not Persimmon is ready to have this onerous conversation with the elephants, she must act now.

Persimmon is shaking as she makes her way to the red curtain. Right before she crawls under the barrier, she hesitates. She takes a deep breath to calm her nerves. This is the hardest thing she's ever had to do. She's lying to all of her friends and she might be about to crush the spirits of these severely abused animals.

Derpoke takes a hold of Persimmon's shaking paw and smiles warmly. "You're not doing this alone. I'm right here with you."

The two friends crawl under the curtain into the holding area, clinging to the hope that somehow they'll come up with a workable plan but sick with fear that they're more likely about to rip away the best chance these elephants will ever have of escaping.

51

THE ETERNAL FRIENDSHIP OF NAYANA & SHEY, PART 4

WHAT HAPPENED TO SHEY

(A Few Months Ago)

ALMOST THIRTEEN YEARS have passed since Samadara was torn from her beloved herd. The elephants never learned what actually happened to her. Their worst fear is that she was taken somewhere and killed. Their greatest hope is that she was taken back to Ceylon to live out the rest of her life peacefully. The humans have rarely been kind to them, though, so they're sure that blissful fantasy hasn't occurred. It's all just speculation anyway; they have no way of finding out. She's just gone. All they know for sure is that they will never see her again and that they miss her every day.

Nayana and Shey kept their promise to try escaping, but each attempt was a failure—a painful failure. Twice, they made a break for it when they were being marched back to the train from an arena. Each time, they barely made it two blocks before humans with guns were on them in droves, so they gave in before things got too out of hand.

They know that a human brandishing a gun is the most unstable and lethal beast on the planet.

One time, the rebellious duo was even bold enough to flee in the middle of a show. They thought that the hysterical crowd might cause enough chaos to give them a chance to run away, but the arena was put on lockdown, so they didn't even make it out the door.

Lorenzo and the trainers were irate after each escape attempt, so both elephants were thrashed severely afterward. They bled profusely from the beatings, but their wounds were covered up with a topical ointment to hide the abuse. Lorenzo jabbed Shey's left ear canal so relentlessly with his bullhook that she is now deaf in that ear.

These escape attempts were an embarrassment to Happy World Circus, so precautions were taken to keep the elephants from attempting to get away during their walks. They are now surrounded with more humans carrying tranquilizer guns, and trainers tie ropes around the elephants' necks to keep them under constant control.

After the last attempt a few years ago, Nayana and Shey were frightened by rumblings that they would be split up to appear in different traveling shows. The threat terrified them more than any beating ever could, so they cleaned up their act instantly. They haven't given up all hope of escaping, but they're waiting until they have a more surefire idea before they attempt it again. They'd rather put up with the physical and psychological torment of circus life together than be shipped off to different locations from each other.

Their worry that they would be separated even prompted Nayana to come up with a clever scheme to make their pairing indispensable. On this summer day, the six elephants are all standing in their usual line chained up before the show so that the spectators can gawk at them. Since Shey and Nayana had been causing so much trouble together, the order of the line has been switched around a bit. Yaso is on the far left, then Shey, Kusum, Padma, Lakmini and Nayana. But the two best friends still find ways to pass the time together.

As they stand around, Nayana turns to Shey and smirks. "Follow my lead."

Always one to play along, Shey perks up in anticipation of whatever naughty prank Nayana has planned. As is the case with best friends, the two have worn off on one another and Nayana has certainly adopted Shey's impish behavior.

When Lorenzo steps over to the elephant area to tell his lies to the audience, Nayana seizes her opportunity. She grabs a baseball cap off of one of the boys standing up against the enclosure.

The boy calls out. "Hey!"

The other people laugh as Nayana throws the hat to Shey, who then tosses it into the air a few times. The crowd cheers, which entices more people to gather.

Shey throws the cap high into the air and the talented Nayana reaches up her trunk to catch it and then comically places the hat onto her own massive head. The spectators applaud wildly.

One of the circus supervisors notices the substantial crowd enjoying the elephants' impromptu performance, so he walks up to Lorenzo. "Wow, that was wonderful! Do you think you could get them to do that in a show?"

Lorenzo scoffs. "I can get them to do anything. In fact, we've been working on that trick for a while now."

Nayana rolls her eyes at Lorenzo taking the credit for her idea, but she nods at Shey. "Let's see them try to split us up when that becomes a huge draw for silly humans."

Shey bows to the savvy Nayana. "I am impressed, my clever friend."

Throughout the rousing stunt, a young elephant was cheering along with the humans. It's Lakmini.

Soon after Samadara was taken away, the circus brought Lakmini in (she was just a baby at the time) to take her place. This infuriated the other elephants to no end—it was as if Samadara were just some object that could be replaced with a newer model—but they of course didn't take out their frustration on Lakmini. On the contrary, just like the herd had warmly welcomed Nayana into the family, they embraced the new little one. And from the get-go, Lakmini was enamored of the feisty Nayana and Shey. Having just been through the misery of the breeding facility, where her spirits were broken, she was thrilled to see two elephants who refused to let the suffocating life in the circus bring them down, and even better, to see two elephants who stood up to the brutal humans whenever they could.

So when Lakmini sees them juggling the baseball cap, she cheers enthusiastically. "Nayana, that was brilliant! You manipulated the humans by playing into their game."

"Well," Nayana responds with a wink. "Let's just say their bullhooks are sharper than their wits."

"Boo! Hiss!" Shey playfully jeers Nayana's bad joke. "Poor taste."

Nayana frowns and Shey laughs heartily—so hard she starts coughing and hacking. Everyone looks at her, surprised. Shey sounds awful, like an old man who's been smoking all his life.

"Yuck," Nayana jests. "Remind me not to make you laugh too often."

Shey laughs even harder and coughs even more intensely. She then sneezes out a thick yellow mucus.

Nayana and Shey immediately stop laughing. They look at the sputum on the ground. This is not funny. It's one of the scariest moments of their lives.

*　*　*

"Shey, you have to eat something," Nayana begs her ailing friend from afar.

Shey looks dreadful. She has been refusing to eat due to feeling so ill, and she's shed tons of weight—so much that her ribs are showing. She wheezes constantly. Every time she breathes, it feels like her lungs are on fire. Her body is attacked by chills and just as quickly seized by sweats. She can't sleep from the unbearable discomfort, but she is so miserable that she is overcome with a throbbing desire to rest every waking moment. Instead of standing erect, she wobbles. A yellow discharge flows out of her trunk incessantly, often stained with blood. Her normally spunky spirit has been stripped away and replaced with a deep depression.

She's riddled with tuberculosis and the humans don't seem to care. They haven't given her any treatment. The only thing they've done is separate her from the other elephants to lower the chances of the disease spreading among them.

The circus is currently stationed in a small town with a smaller than usual arena, so the elephants are being held under a cover in a parking lot. Shey is about twenty feet away from her herd, chained to the back of a semi-trailer truck. She is hunched over, too weak to even lie down. She just stands there pitifully, moaning.

Nayana calls out again since Shey didn't respond. "Shey, you have to eat. I know you don't feel well, but you're only going to feel worse if you don't keep up your energy."

Padma can't bear to look at her emaciated friend. "How long are the humans going to make her suffer like this? She just stands there moaning all day. It's not right."

Kusum, who has become the matriarch in Samadara's absence, calms the herd. "They'll give her the medication soon. I've seen this before. The humans are negligent about taking care of us, but they won't let her die. We're worth too much to them for that. Suffer? Yes. Die? No."

"We have to help her," Nayana insists desperately. "She's in so much pain."

"Nayana, tuberculosis is highly contagious," Kusum warns. "Unless you want to end up as sickly as she is, you'll keep your distance."

Right then, Lorenzo and Daniel—the underling he not-so-affectionately refers to as Nutsack—march around the side of the truck up to Shey, who continues to groan in pain. Lorenzo pokes her in the side with his bullhook. "Quit your bitchin', Peanut."

"Boss, I don't know if she can perform in tonight's show," Daniel says. "She looks like shit."

"Oh, she's performing tonight," Lorenzo dictates. "I don't get to take breaks when I'm sick. Neither does she."

"Well, is she gonna get those meds?" Daniel asks. "She just keeps getting worse and worse."

"Yes," Lorenzo huffs. "But we're in the middle of Hicksville, U.S.A. Do you really think there are elephant vets out here?" Lorenzo pats the teetering Shey on the side. "She'll be all right. I've seen elephants much worse than this. She's just being a diva acting all sniffly and mopey. 'Oh, I'm so tired. Boohoo, my nose is running,'" he mocks.

Shey sneezes out a pile of sputum. Daniel yelps and hops away, covering his nose. Lorenzo lets out a hearty chuckle. "Dumbass! You should be a clown, not a trainer."

"I'm not getting TB," Daniel complains. "I heard some guys in the past have had to quit because they were too sick to work anymore."

Lorenzo rolls his eyes. "Oh, now you're trying to wuss out on me, too, Nutsack? Looks like we got a bunch of pansies working at this circus. You know, there's a reason I've been in this racket for so long. I'm the only one man enough to tough it out."

Lorenzo pokes Shey on the side again with his bullhook. "Rest up now, Peanut, 'cause come show time you better be on your A game."

Lorenzo struts off, assuming Daniel will follow after, but for a moment, Daniel stares at the feeble Shey. She looks in his eyes, wheezing, worn down. She has such a defeated expression, he can't help but feel sympathy for her. "Sorry, girl," he laments and then walks away.

Kusum addresses the anxious herd. "See, they're working on the medication. It's just taking longer because of where the show is located. Maybe by the next town they'll get her the proper medicine."

"The next town?!" Nayana asks incredulously. "Don't you see her? She may not make it that far. They have to help her now."

"If Alejandro were still here, he'd help Shey," Padma laments.

Nayana grimaces. "Emphasis on *if.*"

"He was good to us, Nayana," Padma counters. "You saw how he cried when he told us goodbye. He said he couldn't bear to watch us being beaten any longer and I believe him."

"Yeah, he was kind to us when he was here." Nayana bats at the dirty hay around her chained-up feet. "But then he just abandoned us. Did he ever get anyone to come back and save us like he said he would? No. Once he got out of here, he never looked back."

"Maybe he tried," Padma offers, remembering how sweet he had been to them for those two years. "Maybe any day now he and those other humans out there who hold up signs will come storming in here and rescue us all."

Nayana peers at the moaning, tormented Shey. She's filled with rage and heartache over seeing her beloved friend treated so heinously. "Right about now would be perfect timing."

✷   ✷   ✷

The hallway is spinning. Shey stands in line between Yaso and Kusum in the hall of the small arena. The show has already begun and the elephants are awaiting their second entrance, when they will be doing the majority of their tricks. Shey is so dizzy that she wobbles from side to side. Kusum leans against her to help the sick elephant keep her balance.

"It's okay, Shey," Kusum comforts her. "I've got you."

Lorenzo slams Kusum with his bullhook. "Stay away from her, idiot! You'll get TB, too, and then it will be even more of a headache for me."

Kusum trumpets angrily at Lorenzo. "She can barely stand, you brute! If you'd just give her a break, she wouldn't be fumbling around."

Sleep. Sleep. I just want to sleep. Shey is exhausted from her body working overtime to battle this disease and from malnutrition. She'd give anything for some rest, but the circus can't make money off of her that way, so she's forced to perform despite her frail condition.

"Shey, we're all here for you," Nayana assures her friend from the other end of the line. "Just fight through this show and then you can sleep tonight. It doesn't have to be your best performance. You just have to go through the motions."

Shey wants to make a joke. Normally, she would make a quip about how a true performer always gives her best no matter the circumstances, but she can't muster the energy. She wants to smile to assure Nayana that she's going to be alright, but she can't even feign that. She can tell that her best friend is very concerned for her, so she holds up her trunk to Nayana to signal that she appreciates her support.

A man with a headset shouts down the hall. "Elephant go time!"

Lorenzo, Daniel and the other trainers guide Yaso, Shey, Kusum, Padma, Lakmini and Nayana down the hallway to the arena entrance. The elephants enter to oohs and ahhs from the crowd. Shey is in a daze. All of the sounds of the circus mash together: the audience cheering, the loud pop music blaring, the squealing of excited children. The room spins. Shey trips into Yaso as she walks. Quickly, both Yaso and Kusum steady her with their trunks. Few people notice the tiny slip-up.

Shey follows along with the usual routine, but she's half-awake and unable to focus. *Sleep. I just want to sleep.*

Once, when she twirls around, she bangs her trunk into Daniel, knocking him to the ground. He plays along as if it's part of the show. He hops up and points his finger at Shey, pretending to scold her.

Shey struggles to breathe. The exercise is only worsening her condition. *Please let me sleep.*

It's time for the hat juggling trick. Nayana steals Lorenzo's hat and twirls it into the air a few times. She looks over at Shey and sees that her friend is clearly not up for the routine, so she decides to throw the hat to Lakmini, who catches it with ease and then tosses it to Padma. Unfortunately, Padma isn't quite as coordinated as the others, so the hat flies right past her and drops to the ground. There's a moment of silence as the audience realizes that a mistake may have been made. The savvy Kusum swiftly seizes the moment and stomps down hard on the hat, flattening it like a pancake. The audience erupts into laughter as Lorenzo marches over to retrieve his crushed hat. The trainer pretends to cry and throw a fit, and the audience chuckles again. They've bought the act. The troupe came together to save the day.

The victory doesn't last long, though. Shey's weak legs begin to buckle and she can't stand any longer. She sits down and almost topples over.

Lorenzo steps over to her and motions with his bullhook for her to stand up, but she can't. She just sits there looking beaten down. Lorenzo tries again, tapping Shey on her left front footpad. But she just hunches over even more. She breathes heavily.

The other elephants' hearts begin to race. If Shey doesn't get up, Lorenzo is going to be furious.

Kusum calls out to Yaso. "Follow my lead!"

Kusum turns to Shey and uses her trunk to lift up the back of Shey's body. Yaso helps lift from the other side. The audience begins to applaud, thinking this is part of the show. Kusum and Yaso have Shey standing again, but they're not quite sure what to do next. Lorenzo is fuming and gripping his bullhook. He wants so badly to smack Shey into shape, but he can't do it in front of the crowd.

Nayana quickly rushes over to aid Kusum and Yaso. She stands in front of her debilitated friend and explains calmly, "Shey, we're getting you out of here. All you have to do is walk forward. We'll guide you the entire way. Just follow me and we'll do the rest."

Shey can't gather the energy to speak. She just nods. She is filled with warmth seeing her herd come to her assistance. She trails Nayana as they move forward. To make it seem like this is part of their routine, Nayana trumpets loudly at the humans to get out of their way. The trainers play along, dramatically jumping to safety, and the spectators lap it up and cheer Shey on as she makes her exit.

The elephants make it out into the hallway and then through the doorway to the outside. Padma and Lakmini follow, so now all six elephants are together.

"Come on, ladies!" Nayana rallies the herd. "This is it! This is the moment we've been waiting for! We're finally breaking free!"

Circus workers start crowding around the elephants—trainers, supervisors, roustabouts, even some clowns—attempting to stop the escaping herd. The humans are panicked.

Nayana and Kusum trumpet forcefully to scare the humans out of their way. "Move aside or we'll stomp you, brutes!"

Just then, Shey collapses to the dirt. Immediately, the other elephants form a protective circle around her.

"It's okay, Shey," Nayana calls back to her friend. "Just rest here. Once you can continue, we're going to rush out of here. All of us! We're finally getting out of here!"

Lorenzo hollers at the elephants. "Stop! Now! All of you. Or you'll pay!"

Nayana wants so badly to crush Lorenzo with her powerful legs, but right now she has to guard Shey. She looks back and sees Shey laid out on the ground, struggling to breathe. All of the commotion has drained her enormously, and she whispers to herself, "Sleep. Sleep."

Nayana turns to Kusum. "Keep the humans at bay."

Nayana moves to the center of the circle and Kusum and Yaso immediately fill the hole where she stood. Nayana leans down to her best friend. Shey's eyes are closed. She wheezes, her chest thumping rapidly.

"Shey, I'm right here." Nayana pats her friend with her trunk. "They can't hurt you. Not anymore. No human is ever going to hurt you again."

Shey's breathing slows. She mumbles, but Nayana can't make out what she's saying. Nayana caresses her limp ear. "I know, Shey. You're tired. It's okay. Be still for a few moments. We'll guard you."

More humans have surrounded the elephants, some carrying bull-hooks, pitchforks and tranquilizer guns in case the elephants start a riot. Kusum, Yaso, Padma and Lakmini scream at the humans. "Keep away! We'll smash all of you!"

Shey mumbles again. Nayana comforts her. "No need to talk, my friend. Save your energy for the fight out of here. Just rest for now."

But Shey doesn't want to rest. She's trying to tell Nayana something. She's trying to tell her that she loves her, but Shey can't gather the strength to speak. She wants Nayana to know how much she means to her. How she couldn't have survived without her all these years—through all the physical, verbal and psychological abuse; grueling transport; and humiliating shows. She wants to tell Nayana that she's the best friend she could ever have. She wants to thank her for all the laughter, reassurance and companionship—all of which she so desperately needed. For consoling her when she was hopeless, when she was hurt. For giving her a reason to live. But she's so worn down, so weary, that she can't form the words.

Shey opens her eyes. She needs her friend to know. She needs her to understand. Shey reaches up her trunk and takes a hold of Nayana's. She looks her in the eyes. A tear streams down her cheek and instantly Nayana understands. This is goodbye.

"Oh, my friend." Tears begin to pour out of Nayana's eyes as well. "I know. I love you too, Shey. I love you, too."

Shey closes her eyes. Her breathing slows. She can finally be at peace. No more grueling train rides. No more being chained up all day. No more demeaning performances. No more beatings. No more suffering. No more pain. Just peace.

Nayana falls down beside her friend's withered body. Crushed. Broken. Her heart turns cold and hardens like a jagged rock lodged in her chest.

One by one, Kusum, Yaso, Padma and Lakmini turn around to see Nayana collapsed on the ground beside Shey. They know immediately. Shey is gone.

The humans pounce on the elephants while they're distracted—shooting them with tranquilizer darts and wrapping their legs in ropes and chains.

One by one, the elephants succumb. They would have battled to the end to get Shey to safety, but now… they've lost the will to fight.

As Nayana lies on the ground beside her best friend's corpse, something snaps inside of her. This is the final blow. When the humans tore her away from her mother, it broke her heart. When they ripped away her beloved Samadara, it devastated her. But now this?

There is no recovering from this. Shey was the only one keeping her sane all these years. Now she has nothing left. All hope is decimated.

The tranquilizers start to take effect. Nayana's eyes begin to blink shut. She takes one last look at her sweet friend lying there, motionless. Her only consolation is that Shey is finally free from the torment of life in the circus. Nayana was right when she told Shey that no human would ever harm her again, but now she realizes something she should have known all along—the only freedom these humans will allow is death.

Nayana closes her eyes. The circus has won. It's dominated her entire life and destroyed those that she held most dear. Without Shey, there is no joy. Without Shey, there is no hope. Without Shey, Nayana is unhinged, disturbed, insane. When she wakes, she will spend every minute of every day inconsolably trapped in her own miserable nightmare, oblivious to the world around her.

But... there is one thing. One thing that will stir her back into consciousness again and stoke the hateful fire inside of her.

Unfortunately, Persimmon has no idea that she's about to unleash it.

52

PAW IN PAW, Persimmon and Derpoke step up to the giant elephants. Yaso seems leery of them and Nayana doesn't even notice their approach—she just sways back and forth in a tormented daze. But Kusum, Padma, Lakmini and little Chatura light up at the sight of their two tiny would-be saviors.

"You came back!" Lakmini exclaims with a combination of surprise and relief.

"I told you they'd return," Padma remarks to the herd. "I knew this raccoon was as good as her word."

Persimmon subtly squeezes Derpoke's paw for moral support, trying to hide the guilt she feels over this compliment. She looks up at the colossal creatures towering over her. "Of course we returned. Our plan is to try to get you all out of here. We saw the afternoon show today and it sickened us to see you demeaned like that."

"The humiliation of those shows is nothing compared to being chained up all day," Kusum replies. "It drives us mad not being able to move. But now you're here. So, do you have a plan? Forgive my impatience, but the thought that we might finally break free is the only thing I've been thinking about since last night."

"Well, yes," Persimmon gulps. The sickness in her stomach gnaws at her insides. The elephants stare at her with such earnest anticipation, she hates to let them down. "The plan is already underway. As we speak, we have two teams surreptitiously stealing the keys to open the zebra and goat enclosures. As they do that, Chloe—a very savvy squirrel—is prepping the zebras, goats, horses and camels for their escape. Our plan is to get all of the other creatures out of here first, since it will be much easier to sneak them away, and then Chloe will come rushing in here with the keys to unlock your chains."

Padma and Lakmini cheer, unable to contain their joy.

"It's finally happening!" Lakmini exclaims.

Persimmon's back legs start shaking. She has to bring up her concerns about their escape, but she worries about how they'll react. "So… have you all had any more thoughts about how we can sneak you out of here quietly?"

"Quietly?" Kusum chuckles. "We don't really do quiet. What we have in our favor right now is power and the element of surprise. Once you unlock our chains, just leave the rest to us. You and your team will have done more than enough."

Persimmon was dreading this response. Force is obviously the elephants' most powerful tool, but as she told the team, the commotion they cause may sabotage the rescue of every other creature in the circus—and might even put her own team at risk. She will not put everyone's lives in jeopardy with such a hazardous plan, but how can she just give up on the elephants?

Her heart begins to race faster. She looks from one end of the line of elephants to the other. It's heartbreaking to see their spirits so high. Their exhilaration over the prospect of escaping is palpable and she feels terrible ripping it from them. "But you all will surely get hurt if you just rush out of here. Is there no better way? I just don't want anyone getting injured."

"I understand your concern," Kusum replies. "We have that worked out. Don't worry about us, kind raccoon."

Persimmon attempts to remain calm, but her anxiety is taking over. "Maybe we can…"

Just then, Chloe comes dashing into the room. She darts up to Persimmon, startling the raccoon, who was already on edge. From the squirrel's distressed expression, Persimmon can tell something has certainly gone wrong with the plan. "Chloe! Is everything okay?"

Chloe struggles to catch her breath. Derpoke, Kusum, Padma, Lakmini, Yaso and Chatura all stare at the squirrel, waiting to hear why she rushed in so frantically.

Chloe finally blurts out, "They can't locate the keys. All the trailers are sealed shut. What do we do now?"

Persimmon's mouth drops. What *are* they supposed to do now? That was the most vital part of the plan. Before Persimmon answers, she looks up at the five elephants staring down at her. Everyone is waiting for Persimmon to make a decision. Everyone is waiting for her to save the day.

53

PERSIMMON IS THE only hope for these elephants ever escaping this hell on Earth and everyone knows it. She wants to cry, scream, run away—all at once. She whispers, half hoping they won't hear her. "I'm sorry. I don't know how to save you."

"You're giving up?!" Lakmini howls, the desperation suffocating her instantly. "You can't just leave us. We'll die in here!"

"At least rescue Chatura," Kusum pleads. "He's only a baby. He has half a decade left of being beaten and chained up every day, and once they can't use him any longer in the circus, who knows what they'll do to him? He doesn't deserve this agonizing life. You don't have to save us all, but please save him."

Persimmon is tearing up. "I'm so sorry." She knows that she's betraying them, that she's sentencing them to a life of misery. "It's too dangerous. Even if you escape from this building, where will you go? There's nowhere to hide."

Nayana's ears perk up. She stops swaying. *Escape?* It suddenly hits her. She's been so depressed after Shey's death that she hasn't been thinking straight. But now, a tornado swirls inside of her. All of the hatred she holds for these humans, which has been dulled by her overwhelming sorrow, comes ferociously twisting to the top. These humans have to pay for what they've done to her friends and family for all these years—and especially for what they did to Shey. This isn't about escaping. This is about revenge.

Nayana stomps on the ground, causing a loud thud that reverberates throughout the room. Instantly, the other elephants stop their begging and turn to their raging companion.

Nayana stomps again. She's communicating with the herd.

Lakmini squeals with glee. "Yes!"

"Nayana, don't!" Yaso yells, panicked.

Derpoke curls up to Persimmon, frightened. Persimmon calls out to the elephants. "What's happening?"

"Persimmon, hide," Kusum warns.

Nayana trumpets loudly and shakes the chains around her legs. Persimmon, Derpoke and Chloe rush to the other side of the room and take cover behind a pedestal just as the security guard pushes through the red curtain and marches into the room. "Hey, shut up in here!"

Nayana trumpets at the guard and tosses hay in his direction, taunting him.

"Oh, you wanna gimme attitude?" The guard steps over to Nayana and holds up his bullhook. "You want this stick up your..."

Nayana grabs the guard's arm with her trunk. She lifts him off the ground and swings him around. He screams as his arm pops out of its socket. The irate elephant then drops his body on the concrete floor and crushes his skull with her foot. Blood puddles around his head. The room falls silent.

Persimmon peers up at the large creature, stunned—not blinking, not breathing after what she just witnessed. "You killed him," she finally gasps.

Nayana, who has snapped back to life, speaks to Persimmon calmly and with conviction. "Listen very carefully. Two days ago, this guard hit Padma so hard he made her bleed. He sits in hallways in every arena, relaxing while we're miserable and chained up in dark rooms. He was an evil human and he got what he deserved. Now get those keys off of his belt."

Persimmon stares at Nayana, unable to move.

"Persimmon," Nayana says, remaining composed yet determined. "Any moment now a swarm of humans is going to storm in here. If they see what I've done, they're going to kill me. Please, give us a chance at freedom. You're our only hope."

Persimmon takes a huge breath and gathers herself. There's no going back now. She turns to Chloe. "Run as fast as you can and tell the others that the rescue has begun. I'll bring the keys for the zebra and goat enclosures once I've released the elephants."

Chloe nods and darts out of the room at lightning speed.

Persimmon calls out to her opossum friend. "Derpoke, step outside the curtain and tell me if you see humans coming."

Derpoke scurries over to the curtain, squealing frantically the whole way.

Persimmon rushes over to the security guard's body. She jiggles the keys attached to his belt and, after a few attempts, yanks them free. She then hops over to Nayana. "How do I use these?"

"Take that jagged silver key—the one with the blue plastic cover—and slide it into that slot there on the lock," Nayana instructs.

Persimmon's paws are shaking. She fumbles with the keys and can't steady her fingers long enough to slide the right one into the hole. "I can't do it! My paws won't be still."

On the other side of the curtain, Derpoke breathes erratically. "Oh my gosh. Oh my gosh." He swivels his head back and forth, looking down the three hallways in front of him, hoping that no humans come running his way. "Please, please, please."

Right then, Daniel and another trainer appear around the corner. They rush down the hall toward Derpoke. "Jared? Are you okay?" Daniel yells.

Derpoke hollers back through the curtain. "Humans are coming!"

Daniel and the other trainer stop when they see Derpoke standing between them and the curtain. "What the hell? Is that an opossum?" Daniel asks.

The other trainer examines Derpoke quizzically. "Yep."

Derpoke hisses at the men.

"Whoa!" Daniel flinches. "Do they bite?"

The other trainer lifts up his bullhook. "Guess we'll find out."

Derpoke yells hysterically. "Humans! Humans!" The small opossum bravely holds his position as the trainers step toward him, bullhooks raised.

Derpoke hisses at them again. He curls up, ready for a blow, when WHAM! Nayana smashes through the curtain and pummels Daniel and the other trainer with her massive head.

The two humans smack into the wall behind them. Nayana picks up the men by their legs and swings them at the ground, slamming their heads into the hard floor. Neither human moves after that.

Nayana takes off down the hall. Derpoke watches the whole violent scene with his mouth agape. His heart is pumping hard. This rescue mission is already a bloody mess, and it's only just begun.

*   *   *

Next, Lakmini rushes out of the room. She barrels down the hallway after Nayana, banging into props and metal sets the entire way, making a thunderous racket.

Down the opposite hallway, Derpoke sees another human standing in shock, keeping his distance. The man yells into his walkie-talkie. "Elephants loose! Code black! Elephants loose!"

In the elephant room, Persimmon is finishing unlocking Padma's chains.

Padma thanks her profusely as Persimmon undoes the final lock, then the elephant runs out of the room joyfully.

Persimmon jumps over to Kusum and starts unlocking her chains. "Kusum, I know you have your herd to look after, but I want to ask you one favor."

"Whatever you need," Kusum replies sincerely.

"Can you help us release the other creatures who are stuck in the circus?"

"Absolutely. They are all part of the herd."

"Wonderful," Persimmon says as she finishes unlocking the last chain on the enormous creature's legs.

Persimmon rushes over to Chatura while Kusum watches over.

"I will stay here until you release our little Chatura," Kusum explains. "So help these brutes if they lay a hand on him."

Outside the arena, humans are rushing around, frenzied. Rawly, Bruiser, Scraps, Claudette, Drig, Fisher, Nibbin and Tucker are huddled in a bush covered island in the parking lot, twenty feet away from the arena back door.

"Something's happening. Be alert, everyone," Rawly warns the team.

Right then, Chloe comes darting out of the arena at full speed. She's yelling something, but they can't make it out.

"What's she saying?" Drig asks his companions.

The other team members try to listen more intently, but she's running so fast and is screaming half out of breath, so her words are inaudible.

Chloe finally reaches the bushes and blurts out, "Get ready. Persimmon released the elephants!"

At that moment, two humans slam the back doors shut and lock them.

"Oh, no," Scraps laments. "They're trapping the elephants inside."

Back in the elephant room, Persimmon hurriedly steps up to Yaso—the final elephant in the holding area. Yaso stares at the minuscule raccoon with a concerned expression. "I fear we're all doomed."

Persimmon was rushing to unlock Yaso, but she stops to ask quickly, "So does that mean you don't want me to unlock your chains?"

Yaso thinks about it for a moment. If Persimmon unlocks her, Yaso knows that she will be considered an accomplice and whatever severe repercussions the humans take against the elephants for starting a riot will be taken out on her as well. She has spent her entire life trying to follow the rules just to survive, but that tactic won't work this time. She must take a stand. "Unlock me. You all are going to need my help."

Outside the arena, the team members watch as circus workers scramble around trying to get the situation under control. BAM! Something pounds against the door. The humans freeze. BAM! Another loud thud shakes the door's hinges. The elephants are on the other side taking turns ramming the door with all their might.

A circus worker shrieks. "They're gonna bust the door down!"

"We have to help get that door open," Rawly exclaims to the team.

"How are we going to get past all these humans?" Tucker asks. "Besides, those powerful elephants can't even do it. What are *we* gonna do?"

Inside the arena by the back door, Nayana, Lakmini, Padma, Kusum, and Chatura slam their robust heads into the metal barrier, two at a time. This door is the only thing between them and freedom, and there is no way they are going to let it stop them.

"Come on, we can do this!" Nayana yells to invigorate the herd. "Put your whole body into it!"

Kusum steps back with Chatura and motions for Lakmini to listen as well. "Lakmini, when we smash open these doors, take Chatura and run as fast as you can to the forest. Don't wait for me."

"What do you mean?" Lakmini's voice cracks. "We're all going together."

"Baby, we don't have time to argue over this." Kusum sees the hurt in their eyes and explains. "I'm too slow. The circus ruined my legs. I can barely walk, much less run. But as the youngest of our herd, you two have your whole lives ahead of you and I want it to be a life of freedom. Chatura, you follow Lakmini, okay?"

Chatura clings to Kusum's legs and moans.

"Lakmini," Kusum continues. "Do you remember the way to the woods? We went over this last night. Follow the path we took when the humans walked us from the train to the arena. When you get back to the tracks, you should be able to see the forest from there."

"Yes," Lakmini replies, trying to hold back her distress at having to leave Kusum.

"Get Chatura to safety with the other ladies," Kusum instructs. "That's your job. My job is to stay here and help these other animals. I may never get out of this place myself, but I'm going to do everything in my power to make sure all these other creatures will."

Nayana keeps slamming her head into the unbending metal doors, harder and harder. She's getting exasperated. "Come on!"

Nayana rests while Kusum and Padma take over. The enraged elephant hunches over, trying to catch her breath. She closes her eyes. They've come so far, after so many years. They can't let a stupid door stop them now. She thinks about Randy, Wes, Lorenzo—all of the sadistic trainers she's had since she was a baby. She pictures her mother, Samadara, Shey. How much she misses them. How much she detests these humans for taking her loved ones from her. She must break this door down... for them.

Yaso puts her trunk on Nayana's back, startling her. Nayana stares at Yaso, dumbfounded to see the grouchy elephant joining the herd.

"We may not have seen eye to eye over the years," Yaso explains. "But if we're going to break free from this place, you'll need my help. We're opening this door. Right now. Together."

Nayana perks up. Just when she was beginning to lose hope again, the least likely candidate has stepped up to encourage her.

Persimmon and Derpoke stand at Yaso's feet, staying out of the way of the elephants' assault on the back entrance. The inquisitive raccoon examines the doors closely, remembering when she saw Lorenzo and the now-dead security guard open the same type of door last night when the men took a smoke break. She quickly studies the metal bars that the humans pushed to open the doors and the silver poles that run up and down the length of the thick barriers. Her eyes light up.

Persimmon calls up to Nayana. "I know the door is locked from the outside, but if you look closely, there are metal poles that hold it in place by sticking into the floor and the doorframe." Nayana scrutinizes the door as Persimmon explains. "If your troupe can tear those poles off and possibly break those hinges above as well, maybe it will loosen the doors enough so you can smash through them."

The same light bulb goes off for Nayana. "Of course!" She was so hell-bent on escaping that she focused entirely on using brute force without stopping to be tactical, but this clever raccoon may have just ensured their escape. Nayana rallies the herd, reinvigorated by Persimmon's savvy strategy and Yaso's joining the fight. "Kusum, Padma, Lakmini, Yaso and Chatura, listen up." Kusum and Padma stop ramming the door. "Yank off those metal poles holding the doors to the frame. Break the hinges at the top. We're going to rip these doors out of the wall!"

The other elephants jump into action, tearing at the door. Nayana riles them up as they work. "Picture all the humans who have ever beaten you over the years. All the times they shocked you with electric prods, slammed their bullhooks into your flesh." The herd pulls the metal pieces apart, wildly tossing them on the floor behind them. "Picture the humans tugging you away from your mothers. Chaining you up every single day. Feel that hatred. Feel that vitriol surging through your body and take it all out on that door." Kusum and Padma shred the metal as Yaso, Lakmini and Chatura take turns hammering their heads into the doors with all the force they can muster. "We're so close. Just one door away from freedom. One door away from revenge. Let's make those humans regret ever kidnapping us from Ceylon! Let's crush them!"

Nayana trumpets loudly and the other elephants join her, blaring furiously. Chills run down the spines of the anxious humans on the other side of the door.

Outside of the arena, The Uncaged Alliance watches as humans ready tranquilizer guns. To their horror, they see two humans hop into forklifts and start driving toward the door.

Rawly addresses the team. "If those drivers reach the doors, these poor elephants will never make it out of there. There's no time to waste."

"Rawly," Bruiser tries to talk sense into him. "I wanna get them outta there, too, but it's too dangerous."

"They need our help, Bruiser," Rawly exclaims. "It doesn't matter how dangerous it is."

Bruiser ponders this for a second. Deep down he knows it's true. No matter what, they have to help these elephants. The Doberman nods in agreement.

Rawly smiles and yells wildly. "Uncagers! To no more chains!"

Bruiser, Chloe, Scraps, Claudette, Drig and Fisher all chime in. "No more chains!"

Tucker hollers for his Sweet Pea. "Chloe, don't!" But she doesn't hear him. She's too caught up in the moment.

Before Nibbin can rush off with the team, Tucker grabs hold of the tiny mink. "Not you, little mink. You're going to get yourself killed."

Rawly, Claudette and Drig rush across the pavement, straight toward one of the forklifts. With ease they hop up the side and plow right into the driver's face. Rawly bites and scratches at the man's eyes as Drig tears the flesh on his neck. The man howls violently and falls to the ground, clutching his bleeding face.

At the same time, Chloe, Bruiser, Scraps and Fisher take over the other forklift. Chloe, Scraps and Fisher attack the driver's head while Bruiser grabs hold of the man's pants and pulls him off of the forklift. The man swats at the critters, but he is so taken off-guard that his face is half ripped up before he even knows what is happening.

Both forklifts come to a halt. Victory!

Suddenly, though, the team realizes that they are now out in the open. They look around and see that the circus workers are not facing the doors any longer—the humans are facing *them*.

54

"RUN!" RAWLY YELLS to his fellow Uncagers. He, Chloe, Bruiser, Scraps, Claudette, Drig and Fisher are surrounded by more than a dozen circus workers—all holding weapons, all furious over what the team just did to those forklift drivers.

"They got rabies!" one circus worker shouts. He aims his tranquilizer gun at Scraps and fires, narrowly missing the small raccoon's neck. Scraps maneuvers through another man's legs as a tactic to thwart off a second shot at him. "Don't shoot!" the man screams, so the gun-wielding trainer holds his fire.

Chloe, the smallest and fastest team member, races straight past all of the humans before they can react and makes it safely back to the bushes where Tucker and Nibbin are hiding. Unfortunately, the other team members are larger and make much easier targets.

Two men rush at Bruiser with bullhooks. Rawly and Fisher see this, so they skillfully run circles around their legs to slow them down. The men swat their bullhooks at the raccoons, grazing their fur but luckily not landing any blows. This gives the Doberman time to bark viciously at the men and jump toward them threateningly, which stops the humans in their tracks. Suddenly, the idea of taking on this menacing dog seems like a misbegotten plan.

Claudette runs swiftly past a circus worker who is swinging his bullhook at her. She gracefully avoids his assault by actually jumping straight for his arm that wields the bullhook, which frightens him enough to trip him back onto the pavement. She runs past his legs smiling when WHAM! a tranquilizer dart pierces her side. She squeals and flips over from the blow.

Although Fisher had just made it safely past the humans, he twists around and rushes over to her side. Claudette can barely keep her eyes open. The dart was meant for a giant elephant, so it takes effect quickly. Another circus worker runs up to Fisher and Claudette twirling a bullhook in the air, ready to strike. Claudette can't move, so Fisher charges straight for the man, who swings the bullhook and just misses Fisher's head. The courageous raccoon latches onto the man's right leg and bites down hard, through his jeans and into his thigh. The man wails and falls back. Just then, Drig joins in, hopping onto the man's arm and biting into his wrist. The man screams again and instantly loosens his grip on the bullhook.

Rawly rushes up to his half-conscious sweetheart. "Claudette. Wake up. Please." Claudette moans but is too drugged to walk. Rawly grabs the back of her neck with his teeth and tries to pull her along the pavement. She's too heavy for him, though. "Claudette, please my love. I can't carry you. You have to get up!"

Rawly struggles with all his might to pull her along the ground. He cries as he futilely attempts to drag her to safety. "Please, give me the strength to carry her. Give me the strength. I beg you!" He sees two men running toward them—one with a bat, one with a pitchfork. He yells frantically to his team members. "Someone help! Please!"

Now that Drig and Fisher have debilitated one man, they run toward the two men rushing at Rawly and Claudette. The raccoons get right up to the humans when the man carrying the bat swings and lands a powerful blow to Fisher's skull. The raccoon's body spins in the air and smacks onto the ground with a thud. The man lifts the bat and slams it onto Fisher's head again, smashing it flat.

The other team members shriek in horror as their friend is murdered right in front of their eyes. But there's no time to mourn—they still have to save their own lives.

Rawly desperately attempts to pull Claudette to safety, but he's barely making any headway as the man with the pitchfork runs straight at him. Right then, Bruiser pounces on the man's back, knocking him to the ground. Drig and Scraps follow, biting the man's face and ears. The man howls and drops the pitchfork.

Out of nowhere, another human comes running up and slams his bullhook so hard into Scraps that the small raccoon is sent flying. Bruiser lets out a savage growl and tackles the man to the asphalt. The Doberman sinks his sharp teeth deep into the man's throat and rips out a large chunk of flesh. Blood spews out of the man's neck as Bruiser spits out the flabby skin and quickly darts over to Scraps. He lifts up his little buddy with his teeth and runs at top speed away from the mass of barbaric humans.

Chloe watches, aghast, as her friends are quickly being taken over by the humans. Fisher is dead. Scraps is seriously, maybe even fatally, injured. Only she and Bruiser escaped the mess unscathed, but Rawly, Drig and Claudette are still out there. Chloe is about to rush back to help the remaining team members, but Tucker grabs her.

"Chloe, don't," he pleads.

"Let me go!" Chloe tries to shake him free. "They're going to die out there."

"You can't save them," Tucker begs. "You're just going to get hurt. There are too many humans. Please don't go. I can't lose you!"

Chloe breathes heavily. She can't leave her friends out there to die, but what can she do? More than a dozen humans are rushing at Rawly, Drig and Claudette at this very moment. By the time she gets there, they'll be surrounded and she'll just get swept up in the massacre. He's right. There's absolutely nothing she can do.

Chloe watches, terrified, as humans brandishing tranquilizer guns, bullhooks and pitchforks close in on Rawly and Drig. The two raccoons helplessly pull the unconscious Claudette as fast as they can. Rawly sobs uncontrollably, knowing that rescuing his sweetheart is impossible. He and his friend are simply not strong enough to carry her, and the circus workers are gaining on them too quickly.

The mob of humans finally catches up to the three raccoons and crowds around them—smiling, looking forward to ripping apart these vermin. Rawly and Drig bare their teeth and guard Claudette. They may be about to die, but they're not going down without a fight.

55

CRASH! THE HUMANS halt immediately. A victorious trumpeting fills the air. The people turn away from the three raccoons to see Nayana, Lakmini, Kusum, Padma, Yaso and Chatura come crashing through the arena back doors and out into the open—into freedom!

Most of the humans scatter, forgetting about Rawly, Drig and Claudette. Some of them point their tranquilizer guns at the elephants, but they are so panicked that they fumble with the triggers and miss the giant beasts.

The elephants angrily bellow at the humans. Nayana rams her head into one woman who is taking aim with her weapon. The woman falls back onto the pavement and accidentally pulls the trigger, shooting a dart into the unwitting circus worker behind her. He rips it out of his flesh, but the drug has already penetrated his system and he drops to the ground.

Lakmini swats her trunk at two humans swinging bullhooks at her. It feels so good to finally fight back. "Get out of my way, brutes!" she hollers jubilantly.

Kusum, Lakmini, Padma, Yaso and Chatura veer to the left of the arena where the other creatures are located, but as they push their way through the scrambling circus workers, Kusum notices Nayana heading in the opposite direction.

"Nayana," she calls. "The forest is this way."

"I'm not going to the forest," Nayana replies without a hint of hesitation. She then adds with great admiration, "Good luck, Kusum. Thank you for watching over me all these years."

With that, Nayana runs off before Kusum has a chance to talk her out of it.

* * *

Rawly and Drig continue to pull Claudette toward the bushes. They're exhausted but very close to safety. That's when Rawly sees a man standing over the dead body of the circus worker who just had his throat torn out by Bruiser. The man shakes his head, then looks over at the two raccoons struggling to rescue their companion. He picks up the pitchfork that had been dropped on the ground and heads straight for the trio.

Rawly screams, but before he can try to block the blow, the man jabs the pitchfork through Claudette's chest. She lets out a pained groan and flops her legs, instinctively trying to run away, but her feet aren't even touching the pavement.

The man grins, but just then an elephant's trunk wraps around his waist, hoists him into the air, and forcefully tosses him through the windshield of a nearby car. Nayana looks down at the raccoons, nods, and runs off.

Rawly grabs hold of Claudette's limp body. The pitchfork has fallen over but is still stuck in her chest.

"Claudette! No! No!" Rawly wails. He pulls her lifeless body off of the pitchfork and wraps his paws around her. "My love!"

Persimmon and Derpoke rush over. They witnessed Claudette's murder from the arena doorway. Now that most of the humans have dispersed to follow the elephants, they are finally able to join the rest of the team. The two friends watch Rawly weep as he hugs his sweetheart tightly. They want to console him, but they have no idea how. That's when Persimmon notices the other unsettling mayhem in the parking lot: Fisher's dead body smashed into the ground, the human that Bruiser killed, the human Nayana smashed into a car, and the two forklift drivers clutching their faces as they're being carried away.

"Oh, no!" Persimmon gasps. Her worst nightmare has come true. Two of their team members have been killed and humans are both dead and injured, all because she released the elephants. But what was she supposed to do—leave them chained up to suffer? She drops the keys she had been carrying. Sadness, confusion and guilt sweep through her. Everything has fallen apart.

Chloe, Tucker and Nibbin dash over to the team as well.

Persimmon is flummoxed by the tragedy that just unfolded. "What happened here? How did the humans surround you all?"

Chloe reveals in a state of shock. "They were going to block the doors with those vehicles. We couldn't just stand by and watch, so we attacked the drivers. And it worked. The elephants broke free, but by that point the humans had surrounded us. And they just kept hitting us and hitting us. There was nowhere to run."

She is shaking, so Tucker embraces her.

Persimmon is suddenly overcome with a sick feeling. "Where are Scraps and Bruiser?"

"Scraps got hit with one of those sticks pretty hard, so Bruiser picked him up and ran off that way," Tucker explains, pointing in the direction the Doberman ran.

"Is he okay?!" Persimmon asks, panicked.

"I don't know," Tucker replies nervously. "He got hit really hard. I'm sorry."

"I have to find him," Persimmon says, starting to move away.

Chloe calls after her. "What should we do? The other creatures are still trapped."

Persimmon halts. She wants to make sure her brother is safe, but can't abandon her leadership duties. The team is counting on her, and so are the horses, zebras, goats and camels.

"Go check on the other creatures," Persimmon instructs. "The elephants said they may help us release them. But do not in any way put yourselves in harm's way again. I mean that. Assist where you can, but no irresponsible heroics. I'll be back as fast as I can."

With that, Persimmon runs off after Bruiser and her injured brother.

Chloe, Tucker, Nibbin and Derpoke turn around to start their expedition. In front of them, Drig stands near Claudette's lifeless body, but Rawly isn't there any longer. Where did he go?

Then Chloe sees Rawly in the distance, running away. She can barely make out the raccoon's outline but sees something surprising dangling from his mouth—the keys.

56

SMASH! KUSUM YANKS up and down on the metal fence to the goat pen with her muscular trunk, tearing at the hinges. The goats huddle in the opposite corner, cheering.

"Rip it apart, Kusum!" Mirabel roots her on. "Destroy it!"

Padma and Yaso guard Kusum, charging at any humans who attempt to stop their courageous matriarch. Most importantly, the two protective elephants focus on knocking down any circus workers carrying tranquilizer guns. So far none of the elephants have been hit, but they've had a few close calls.

WHAM! Kusum pulls once more and the gate rips apart. The goats, led by Mirabel, applaud her efforts and immediately dash off toward the street. They're not going to pause for even a moment now that they have their chance to escape.

The circus workers rush to grab the goats, but the stampeding creatures just plow right into them with their thick skulls, knocking the humans back on their behinds.

Chloe, Drig, Tucker and Nibbin come running around the bend just in time to see the goats freed. They can't believe their eyes. The amazing elephants are risking their own lives to save these other creatures. The team shouts merrily. "Hooray!"

"Tucker, try to catch up to the goats and guide them to the forest," Chloe calls out.

Tucker nods and rushes after them.

As the team runs past a few humans, Chloe yells, "Drig, while the humans are distracted, let's get started on those horses' buckles."

"Got it," Drig replies as he follows along with Chloe and Nibbin. They weave in and out of the oblivious humans, who are too distracted by the rampaging elephants to pay them any attention.

Kusum has moved on to the zebra enclosure. She yanks at the gate just like she did with the goat pen. One of the trainers has caught on to her plan, though, and instead of taking on these gigantic creatures, he decides to shoot the captive zebras with his tranquilizer gun. He figures that even if the enclosure is opened, they'll be too drugged up to run away. The man loads his weapon with another dart.

Somersault neighs loudly and runs toward the gate where the man is readying his weapon. Chloe and Nibbin see this, so they run through the man's legs, startling him. He pulls the trigger and, unfortunately, a dart hits one of the other zebras. The creature squeals and shakes his fur to try and knock it off, but no such luck. Within a few moments, he slumps to the ground, knocked out.

Padma storms over to the man as he reloads his tranquilizer gun and rams her thick head into his chest. He flies back, going limp as his skull hits the pavement.

Four men surround Padma and begin beating her violently with their weapons. One has a pitchfork and stabs it repeatedly into her back left leg. Padma screeches. She swings her trunk around, knocking another one of men to the ground, but the others keep tearing at her flesh with their lethal hardware.

Yaso charges at the humans abusing her friend. She picks up the man carrying the pitchfork and swings him around by his leg before slamming him down on the fence. A loud crack fills the air as his spine breaks in half.

Padma then pounds her head into the three remaining men, knocking them to the ground and crushing their insides. They shriek as the life is squeezed out of them.

The entire time, Kusum continues to shake the gate of the zebra enclosure, but the metal just won't bend. To the team's great dismay, more circus workers are running toward them. This may be the end of their rampage. How will they stave off all of these humans long enough to rescue the other animals?

$$* \quad * \quad *$$

The arena hallways are in shambles. The circus sets are twisted into metal shards. Props are crushed and torn to pieces. Balloons are popped. Green and gold pedestals are now just green and gold piles of junk. A bullhook lies here. A whip lies there. All of the instruments of torture the animals have feared for so many years have finally been demolished.

And in this clutter creeps a seething mess of a raccoon, consumed by an unfathomable rage he has never known before. Not a human is in sight. They're all outside of the arena, flailing around and attempting to contain the rioting creatures they've dominated for so long.

The eight caged tigers have been watching Rawly prowl toward them since he appeared down the hall, mesmerized by what he is carrying in his teeth.

Rawly steps up to the cage of the head tiger, Yarick, and drops the keys in front of his enclosure. Yarick's pupils dilate as they home in on the shiny metal objects. The tiger licks his lips. "You have my attention."

Rawly's face is still wet with tears, but the sorrow has been stripped away and replaced with hatred. "I could change your entire life right now, but in order to make that happen, I have two demands."

Yarick leans in closer. He could reach through the cage and instantly slice Rawly to shreds, but he's enthralled by the raccoon's gall. "I'm listening."

"One," Rawly begins. "Upon your release, you won't harm any of my friends or any of the other creatures stuck in this circus."

"You have my word," Yarick responds resolutely. "And two?"

Rawly grinds his teeth and scratches the concrete floor in front of him. "You must kill any humans that you see."

Yarick flashes a devilish grin. "With pleasure."

57

"SCRAPS! BRUISER!" PERSIMMON races through a vacant section of the parking lot, sniffing the ground and shouting for her brother and loyal friend. Her heart is pounding. She can't think straight. The fear that she might find her little brother dead by Bruiser's side haunts her. *Please be okay. Oh, my sweet brother. Please be okay.*

Persimmon stops in her tracks. Droplets of blood litter the pavement. "No." She becomes dizzy. The ground tilts. Is he dead already? Will she not even have the chance to say goodbye?

"Persimmon!" Bruiser calls out to the panicked raccoon from the cover of a bush. She darts over, lightheaded and wobbling slightly.

When she crawls inside the foliage, she sees Bruiser standing over her brother just as she had feared. The Doberman licks the tiny raccoon's fur, which is smeared with blood.

"Scraps!" Persimmon grabs hold of her sweet little brother and weeps. "No! My brother!"

Scraps hugs his sister back. "Persimmon, it's okay. I'm all right."

Persimmon sits back, stifling the tears. "What?!"

"I'm all right," Scraps assures her. "I just got knocked out from being hit. My side hurts like crazy, but I'll fight through it."

Persimmon looks at his blood-soaked fur. "But there's all this blood."

Bruiser speaks up, sheepishly. "It's not Scraps' blood." The Doberman sighs. He's worried how his raccoon friend is going to take this. "It's human blood. Persimmon, I killed one of the humans. He was 'bout to crush Scraps and I attacked him. I couldn't let him hurt my lil' buddy."

Persimmon teeters, stunned. "You killed that human? I thought the elephants had done that."

Bruiser attempts to explain, "There was no other..."

Persimmon cuts him off and hugs the large dog's right front leg. "Bruiser, you saved my brother's life. I am eternally grateful. You don't need to justify it. If I had been there... I would have done anything to save him... to save any of you."

Persimmon holds out her arm for Scraps to join in the hug. He crawls over and wraps his arms around his sister and their trusty friend. She rests her head on her brother's head. "I'm just glad you two are safe."

Persimmon holds the hug for a moment, basking in the relief that they are both alive. She then says, "Okay, I need to get back and help the rest of the team release the other creatures. You two stay hidden."

"Are you kidding?" Scraps complains. "We're going with you. You need our help."

"You were almost killed, Scraps." Persimmon counters. "It's too chaotic. Things have gone completely awry. Poor Fisher and Claudette are already dead."

Scraps and Bruiser gasp. The small raccoon remarks, shaken. "Claudette was killed, too? Rawly must be devastated."

"He's destroyed," Persimmon replies. "I don't know how he'll ever recover. I would be just as devastated if I lost either of you, which is why I don't want you two going back out there. The humans are out for blood over us trying to release the creatures."

Scraps takes his sister's paw. "Persimmon, I know how unsafe this is and I promise you that I'll be careful. I won't make any more risky choices, but those horses and camels are counting on us to unbuckle their halters and you need my help to do that."

"And you better believe I'm not just sittin' by while the rest of the team does all of the work," Bruiser adds.

"Ahh!" Persimmon shakes her paws in the air, frustrated. "This team is impossible." She scratches her ear anxiously and finally gives in. "I know you're not going to listen to me anyway. You two can come, but here are the conditions. Scraps, absolutely no running into the middle of any more swarms of humans. And Bruiser, since the humans are going to be on the lookout for you, I think we need to station you away from the arena. Tucker and Chloe were supposed to help lead the rescued animals through the streets, but we're going to need Chloe's help unbuckling the horses and camels. So maybe you can help Tucker instead. I think most of the elephants have run off already, but the rest of the creatures are going to need guidance."

"Deal," Scraps and Bruiser agree.

With that, Persimmon, Scraps and Bruiser rush back toward the arena. It's time for phase two.

✳   ✳   ✳

CRUNCH! Nayana slams her thick head like a battering ram into the side of a trailer. The thin metal buckles easily and the two humans inside shriek as their legs and arms are crushed. Nayana is obliterating rows and rows of RVs and trailers. Some of the circus workers who were hiding inside them were smashed and killed. Behind her is a trail of bodies—workers who tried to stop her in her tracks and paid the price.

"Where is he?!" Nayana screams with a ferocity from deep within.

In the alley between two of the RVs, a woman runs up to Nayana and shoots a tranquilizer into her backside. The rampaging elephant screams angrily, grabs the woman's torso, and smashes her into the side of one of the trailers. The woman drops the tranquilizer gun and pounds her fists into Nayana's trunk. The elephant fights back by slamming the woman's head into the trailer, smacking her into an air conditioner that juts out of the vehicle's side and snapping the woman's neck. As Nayana drops the woman's lifeless body onto the ground, another circus worker jabs a bullhook into the elephant's ear. She swings fiercely at the man, knocking him into the trailer behind him and he drops to the ground, moaning.

"Keep trying, you brutes!" Nayana hollers. "I'll crush you all!"

She bangs her head into the trailer beside her, flipping it on its side, revealing… Lorenzo, who had been hiding behind the vehicle. Nayana trumpets in triumph. There he is—her mortal enemy—with his stupid black, braided beard dangling from his chin and his ridiculous black leather vest.

Lorenzo stands there holding his favorite bullhook, ready to take Nayana down. But when he sees that raging look in her eyes, he turns around and darts back to his trailer. He's not running away, though—he's going for his handgun.

Lakmini and Chatura run through the streets at full speed. It's past midnight in the very early hours of the morning, so luckily there are only a few cars driving by, but each one screeches to a halt or crashes into parked cars to get out of the way. The drivers stare in amazement at these two exotic creatures barreling through the middle of the city.

The two escaping elephants are sobbing. They miss the rest of their herd and feel awful about leaving them behind. They're also lost and too hysterical to think straight. Tucker would have been happy to guide them to the forest, but the elephants burst out of the arena and ran off before the team had time to coordinate with them.

"Chatura, don't look back," Lakmini calls out to her young companion. "You have to run faster. We'll never get to the woods at this pace."

A car idly turns the corner and when the driver sees the elephants, she accidentally hits her gas pedal instead of the brake. Her car hurtles toward a building and crashes into the brick wall.

Another driver, who has already stopped his vehicle, is yelling into his phone. "You gotta come quick! There are two elephants in the middle of the street. They're tearing apart cars! They're gonna kill us all! You gotta get here now!"

Chatura stops abruptly and plants his feet.

Lakmini turns around. "Chatura, we have to keep going. Please. I know we're lost, but we'll find the woods eventually if we just keep running. Kusum would want you to. She wants you to be safe. *I* want you to be safe."

Chatura weeps, confused and overwhelmed.

Two teenage boys—out way past their curfew—hold up their cell phones to record video of the elephants. "This is so cool!"

One of the boys yells at Lakmini and Chatura. "Come on, do something cool. Step on one of those cars!"

Just then, an orange tabby cat comes rushing up to the elephants. It's Apricot. "Elephants! Follow me!"

Lakmini and Chatura stare at her, dumbfounded. Lakmini whispers to Chatura. "Is that the cat from last night?"

"Elephants! Come on!" Apricot yells energetically. "I'm helping The Uncaged Alliance. Follow me."

Lakmini and Chatura exchange glances. What a relief! This plucky team never ceases to amaze. They happily follow the cat as she darts off down the street.

"Out of my way, humans!" Apricot commands. "Oversized load coming through!"

*　　*　　*

Derpoke tiptoes down the messy arena hallway. Since he's too slow to help release the zebras, horses and camels, the team has decided that he should try to retrieve the coveted keys from Rawly.

"Rawly?" Derpoke calls out, his voice echoing off the walls. "Rawly, we need the keys to release the zebras and goats." The opossum has no idea that the lucky goats are already far down the street—halfway to freedom.

Derpoke is crawling around the remnants of the circus props when two humans step through the back door and head down the hallway.

One of the humans stops, stunned at the sight before him. "Whoa! It's gonna cost a fortune to replace all this stuff."

"Come on, you're wasting time," the other circus worker reprimands as they walk past the hidden opossum. "We have to get those other tranquilizer guns from the elephant holding area."

Suddenly, a bone-chilling roar reverberates throughout the arena. Before the men can react, eight fearsome tigers bound down the hall straight for them. The men shriek and run in the opposite direction.

Derpoke hunkers down under some debris as the big cats sprint toward him. The opossum freezes with fear, but he can't help but be mesmerized by the sight of these stunning predators gracefully gliding through the dimly lit corridor.

The two men barely make any headway before the enraged beasts pounce on them. The tigers rip and tear at the humans' flesh until they're just a pile of blood, guts and shredded clothes.

Derpoke shakes fearfully as the tigers leap away down the hall, but one, Yarick, turns and glares at the hiding critter. Blood drips from Yarick's mouth. Derpoke, breathing erratically, lets out a quiet squeal. This is it. He's going to be sliced to pieces just like those humans.

Yarick hisses, "They won't be whipping us any longer."

Then the big cat sprints out the back door with his fierce brethren. Just like Nayana, they're on a mission for revenge. For every day these tigers were caged and for every time they were whipped, these humans are going to pay severely.

Derpoke's mouth is agape—tongue drooped out. He falls over on his side, not quite sure how he's still alive. He wants to hop up and help with the rescue mission, but he's going to need a few moments to recuperate. It's not every day that you come face to face with a tiger and live to tell the tale.

58

PADMA WOBBLES AS she stands between the horse and zebra enclosures. She has been shot numerous times with tranquilizer darts and is starting to feel woozy. Half a dozen circus workers crowd around her, jabbing her with bullhooks. They could just let her succumb to the sedative, but the humans are in attack mode. They want to teach her a lesson after all the chaos she's caused.

Yaso tries to bat the humans away from Padma, while also attempting to protect Kusum, who is still struggling to tear open the zebra enclosure.

"Kusum," Yaso yells as she fights off the advancing circus workers. "We have to get out of here! We're being overrun!"

"No," Kusum responds defiantly. "I'm not leaving these zebras in here."

At the same time, Drig has managed to unbuckle two of the horses' halters. Chloe and Nibbin have also worked as a team to undo one more, but it's much more difficult for the squirrel and mink since their paws aren't as strong as the raccoon's. The horses haven't run away yet, though. If even one of them suddenly darts off, the humans will notice that they are being set free right under their noses.

"We're not going fast enough!" Chloe yells to Drig as she watches the poor elephants fight for their lives. "At this rate…"

Just then, Persimmon and Scraps come dashing out from behind the semi-trailer trucks where the camels are tied up. Chloe lets out a sigh of relief.

The miniature horses lean down to let the two raccoons climb onto their necks. Persimmon waves at Chloe to let her know that help has arrived.

Persimmon, Scraps, Chloe, Drig and Nibbin frantically rush to unbuckle the patient horses' halters. All of the noise in the parking lot is spooking the horses, but Charlemagne keeps his companions in line with encouraging words. "Hold steady, my friends. Focus forward. Our freedom hinges on our ability to remain calm."

Persimmon addresses the horses. "We'll get you out of here in no time! As Chloe probably told you, remember to follow Tucker the squirrel and Bruiser the dog down that road over there using the building with blue lights as your guide. That'll lead you safely to the forest."

BOOM! A shot rings out. But this isn't a tranquilizer gun—it's a semi-automatic rifle. Two police officers have arrived and one has unloaded a real bullet into Kusum's back. The mighty matriarch lets out a pained scream. She shakes, but instead of attacking the man, she keeps tugging at the zebra enclosure. She's so close, she's not stopping now.

"Hell yeah! Nice shot!" a circus worker callously rejoices. "Now aim for the head, officer!"

Somersault pleads from inside the zebra pen. "Run, Kusum! They're going to kill…"

BAM! The police officer shoots another bullet into Kusum's flesh. The noble creature howls again. Blood trickles out of the two holes in her weathered skin, but that only makes her pull harder on the metal gate. She knows that she may not make it, but she refuses to give in.

Yaso charges at the cops, but just as they're about to fire a hail of bullets at the elephants, two tigers leap into the air, sink their razor-sharp claws into the men's torsos, and tackle them to the ground. The officers shriek as the fearsome tigers rip at their skin.

Everyone else stops immediately, The Uncaged Alliance and circus workers alike. They can't believe their eyes. How did the tigers get out?

Suddenly, six more enraged tigers pounce on the circus workers and all hell breaks loose. The humans scatter wildly. The tigers gleefully jump from one frantic person to the next, biting off chunks of flesh. Bloodcurdling screams fill the air and, just like that, the area with the captive horses, zebras and camels is mostly cleared. All of these creatures who have been trapped for so long—who have been beaten on a daily basis for countless years—cheer. The day of reckoning for these vile humans has finally come.

As all of this mayhem is occurring, Rawly is perched high above on the arena roof, watching the carnage. He wears a devilish smile, reveling in seeing the humans torn apart by these impressive predators. He knows that their deaths won't bring back Claudette and Fisher, but the vindication he's feeling right now certainly numbs some of the anguish that's eating at his insides.

Persimmon, Chloe, Drig and Nibbin are rendered immobile, unnerved at witnessing the circus workers dismembered right in front of their eyes. Persimmon finally calls out. "Snap out of it, team! We have to get these creatures to safety. Keep unbuckling the horses. The camels are next!"

The other team members pop back to reality. Despite the uproar behind them, they have a job to do. This is their best chance at getting these animals out of here.

✳ ✳ ✳

Padma watches the team work diligently to extricate the horses. She's pleased to see more of the animals coming closer to freedom and to know that she has played a part. She looks over at Kusum, who is still struggling to break open the zebras' gate. Padma wants to help her dear friend, but her eyelids feel so heavy. The ground begins to spin and she crumples to the asphalt, overcome by the tranquilizers.

Yaso immediately rushes up to the injured elephant. She peers helplessly at Padma's numerous wounds. Deep holes have been dug into her skin by bullhooks and pitchforks. She is covered in blood. "What have those disgusting brutes done to you?" Yaso wants to comfort Padma somehow, but doesn't even know where to begin. "What can I do to help you?"

Padma groans. "I feel so dizzy."

"I'm so sorry, Padma," Yaso laments. "I tried to protect you, but there were too many of them to fight off."

"It's okay, Yaso," Padma wheezes, half asleep. "You are so brave. But don't waste time with me. Go help Kusum release the zebras. Make all this worth it."

Yaso is heartsick. Is this it? Is Padma dying? Can she survive all these injuries? "Padma, I..."

Padma cuts her off. "Go, help her. It's okay. Let me sleep."

Yaso pats Padma with her trunk affectionately and then turns to face the zebra enclosure. With all the energy she can muster, the giant elephant rushes at the pen where Kusum is still trying to pull apart the gate. Yaso takes her powerful trunk and, finally, the two lift the heavy fence above their heads.

"Run underneath!" Yaso hollers to the zebras. "Now!"

Somersault and the rest of the zebras dart under the dangling metal, calling out their appreciation as they run past. After everyone has made it, Yaso and Kusum drop the gate to the ground. They did it! The zebras are finally free.

Moments later, Persimmon unbuckles the last of the horses' halters. The Uncaged Alliance members hop down, and Charlemagne, Ramses and their companions kick their legs out in celebration and gallop toward the main road.

"Thank you, Uncaged Alliance," Charlemagne calls out to Persimmon and her team. Then, as he charges off, he rallies his troops. "Forward! Top speed!"

"Woohoo!" Bruiser hollers as he sees them coming toward him. "Follow me!"

The Doberman darts off down the road, followed by the pack of zebras and horses. The circus workers, who are hiding from the tigers in parked cars, are astounded to see their prized equines racing away.

"What the hell is going on?!" one trainer yells to another.

The other trainer just watches in amazement as the beautiful beings stride through the night, finally free from their lifelong prison.

The horses and zebras are faster than Bruiser, so the dog starts to lag behind as they get farther into the city. As they speed away, Bruiser yells after them. "Keep goin' toward those blue lights! Run as fast and as deep into the woods as you can, and you're free!"

"Much obliged, Bruiser!" Charlemagne whinnies before picking up his pace.

Tucker, who is rushing back to the arena, watches as the horses and zebras gallop at full speed. He is surprised to find that the clip-clopping sound of their hooves is music to his ears. He's been focusing so much on his fear over the team members getting hurt during these rescue missions—especially Chloe—that he neglected to think about the true importance of The Uncaged Alliance's cause: to help these creatures win their liberty. Tucker can't help but get swept up in this exhilarating and rewarding moment, witnessing these majestic equines racing away to better lives.

"Hooray!" Tucker shouts. "Freedom!"

Bruiser and Tucker convene on the sidewalk, both completely out of breath. They pant, gulping in air, and then Tucker says, "Wonderful! What an awe-inspiring sight to see them free."

"You bet," Bruiser agrees. "How'd it go with the goats? They get to the woods?"

"Yep," Tucker exclaims proudly, feeling a renewed bond with the team. "I guided them the whole way there. I wanted to make sure they made it safely. They're remarkable creatures. They were jumping onto cars and hopping all over the place. Who knew those odd-looking beings would be so agile."

"Great," Bruiser remarks. "Did you see any elephants come this way? I only seen three of them back at the parking lot, but I don't know where the other three got to."

Tucker shakes his head. "No. Maybe they took another route to the forest. I hope they're okay."

"Hmm," Bruiser ponders. "Let's get back to the arena. There's still work to do."

The Doberman and squirrel are about to rush back toward the arena when Bruiser halts and warns, "Oh, watch out for the tigers. They got loose."

Tucker thinks it's a joke at first, but then he sees the serious expression on his friend's face. Nope. No joke. There really are tigers loose. A shudder runs through Tucker's tiny body.

"Is Chloe okay?" Tucker inquires, disquieted.

"From what I saw, the tigers were havin' a good old time feastin' on those humans," Bruiser answers as he dashes off down the road. "I don't think they're much interested in us critters who are actually there to rescue 'em."

But the squirrel isn't convinced that Chloe's safe. His exultation at seeing the horses and zebras run free is quickly overshadowed by thoughts of thrashing tiger claws, so he quickly follows after the Doberman.

$$* \quad * \quad *$$

One of the tigers, Naresh, saunters up to a medium-sized tree in the middle of the parking lot. He glares up at a human clinging for dear life to a branch above him and shakes his head, unimpressed. "Silly human."

With ease, Naresh jumps onto the trunk of the tree and crawls his way up to the shrieking circus worker. The man frantically attempts to scramble higher into the tree, but the nimble tiger approaches quickly. Naresh swats at the man's legs with his right paw and then sinks his claws into the man's calf, pulling him down hard. The man loses his grip on the branch and plummets to the grass below, landing directly on his right arm. A loud crack fills the air as the bone splits apart.

The circus worker writhes around and begins to crawl away, using his left arm to pull himself along the ground. Another tiger, Timir, leaps up and puts his strong paw on the man's back, holding him in place.

Naresh hops down from the tree and crouches beside the screaming man. "Timir, how many times did we see Tony here punch those poor horses in the face?"

"Too many," Timir growls.

"My thoughts exactly." Naresh opens his mouth wide and places it over Tony's head. The man screeches wildly as Naresh bites down with his mighty jaw. Tony's skull cracks under the pressure, and he stops quivering and falls silent.

Blood drips from Naresh's mouth. "One less human means a little less cruelty in the world."

Simultaneously, Yarick scratches viciously at the door of a nearby car. He growls with seething hatred.

The man inside the automobile shakes in fear. It's Bob, the big cat trainer who has spent years tormenting Yarick and the other tigers. This pompous man whipped these creatures raw, pumping out his chest each time as if he were their master, but now he cringes in the passenger seat, so afraid he's about to wet himself.

"Come out and fight, coward!" Yarick roars. "Man versus tiger. No weapons. Just us. Then we'll see who dominates whom!"

Yarick scratches again at the window and the side of the car. He's ripped off two toenails during his assault, while the craven man hides in the vehicle. Yarick would give anything to tear open the automobile—to kill this man who has caused him so much pain, who has ruined his life and the lives of his fellow cats—but the car is impenetrable and there is no way Bob is setting one foot out of the only safe environment within range.

Yarick leaps onto the hood and tries to look Bob in the eyes, but the petrified man just lowers his head down into the driver's seat. The tiger rages, "You sniveling bully. You're nothing without your whip. Nothing!"

Yarick suddenly stops his rant and listens intently to the sound of police sirens off in the distance. The tiger slams his paw against the car angrily. Just an inch of glass stands between him and making Bob pay for all the torture he inflicted, but now this loathsome man will continue on without retribution. Yarick grinds his teeth. He will have to let this one go.

Naresh and Timir bound over to the car.

"It looks like our fun is coming to an end, brothers," Yarick says to them.

"Should we run?" Naresh asks.

Yarick shakes his head. "No. They'll hunt us down and either murder us or capture us again, and I'm not letting them have the pleasure of putting me back in a cage. Our days of being imprisoned are over."

Yarick ferociously thunders at Bob through the windshield. "You hear that, scum?! You're never whipping us again!"

Bob keeps his head hidden against the driver's seat, not daring to look up at the raging tiger.

"So we stay and fight?" Naresh asks.

Yarick grins. "So we shall."

59

THE POLICE SIRENS get increasingly louder as Persimmon, Chloe, Scraps, Drig and Nibbin run toward the semi-trailer trucks where the camels are tied up. The raccoon calls out to her friends. "Start unbuckling the camels. I'll be there shortly."

Persimmon darts past Padma, who is completely knocked out but still breathing. The raccoon also navigates around a number of dead humans who are strewn about on the pavement. As she does this, tigers sporadically bound through the area, searching for more humans upon whom to prey. In the distance, she can hear faint screams as tigers pounce on their victims.

Persimmon steps up to Kusum, who has collapsed on the ground. A grief-stricken Yaso is also there, standing over her mortally wounded matriarch.

Persimmon, who looks minuscule next to Kusum, sees the blood pouring out of the bullet holes in the elephant's side. "What can I do to help you?"

Kusum looks over at Persimmon, drearily. "Little raccoon, don't worry about me. Just free the camels. They're the last creatures still trapped in this despicable place."

"But surely there must be something I can do for you," Persimmon offers, upset at seeing the life drain from this remarkable creature. "It's not fair. You fought so bravely."

"There, there, little raccoon," Kusum responds, weaker every moment. "All I ask is that you don't forget what you saw here. This is not the only circus. There are many, many others. And wherever there is a circus, there are elephants, tigers, zebras and so many other poor animals suffering horribly. Today must be only the beginning of your rescue missions to save our kind."

Kusum places her colossal trunk on the heartbroken raccoon's back. "Because of your efforts, the horses, goats and zebras are running free. Lakmini and Chatura are running free. It crushes me to think that they may be recaptured. It hurts my heart to think of all the creatures who lost their lives today, but this fight, *our* fight, will not soon be forgotten. The sadistic humans who lost their lives today will serve as a warning to all humans that they cannot keep us trapped any longer. The days of circuses are numbered, thanks to you and your courageous team."

A tear rolls down Persimmon's furry cheek. "I will never give up this fight, Kusum. I promise you that."

Kusum pats the raccoon with her trunk, then closes her eyes. She doesn't have the energy to talk any longer.

Moments later, Persimmon hears Chloe, Scraps, Drig and Nibbin cheer. She looks over to see the camels fleeing toward the road. Four more creatures racing to freedom, because of what her team has accomplished here today. She wants to celebrate, too, but how can she when the regal Kusum is dying a few inches from her?

Persimmon surveys all of the dead humans scattered throughout the parking lot—a bunch of bloody messes of torn skin and tattered clothes. *Will these lives lost teach other humans to give up circuses altogether? Are they intelligent enough to learn from this deadly fiasco? I just*

*hope all of the creatures we freed here today make it to the forest. I hope
even more that getting to the forest will actually mean they're safe.*

A whole squadron of police cars comes screeching to a halt, creating a perimeter around the entire block.

Persimmon peers up at Yaso, concerned. "Aren't you going to run away? Soon this place will be swarming with humans. And if they're anything like those other people wearing blue uniforms, they will have guns, too."

"An elephant does not leave her herd," Yaso states. "I spent too many years bowing down to these ruthless brutes. That ends today. No matter the cost."

Persimmon wishes she could guide Yaso to safety but knows that she cannot. She also knows that Yaso will not leave Kusum anyway.

"Good luck, Yaso." Persimmon is gravely aware that this will likely be the last time she sees this valiant creature alive.

"Thank you, Persimmon," Yaso responds as she watches the hordes of police officers approach with their guns in hand, attempting to secure the area. "Although, I'm not so sure luck has ever really been on my side."

60

NAYANA RACES DOWN a corridor in between two rows of RVs, straight toward the malicious Lorenzo. She charges forward with the speed of a freight train, gaining on him. Just before she reaches him, though, the sneaky man dives under one of the trailers. He scrapes layers of skin off of his knees and drops his ever-present bullhook, but he's alive. The panicked trainer rolls on the ground and out the other side, hopping up immediately and darting down a parallel pathway between another row of RVs.

Nayana rushes down the path before her, knocking people out of the way as she goes, always keeping an eye to her right to see if Lorenzo is still running.

Nayana hollers at the terrified man. "You think you can treat us this way and just get away with it?! I'm coming for you, Lorenzo!"

The frantic trainer stops running and rips open the door to his trailer. Nayana instantly pulls to a halt. She bashes her way in between two RVs to enter the parallel alleyway.

The enraged elephant sprints straight for Lorenzo's trailer and slams into it with all her might, knocking the mobile home onto its side. Inside, Lorenzo squeals. Nayana attempts to grab the door with her trunk to pry it open, but she's having difficulty gripping the small handle.

Without warning, three circus workers rush up from behind and whack aluminum baseball bats into her back legs. Nayana yowls and twists back around, swinging her trunk at the attacking humans.

"Get off of me!" Nayana shouts.

Two of the men drop their bats and race for safety behind a nearby trailer, but Nayana trips the third man with her trunk, sending him to the pavement. She quickly stomps her foot down on his skull, cracking the thick bone. She then turns back to the task at hand—stopping Lorenzo once and for all.

Nayana uses her massive head to ram the weak frame of the caravan. If she can't pull this vile man out, she'll crush him while he's still inside. She bangs her head over and over into the RV, bending it as effortlessly as if it were made of paper. Her fragile skin is soon covered with blood and gashes from the shards of metal, but she will not be deterred.

"Help! Help!" Lorenzo shrieks.

"Keep screaming, brute!" Nayana threatens. "There is no escape!" She smashes her head into the trailer, and the thin metal buckles. "I'm going to make you regret ever laying a hand on us. And when I'm done with you, you'll never be able to abuse another elephant again. Never!"

Suddenly, a hail of bullets blasts through the trailer door. Lorenzo is unloading his 9mm and the bullets pierce Nayana's head and neck. She trips back, shocked and wounded, staggering to stay upright.

With Nayana temporarily stunned, Lorenzo quickly opens the door, crawls out and jumps over the side of the trailer. Nayana is dazed from the bullets lodged in her skull and as she turns to follow Lorenzo, to her horror, there is a line of police officers facing her, guns raised.

"Now!" the lieutenant barks, and the officers shoot round after round of bullets into Nayana's flesh.

The overpowered elephant screeches as the barrage of bullets rips through her body. From behind the cops, Lorenzo watches with relief and sadistic delight as Nayana wobbles and screams, having nowhere to run.

"Hold your fire!" the lieutenant commands.

Gun smoke fills the air. The humans watch as Nayana struggles to keep her balance. "Shey! I'm sorry. I couldn't save you and now I let him get away. I tried, Shey. I tried!" she cries as blood pours from her bullet-ridden body. She cannot stand any longer. She collapses to the ground.

Nayana lies there with punctured lungs, her chest pumping up and down, gasping for air. A pool of warm blood trickles around her torso. She tried so hard to end Lorenzo's evil reign, but now countless other elephants will suffer at his hands. She let them *all* down.

One of the officers turns to Lorenzo and laughs. "Damn, man, that elephant sure had it in for you."

Lorenzo shrugs. "Bitch doesn't appreciate all I did for her. She got what she deserved."

Just then, Lorenzo and the police officers hear shouts nearby and turn to see what the fracas is about. Yaso smashes through the trailer right next to Lorenzo, and before any of the humans can react, she picks him up with her powerful trunk and smashes her bulky body right into the line of cops. The officers jump for cover, some dropping their guns. Lorenzo shrieks as Yaso tosses him onto the pavement in front of Nayana.

Nayana is losing blood quickly, but with her last ounce of energy, she reaches out with her trunk and wraps it around Lorenzo's neck. Like a mighty boa constrictor, she squeezes Lorenzo's throat tighter and tighter. The terrified trainer grabs and punches her trunk, but she holds her death grip firmly.

A few of the cops shoot at the two elephants, trying to avoid hitting Lorenzo. Yaso kicks at the officers and swings her trunk at them as more bullets lodge in Nayana's head and cut through her ears.

Lorenzo kicks frantically as blood oozes from of his mouth, eyes and ears. Nayana squeezes with all the hatred she has for this loathsome man. And finally he stops kicking and lies flat. It's done. He will never harm another elephant again.

Filled with hot metal, Yaso falls to the ground beside Nayana and both elephants take their last breaths. A thousand thoughts cross Nayana's mind in her final moments. She realizes that she never did see her mother again. She thinks about how sweetly affectionate Samadara was toward her. She wonders if it's cruel of her to have no regrets about the humans she just killed. She fawns over the brave Yaso, who—despite years of clashing with her—came through when it counted most. And she thinks of Shey. Her dear Shey who was always there to cheer her up with a mischievous prank. Who loved nothing more than trying to make Nayana happy to help her survive this wretched existence in the circus.

Nayana knows that killing Lorenzo doesn't make up for all the torture he put them through. And she's not foolish enough to think that a depraved new trainer won't just take his place. But still, a peace comes over her. Their tormentor is dead. She and Yaso lie there as two victorious warriors. And in their last few moments, that comforting thought is enough

Nayana closes her eyes. A slight smile comes over her face as she realizes that she will never have to spend another day in the circus. She lets out one last sigh of relief and stops breathing. She might not have made it to Ceylon, but she is finally free.

61

PERSIMMON, DERPOKE, SCRAPS, Chloe, Drig and Nibbin have gathered underneath one of the trucks to which the horses used to be tethered. Derpoke has finally caught up with the team, and they're all waiting for an opportunity to slip away, but the police have set up a perimeter around the block, so there's no way for them to sneak out.

Off in the distance, gunshots fill the air, and the team freezes.

"Do you think the humans are killing another creature?" Scraps asks fearfully.

"I don't know," Persimmon answers, trying to avoid revealing what she really thinks. "But we can't focus on that right now. The more humans who show up with guns, the more dangerous this place is for us. We have to get out of here immediately."

"What about Rawly?" Drig inquires.

"I did my best to find him," Derpoke explains. "But as I said, once those tigers came at me, I wasn't about to continue my search."

"Rawly knows the meeting place in the forest," Persimmon states. "If he's going to put everyone's life in danger by releasing those tigers, then he can get back there on his own."

"We don't know for sure that he released those tigers," Drig counters heatedly.

"Drig," Chloe cuts in sincerely. "I know he's your friend, but we saw him enter the arena with those keys. And we all know how devastated he was over poor Fisher and Claudette. It makes sense that he would have released the tigers. I understand why he did it, but it was reckless."

Drig looks like he's about to say something else, but he stops himself. He feels compelled to defend his good friend, but he's pretty sure Rawly did it, too.

The team sees Yarick, Naresh and Timir sneaking around parked cars toward a group of police officers. The predators stay low to the ground and don't make a sound. The officers have no idea that the three fierce cats are headed their way.

"Scraps, don't watch," Persimmon warns.

In a flash of fur and teeth, the tigers pounce on the unsuspecting cops. The officers scream and fire their weapons into the air, missing the tigers. More police officers rush to the scene and shoot at the attacking creatures, trying not to hit their fellow cops. The team members watch in horror as these beautiful beings are shot countless times.

Despite the disturbing sight, Persimmon's attention is on her team's safety, and this diversion is their one chance. "Everyone disperse with your partners. We'll reconvene in the forest. Be careful. The sun is coming up, so many more humans will be milling about."

Persimmon and Scraps rush to a group of parked cars while Drig and Nibbin head over to a bush in one of the parking lot's islands. Chloe and Derpoke scurry in the opposite direction toward the main street. Chloe is hoping to run into Bruiser and Tucker on the way to the forest. Of course, having Derpoke with her is certainly going to slow her down, but someone needed to partner with him.

While the officers are preoccupied fighting off the brave tigers, the team members swiftly maneuver their way past the police cars. Each gunshot they hear jolts them, because they know that the moment those ear-piercing sounds end, the tigers will be no more. The death toll for this mission continues to rise and the team still has a long way to reach safety.

* * *

The sun has now fully risen. Cars zoom along the roads. People walk down the sidewalks on their way to work, sipping coffee and chatting idly. Suddenly, a herd of horses and zebras comes barreling toward them. Bystanders scream. Cars crash into one another.

Charlemagne is well aware of the congestion in the streets. Someone is going to get seriously injured if they keep this up. He calls out to the troupe. "Everyone split up!"

In an impressive synchronized feat, the horses and zebras separate and take off down different alleys and streets. It happens so quickly the humans can't believe their eyes. One second there were a dozen equines; the next they've disappeared.

A few minutes later, the horses and zebras see their first glimpse of the forest. What a sight! Each of them gallops as fast as their legs will take them through the neighborhood and into... freedom!

When they get to the edge of the woods, some leap merrily onto the soft grass. They've been standing on hard pavement their entire lives, rarely getting to feel a gentle surface under their hooves. It is a pure delight.

As Ramses zigzags around the trees, he sees Charlemagne rushing joyously a few feet away. "We did it!" Ramses cheers.

"What a day!" Charlemagne celebrates. "We'll run as fast and far as we can until we practically collapse. Let's see if you can keep up with me, Ramses."

"Ha! Don't flatter yourself, old horse," Ramses calls out as he picks up his pace. This is the first time they've ever been able to roam free, and it feels superb. No human will ever ride them again and the possibilities for the future are endless. What a grand day indeed!

*   *   *

Chloe and Derpoke scuttle down the road as quickly as they can, but it's slow going since the well-meaning opossum isn't exactly known for his speed. More and more cars and people are appearing on the roads and sidewalks, so Derpoke finally suggests, "Chloe, just go ahead without me. I'll have to hide here until nightfall."

Chloe stops running and she leads Derpoke into some foliage beside a brick building. "No way am I leaving you here," she argues. "We can make it. I'll just go slower so you can keep up."

"It's too risky," Derpoke counters. "All these people won't think twice about seeing a squirrel trotting down the road during the day, but an opossum? I don't trust these humans to leave me be."

Chloe knows he's right. They've lost enough friends in the past day. No need to push their luck this late in the mission.

Just then, Chloe sees her lovably grumpy partner dash by with Bruiser. She jumps back out onto the sidewalk. "Pupsy!"

Tucker screeches to a halt. There's only one being on this Earth who calls him that. "Sweet Pea!"

Tucker races toward his sweetheart and embraces her. "You made it! You weren't eaten by tigers."

A woman walking nearby notices the squirrels hugging and gushes. "Aww. Too cute!"

The squirrels sense that they've been spotted, so they hop into the cover of the bushes.

Tucker is surprised to be face to face with Derpoke. "Well, hello!"

"Hello back at you," Derpoke responds. "Good to run into you. Did any of the creatures make it to the forest?"

Tucker smiles. "I'm happy to say that the goats made it safely to the forest, and as long as everything went according to plan, the horses and zebras should be there by now as well."

Bruiser crawls into the foliage with the other team members. He's a bit too big for the bush, though, so he's crammed up against Derpoke and his tail pops out onto the sidewalk.

"Hmm," Bruiser remarks, "This may not have been the best idea."

"What an astute observation," Derpoke replies snidely as the Doberman's nose smashes up against his gray tummy.

Tucker guides Chloe deeper into the bush for some privacy. "I want you to know that I was so proud watching you lead the team in getting those creatures out of the circus."

"Oh, Tucker," Chloe beams. "It means so much to me to hear you say that. I was actually going to say the same to you! You were wonderful guiding everyone through the city."

Tucker smiles shyly. "I understand now what you mean by us being a team to rescue these other animals. You are a born leader and were meant to do this. And because *we're* meant to be, I want to support you in these missions. It seems that everywhere we go, there are so many mistreated animals and they need all the support they can get. Although I'll never be as brave as you are, I know I can help in my own way."

Chloe licks his face repeatedly. "That's all I ask, Pupsy."

"Okay, you two," Derpoke cuts in, slightly annoyed since Bruiser's snout is still poking his stomach. "Enough licking. Everyone is going to be looking for us at the meeting spot."

"So you're going to come with us now after all?" Chloe asks.

Derpoke frowns. "Good old Bruiser here has an idea. I have my reservations, but..."

Before Derpoke can finish, Bruiser lifts the opossum up with his teeth and carries him as if Derpoke were his prey. The Doberman charges out of the bush and down the sidewalk at top speed. As they weave around the pedestrians, Derpoke complains. "This is disturbing and gross."

"Hush up," Bruiser says through his teeth. "Carcasses don't talk."

*   *   *

Lakmini and Chatura race down the road behind Apricot, but the congestion of cars slows their pace to a crawl. People shriek at the sight of the elephants and flee their vehicles for cover. Lakmini tries to push her way around the abandoned automobiles, but it's a struggle.

"Get out of our way, humans!" Apricot commands.

Right then, a group of police vehicles zooms down the street and surrounds the elephants. They contemplate fleeing but realize they would have no chance, so they come to a halt.

Lakmini curses. "No. No! Stupid humans."

Cops jump out of their cars, yelling at the people on the streets and sidewalks. "Get outta here! These elephants are killers. Take cover! They're deadly."

"Deadly?" Lakmini looks down at the smaller Chatura. "We're just trying to get to the forest. We haven't hurt anyone."

The civilians duck into nearby stores while the police create a semi-circle around the elephants with a van and a building blocking their escape from behind. The cops approach the confused creatures, guns drawn and yelling frantically at one another.

"Watch out!"

"Get back! Don't get too close!"

Lakmini steps in front of Chatura. "Get behind me, tiny one. These humans have lost their minds." Lakmini concedes to the unruly police. "Okay, okay, humans. We stopped running. We give up. No need to point all those weapons at us."

Apricot stands a few feet in front of the elephants and hisses at the police officers. She arches her back, fuming. One of the cops aims his gun at the irate feline. Lakmini calls out to her. "Cat. It's no use. There's nowhere to run. We were foolish to think that we could actually escape. Hide before you get hurt!"

Apricot reluctantly scurries underneath a nearby car, disappointed that she wasn't able to lead these poor creatures to safety.

The police are frenzied. They bark orders at one another. Almost two dozen cops have their guns pointed at the terrified Lakmini and Chatura, whose backs are pressed up against the parked van. They stare at the hysterical humans, bewildered.

"These people are insane. We're just standing here." Lakmini looks back at her frightened companion, who is snuggling up to her legs. She nuzzles him in return. "It's alright, Chatura. They're just silly humans, overreacting as usual." She pauses. "I'm sorry I got us lost. Now we're going back to those chains, to performing idiotic tricks. And I'm afraid to find out what happened to the others. They're going to be so dismayed that we didn't get away."

Lakmini lets out a deep sigh. "For a brief moment, it felt so good to be running free, though, didn't it? I wanted so badly to make it to the forest just to feel the dirt on my feet. Maybe one day..."

"Fire!" the sergeant hollers the order and all of the cops unload their rifles and handguns into the two helpless elephants. Lakmini tries to shield Chatura, but there are too many officers shooting too many weapons. The elephants shriek as the bullets rip into their flesh.

Apricot yowls, horrified and sickened. The civilians scream as well, shocked to see these magnificent creatures massacred right in front of them. Many of the onlookers—some of whom had seen Lakmini and Chatura perform in the circus over the last few days—weep. Young children on their way to school hide in their parents' arms. They've seen violence in TV shows, movies and video games, but this is visceral, grotesque—irreparable. They can't just shut it off.

Lakmini and Chatura fall to the ground, dead before they even hit the pavement. Their lifeless bodies, covered with blood and riddled with bullet holes, lie there for all to see.

Apricot crawls out from under a car, aghast, and hobbles over to the corpses of the two innocent elephants. She turns to the line of cops and howls. "They surrendered. Why did you kill them?!"

Most of the police officers ignore her, so she hops up on the hood of a nearby car and peers into the stores where onlookers had sought refuge. The people stare back, traumatized. "*You* did this! You pitiless savages! *You* killed them by supporting the circus. Their deaths are on you!"

A few police officers have stopped to watch the seething cat as she hisses viciously.

Apricot continues her tirade. "Worse, I bet all of you barbarians who have attended the circus in the past will callously go again next year. Hypocrites!"

One of the cops points his gun at Apricot. Immediately, one of his fellow officers puts her hand on the man's arm. "Robert, it's just a cat. What are you doing?"

"The damn thing is going crazy," Robert retorts, gun still raised. "It could hurt someone."

The female officer looks Robert in the eyes and points at the people staring through the store windows and from inside their cars. "You want all these civilians seeing you shoot a cat? How do you think that would make us look?"

Robert peers at the crowd, who all look completely appalled. Then he looks back at Apricot, who is glowering at him. He lowers his gun.

"Fine," Robert acquiesces, and then calls out to Apricot. "Looks like you just used up one of your nine lives, cat."

Apricot keeps her glare focused on Robert, wishing she were a tiger so she could rip his throat out. She hops off of the car to go search for the team. This unnecessary and brutal butchering just sealed her decision: She's joining The Uncaged Alliance.

62

PERSIMMON LIES SPRAWLED out in some leaves on the forest floor beside Derpoke, Scraps, Bruiser, Drig and Nibbin. They are hidden in thick brush and each of them is panting heavily, completely spent from the stressful events that just unfolded.

Chloe and Tucker are curled up in a tree just above the rest of the team, already asleep with smiles on their faces. It feels so comforting to be in one another's embrace again.

Just then, there's a rustling in the foliage. Something is crawling toward them. What now?

The entire team sits up to see who it is. Rawly pokes his head through the bush.

"Rawly!" Drig rushes over to his weathered friend.

Rawly collapses on the leaves, fatigued beyond belief. Any sense of joy has been stripped from him, leaving nothing but an exhausted shell.

Persimmon has a great deal she'd like to say to him, but now is the time for sleep. They've all earned it after their nerve-racking rescue. She'll have her sure-to-be contentious discussion with him later.

✱   ✱   ✱

Persimmon sits at the edge of the forest, gazing at the suburban neighborhood before her. It's night, so the roads are mostly empty and the humans are inside their homes asleep. The view is uneventful, which is fine by her. She's not there to sightsee; she's waiting for someone.

The rest of the team is back at their meeting place in the forest. It has been almost a week since the chaotic and deadly circus mission and she's eager for an update on how the various creatures are faring. Which of them have been recaptured? What is the official death toll?

She would have gone to the arena herself to find the answers, but it's too risky. The humans are on high alert for any suspicious activity, and since her team made such a stir the other night she fears that they'll be on the lookout for any more "rabid" critters. Which is where Apricot comes in handy.

Persimmon watches the feisty cat stroll down the street toward the edge of the forest and notes to herself, *There are some bonuses to being a creature to which humans have become accustomed: cats, dogs, squirrels. You can mostly roam free without raising any suspicion. We need more creatures like that on our team.*

Persimmon has not had her conversation with Rawly yet. She's waiting to assess the full damage of the circus rescue before laying into him about releasing the tigers. He has also been so distraught all week that she wanted to give him some time to mourn the loss of his sweetheart and friend. Tonight, though, she'll finally confront him, despite how awkward or intense their talk may be.

As Apricot approaches, Persimmon's nerves start to get the best of her. She scratches her ears anxiously. She's afraid to hear what the cat has discovered about the fate of all the creatures they tried so desperately to free.

Apricot crouches down beside her. "I made contact with Somersault."

"Oh, no," Persimmon laments. "They caught him."

"Yes," Apricot reports sadly. "That's some of the bad news. In fact, it's mostly bad news, although there is an inkling of good. I'll start by telling you the good. The horses and goats are still running free somewhere. It looks like those savvy creatures did a wonderful job of assimilating into the wilderness."

"That's encouraging," Persimmon says, but she holds off celebrating, knowing that the impending bad news is going to knock the wind out of her sails.

Apricot continues. "Unfortunately, because they don't blend in, the zebras and camels were recaptured."

Persimmon's heart sinks. "All of them?!"

"Yes," Apricot responds. "Every last one."

Persimmon bats at the leaves on the ground in front of her in frustration. "I knew those poor creatures wouldn't be capable of hiding around here. How dare those selfish humans take them so far away from where they belong!" The dispirited raccoon falls silent for a moment. She knew the chances of them being recaptured were very high, but that doesn't in any way lessen the blow.

Apricot clenches her jaw. She can tell Persimmon is taking all of this very hard, and she hasn't even told her the worst of it yet. "You asked about the death toll..."

Persimmon stops breathing. She already knows that this news is going to hurt the most.

"There's no way to be delicate, so I'll just say it straight," Apricot asserts somberly. "The elephants and tigers are all dead."

"No." Persimmon almost topples over. It's even worse than she thought. "Are you sure?"

"Positive," Apricot responds gravely.

Persimmon lays her head down on the leaves, which crinkle under her weight. She whispers to herself, "The humans murdered all of them?" The dejected raccoon refuses to believe that they're really all gone, so she continues her questioning. "What about Padma? I thought she was just tranquilized."

"Somersault overheard the humans discussing how they didn't think it was worth the money to fix her up. She had so many wounds from when the humans attacked her, they felt that even if she did get better, she wouldn't be able to perform as well any longer, so they just killed her."

Persimmon, full of despair, squeezes a pawful of leaves. "What about Nayana? She ran the other way. And the tigers? You're telling me they didn't recapture even one of them? They just shot all of them to death? There were eight of those formidable cats."

"Do you really want to hear all the gory details of their demises?" Apricot asks. She herself doesn't want to go over all of them. It's too depressing.

Persimmon closes her eyes. "No. I want them to be alive. There must be a better way to conduct our rescues. We led so many of these creatures to their deaths. We told them we would rescue them... and instead..." Persimmon trails off. She can't bring herself to say it again.

Persimmon keeps her eyes closed, wishing she were asleep and not hearing this tragic news. "I'm finding that there are no easy answers in what we're doing, Apricot. If we had left those creatures in the circus, they would have suffered every day for the rest of their lives. But when we released them, they were just killed or brought right back to the circus. There was no way to win this one. Not when humans care so little about other animals' well-being."

Apricot tries to cheer Persimmon up. "I did save some good news for last. At least thirty or more humans were killed."

Persimmon pops her eyes back open, surprised. "Good news? Apricot, I do not condone killing humans."

"But the humans trapped and beat those poor creatures their entire lives. They deserved to die for all the pain they caused," Apricot replies, confused.

Persimmon positions herself so she faces the cat directly. "I want to be very clear with you on this. The Uncaged Alliance was established to rescue animals who are suffering. The goal of every mission is to sneak the animals out unnoticed with zero casualties on either side. If we have to, we will defend ourselves and the other creatures from humans, but we do not rejoice when they are killed."

Apricot becomes agitated and her pupils narrow. "But these are not decent human beings. They tortured those creatures for years and then murdered them."

"And how many creatures have you killed, Apricot?" Persimmon snaps. "Should the team murder *you* for that?"

Apricot is stunned. She wasn't expecting to have to defend her own actions. "But that was mostly for food."

Persimmon places her paw on the orange tabby cat's paw. "I'm sorry. I just wanted to make a point. I don't excuse the humans in any way for what they did to those helpless creatures. They are despicable. Maybe it's better that some of those humans aren't around any longer, but they also live in a society that supports that type of cruelty. Extinguishing them is not the right way to fix this problem in the long run."

Apricot turns away. Persimmon can tell the cat is offended. The raccoon asks directly, "Are you sure you want to join this team? Clearly what we do is very dangerous—even deadly. You have such a comfortable life with your humans. No one would fault you for not wanting to give that up."

Apricot nods, thinking fondly about her life with her humans. "The Kojimas *are* very loving. They adopted me when I was just a kitten. But last week when I ran home before the rescue began—after I got upset over you and the team not wanting to release the tigers—I had a revelation. Upon my return, my humans cuddled and kissed me, as usual. Normally, it annoys me when they're too affectionate, but this time, I was actually happy to see them after witnessing all of those poor creatures locked up. I curled up on Evan's lap, sprawled out on the comfy sofa. It was so relaxing."

Apricot stretches out her front legs as if she's reliving how soothing it was. "But I couldn't erase the vision of all the poor creatures trapped in the circus. How they're chained up all day. Whipped. Beaten. I tried to move to different locations to sleep better—on top of the book shelf, the kitchen chairs and even my favorite spot on top of the warm cable box—but one thought kept nagging at me: How could I live such a luxurious life when they're imprisoned? I guess I felt... sympathetic. I knew then that I had to return to the circus and help you all. And after seeing Lakmini and Chatura needlessly massacred, I'm done with humans."

Persimmon starts to say something, but Apricot cuts her off. "One last thing. I didn't tell you this before because I didn't want you thinking poorly of my humans, but they actually went to the circus a few days before you arrived. That's how I knew it was in town. And that's how I knew I couldn't live with them any longer. I adore them, and will miss them very much. But I can't understand how the Kojimas are so doting toward me and yet they support the torture of other animals in the circus. I can't be part of their family if they condone such cruelty. The Uncaged Alliance is my family now."

"We're grateful to have you," Persimmon says thankfully. "Come on, there's someone I need to talk to."

63

THE ENTIRE TEAM is silent. Persimmon, Derpoke, Scraps, Bruiser, Rawly, Drig, Nibbin, Chloe, Tucker, and Apricot sit on the decaying forest floor in a daze. Persimmon has just relayed Apricot's news about the creatures who were recaptured and killed. The team members know they did their best to save the animals in the circus, but guilt gnaws at them. Could they have done anything differently to prevent such a massive tragedy? The group feels even worse remembering how ecstatic the circus animals were when they heard the news that they were being rescued. The team can't imagine how much those animals must have suffered all these years and now most of them are just... dead.

With everyone lost in thought, Persimmon casually steps over to Rawly, attempting to be inconspicuous. "Rawly, can I speak to you privately?" she whispers.

Rawly replies indignantly, loud enough for the rest of the group to hear. "Anything you have to say to me can be said in front of the group."

Persimmon grits her teeth. She peers at the other members of the team, who are now staring at them. She feared this incorrigible raccoon might not make this easy.

"Fine," Persimmon sighs, annoyed that she can't conduct this conversation on her own terms. "This ordeal has been incredibly hard on all of us, but especially you, Rawly. You not only lost one of your great friends, but you lost your true love. I can't imagine the sorrow you're feeling."

Rawly is taken off guard by Persimmon's condolences. He waits to see where she is going with this before he says anything.

Persimmon continues. "And given the shock of your loss, I think it would be wise for you to take a break."

"I think it would be wise for *all* of us to take a break," Rawly counters, hoping to get her to say what he knows she is delicately dancing around.

"True." Persimmon pauses, trying to figure out how best to word this next part. "But I also think you need to take a longer break. I think it would be in everyone's best interest if you took some time to recuperate while the rest of us conduct our next mission."

Rawly nods his head and quietly laughs to himself. He knew this was coming and he was more than ready for the challenge. "Are you kicking me off the team, Persimmon?"

The rest of the group has moved in closer. Things just got very interesting, and they're curious about where this disagreement is headed.

Persimmon responds carefully, not wanting to antagonize him. "In light of your actions on this last mission, I don't think you're in the right frame of mind to be a part of our rescue operations at the moment."

"Because I released the tigers?" Rawly barks back. "How about the fact that those tigers risked their lives to allow you to free the horses, zebras and camels? And they distracted the humans from killing any more of us. Did that thought cross your mind?"

"Yes," Persimmon responds, trying to keep her cool. "And you know what else crossed my mind? The thought that those tigers could also have eaten any one of us."

"Don't even try it," Rawly growls. "Those tigers are heroes. They vowed not to attack any of us or any of the other animals stuck in the circus. And they kept their word—and fought valiantly. The only animals they harmed were humans who, I might remind you, had spent years and years whipping and caging them. Those humans deserved to die."

"We are *not* killers," Persimmon says, raising her voice for the first time in this argument. "By releasing those tigers, you set them up to murder those humans."

Rawly snaps right back. "Speaking of murder: How many creatures do the humans have to kill before you realize that they are a danger to all other animals? They're irredeemable and they must be stopped."

"I'm glad you brought that up." Persimmon knew Rawly would take that extreme stance and she's prepared to shut him down. "Just a little while ago, Apricot told me something very interesting. Do you know who the humans are blaming for releasing the creatures from the circus? Animal rights activists. And do you know who they are? They're *humans* who advocate for other animals. This isn't the first time we've heard of this, either. Vincent told us about humans who freed the minks. So it doesn't make sense to hate all humans, because there are those who would risk their lives to save *you*. With that in mind, do you want to adjust your statement about all humans being a danger to other animals? Does this make you think twice about letting the tigers loose to go on that killing spree?"

"I'm not saying *all* humans are evil," Rawly replies, addressing the group as much as he is speaking to Persimmon. "But we must stop the ones who are. And the creatures we try to save on our rescue missions are going to continue to die unless we take more aggressive measures. On this mission, for example, we should have released the tigers first so that they could have taken care of the humans. Then we could have more easily snuck the other creatures out of there."

"Did you learn *nothing* from this tragedy, Rawly?" Persimmon asks with a hint of condescension. "Most of those creatures were never going to make it. The elephants, tigers, zebras *and* camels are not from this land so they couldn't have blended in once they were released. And, as I predicted before the rescue even got under way, all of those creatures are now dead or recaptured. But you refuse to give up your misguided stance."

Rawly steps closer to Persimmon, determined not to let her win this dispute. "And let me remind *you* once again: The elephants said they'd rather die than live through the torture of the circus, and I bet all those other creatures would have said the same."

Rawly sighs. He decides to try a different tactic. He wipes the grimace from his face and speaks as earnestly as he knows how. "Persimmon, I know you think I'm thick-headed, but I promise that I'm not just disagreeing with you to give you a hard time. I genuinely wanted to get those creatures to safety. For one second, put yourself in their position. They're..."

Persimmon blurts out, "I did..."

"Just listen to me for a second," Rawly implores. "Imagine you're them. *Really* imagine it. You're chained up all day. Beaten until you're willing to dance in circles just so you won't be beaten any longer. At some point, being trapped in the circus becomes worse than death. To reiterate, you'd rather *die* than live another day stuck in there."

Rawly pauses to drive home that point and then looks at the other team members, who are listening intently. Both Persimmon and Rawly are making compelling arguments and the others are trying to figure out how they really feel about all of it.

"Yes," Rawly continues. "It would have been wonderful if our team had had more time to plan the rescue, but we didn't. Those poor creatures were being tormented and held against their will, and when they finally escaped, the humans murdered them for it. I don't for one second regret my decision to release those tigers. At least they got to have their revenge before they died."

"You mean you got to have *your* revenge," Persimmon sneers.

Rawly angrily kicks the leaves on the ground in front of him. "Yes, I also got to have my revenge. If I could have, I would have ripped apart every one of those humans myself. They're filth. And I'm glad they're dead."

"This isn't you, Rawly." Persimmon reaches her paw out to make peace, but Rawly shrugs her away. She pulls back her paw, accepting his boundaries. "You're not a killer. You're just hurting right now and I understand. You've been..."

Rawly talks right over Persimmon. "I bet you blame me for Claudette's and Fisher's deaths. Don't you? And probably for Scraps getting injured. Because I'm the one who encouraged the team to take on those humans."

"That's not true," Persimmon clarifies. "I think it was brave of you to lead the team in trying to help the elephants escape. Your heart was in the right place. If you feel guilty about..."

"It wasn't my fault!" Rawly hollers. "I did everything I could to get Claudette out of there. I was too weak. I couldn't..." Rawly cuts himself off. He's getting emotional but doesn't want everyone to see him weep again. After a pause, he exclaims proudly, "I even decided to stop eating other animals in Claudette's honor. Not that you'd give me any credit for making that change."

Persimmon is surprised, even impressed. "I think that's..."

Rawly lashes out before she can finish. "You know what *I* think? I think it's very interesting that you act all high and mighty when you're the one who released the elephants. How many humans did *they* kill?"

"The difference is our intent," Persimmon snaps back. "I released the elephants to free them. You released the tigers to kill people. There's a major..."

Rawly pushes on, talking over her. "Bruiser tore out a man's throat with his own teeth, but I don't see you kicking him off the team. As usual, you're playing favorites, Persimmon."

"Bruiser was defending Scraps and himself," Persimmon replies, exasperated. "He…"

Rawly cuts her off again. "You never wanted me on this team because you can't stand anyone questioning your authority. You know what, Persimmon? *I* can't stand being a part of The Uncaged Alliance any longer. No need to kick me out. I quit."

Rawly turns to the rest of the team. "Who's with me?"

64

A LINE IN the sand has been drawn, and each team member knows it. The question is, who will step over that line to join Rawly?

He surveys the group. "I'm leaving right now. Who's coming?"

Rawly looks at his right-hand raccoon. "Drig? Will you join me, my friend?"

Drig walks over to Rawly's side. "Persimmon, I greatly admire you as a leader, but if this team is parting ways, I gotta go with Rawly. I hope you understand."

"Of course, Drig," Persimmon replies, trying to hide her disappointment. "Thank you for being such a valuable member of the team. You will be missed."

With that, the team is officially splitting up. Derpoke, Scraps, Bruiser, Nibbin, Chloe, Tucker and Apricot stand unnaturally still, afraid to move for fear it will indicate that they're taking sides.

Apricot takes a deep breath and then steps forward. "Rawly, do you have room for a sassy, mischievous cat?"

"Absolutely!" Rawly perks up. He's gaining followers by the minute. "With your keen eyes and natural predatory skills, you'll be quite an asset."

Persimmon feels a sickness in her stomach. She tries not to show it, but it's a gut punch for anyone to go with Rawly. It feels like a criticism of her leadership abilities, so she can't help but take it personally. She's done her best to lead this team fearlessly without being irresponsible and passionately without being overzealous, but perhaps she was too cautious. Perhaps in trying so hard to keep her team members safe, she led them to their deaths. As her team begins to splinter, those thoughts eat at her insides.

Before heading over to Rawly, Apricot turns to the dismayed raccoon. "Persimmon, I hope you don't feel slighted by my decision. It's just that after what happened to Lakmini and Chatura, I see what humans are truly capable of. And if taking the offensive against them is the best way to rescue other animals, so be it."

Persimmon wants to contest Apricot's reasoning, but she stops herself. She's tired of debating the same points over and over. There's nothing left to be said. If she hasn't convinced them by now, she'll only be wasting her energy by continuing the conversation, so she just nods. "Be safe. Rawly's lucky to have you on his team."

With Apricot by his side, Rawly starts to feel cocky about who else might defect. He looks at the Doberman. "Bruiser? You're the most powerful fighter here. We could use your help. And after what humans have done to you, I know you can't stand them."

Bruiser responds affably but without hesitation. "Persimmon saved my life, Rawly. Where she goes, I go."

"Fair enough," Rawly replies, disappointed.

Persimmon looks over at Bruiser, who is sitting a few feet away. She smiles, appreciative of his unwavering support.

"Persimmon?" Scraps puts his paw on his sister's arm. Persimmon's heart stops. Her little brother?!

"I think Rawly is right," Scraps says. "These humans have to be stopped. We can't..."

"Scraps, no. No." Persimmon shakes her head, so upset by the prospect of losing her brother that she almost breaks down. The other team members hold their collective breath. None of them saw this coming and it pains them to see Persimmon on the verge of being abandoned by her own little brother.

"Let me explain," Scraps remarks. "Maybe we can stay together as a team but just adjust our tactics. Did you see the look on those humans' faces when they were jabbing and shooting the creatures in the circus? They looked like they enjoyed hurting them. People like that would never let animals go without putting up a massive fight, so maybe the only way to do a successful rescue against those types of humans is to be more aggressive."

"Don't start, Scraps," Persimmon shoots him down. "Attacking humans is not the answer, and I will not argue with you about this right now."

Rawly interjects. "Let your brother talk. He has a right to…"

Persimmon snaps at Rawly with a fury the team has never seen before. "Shut up, Rawly, or I will thrash you right here." She steps toward him, threateningly. "You're not taking my brother from me. Period."

Rawly holds his paws up in surrender. No need to push the issue. He knows that tiny Scraps wouldn't contribute much tactically to his team anyway, and besides, he doesn't want to demoralize Persimmon by taking away her sibling.

After Persimmon's heated outburst, Scraps realizes that it's no use trying to reason with her at the moment. He supports his dear sister, but he thinks Rawly has a solid point, too. He figured he could persuade Persimmon to rethink her strategy instead of letting the team be dismantled. Obviously, the topic is no longer up for debate, so he holds his tongue.

Rawly addresses the rest of the team. "I know Derpoke's a lost cause, but…"

"Why don't you just get out of here already?" Derpoke hisses.

"I'm leaving shortly, my good old friend," Rawly responds. "But first I want to give everyone a chance to decide for themselves. So is there anyone else who wants to join me? Chloe, Tucker... young Nibbin?"

Nibbin hides behind Bruiser's muscular legs.

Chloe, though, speaks up. "I uprooted my entire life—and continue to put my life on the line—because Persimmon is the most noble and selfless creature I have ever met. No offense, but she's the only one I trust to lead this team."

Tucker nods in agreement. "That makes two of us."

Rawly grits his teeth, trying to pretend that Chloe's comment doesn't sting. "Okay then. Looks like this is farewell."

The two sides—Rawly, Drig and Apricot on one; Persimmon, Derpoke, Scraps, Bruiser, Nibbin, Chloe and Tucker on the other—stare at each other for a moment. It's tense and awkward, and it feels as if there's a thousand-mile gorge between them. The team is divided, and it happened so quickly that they're all a little stunned.

But then Persimmon walks up to Drig and Apricot and hugs them, breaking the tension. They made such an extraordinary team, there's no need for hostility now. Even with the animosity between Persimmon and Rawly, the rest of the group are still wonderful friends who did amazing and important work together. That demands a fond farewell, so the two new teams take a few moments for heartfelt good-byes before they head off on their separate adventures.

Rawly saunters over to Persimmon hesitantly. "You probably hate me and don't want..."

"This isn't about you and me, Rawly," Persimmon remarks coldly but calmly. "It's about the best way to save other animals. And we obviously have differing opinions on how to do that, so let's leave it be." Persimmon pauses, then adds one last bit of advice. "I will say this: Be safe. Now that you're leading your own team, Drig, Apricot and whatever other members join you are putting their trust in you to make intelligent choices and keep them out of harm's way. Remember that when you're planning your rescue missions."

Persimmon turns to walk away, not wanting to speak with Rawly any longer.

Rawly calls after her. "Persimmon, thank you for opening my eyes to the truth about what lies beyond the forest." Persimmon stops walking but doesn't turn around. Rawly continues. "You've started something remarkable, inspiring others to help those in need. And you made me a more compassionate raccoon. I will never forget that."

Persimmon stands in place for a moment, still not turning around to face him. She's proud that she has inspired others to be more compassionate—a beautiful thing—but she's concerned about what happens when her good intentions get twisted by others—like Rawly—into unintended, even dangerous, results. Suddenly, she has an epiphany. She flips around to face him.

"You can keep the names The Uncaged Alliance and Uncagers for your team, Rawly. They better represent what you're doing. I'm going to come up with a new name for my team. One that better reflects our approach."

With that, Persimmon spins back around, confident that she'll prove Rawly—and his aggressive tactics—wrong.

65

"PERSIMMON! WAKE UP!" Bruiser yells frantically at the sleeping raccoon, who is resting in a hollowed-out tree stump beside Derpoke and Nibbin.

Persimmon stirs. "What? What's wrong?"

"Scraps is gone!"

Persimmon pops up and looks at the empty spot beside her where she last saw her brother. Her heart tightens and a searing pain shoots through her body as panic sets in.

Bruiser continues, clearly upset. "I followed his scent into the forest. He went in the direction of Rawly's group. If Scraps left soon after we dozed off this mornin', that means he's been travelin' all day, so if we search through the night, we can probably catch up to 'im by daybreak tomorrow. But we gotta leave right now."

Without hesitation, Persimmon and Bruiser dart into the woods. She calls back to Derpoke. "Tell everyone to wait here. We'll be back!"

Persimmon and Bruiser track Scraps' scent deep into the dark woods. Sure enough, he has followed Rawly, Drig and Apricot's trail. As they run, Persimmon breaks into tears. *He's going to join Rawly's team? How could he just leave me like that? Doesn't he know that we may never see one another again? And why would he want to join Rawly's team? Does Scraps really think that the way to save these other animals is to attack humans?*

As the raccoon and Doberman sprint through the forest, Persimmon's emotions run the gamut from anger to hurt to despair. What will she say to Scraps when they find him? How can she convince him to stay with her?

After running for so long that their lungs hurt, Persimmon and Bruiser finally have to stop. They collapse on the ground, trying to catch their breath.

Persimmon bursts into tears again. Bruiser decides not to bother her. There's nothing he can say to console her. The only way he can help is to find her brother as quickly as possible. He and Persimmon have already been through a world of heartache in the time they've known one another, but he's never seen her more grief-stricken than she is right now.

✳   ✳   ✳

Scraps freezes in place. He had been taking a quick break from trying to catch up to Rawly's team when he sees Persimmon and Bruiser staring at him from a few feet away. The defiant raccoon clenches his jaw. "You can't talk me out of going, Persimmon. Those awful humans ruthlessly killed all those creatures and it's not right. It's not enough to just save these other animals. We have to stop humans from causing so much suffering in the first place. I'm joining Rawly and there's nothing you can do about it."

"I'm not here to talk you out of going, Scraps," Persimmon replies with sorrow in her voice.

"You're not?" Scraps is flummoxed. Even Bruiser is surprised.

Persimmon walks along the cool dirt, closer to Scraps. Even her movements are filled with gloom. She shakes her head. "I cried the entire way here because I was so scared of losing you, but then I cried even harder when I realized that I had already lost you." Persimmon stops next to her little brother, anguish carved into her face. "The reason I had to find you was to say goodbye. You can't leave me without at least saying goodbye."

Scraps starts to sob. He was so caught up in not wanting anyone to talk him out of going that he didn't even let himself think about how he'd feel about parting ways with his beloved sister.

Persimmon opens her arms and Scraps instantly curls up in her embrace.

"I'm sorry, Persimmon," Scraps cries. "I wanted to say goodbye. I just..."

Persimmon caresses his head. "It's okay, little brother. You don't have to explain."

"No, I want to," Scraps replies. "I am so angry with these humans. When we first started our missions—that feels so long ago—I was naïve. I thought the adventures would be exciting. But now... our rescues feel essential. Humans can't get away with how they abuse other animals. Someone needs to teach them that."

"I agree," Persimmon states. "Humans act like they own the ground, the air, the water and all the wonderful creatures that live in those places, but they're wrong. We're all equal and we can live in peace. But, like I told Rawly, we fundamentally disagree on how to bring about that peace. I don't want our farewell to be soured by a debate, though. I love you very much." Persimmon sighs and scratches Scraps' ears. "I never thought we'd part ways, little brother. You've been with me since the day you were born."

Scraps looks away for a moment, thinking. He has something to tell her, but he's trying to muster the courage. "I was never going to tell you this, but it feels like the right moment, because I need you to know how much you mean to me."

Persimmon's paws are shaking. Her nerves are already shot from all the stress of the night so far. What is he about to say now?

Scraps nervously takes a breath and then blurts out, "I know Mom was going to leave me to die."

Persimmon's mouth drops open in shock.

"I figured it out," Scraps explains. "After I was born, she was gonna leave me in that tree, because I was so small and weak. I pieced the story together over the years. You were always so mysterious when I asked about Mom, so since you wouldn't directly answer my questions, I started to inquire about it without you knowing what I was doing, and then one day it all came together: You were already two years old when Mom had another litter with me in it. She left me to die, thinking I'd never survive into adulthood, but you stayed with me. You saved my life."

Persimmon is speechless. She had no idea that Scraps knew. She had tried to protect him from the truth, but he's too clever.

Scraps takes Persimmon's paw. "Every day you've been the best sister I could ever hope for. Please don't hate me for leaving."

"I could never hate you," Persimmon says as she hugs him close. "I love you with all of my heart, as if you were my own little pup."

The siblings hold their embrace for a while. This could very well be the last time they ever see one another. It's not the first time their lives have been upended by fighting for this cause—and it will not be the last

66

DERPOKE, CHLOE, TUCKER and Nibbin have been waiting anxiously for Persimmon and Bruiser to return, and all of their hearts sink when the raccoon and dog appear through the trees without Scraps. The foursome knows instantly that Scraps will not be returning.

Derpoke is about to say something to Persimmon as she walks by, but Bruiser motions for the opossum to give her some space. The dejected raccoon disappears into her hollowed-out tree stump.

"We should leave her alone for a few days," Bruiser explains. "She's crushed over losing the little guy. Nuthin' we say will change that."

Derpoke nods. He has cried on and off all night. He's known Scraps for years—they were basically brothers—so this is a shocking loss for him as well. "Things just keep getting worse and worse. I never liked the idea of letting Rawly join the team. Someone that arrogant is always going to cause trouble." Derpoke looks over at the sullen Doberman. "You and Scraps were close too, Bruiser. Are you alright?"

Bruiser looks at the ground. Being chained up in that backyard had severely hardened him, but this loss cuts him deep. He clears his throat. "I never thought I'd love a raccoon as much as I loved my little buddy. Ain't no fillin' that hole in my heart. Never."

Derpoke and Bruiser crawl into the foliage and lie down to sleep through the rest of the day. After all of the turmoil they've been through, they need some time to recuperate, physically as well as emotionally.

* * *

Persimmon tosses and turns in her small burrow. She finds it difficult to sleep without Scraps, Derpoke and Nibbin curled up by her side, but even though she's lonely, she prefers some solitude for a while—to wallow, to mourn, to heal… if that's even possible.

Part of her wishes she could quit the rescue missions. All she wanted to do was help other animals—to save them from a life of misery—but it's been such a heartbreaking journey, full of tragedy, disappointment and so much death. And now she's lost her sweet brother. He's not even the same sprightly raccoon any more. These missions have changed all of them—worn them down, made them cynical, shaken them to the core.

But despite her thoughts about stopping these missions, she's aware that it's just self-pity. Deep down she knows she can never give up. She thinks of Gilby and the helpless calves, Vincent and the tormented minks, Nayana and the battered elephants. Then she pictures all of the other innocent creatures out there right now who must be in immense pain, subjected to unimaginable torment at the hands of humans. She can't abandon them no matter what happens to her or her friends, because there are so few courageous critters out there willing to dedicate their lives to freeing these abused creatures. These animals desperately need her help. And she knows that no matter how much she may suffer trying to save them, it's nowhere near what they endure every single day. This fight is bigger than she is. It is the most important thing she could ever do—the most important thing she *will* ever do. So after two weeks of restless sleep, occasional crying, pondering and planning, Persimmon steps out of her den.

The rest of the team immediately huddles together. They've been waiting anxiously for her to reappear. Derpoke, Bruiser, Chloe, Tucker and Nibbin all look at her with eyes wide open, full of anticipation. What does she have planned for them next?

The raccoon looks over her faithful team. "My friends, our journey so far has been arduous and devastating. We have seen unforgivable acts of cruelty toward other animals that I never even thought possible. We lost two of our dear team members and have now parted ways with almost half of the rest. Yet, here we stand. Strong. Dedicated. Refusing to give up on our mission no matter the consequences. I could not be more proud to be on the same team with each and every one of you."

She beams with pride as she scans this remarkable group and decides it's time to share her news. "During all of this, we've grown both personally and as a team, which is why I think we've outgrown our name—The Uncaged Alliance."

The team members are surprised. They had really embraced that moniker.

Persimmon continues. "Our mission is to save all suffering creatures, but just uncaging them won't free them permanently. The only way to make lasting change is to enlighten humans that they should treat *all* creatures with respect. They shouldn't eat them, steal their skin and fur, force them to do tricks for entertainment, and so on. They should treat them all with kindness. I know it seems like they should know this naturally, but don't forget, we used to be just like them. For example, we used to eat other animals. But we changed, and I think they can change, too."

Persimmon notices the team shifting in place with doubt in their eyes. "I know it seems like a daunting task—even an impossible one—but if anyone can do it, it's the six of us."

Persimmon declares enthusiastically. "So come on, Enlighteners. Innocent creatures need rescuing, and it's our job to set them free."

One by one, each team member breaks into a bright smile. Excitement surges through them. They like the sound of The Enlighteners as a new name, and Persimmon's updated strategy makes total sense—the key is to somehow teach every human to be compassionate toward other species. The team isn't sure yet how they'll do it, but they *are* sure that is the only way to bring about true change. This is their destiny.

Chloe cheers. "To The Enlighteners!"

The rest of the group follows suit with joyous affirmation. "To The Enlighteners!"

Persimmon, Derpoke, Bruiser, Chloe, Tucker and Nibbin gather together and head off into the forest, more determined and united than ever before. They have no idea what horrific abuse toward other animals they will bear witness to on their journey, but they do know one thing: No matter how awful the hardships—and there will be many—they must charge forward until every terrorized creature has been emancipated. Until all the other animals of the world are safe from humans.

Right now—everywhere—creatures are trapped in cages, chained up, hacked apart, skinned alive, beaten, neglected, sliced open, experimented on and slaughtered by the billions. These helpless animals are crying out for someone to save them and The Enlighteners must answer their calls. Each member of the team knows that they cannot stop—*they must not stop*—until every animal is liberated.

Because no animal is truly free until every animal is completely free.

END OF BOOK ONE

ACKNOWLEDGMENTS

MY WIFE, MY muse, this novel is a love letter to you—every page makes that clear. I admire you. I am enamored of you. I will be forever grateful to you for your countless contributions to make this novel a reality. We are we!

Mom, your love of the arts inspired my love of the arts, and helped nurture my lifelong passion as a writer. How fortunate to have a mother who is also a brilliant educator!

Dad, thank you for always being such a champion of my creative endeavors (attending every school play!) and for the stability and serenity of our "bachelor" years.

Beth, my big sister, thank you for your ever-present encouragement and sage counsel over all of these years.

Mike, Coconut Brothers forever! Enough said. Oh, and yes, we can play tennis next week.

Marina and Arun, thank you for your kind support during the very long process of creating this novel. Here's to many more adventures together as a family!

Mena, Sonia, Christopher, Michael, Mickayla, Tigg and Myka, may this novel inspire you to be the next generation of animal advocates!

Tin Tin, Midge and Cupcake, I couldn't ask for more lovable little beasties. You make me a warmer person. It is an honor to be your father, little ones.

CHRISTOPHER LOCKE

L.A. Watson, what a unique artistic talent you are! And what a delight and honor that people will judge this book by its cover.

Katie Frichtel and Troy Farmer, founders and creative directors of raven + crow studio, not only are you gifted designers (I so love that raccoon mask logo on the spine!), but you also use your gift to make the world a kinder place. Now that's an admirable team.

Jennifer Brenner, this book is the most important creative endeavor of my life, and therefore you are the only person Jaya and I trusted—and wanted—to give the book a masterful polish with your copyediting skills.

Katie Vann, I was so stressed about the prospect of having to design my own website and then you saved the day! On top of that, you provided clever marketing advice. Talk about multi-talented.

Sean Haeseler, you captured two of the most important experiences of my life with your lens, sir. I can't imagine working with a more talented artist.

Bryan Monell and Matt Rossell, you are true heroes. The animals of the world are lucky to have you on their side, and *I* was lucky that you were gracious enough to share your valuable insight into the circus and fur industries, respectively.

Megan Grigorian and Jenny Woods, your knowledge about the circus industry and the exploitation of animals for human entertainment was crucial to this story. Thank you for being such avid animal advocates and for working on the front lines.

Philip K. Ensley, thank you for speaking out on behalf of captive elephants and for guiding me to very helpful resources regarding the treatment of animals in circuses.

E. Van Lowe, thank you for believing in me and mentoring me over the years. You are the most hilarious and fun boss I will ever have. Your guidance about marketing and the publishing industry has been vital.

Dave Simon, thank you for your sound advice about the publishing industry and for being such a powerful voice for the animals, including writing *Meatonomics*—an absolute must-read for anyone interested in furthering this important cause.

Robin Lamont, author of *The Kinship Series*, your encouragement has meant a great deal to me and your advice about self-publishing gave me the tools and support I needed to choose this path.

Hope Bohanec, author of *The Ultimate Betrayal: Is There Happy Meat?*, thank you for being kind enough to share your expertise regarding self-publishing and for writing the definitive book debunking the humane meat myth.

Andrew Lyons, your encouragement to follow my dreams right after I made the nerve-racking leap to leave my stable job was truly inspiring, and your advice on marketing and the publishing industry was extremely helpful.

And thank you to everyone who kept asking excitedly when they could read this story. Your enthusiasm was very much appreciated! I hope it lives up to your expectations.

Thank you to the following organizations for providing resources that were indispensable while I was writing this book, and for your tireless efforts, against all odds, to save billions of lives:

Animal Defenders International
Born Free USA
Farm Sanctuary
The Humane Society of the United States
Mercy For Animals
People for the Ethical Treatment of Animals

Made in the USA
Charleston, SC
29 May 2015